Kathryn Flett is a journalist and the author of a memoir about divorce (*The Heart-Shaped Bullet*). She has written for numerous international publications and makes regular TV and radio appearances as a critic and pundit. *Separate Lives* is her first novel.

KATHRYN FLETT
SEPARATE LIVES

Quercus

First published in Great Britain in 2012 by Quercus

55 Baker Street
7th Floor, South Block
London W1U 8EW

A CIP catalogue record for this book is available
from the British Library

ISBN 978 1 78087 186 8

10 9 8 7 6 5 4 3

Printed and bound in Great Britain by Clays Ltd, St Ives plc

Typeset by Ellipsis Digital Limited, Glasgow

For Shirley Nathan

PROLOGUE

June 2009

Susie

I know it's a cliché, but it was the text on Alex's phone that did it. And yes, obviously I shouldn't have been reading his texts, but if you dared look me in the eye and tell me you had never done the same thing, frankly I wouldn't believe you. Because we all have.

The text simply said: *Start living a different kind of life ... P :-) xxx*

Several thoughts jostled for my undivided attention simultaneously.

Who the hell is P? And what's with the smiley? (And how come they forgot to *LOL*?). Three kisses. P's a She ...

Shit – Alex is getting out of the shower.

I tapped the phone in an attempt to return to the blank screen but only succeeded in opening the new *Up* iPhone App that Alex had got for the kids. It was tempting – though only for a moment – to see what level they were 'up' to. Instead, I shoved the phone back into Alex's jeans and rearranged a simulacrum of the heap of clothes he'd left on the bedroom floor. By the time he appeared I was tidying my knicker-drawer. And humming. It occurred to me that tidying a drawers-drawer is pretty much at the bottom of the list of desperate displacement activities. And humming while doing so means you may as well have the words 'GUILTY OF SOMETHING, M'LUD' tattooed on your forehead. In this case, pants-placement-plus-humming was just the easiest plausible thing I could pretend to be doing under the guilt-inducing circumstances. It was just as well that Alex remained completely uninterested by my presence. As was, increasingly often, the case.

'Nice shower?'

But before I'd even got past 'nice' to 'shower' I knew this was the most absurd non-question I could have asked. It sounded like something a guilty somebody might say in a soap. Alex, still dripping a little and clad only in a too-small towel that did nothing for his incipient paunch, frowned and looked at me as though I were a particularly stupid and annoying child to whom he wasn't even related.

'Yeah, you know – hot water, shower gel, that sort of thing.'

Alex leaned over to pick up his clothes. Relieved, I turned back to my drawers, unearthing a black Myla thong that had been in my Christmas stocking three – maybe four? – years ago, in the days when Alex probably didn't get smiley-face xxx texts from 'P' and the prospect of hot, thongy sex with the missus wasn't the sexual equivalent of being forced to undertake a Bushtucker Trial on *I'm A Celebrity*. I pushed the thong to the back of the drawer. It would probably be another four years before I'd see it again.

'Right,' said Alex, 'I'm going to drag the kids away from the TV. Hurry up, would you?'

'Yes, give me five minutes.'

As Alex went downstairs, I walked into the bathroom and looked at myself in the big old Venetian looking glass, the only mirror I'd ever owned that always seemed to go out of its way to flatter me. I tried not to wear my 'mirror-face'; that pseudo-blank (yet ever-so-slightly Joan Rivers) make-up-application expression which, in the best light and with the right tools, means that reinvention isn't entirely beyond the realms of possibility. As I slowly began to apply my face-the-world mask to the blank canvas, the face peered back. I let it droop a little, stopping short of pulling the totally bonkers expression that might reveal the brutal, animated truth: that today I looked every minute of my thirty-nine years.

It was not a face that had ever been described as pretty – at least not since I'd hit puberty, shed the puppy fat, acquired cheekbones and suddenly appeared a lot closer to a legal sixteen than a jailbaity twelve – but it was still a good sort of face and usually scrubbed up OK. I'm a blonde, but not naturally – half-head-highlighted and therefore what my sort-of sister-in-law once described, slightly cruelly but entirely accurately, as 'a school-run blonde'.

So: green eyes set slightly too far apart, pale Celtic skin, a neat nose and a serviceable sort of mouth currently distorted by being bitten at one side, my face arranged itself into a stillness that managed not to refer too obviously to the churning in my solar plexus. But there was definitely something in the eyes – a sort of panicky, adrenalized look, offset by exhaustion and the knowledge that this being Saturday morning, there were another forty-eight hours of varying degrees of domestic discomfort to be borne before Monday morning would allow me to reclaim my grown-up head and think properly about 'P's text and the emotional ramifications thereof.

Pippa

Dear Mum,

It's been a while since I've done this, so where to start? Where to finish? Maybe it's just best to write until I run out of words. No idea where that will end up, but ... I should probably start with the text from Lisa, inviting me to dinner with her and Guy. I nearly turned it down at the last minute because it was – a bit randomly – on a Wednesday and I'm often a bit done-in on Weds after the gym. And then there was Hal's senior school interview, at College Hall, on the same day, which meant that he'd either be all wired and wanting to be on the Wii all night, or morbidly miserable because he'd screwed up ... and wanting to be on the Wii all night. So either way I didn't feel as though I should be going out. And then the weather was starting to get me down – that last-gasp-of-spring sort of weather that always seems to turn up just when you think summer is finally under way and it starts raining and looks as though it will never ever stop.

So I wasn't going to go but then it turned out that Hal was cool with the whole College Hall interview thing, and said, 'Don't stress, Mum, I've totally walked it' (twelve-year-olds), then he actually said, 'You should go out, Mum – you deserve it.' (Er, hello?) And so I got Marta to babysit at the eleventh hour and just chucked on the first clean pair of skinny jeans I could find and didn't even bother washing my hair and turned up at Lisa and Guy's place in West Hampstead with a bottle of wine.

It was just six of us – Guy and lovely Lisa, obviously, and Guy's mate Steve, who used to be the Harlequins' physio but is now the go-to personal trainer for about six north/north-west London postcodes (luckily I'd seen him in *Grazia* just last week so I was up to speed), and Steve's sweet wife, whose name I've already forgotten – she's a senior stylist at John Frieda who has just got an OU degree in Eng Lit. And then there was Guy's twin, Alex, whom I'd heard about from Lisa but never actually met. I think he was there by accident, having stopped by to see Guy after work, before Lisa persuaded him to stay for the chilli.

So it was a good evening. Easy. No big deal – just a bunch of people chatting about this and that. No politics, or religion, or political religion (thank God!) and I really hardly spoke to him until dessert (Ben and Jerry's or cheese – it was totally Wednesday) and when we first started talking it was just the usual polite probing: 'So,' (me to Alex) 'what do you do?' 'Oh I work in magazines. I'm the publisher of *Excellent*, *Excellent Fitness* and *Max Men*. And you?' . . . 'Oh that's cool. Well, I used to be a model agent – Lisa was one of my "girls" – but now I'm mostly a mum, and not so yum.' And Alex said, 'From where I'm sitting you look pretty yum,' and I laughed, and Lisa overheard this and raised an eyebrow across the table at me, as if to say 'wooooah!', but I'd had three glasses of a delicious Bordeaux (not mine, incidentally – mine was a so-so Sauvignon) and it was only 10 p.m. and I knew Marta was good till 1 a.m., and tomorrow wasn't exactly looking busy, so, whatever (as Hal would say. And now, apparently, do I).

Anyway, Lisa was kind of locked into a conversation with . . . um, I wish I could remember her name . . . and

6

Guy and Steve were off on one about some great rugby match, which just left me and Alex to shoot the breeze. And after the breeze had been well and truly blown away, it got a bit personal.

I didn't really want to talk about David, but once I'd explained that I was a single mum of a twelve-year-old boy and Alex asked what had happened to Hal's dad, I ended up (and I blame the Bordeaux) telling him all about meeting David at one of those model-heavy parties (perhaps model-lite is a better description, given the amount of canapés they weren't consuming) I hadn't really wanted to go to, and how he'd pretty much swept me off my feet (not least by saying that models didn't do it for him ... anymore). How our first date had involved David chartering a private plane and taking me for Sunday lunch in Le Touquet, and how we'd walked along the dunes and he'd explained what a hedge fund was in language I could actually understand and then said that while he loved his work he wasn't ever going to be defined by how much he earned, that there was a big world out there and more than anything he was looking to meet the mother of his children because, without a family, what was the point of all that hard work – and money? And how I'd actually fallen for all of that.

Anyway, on I went and Alex was a really good listener. Such a good listener, in fact, that I made him listen when I would have been better off changing the subject. Instead I told him about the engagement ring in the soup six months later at the Aman in Bali, the wedding six months after that at Luttrellstown Castle, falling pregnant with Hal on our honeymoon in the Maldives, moving into the house (that bloody house) in Hertfordshire ... I had practically got to the end of the marriage before I remembered to ask Alex about himself. Which is not like me, but he made it too easy. Though I did tell him other things too – all the family got brief name-checks, in case you're feeling sidelined, though I may not actually have covered all the pets. And no, I didn't tell him about the really important stuff, didn't fill in the biggest gaps. My tongue was a bit loose, but there are limits.

So Alex told me about magazine publishing (about which I pretended to know less than I do, because even you know model agent = models = magazines) and he told me about his kids and his house and ... he didn't say much about his wife, which was, for a married man, a pretty glaring omission. But I tried not to notice the glare and we just chatted and eventually it was eleven thirty and people started making time-to-go noises and even though I didn't want to go I knew it was a school-night for everybody else, so, weirdly, I ended up being first out of the door, mostly so I wasn't the last. Alex gave me a peck on the cheek and said it had been lovely to meet me. And Lisa gave me a kiss and a bit of finger-wagging. Not that she needed to because that was that. Really nice guy. Married. End of. I don't do married. No woman who's had it done to her is ever going to do married men, are they, Mum? Especially not a second-generation dumpee.

Alex

Thursday 4 June 2009

From: alex@foxmail.co.uk
To: guy@guysports.com

Good to see you and Lisa last night. Didn't realize I was crashing a dinner party – sorry. Still wanna meet up for a beer tho. Stuff to talk about. Value your input. A

From: guy@guysports.com
To: alex@foxmail.co.uk

No worries, mate. You looked like you were having a good time anyway?! Thought you must have met Pip before at our place, but obv not! Anyway, can do quick beer after school 2moz, if that's OK?

From: alex@foxmail.co.uk
To: guy@guysports.com

Roger that! The usual, 6.30?

From: guy@guysports.com
To: alex@foxmail.co.uk

10-4.

Friday 5 June 2009

From: alex@foxmail.co.uk
To: guy@guysports.com

Sorry bruv – have to blow you out tonight, big stuff going down at HQ with the Germans. Will prob be working late anyway and better get home. Don't know exactly why I'd better get home, but I feel I should. A

From: guy@guysports.com
To: alex@foxmail.co.uk

No probs. And you've got to get home because home is where the heart is, right? G

From: alex@foxmail.co.uk
To: guy@guysports.com

So they say! A

Thursday 11 June 2009

From: alex@foxmail.co.uk
To: guy@guysports.com

Just tried your phone but no joy. Listen, really need to talk. Things not quiet on the Western Front. Or the Eastern Front. Or indeed any fucking Fronts ... Call me when you pick this up? A

From: guy@guysports.com
To: alex@foxmail.co.uk

Out of this twunting meeting by 5. Call you then ... G

From: guy@guysports.com
To: alex@foxmail.co.uk

Just got to say, further to our chat? Holy shit. Hang in there. We're just talking about a hunch, nothing hard-and-fast. Don't let it eat you up. No need to steam in and say anything until you've got something to say, right? Thinking of you. Let's just get this party out of the way then we can all breathe easy. OK, easier ... G

From: alex@foxmail.co.uk
To: guy@guysports.com

Thanks. It'll be fine. Grateful for input, as ever. Home now ... A

CHAPTER 1

Susie

'Susie. HURRY UP.'

I glanced at my watch – the Cartier Tank that had been an eighteenth birthday present from my father and which was in permanent need of a service, having run six minutes slow since the late twentieth century. I'd been in the bathroom for four minutes.

'Coming.' I made it sound bright and efficient and I'm-on-top-of-all-this-Saturday-stuff. This was a lie.

I slicked on some tinted moisturizer, slightly cloggy mascara and the muted Mac Viva Glam gloss that I felt was appropriately 'Saturday morning'; the kind of non-colour on which I had relied since motherhood had somehow mysteriously dictated I leave the hot pinks and vampy reds behind.

And while I'd assumed that having babies was responsible for the muted lips, here, now, in front of this mirror a zingy lightbulb moment of clarity indicated that this might not in fact be the case. Perhaps it had been the moment I'd swapped my trademark bright red lips for tastefully grown-up gloss that indicated the passing of the Susie I had been and announced the arrival of the Susie I had become: a woman who asked her partner of ten years – her apparently straying, semi-stranger of a partner, the recipient of smiley-face texts from a red-lipsticked mystery woman (P almost certainly hadn't left vampy reds behind) if he'd had 'a nice shower?'. For fuck's sake.

A last glance in the mirror and a comb through the dirty-blonde bird's-nest. Noises were now coming up the stairs. Specifically the noises of a recalcitrant four-year-old male child – Charlie, aka Chuck – being reluctantly persuaded into a pair of shoes which, maternal multi-tasking brain effortlessly clicking into gear, I recognized were almost certainly the ones he had just outgrown.

'Alex. Those SHOES,' I shouted down the stairs. 'They don't fit him anymore. I meant to tell you.'

At the bottom of the stairs Alex was kneeling on the floor pushing a small foot into a smaller shoe, while Chuck was wearing an expression like a freshly smacked bottom – puffy, red, with a hint of grizzle. I sighed, pushed – almost elbowed, but not quite – Alex out of the way, removed the shoes and found an emergency replacement pair of *Bob the Builder* trainers that had been gifted by a friend with no taste and no children.

'There,' I said soothingly. 'Lula, where are you?'

Lula is my – our – eight-year-old daughter. What with the postnatal hormones, she was very nearly Tallulah, after Jodie Foster in *Bugsy Malone*, but when I finally got around to registering her birth relative sanity had thankfully prevailed.

'Your daughter,' said Alex – she was always 'my' daughter when he couldn't relate to her – 'is watching *Hannah Montana*. As per.'

I went into the living room where she was indeed curled like an apostrophe on the sofa, sucking her thumb and staring at Miley Cyrus with a kind of crush-fostering girl-longing I entirely understood – I'd felt pretty much exactly the same way about Jodie in *Bugsy Malone*. Just for a moment I was disarmed by her loveliness. My straight light-brown hair had, when combined with Alex's conker-coloured curls, given Lula a genetic leg-up. Those long thick honey-coloured strands (one of which was being chewed and which may or may not have been harbouring a nit), the delicately olive skin (Alex's), Bambi legs (Alex's) and green eyes (mine) made Lula the kind of child people first stared at and then smiled at in supermarkets, their days apparently bright-ened. Anyway, until recently Lula would have sneered at *Hannah Montana* as being 'yuck! For girly-girls' but something had shifted recently and a newly emerging Lula had started saying unnerving things like 'when I grow up I want to be Cheryl Cole'. So much for the vet-cum-part-time-firewoman.

'Lula, let's go. Like, now.'

The drive from north-west London to Suffolk was long and leavened only by Jonathan Ross on Radio 2, the occasional lingering shoe-related grizzle from Chuck before he decided to conk out and the bleep of Lula's Nintendogs. Alex seemed to be lost in his thoughts – red lipsticked, thong-wearing thoughts? – so I was left with mine. Which, with autistic-spectrum variety, ranged from the banal to the hyperventilatory.

'You're quiet,' said Alex at one point, just as we pulled into our preferred motorway services pit-stop for the trad-itional mid-morning caffeine-and-wee.

'I am. You're not wrong. I'm very quiet. On the outside.'

Alex glanced at me quizzically.

'And what does that mean, precisely?'

'I think it means just that. Not talkative. On the inside, however, I'm practically Jonathan Ross.'

He left me to it.

My outlaws, Mr and Mrs Fox – to whom we were heading for a family gathering in honour of (brace yourself for the irony) their golden wedding anniversary – live in a rambling, low-slung house painted Suffolk Pink, which is about two shades the bearable side of Barbie but still very much on the Disney Princess spectrum. It is the kind of house that looks unarguably attractive in estate agent's windows or on *Location, Location, Location* but which has always struck me as absurd for anybody less than 300 years old to actually live in.

I grew up in London, in an Edwardian mansion flat, and have always been about high ceilings and cornices and lots of light and never particularly charmed by a beam, which always makes me think I'm in the kind of hearty, engraved-tankards-behind-the-bar pubs I invariably want to leave immediately. The Foxes, on the other hand, are into their inglenookery and have spent their entire lives collectively banging their heads on lintels, which may explain a lot but, nonetheless, is all the more perverse because they are a family of giants – the shortest person in the family, Alex's mother, Joan, is five foot nine.

The Foxes habitually refer to the family homestead as The Pink House, though it is in fact called (gag-reflex alert) 'Whispers', after the sound of the East Anglian winds breezing through the fronds of the Weeping Willow by the stream. If I had been an American marrying into this family, I would probably have died of the joy of Englishness when I first heard this. However when Joan first told me about Whispers I had to suppress a snort and retreat to the loo. For ever after, if only by me, The Pink House was referred to as 'Careless Whispers'.

The most annoying thing about Careless is not the

low-slung ceilings (I'm five foot seven so it's navigable with minor stooping) but the fact that every room leads off every other room and none is quite big enough to contain everybody comfortably, especially if 'everybody' is more than six people, which it invariably is, what with Mr and Mrs Fox having four offspring and, thus far, seven grandchildren.

However, I do appreciate the gardens, even though, as a confirmed Londoner, I have never seen the point of having more garden than house. Houses are the bit that matter, gardens a luxury. And gardens with lawns that have to be mowed by small tractors (the Foxes have three acres) are a luxury from which I am pretty certain I shall forever be excluded. Owning a proper garden is, to me, a bit like waking up one day and suddenly finding oneself welded to a trug, yearning to vote Tory and knowing how to pronounce 'tsk-tsk'. But the kids, needless to say, adore Careless, and as we pulled into the gravel with just enough wheel-spin to announce ourselves, even I had to admit it scrubbed up pretty well for a 300-year-old, without recourse to lip-gloss, and on this warm mid-June day, with its 'anyone-for-tennis' lawns and herbaceous border ablaze, Careless had never looked more like a double-page spread from *Country Living*. Or, indeed, a particularly pastel scene from *Fantasia*.

Nigel Fox – Alex's father – was already at the (wisteria-festooned, obviously) door, glass in hand.

'Aha. Alex. Susie. Offspring. You're last. Welcome.'

Nigel does actually talk like this, in short barked sentences. He was one of six children so presumably while growing up he rarely got a word in and it was a habit that stuck. When he joined the RAF it was probably considered an asset.

'Dad,' said Alex, with no particular inflection or warmth, and I noted, not for the first time, that Alex instantly deflates from his habitual Alpha-maleness as soon as he comes into contact with his father. I used to worry about it a bit, feel for him – but not these days. I've had more conversations with Alex about his ego-puncturing relationship with his father than I can count and I wasn't particularly looking forward to the one we'd almost certainly be having on the drive home tomorrow. The contents of my empathy cup, far from running over, had all but evaporated.

'Grown,' barked Nigel, pointing at his grandchildren, 'haven't they.' Statement not question.

'They do tend to,' I said. 'I've tried pruning them but it's no good.'

'Ha. Susie. Funny.'

Inside Careless, a skulk ('it's the collective noun', Nigel had told me, the first time we'd met) of Foxes 'Hi'd and 'How are you?'d and jostled for some kissing. A newly reinvigorated Charlie instantly disappeared with his five-year-old cousin, Jack, Isobel's second 'miracle' IVF baby, and the one for whom that Mumsnetty term 'Little Emperor' could have been coined. I have always failed to be charmed by Jack but Charlie worships at his (designer-shod) feet. Lula, meanwhile, had already paired off with her eight-year-old cousin, Isobel's daughter Chloe, a bright, devastatingly plain, tomboyish dogs-and-ponies girl of whom I was extremely fond, though I feared that now Lula was coming over all Girls Aloud she and Chloe were bound more by familial ties than by any shared interests. But still, vanishing children was one of the upsides of a Fox family gathering. It meant I could conceivably reclaim a portion of otherwise-occupied brain for myself.

So, apart from Nigel, who thinks kissing is common, in no particular order I kissed:

* Prickly, put-upon, wildly clever Isobel, Alex's older sister, successful human rights lawyer and single ('through choice! MY choice! And my choice of donors too!') mother to Chloe and Jack.

* Guy, Alex's older-by-five-minutes twin brother. Handsome, charming Guy, a professional rugby player turned sports agent who had not only retained his genetic share of Alpha-maleness but somehow kept on acquiring even more. One day I imagined the potentially flammable combination of success and testosterone might cause him to explode in a puff of machismo.

* Guy's brand-new, as of last weekend – though they had been together three years – fiancée, the no-longer-borderline-anorexic and therefore even more exhaustingly beautiful American ex-model turned hip boutique owner, Lisa, who predictably thought Whispers was 'like, *toadally* heaven'.

* Guy and Lisa's (runs in the family) twins, six-month-old Stanley and Poppy, who virtually at birth had been dubbed Pea and iPod by Isobel – nicknames that were in danger of sticking.

* The Fox firstborn, Will, an RAF officer and owner of an upper lip so stiff that on the rare occasions when he smiled, as now, it appeared to if not actually crack then certainly creak a bit. Will had suffered a horrible loss when his childhood sweetheart, Marianne, died of breast cancer when they were both thirty (he is forty-seven now, so I never knew her). Their son, Luke, meanwhile, was just nine months old when his mother died and Will has brought him up alone and, despite the demands of his job, quite brilliantly ever since. Still single, though stalked by squadrons of women bearing both sympathy and, no doubt, Myla thongs, Will is an acquired taste but one worth acquiring. Alex, interestingly, is not remotely close to his big brother.

* Finally, in the kitchen – the only part of the house that references the twenty-first century because, despite the Aga, it's surprisingly un-farmhouse-y and, with its limestone work surfaces and handle-less drawers and cupboards, rather more Bulthaup-y – I found Joan doing her usual bossy matriarchal thing alongside four young cooks hired for the occasion: tonight's sit-down dinner for a hundred in a marquee which, I could now see through the French doors, was being erected, distractingly, by numerous topless men.

'Darling. Susie. Just the woman. Come and kiss me. But I'm very floury.'

If Will is a taste worth acquiring then Joan is a taste that may well be a lifetime's work, like learning to appreciate hundred-year-old eggs. On the surface we get on very well – she's clever and funny (if Will is Nigel Junior then Joan is Isobel Senior) and very much the flame around which her family gathers for warmth. However, if she didn't actually give birth to you and you try to get a bit too close then you're always in danger of meeting a moth-like fate.

After ten years of dealing with Joan and more than a few slammed doors and stamped feet (on both sides), not to mention a handful of 'Alex, your fucking mother is driving me MAD!'s, we've now reached a kind of truce. If she can avoid competitively criticizing my parenting skills, or lack thereof, and stick to the stuff we both agree on, i.e. food, which is Joan's great passion and happens to be my career, we're fine.

I'm a restaurant critic. Did I tell you that? Apologies – distracted. If push came to shove I could probably struggle by without sex, but I couldn't cope without having food at the centre of my life. If I couldn't have either, I would become a recluse and retreat to a darkened room where I'd grow twelve-inch fingernails and watch films like *Tampopo* (foodily erotic) and *Babette's Feast* (erotically foodie). And even though I think *Last Tango In Paris* is about as sexy as a cholesterol test, remaking it with *I Can't Believe It's Not Butter* would've been a disaster. Anyway.

'This looks very good, Joan. Anything I can do?'

'No, darling. I have these wonderful girls,' (at which point Joan waved an arm proprietorially around the kitchen), 'and they're doing marvellous things, but of course I always appreciate your expert eye!'

Of course. This is the form in Joan's kitchen. A proper control freak (and it takes one to know one, so, like, *respect*) she habitually both welcomes and excludes at the same time. Today my head is crammed full of so much other stuff that I really don't mind being let off the culinary hook, but it's very important to make all the right noises.

'Well, just shout if you need me. And those volleyballs are looking magnificent.'

'It's really all down to the girls. You'll have heard of them, I'm sure – "Hot Sausage and Mustard"?'

This information checked my social autopilot for a moment. 'Hot Sausage and Mustard' are the indubitably twee-ly named county caterers *du nos jours* – the last word in 'our home cooking, cooked in your home' comfort food for fans of 'robust English fare'. And for avoiding adding a 'y' to 'fare', food writers remain very grateful. But more important even than this is the fact that HS&M is the brainchild of a woman called Harriet Harvey, who is the only person in the whole world I have ever actively hated. Momentarily stumped for an appropriate response and in the absence of worry-beads, I picked up a wodge of stray pastry and attempted squidgy origami.

'You must know of them, Susie? They're all over the press, aren't you, girls?' There is mumbled assent from the 'girls', the youngest of whom is probably mid-twenties. None of them, I'm relieved to see, is Harriet.

'You'll meet Harriet Harvey in a minute, I'm sure. Hot Sausage is her "baby",' (here Joan did air-quote fingers, which she considers groovy), 'I think she's outside with the van.'

'Lovely,' I said, dropping my pastry crane. 'Long journey, Joan. Excuse me – loo.'

Since the time Joan told me about naming the house Whispers and I had had to retreat to quell my giggles, I have spent large chunks of the last decade in the Foxes' downstairs loo. Usually I've been dealing with countless nappy-changing and toilet-training emergencies, though there was the memorable – to me, anyway – incident when Alex had announced our engagement at a family gathering on New Year's Day and I'd overheard Joan's stage-whispered response: 'Alex, darling, are you really *sure* about this one?'

Now here I was again, staring blankly at the framed Klee print and selection of ancient yellowing *Punch* cartoons (the loo apparently having been time-capsuled in about 1976 – something which, as an only child without a life-time's worth of 'home' to call my own, I found quite comforting) and contemplating the fact that I was within moments of meeting my teenage nemesis, 'Heinous' Harvey. A woman from whom I'd only recently received (and delightedly ignored) an emailed press release alerting me to the success of 'Hot Sausage', with an added personalized note: 'Long time, eh?! Anyway, thought you might be interested, Love HH.'

'Love?' I'd thought incredulously. How dare the woman who, with the assistance of her hapless weak-willed crony, Clare ('Hunchback') Hutch, once mugged me behind the sports hall, stealing not only an unread copy of *Smash Hits* and the Keith Haring Swatch I'd got for my fifteenth out of my backpack, but also my diary. An event about which I could still feel a surge of psychic pain if I dwelt on it for more than a moment. How dare 'Heinous' pretend to 'love' me, I'd thought before consigning her email to the desktop Trash with a flourish.

A knock on the door. 'Mummmmeeeee. Is that yooooo?'
Chuck.

'Yes, it's me. Are you OK?'

'What are you doing in there? I need a weeeeeee. Are
you hiding?'

'No, no of course I'm not hiding. I'm having a wee, too.'

'A wee and a number two?'

'No, sweetie. Not a number two.'

I sighed, unlocked the door. Charlie was hopping from
foot to foot holding his father's hand and though Alex
wore an expression of boredom coupled with indifference,
Charlie was clearly about to cry. I watched helplessly as
a dark wet patch spread across his crotch.

'Alex, surely one of the great things about both big and
small boys who urgently need a pee is that if the loo is
busy they can do it in the garden?'

Alex pulled a face. I interpreted this to mean that the
idea of al-fresco peeing at Whispers was totally beyond
the pale. He was always intractably up-his-own-arse about
all things lavatorial. I blame Joan, but then I blame Joan
for a lot of things.

'Whatever. I'm pretty sure I – no, in fact make that we.
As in pee – forgot to bring a change of trousers,' I muttered,
and Alex shrugged, immediately altering his expression
to reflect the belief that remembering to bring a change
of trousers for a four-year-old was pretty much 150 per
cent not within his parenting remit. At which point (and

not for the first time) I felt the onset of a particular kind of resentment familiar to all mothers of small children whose partners not only *just don't fucking get it* but automatically assume women are genetically pre-programmed to remember this stuff. We haven't in fact been forced to delete numerous interesting files in our brains labelled 'Shakespeare's sonnets' or 'quantum mechanics' or 'Kerry Katona's private life' in order to download 'Always remember to take a spare pair of trousers to the outlaws' golden wedding anniversary party just in case the four-year-old wets himself'.

I removed Chuck's trousers and pants and figured that if I stuck them in the rockery they'd probably be dry in an hour. In the meantime Joan was bound to have an ancient (which predates 'vintage' by about twenty-five years) pair of children's velvet knickerbockers folded in tissue paper inside a drawer full of handmade lavender pouches.

Thus far the day was not going particularly well; however, I was grateful that in the garden there was no sign of Heinous, just a lot of fit blokes with their tops off doing butch stuff with tarpaulin and ropes. I lingered awhile. And though I doubted if any of these men had ever remembered a change of trousers for a four-year-old either, I wasn't living with them, just ogling. Like a sad on-the-threshold-of-middle-age woman with a husband who was probably having an affair with a piece of work called 'P'.

Which reminded me. After I'd hung Charlie's clothes out to dry on a small palm, I walked around the end of the marquee in an attempt to spot the 'Hot Sausage' van, but without being seen. And lo – there was Heinous, sitting half in and half out of the passenger door, wearing a magnificent pair of boots and shouting into her mobile.

'You know what? I don't bloody care. I totally do not fucking care one iota what you think, OK? Actually, strike that "OK". If I didn't in fact totally not fucking care, I'd definitely hope it was not OK. OK?'

Which semi-articulate sentence of rage did rather impress me. It sounded good, sounded a lot like I was feeling. And then I thought about it a bit more and realized that it actually did make sense, so kudos to Heinous. Anyway, this was the point when I should have ducked out of her sightline, but when she hung up with a robustly delivered 'so just fuck off', almost inevitably she happened to glance my way. She squinted and grinned. Busted. This was it – twenty years of emotional baggage was about to be fly-tipped all over Whispers' freshly raked gravel drive.

'Susie *Poo*? Is that really you?'

See? One of the very best things about being proposed to by Alex had been the prospect of dumping my old surname and high-tailing it down to the post office to have my passport rebranded as Fox. As would the Righteous Post-Fem squad if their surname had been Poe and they were at school with Heinous.

'Hein— er, hey.' I scuttled – I don't think I've ever scuttled before – out from behind the marquee. 'How's tricks?' And no, I've no idea where 'How's tricks?' came from because I'd never said it before; however, there always had been something about Heinous that made me turn into a character from her movie, not mine.

'Tricks are fine. Tricks are good.' Heinous glanced at her phone. 'Good-ish. How are your "tricks"? And look, Susie, I'm sorry about the diary.'

For one disarming moment it looked as if she were about to lunge at me for a hug, before thinking better of it and thrusting out a hand, which I ignored. It was going to take more than a bloody handshake to eradicate the memory of Heinous removing pages from my diary and posting them on the common-room noticeboard.

'It's haunted me for years. You may be relieved to know that I am no longer that girl. Not anymore. I'm properly sorry.'

'OK, thanks. But it was a shit thing to do. When Tara Maplethorpe . . .' (aka Maple Syrup, because we were at an all-girls school and had read too much *St Clare's* at an impressionable age) '. . . found out I'd got off with her boyfriend – what was his name? Mark Thingy? – while we were both waiting for the night bus after the St Benedict's disco, she never spoke to me again. And I'd only got off with him to keep warm because Mark Thingy was wearing a puffa. And you also nicked my Swatch.'

It was amazing how much I sounded exactly like my sixteen-and-a-half-year-old self. Heinous must've thought I'd gone mental. Possibly as a direct result of her actions.

'Totally accept that. Totally out of order. But actually the Swatch was Clare. She's probably still wearing it. And not in a cool, retro, referencing-the-eighties way.'

Against all my instincts this made me laugh. Heinous too. It suddenly occurred to me that my day was already so shit there was no point in making it any worse.

'OK, Heinous Harriet Harvey. Whatever. Bygones. Shall we seek some closure?'

'You know, that would be a massive weight off my mind. Thanks.'

'I'm not saying I've forgiven and forgotten. Just that I'm probably grown-up enough to try.'

'Good enough for me. So, your bloke is somebody here?'

'Yes, though he's still my bloke only by the skin of my – his – teeth.'

This was slightly mad of me. It was clearly going to take a while to adjust to this new, quasi-likeable Heinous, one who suddenly felt like somebody I could talk to. Perhaps because her surname wasn't Fox? Or maybe because we were bonded by so much history. And Hockey. And Latin. Anyway.

'I'm sorry. And there's a man heading this way.' I liked that Heinous sort of hissed this, collusively. I turned.

'Alex. You won't believe it but . . . this is Heinous Harvey. You know . . .'

'Yeah, I've heard all about Heinous Harriet Harvey, Scourge of the Sixth. And you're actually speaking instead of sticking chewing gum into each other's hair during Prep?'

'We are. She's apologized.'

'Better late than.' Alex thrust forward a hand. 'Alex Fox. You still got the Swatch?' He was suddenly all charm and smiles and twinkling eyes and really quite handsome. Like somebody else's husband.

'No, that was Hunchback. I was just saying to Poo – Susie – that she's probably still wearing it.'

'Very funny. So you're the sausage woman?'

'That's one way of putting it.'

'Well, good to meet you. You're not half as hideous in real life.'

She had the grace to laugh. Probably because whatever she now was, 'Hideous Heinous' she definitely wasn't. She was looking great. I knew she'd just turned thirty-nine, on the first of June. There are some bits of pointless information you really try to forget – or imagine will get lost inside a head filled with spare pairs of toddler's trousers – but weirdly, Heinous's birthday wasn't one of those things.

The rest of the day was entirely bearable, the afternoon a sunny, 'Whispery' blur of family small-talk with a smattering of small-p politics and some gossip. I spent nearly an hour with Isobel, who was excessively interested in some rumours about a Michelin-starred chef who was apparently putting it about a bit, to the predictable displeasure of his TV weathergirl wife. Turned out Isobel had met the chef at a mutual friend's dinner party. Apparently 'there were definite sparks'. And, Isobel eventually revealed, definite texts.

'In the interests of research,' I told Isobel, 'I went out with a chef, back in the 1990s when they were still just blokes who cooked for a living. He liked doing it *al fresco, al forno, al dente* – basically as often as possible, everywhere. And being a creative soul, in all sorts of ways, with lots of olive oil.'

'I am *so* listening.'

'OK, so the morning after one particularly memorable night before he made me a cooked breakfast in the nude – my own naked chef, back when Jamie Oliver was still burning water. He tried to get me to assist, but I said that if the nudity was compulsory I'd rather just lie around in bed rather than end up hauling my second-degree postcoital glow off to A&E.'

'Yeah, I can see that wouldn't be a very good look.'

'Anyway we split up shortly after that. He said it was because he was emigrating, but I've always wondered if it was because I refused to make bubble and squeak in the buff.'

'These days I'd be perfectly happy to make bubble and squeak in the buff,' said Isobel. 'Though it would be my poor kids who'd probably end up emotionally scarred for life. Mind you, when they leave home I may feel a sudden compulsion to cook something complicated in my smalls. *Nostalgie de la bouillabaisse*. Bring it on.'

I tried to persuade Isobel that the chef, though undoubtedly good with his hands (and other extremities), was a tosser, but perhaps when you've been single for as long as Isobel then having breakfast cooked for you by a naked celebrity tosser is a prospect worth entertaining.

And so the day rolled into the evening, and because I'd drunk the Pimm's lake pretty dry, everything was very nearly sort of lovely when we finally sat down to dinner. Lula was entirely occupied by the presence of her cousin, while I fed sausages and mash to Charlie, who fell asleep on my lap before being spirited away to our sleeping quarters by one of the nannies Nigel and Joan had thoughtfully hired so that we grown-ups could fulfil our adult destiny, i.e. get even more spectacularly pissed, especially during the speeches, when Nigel referred to Joan as 'less Joan of Arc, more Joan of My Heart', which in turn made me snort snottily. Eventually (and surely it was Tuesday by now?) everybody hit the dance floor, commandeered for the purposes of total embarrassment by Ipswich's own DJ Jeff and his Spectacular Strobe, and threw their version of middle-class-white-people-can't-dance shapes to 'Brown Sugar', and thus the proverbial Good Time Was Had. Meanwhile, Alex and I barely exchanged a word.

After the apparently endless Stones medley, which featured a bit too much air guitar for me (any air guitar being too much air guitar, frankly) and a mass outbreak of non-ironic lighter waving during Boston's 'More Than a Feeling' (who knew so many people still had lighters?), it was time for a head-clearing perambulation around the garden. I was pissed enough to feel not-unhappy, but then the memory of this morning resurfaced and my heart sank, assisted by heavy sausages.

And then, sitting beside a willow smoking a surreptitious fag, I found Heinous.

'Hey,' she said. 'I don't really smoke. I'm just a bit ...'

'Stressed? I heard your rant into the phone earlier. Domestic?'

'More of a post-domestic, really. My ex, Jonathan – father of my daughter. Did I tell you I had a daughter?'

'No, what with getting stuck in the 1980s you neglected to. Also, I'm properly pissed. And sausaged. Very good sausages by the way.' I sat down, landing heavily on my (by now) Hussein Chalayan-clad arse.

'Thanks, we give good sausage. Yeah, my daughter, Edie. Same age as yours, give or take.'

'Really? Well, maybe ...' (and I surprised myself with this one) 'we should get them together? Let them nick each other's Lelli Kelly shoes, or something. It would be a shame to break the cycle.'

Heinous laughed. 'I think that would be great. If you ever a fancy a daytrip down to Random-on-Sea ...'

'You don't live in London?' I was slightly surprised. I assumed she did, but then I'm so London-centric I assume everybody does. 'Where's Random-on-Sea?'

'South coast. Not Brighton. From London, it's down and left a bit, just before East Sussex peters out and Kent kicks in. Arse-end-of-nowhere and a bastard for travel links but we've been there five years now, since I left Jonathan, and it suits us. You get a lot of house for the price of a two-bed flat in "Media Vale".'

'Sounds lovely. Really.' I meant it. 'Look, I'd better go and do the family thing. It's been . . .' I scrambled to my feet and sort of hovered with my arms outstretched. 'It's been good. It's been real.'

And this was the point in the evening when Heinous Harvey and I actually hugged, right there under a willow at Careless while The Moody Blues' Justin Hayward sang 'Just what the truth is, I can't say anymore'.

'It pains me to admit it,' I said, 'but you're OK. And I love your boots. And I'll stop now because I'm pissed and I don't actually have lesbian tendencies. Not that there's anything wrong with lesbian tendencies. They're great, possibly even enviable. I just don't have them. Sorry if that's a terrible disappointment.'

'I'm devastated, obviously,' Heinous deadpanned. 'But the boots are by Georgina Goodman and I happen to know they're now on sale, reduced from a slightly challenging £595 to a not-entirely-unaffordable £245.'

And even as we both convulsed into hiccupy sixth-form giggles I wasn't so pissed that I didn't make a mental note to check out the boots online first thing Monday morning. Or possibly second thing. Just after a nice big row. It was something to look forward to.

Inside the marquee, people were now slow-dancing in couples. I sat back down at our table and attempted to make eye-contact with Alex, who was deep – extremely and obliviously deep – in conversation with Guy. A wave of misery rolled over me as I sat next to my partner, yet entirely alone, when Jeff spun the slow-dance-from-hell, the song that could make even big girls cry – 10cc's 'I'm Not In Love'. After what felt like an eternity of aeons but was probably only as long as it took to get to the end of the first verse, Alex turned to me.

'I'm going to sit this one out with Guy. We're talking. That's OK, isn't it.' It wasn't a question but a statement.

'Yeah.' I couldn't bear the fact that my eyes were watering. And I just hoped nobody could see. Or if they did that they were so drunk they'd mistake my duct-excretions for tears of 10cc-related joy.

A tap on my shoulder.

'Susie. The father of your children is clearly pressingly engaged. Dance?'

It was Will, whom, it occurred to me, I had never actually seen dance. Maybe it had been a Careless Whisper-style

'I'm never going to dance again' situation after Marianne had died? Either way I nearly fell off my chair.

'Whoops. I hope you're better on the dance floor.' Will grinned as Alex nodded in assent, as though it had ever been sought.

'Yeah you go for it, bro. Just keep your hands off the missus's arse.' Alex was weirdly faux-cheery-to-the-power-of, but clearly distracted and instantly back in earnest sotto-voce conversation with Guy. I'd learned never to gate-crash the twin-thing.

Slow-dancing in public with Will meant I was forced to adopt a kind of close-but-not-too-close technique I'd never previously attempted. The way to pull it off seemed to be to do all the usual slow-dance moves with extra crotch-avoidance, while making small-talk straight out of Austen. And then there was the fact that Will smelt of Creed's Green Irish Tweed, which was lovely but also confusing, because not only was it my favourite men's aftershave but also, rather wrongly, my father's favourite too.

'So, Will, I meant to ask you – where's Luke? I appreciate that Careless is the last place a cool eighteen-year-old male would want to be hanging on a Saturday night but I assumed there was a three-line whip?'

'There would have been, but he's up to his eyeballs in A-levels.'

'Of course, I'd forgotten, yeah. Poor Luke.' I wished I

could be a bit more articulate but the situation was too distracting. Rather needily, I always wanted to impress Will with my wit and intelligence, though this was probably neither the time nor the place to do it.

'He already has a place at Oxford in theory, so after his exams he's off to Costa Rica with Operation Raleigh, during which he'll turn himself from a smart boy into a well-rounded young man.' Will paused, rolled his eyes. 'With all that that entails.'

'South America? It's all red hot chilli chicks and Class A's, surely?'

'Yeah, pretty much the perfect training for three years of PPE.'

Big boys don't cry breathed the 10cc girl as 'I'm Not In Love' shifted a musical gear from merely soppy to properly clinchy. My embarrassment was palpable.

'I get the feeling that us dancing to "I'm Not In Love" in front of the father of your children is possibly too big an ask? I can hardly blame you.' We pulled apart, relieving ourselves of the enforced intimacy – and relieved by our relief.

'That was nice. If wrong-feeling.'

'Well, maybe. But you looked like you wanted to dance. Come on, let's get you some air.'

'"I can feel it coming in the air tonight" . . .'

I was singing Phil Collins. To Will. Shit. Nonetheless, I allowed myself to be gently steered out of the marquee and back down to the willows – fast becoming a place where surprising things could happen.

'Look, Susie. I asked you to dance because I wanted the chance for a quick word. And though I hadn't anticipated you'd be quite as pissed as you clearly are, I'm going to seize the moment anyway. So help me God. And the only reason I'm doing this is because you're you, and I care. You know I do.'

'I do know that. Yes.'

'And I don't want you to get hurt – or indeed to do any hurting because you've been hurt. And I'm almost certainly talking out of turn because I have had one, possibly even two glasses of wine, never mind the Pimm's. And I want you to know that whatever's going on with Alex – and it's pretty obvious something's going on – I think you shouldn't attempt to sweep it under the carpet but address it. As soon as possible. And that's about all I've got to say. At least that's all I'm able to say, here, now.'

'But?'

There were many questions jostling for my undivided attention simultaneously. Again.

'No "buts". Not now. Just sort things out with Alex before it's–' He stopped short.

'Too late?'

'Yeah, OK. Too late.'

It was a bit too much, prompting an uninvited tear – a hot, fat, saline tear, the precursor, presumably, to many more, hotter, fatter, infinitely wetter and saltier tears. Will put an arm round my shoulder in an appropriately 'chin-up, sis' kind of way while I sobbed a bit into his armpit. Then I pulled back, reached up on tiptoes and kissed him quickly – very quickly – on his stiff upper lip. Which was not very stiff at all.

'Thanks, Will. I hear you. Which also means I know that I need – no, not need, want – a drink.'

Back inside the marquee, I did have a drink. Possibly two. And then I stumbled the fifty yards to 'our' quarters – the studio room over the stable-block-turned-garage, where Lula was already curled up on a sofa-bed alongside Charlie – and I slept right through the departing 'Carriages at One' (minicabs by any other name) and then for another eight heavily dream-laden and unrefreshing hours.

Sunday morning arrived looking blurry. Thankfully the kids slept late (for kids) and Alex, who I presumed had come to bed at some point if only because there was a dent on his pillow, had already left the building. I was slightly surprised – and heartened – by the fact that on the bedside table there was a glass of water and a sachet of Resolve. Thoughtful. Suspiciously so? Or was I now just programmed to be suspicious? It could just have been kindness laced with a dash of self-interest. After all, a Susie with a sore head was always going to be less of an attractive proposition on a Sunday morning than, say, a Susie with a sore head that was becoming marginally less sore.

When I emerged from the shower with last night's mascara panda-ing my eyes, the kids were awake.

'Hi. Big night, eh? Fun?' I could just about do chirpy, though preferably monosyllabically.

'Where's Chloe, Mum?' said Lula, yawning and stretching; a Pixar lion cub. 'And what happened to your eyes?'

'OK, my eyes demonstrate the fact that when you are a grown-up and have been to a party and had a whole glass of wine, you must always remember to remove your make-up. It's an important life lesson for all females.' Lula looked suitably bemused. 'I expect Isobel, Chloe and Jack were sleeping in Isobel's old room, so why don't you go and look for them? I'm sure those posh pyjamas from Grandma Joan are acceptable attire before noon.'

In a streak of candy-striped cotton, Lula disappeared, though a thumb-sucking Chuck was less easily persuaded out of bed.

'Come on, Small. Bet there's bacon butties.'

I carried him down the stairs, negotiated the gravel in my bare feet and entered the kitchen through the back door, to be confronted by a sitcom's-worth of Foxes and the aroma of upscale frying. Inside the 'Careless Cafe' Joan was in charge of bacon, Guy was toasting, Alex was on coffee duty, Isobel was arranging condiments, Will was washing up and Nigel was wearing a novelty apron that said 'How can you help? GET OUT OF MY KITCHEN!' and beaming the smile of a man who had been married for fifty years and was miraculously still both compos and mentis.

'Ah, Susie. Charlie. You're here. Butties?'

And I felt a kind of sharp stab somewhere in my chest, albeit more of a metaphorical stab than an actual physical pain, and I knew it was because I was both moved by the familial warmth and sheer cosiness of the domestic scene unfolding in front of me and yet also somehow disconnected from it. In that moment I felt quite clearly that one of the reasons – perhaps even, in retrospect, the most compelling reason – I had wanted to accept Alex's proposal nine years ago was that marriage would give me instant all-areas access to a proper family, one that seemed, to all intents, and at least from the outside, to be convincingly functional. It was at times like this that I felt both very privileged to belong and, weirdly, almost entirely alienated. Half in, half out. Story of my life.

All through my only-childhood I'd been obsessed by notions of family and had gravitated to books in which siblings interacted in slightly baffling yet thrilling ways, sucking up stories of brothers and sisters who did stuff together, who fought and fell out and then found each other again. Using children's fiction as a template I probably grew up with a pretty warped perspective on what constituted A Family (fifty per cent *The Chronicles of Narnia*, fifty per cent *Little Women*) but it was also a very potent one. My parents had both emigrated from Australia in the early 1960s, as groovy middle-class Australians of the era were wont to do, and their eyes had met over a tray of Lamingtons in the flat of another Earl's Court émigré, so being a three-person family with no close relatives nearby we were a tight little unit, forever on the outside of other people's parties, looking in.

When I was seven my parents split up. And that my advertising copywriter father, Derek, ran off with his secretary is a source of eternal disappointment, if only because – and this is nothing to do with the secretary, Cathy, of whom I was, and remain, properly fond – it was the single unimaginative act of a man whose imagination had made his fortune. Anyway this was the point when the family triangle – our impenetrable little pyramid – was irreparably broken. After that we were no longer A Family, just three individuals trying to find our way and bumping into each other occasionally en route.

After the split I lived with Pauline, my mum, seeing Dad every other weekend. By the time I was eleven Mum had met my soon-to-be-stepfather, another divorced Aussie (not to mention the first Australian I'd met who was actually called Bruce) and the two of them started planning a return 'home'. I was invited, of course, but it was a no-brainer: Pauline and Bruce were planning to live in a country 'town' (one pub and a petrol station, apparently) while I had spent my entire life a ten-minute drive from Selfridges.

When Mum and Bruce finally left for Australia the week after my fourteenth birthday, I moved in to Dad and Cathy's St John's Wood townhouse. Dad had worked hard to turn a spare bedroom into a cool 1980s girl-den, installing an entirely impractical but massively desirable white wool carpet and painting the walls egg-yolk yellow. Gone were the 1970s brown-on-brown-with-accents-of-beige Laura Ashley print curtains of my old bedroom, replaced by 'funky' blinds decorated with big red poppies. On one wall I had a long set of shelves already loaded with books, a pine dressing table-cum-chest of drawers next to the bed and a free-standing pine wardrobe. This sophisto-teen universe was set off by a yellow corduroy modular sofa beneath the shelves and, within minutes, my walls were Blu-tacked with pictures culled from the pages of *The Face* and *Smash Hits*. On the day I moved in, there, waiting for me on my sofa, was a pair of red and white Converse-style high top roller skates with orange Kryptonic wheels, from Slick Willies in Kensington High Street. Obviously I didn't have the heart to say that I was already over roller skating, an obsession of the previous two years, and was infinitely more excited by the girl-heaven that was my own en-suite bathroom, in which I could (and did) fail to remove eye make-up at my leisure.

Cathy worked hard at being sweetness itself. As she was

also a sublime amateur cook, we bonded in the kitchen. (Years later she'd watch *Masterchef* with a permanently wistful look, but, being hopelessly self-effacing, always refused to apply). Mum, on the other hand, wasn't much cop as a cook, though she was useful in other ways – it was she, for example, who had instructed me always to remove my make-up after parties. Anyway, the point is that this new fractured family reconfiguration may have turned out to be a triangle – and a pretty good triangle – but because it was more isosceles than equilateral it was just not my triangle of choice.

So I stood in Joan Fox's kitchen, bacon butty in hand, surfing an invisible wave of wistfulness and feeling something dangerously close to sorry for myself. And not even for the obvious reason – a potentially vanishing partner – but because *if I lost him, I'd also lose all of this*. At that precise moment I wasn't sure which was worse; all I knew was that if I lost this I had also lost my shot at belonging to a family. And I don't think I'd ever realized quite how much that meant to me, far less ever articulated it.

The rest of the morning was spent mucking in, tidying up, debriefing and re-running scenes from the previous night. I seemed to have missed a lot. Apparently Nigel's golfing buddy and near-neighbour Adam Purves had turned up to the party with somebody called Jennifer who had implausible Mrs Slocombe hair, while Mrs Purves was apparently sitting at home weeping into a Campari and soda. Adam and Jennifer had met while tackling a tricky bunker a month ago and had been inseparable ever since. However, everybody whose surname was Fox, or nearly-Fox, agreed that introducing your amusingly coiffed mistress to the world at your best friend's golden wedding party pretty much ensured golf-club-related social suicide.

Then, to a roomful of laughter, Alex shared the story of my history (and subsequent reconciliation) with 'the sausage woman, aka – wait for it! – "Heinous" Harriet Harvey, Scourge of the Sixth.'

'But Susie, dear, you really should have said!' exclaimed Joan with slightly more glee – a hit TV series-worth of *Glee*, in hindsight – than she might have done. Or perhaps I was just being a bit thin-skinned.

'You know how it is, Joan. Lot on my mind – didn't want to burden you on the big day.'

And I don't think I imagined the triangle of quick glances and furrowed brows that followed this unremarkable statement. A blink-and-you'd-miss-it from Guy – firstly to me and then to Alex. And then from Alex back to Guy, and swiftly on to me. It was almost imperceptible, but not quite imperceptible enough.

'Oh, it wouldn't have been a burden, it would have amused us all!' said Joan, oblivious to all the glancing, which, not knowing whom to trust, felt like the start of a potentially messy game of 'wink murder'.

And on it rolled, until we eventually departed after a lunch of leftovers and some overly complicated send-offs, plus kissing.

* From Isobel: urgent whispered demands not to 'breathe a word to Alex about you-know-who. Promise? Strictly *entre nous*, yeah?'

* From Guy: 'Remember, please don't tell Lisa what I told you about the, y'know, thing!' Which only confused 'things' because I couldn't actually recall having had a conversation with Guy at all last night, so I was now entirely up Willow creek without a paddle – or indeed a 'Thing'. But I nodded and assured him I wouldn't breathe a word.

* From Lisa: 'Hey, hon, Guy doesn't know I know but actually I do know, so it's toadally fine. But isn't that like hilarious?' *Toadally*. If I'd known what she was on about. However, I grinned and winked. 'Everybody's secrets are safe with me.'

* From Will: a briskly whispered 'Hang in there, Susie. You'll be fine.'

* From Joan: 'So lovely to see you and the children. I must say you're looking a little pale and peaky but perhaps

that's to be expected. Though you're not skinny at all.'
What the hell did that mean?

* From Nigel: 'Susie. Lovely. Safe home. Bye.' Dear Nigel,
the definition of uncomplicated. Such a relief.

Having burnt out on the combination of extreme excitement, excess sugar and lack of sleep, Lula and Charlie had
both drifted off even before we hit the A12.

'You're quiet,' said Alex after a mile or two.

'It's been a pretty noisy weekend, so ...' I tailed off. 'I
hardly saw you. Have a good time?'

'I guess. It was all about the folks, really, and they definitely had a good time. I haven't seen Dad looking quite so
chuffed since ... maybe since Will got his starred first, or
Isobel was called to the Bar, or Guy scored his first try for
Harlequins.'

It was Alex's turn to tail off and I felt, despite myself
– despite everything – an unexpected surge of warmth.

'I seem to recall he was completely delighted when you
became Publishing Director.' (Did I tell you that Alex is
the publisher of three men's style magazines? Apologies,
distracted.)

'Maybe.' Alex sighed. 'You want music?'

Sunday afternoon, Radio 2, Johnnie Walker's *Sounds of
the Seventies*.

I'm not in love, so don't forget it. It's just a silly phase I'm going through. And just because I call you up, don't get me wrong, don't think you've got it made . . .

Alex punched the retune button. 'I hate that song. Always have.' He stared straight ahead while navigating a roundabout. His expression . . . expressionless, unfathomable.

'I like it.'

'Yeah, you would.'

I didn't know what he meant by that but I did know it wasn't the best time to ask, so we drove the rest of the way home accompanied by Radio 4 while, inside my head, I started practising the beginning of an entirely different conversation. After numerous versions – the traffic was bad – I eventually hit on one that seemed to strike the right sort of tone: potentially quite light but with hidden depths. It went like this:

'So, anyway, Alex, um, I was just wondering . . . who is this person whose name begins with P who wants you to live . . .' (at which point I would do air-quotes with my fingers, so help me Joan) ". . . a different sort of life?" A life which apparently includes smiley emoticons and three kisses?'

Now all I had to do was pick my moment. Fingers crossed.

CHAPTER 2

Pippa

Dear Mum,

After the dinner at Guy and Lisa's, I was at home and in bed by 12.30, having checked up on Hal, who had fallen asleep with his light on and the new iPod Touch on his pillow, so it had probably already fried his brain (does that date me, thinking that all electronic devices are potentially mini-microwaves? Probably), in which case David would be spared the school fees, should Hal ever actually get in to College Hall, north London's most over-subscribed fee-paying-guarantee-of-a-place-at-a-pukka-uni. Though, knowing David, he'd probably offer the bloody school a new IT building. Come to think of it, he probably already had. And I can't believe I've only just thought of that. No wonder Hal was so chilled. 'Walked it'? Daddy probably walked it for him.

I worry about Hal. He's a good kid mostly, but like all his mates he's also what used to be described as 'spoilt'. 'Little Emperors' they call them on Mumsnet (the website? Are you up to speed?): the children of parents for whom belt-tightening is what you're able to do when you've lost another precious pound at the gym. They have *every-bloodything* they want, and loads more they don't want, even in the middle of this recession-what-recession. And then it's all about the screens. I think I'm pretty multi-task-tastic, frankly (and this I definitely get from you), but kids now (kids now? I am turning into you) are super-multi-taskmasters. I'll watch Hal playing a game on his laptop while keeping one eye on the telly as he texts his mate Dom and I just think . . . *give yourself a break*. Though to be fair I did find him in bed the other night actually reading a book. And not even on his Kindle – a proper book made of ye olde dead trees. According to Hal, 'sometimes reading's wicked, Mum'. Thank Christ for that, eh?

So Hal's probably mostly OK, even though he leads this weird other life when he's with his dad and the current Mrs Ashford. Whatever else is going on in my life, it's really important for me to keep his feet on the ground because having a filthy-rich mostly absent father is probably grounds for decades of therapy. He has his dad on a pedestal – and you know that on a pedestal is probably where David is happiest.

Anyway, I'm making it sound as if me and David are

still at loggerheads when we're actually sort of OK (did I tell you that?), mostly, kind of, on a day-to-day basis. If only because there isn't a day-to-day basis. I haven't seen him since Hal's handover at Christmas and with a bit of luck I won't see him again until Speech Day, and email actually does seem to work for us, even though so many other divorced parents say it usually makes things worse, because of the possibility of misinterpretation. You know, take an ordinary misunderstanding, multiply it by a thousand, light blue touch paper and retire. The trick is to keep emails brief, factual and polite and to stop yourself telling the ex what you really think of them. I have always been the mistress of email – you know that, even though I'm writing this letter in the old-fashioned but post-handwritten way, via printer ink on paper. Whatever, email is just about all I ever intended to be the mistress of.

I've got a horrible feeling I may have done my email-spiel to Alex at some point, but with a bit of luck he forgot because it's not like it's relevant. And I'm sure he's the master of email – he works in publishing, FFS (don't know if you know what FFS stands for? For fuck's sake. But you don't say it aloud – it's only written down).

So anyway I met this man called Alex over a bowl of chilli at Lisa's and ... I chose to forget about him almost immediately. I do believe it's possible to choose to put somebody out of your mind – it's probably one of the things that mark you out as a grown-up. But it was easy enough to do it because, two days later, I was going on a proper see-you-at-eight date with somebody who wasn't married. OK, so I hadn't actually met him when we made the date and therefore couldn't categorically say he wasn't married, but I had to believe him when we spoke on the phone to arrange it and I said something like 'don't forget to take your wedding ring off' and he laughed, but said (quite earnestly), 'Trust me, I'm definitely totally one hundred per cent divorced. Shall I bring my decree absolute?'

Internet dating. I honestly never thought it would come to this – and I took a lot of persuading, believe me – but when I finally caved in, well . . . where do you go if you're in my position? I'm forty-two, I can't hang out in bars or clubs and I don't have an office to go to anymore. And even if I did it would be full of teenage girls, middle-aged women and gay men, which is great if you want to gossip about *X-Factor* or how much cosmetic surgery Madonna is still not admitting she's had, but not if you're looking for love.

So I bit the bullet. Signed up to imnotinlove.com, spent an entire Friday evening working my way through a bottle of red (two-thirds, actually, just in case you think I'm losing the plot) and constructing a profile.

It's weird, selling yourself. You have to be upbeat and accentuate the positives without being entirely unrealistic. Before I started, I read a few by women my age and they were so unashamedly 'Look at me! Look at my tits!'

that I nearly gave up, though eventually I constructed something that felt honest but not too honest and found a great snap that Lisa had taken of me in Chamonix last Easter – bit of a ski-tan, not TMI tit-wise (TMI? Too Much Information: the basic currency of the dating website) – and just as I was starting to wobble and think this really wasn't for me, I hit Send and then there I was: a pretty good-looking, fit forty-two-year-old brunette single-mum-of-one with her own teeth (underneath her veneers) and a nice house in Belsize Park and no mortgage and no pressing need to work (not that I don't want to, but have the choice), who loves yoga and the gym and skiing and who recently ran the London marathon for a breast-cancer charity but who isn't averse to quiet sofa-spud nights in front of the telly, and can appreciate a film with subtitles (occasionally) and is happy to eat her own bodyweight in carbs over dinner as long as she can get down the gym the next morning, and ...

Was it Robert Louis Stevenson who said it is better to travel hopefully than it is to arrive? Whatever, the point is that, wherever I was headed with the internet dating, the next few days were fun and checking my messages on the website became quite addictive. I don't know what it is about the net that gives you this false sense of security and inspires you to open up and ... well, if not let it all hang out, then certainly push your boundaries a bit. Within a few days I'd narrowed the fifty-six (I know!) contenders (in fact I'd had more replies, but these were the ones who didn't sound like wannabe serial killers and who could write whole sentences with punctuation) down to a workable ten, and then I'd messaged them and we'd started chatting by email (I couldn't cope with instant messaging; it felt too in-your-face), and then five of those fell by the wayside. Why?

* One of them revealed he'd read the entire Jeffrey Archer oeuvre. I can understand reading one Jeffrey Archer out of curiosity or because you'd found it in a hotel room. But all of them?

* Another described his ex as a 'mad bitch'. Enough said: two sides to every story; save it for therapy.

* Another (and I can't quite believe I'm telling you this, but you lived through the 1960s so . . .) admitted he'd like a threesome. It's not a giant crime (I don't suppose there's a man alive who wouldn't) but still, we hadn't even met.

* One bloke (who I'd really liked the sound of – 'GSOH', etc. – said he'd recently been forced to move back in with his mum after both his business and marriage had failed. I probably shouldn't judge (he said it was only temporary) but I did. Is that bad? Too late.

* And then the last one admitted he'd let his previous date pick up the restaurant tab 'because she'd offered and I thought she'd be offended if I argued the toss'. This was a tough one because of course it's fine to offer to pay – almost compulsory if you're a grown-up working woman – but you don't want to have to, do you? I'd be fine with splitting it on a first date and if he seemed really keen to pay – as if it was an affront to his masculinity not to – I wouldn't 'argue the toss', but I'm old enough to think that a reasonably solvent adult male shouldn't let a woman pay. I wonder what you think, Mum?

Anyway, once I'd weeded out the bitter and twisted, tight-fisted, sex-addicted Jeffrey Archer-reading Mummy's boys, I was left with five perfectly reasonable-sounding men, so I picked one and went for it.

His name was Gary. He was forty-four, worked 'in finance' (better the devil . . .) and lived in Islington. He'd been divorced for three years after having been married for thirteen, with two daughters of eleven and eight and had had one 'rebound relationship that lasted a year – lovely woman, just wasn't meant to be . . .' He had even been in Chamonix last year, just the week before I had. He sounded totally unscary, normal, and he was good-looking but not too good-looking, if you know what I mean? Not vain-looking. So.

We hooked up at a quiet-ish bar in Soho on the Friday after I'd met Alex at Lisa's, had a couple of drinks and made polite small-talk before going round the corner for dim sum at a Chinese we both knew, and then we loosened up a bit. And he was properly nice, funny but not wannabe-stand-up funny. He looked good too, not uptight (Richard James suit, John Smedley sweater underneath) and he smelt delicious. He was losing his hair but that's not a problem and he was, on first impressions anyway, really quite lovely and we were getting on brilliantly. He kept touching my arm over the table – just fleeting little touches, not lingering clings – and though he talked about work (he's a man) it was just the right amount. And he spoke very well of his ex-wife and was good with the eye-contact.

And so, after dinner, when he suggested a nightcap at a members' club he belongs to round the corner, I was up for that. And quite surprised he'd belong to that sort of club, frankly, being a city boy. But he said that his work involved a lot of media contact and not all city boys were obsessed with numbers to the exclusion of all else. 'Some of us are actually interested in the world outside the square mile.' And obviously I liked that, having been Mrs David Ashford. (And no, if you're wondering, I didn't flag up the Mrs-David-Ashford thing. I just said I'd been married to a man called David who worked in finance and hoped his radar wasn't that attuned, and luckily it wasn't. I mean, I don't think I send out Ex-Mrs-Hedge-Fund vibes. Not anymore.)

In short it couldn't have been going any better. And I really did think *this internet dating lark is great. What took me so long*? So we were inside the club, having another drink and feeling pretty relaxed, and Gary introduced me to a couple of people and it was all very easy and fun and by midnight he had introduced me to another friend as 'my hot date. Didn't I do well?' and I didn't mind a bit and was even thinking: if he tries to kiss me later, I'll just go with it.

By about midnight (it was Friday night, so what the hell) we were quite a little gang on the sofas. Two other couples, plus two former colleagues of Gary's, and a couple of their friends. It was all very convivial and gossipy and pleasant. Made me realize how much time I've spent alone. Made me realize I don't want to. Anyway, eventually I needed to go to the loo and one of the other women, Amanda, to whom I'd just been talking – one half of one of the couples – said she'd come too, so, we were in the ladies', doing our lips (that tube of Mon Rouge you gave me still hasn't run out) when Amanda suddenly said – blurted – 'So, you and Gary? How's that going?'

And I said, 'Well, for a first date I think it's going pretty well. What do you think? You know him better than me.'

And she pulled an odd face, a kind of smile-cum-grimace. And then she kind of checked herself, before saying: 'I think you look very comfortable together. Listen, Gary is a man any woman would want to have as a friend.'

And I looked at her quizzically. It seemed to me that (and even after X glasses of whatever) she was trying to tell me something.

'Friend? But not boyfriend?'

'No, not boyfriend. Look, I'm sorry, I'm talking – the wine's talking – out of turn and I'll shut up now. Please don't get me wrong – Gary's a lovely bloke, he really is. You'll work it out.' And then she was gone.

'You'll work it out?' Did she mean Gary and I would work it out? Or did she mean I'd work out why Gary wasn't good boyfriend material? I lingered in the loo for a couple more minutes, grappling with this information. And then I thought *sod it, I'm having a fun evening* . . . and went back upstairs.

It was after 1 a.m. when the party started breaking up, and eventually it was just me and Gary, and he had an arm round my shoulder by now – but not in a creepy way. And I said, 'Well, it's been great but I'd better be going. Babysitter.' And Gary said, 'Yes, of course. Look, Pippa, I've had a fantastic evening, I really have. And I hope I'm not being presumptuous but I think you might have done too – they're a good bunch, aren't they? – and . . . I would really, really love to see you again. Very soon, if you think . . .'

And I dived in. 'I'd love to; it's been great.' And I was both delighted and relieved, because I definitely wanted to see Gary again but I wasn't quite drunk enough to feel comfortable about the your-place-or-mine routine. As first dates went, though, it had been pretty perfect, so why screw things up? I'm forty-two. I can do delayed gratification. And apparently so could he.

Gary said, 'I'll get you a cab,' and we stood on Old Compton Street and waited and when a free cab appeared he opened the door and then he kissed me lightly on the lips and put a hand up to my cheek and said, 'I think you're great, Pippa. Thanks for a lovely evening. I'll call you. Or you can call me. I don't play games,' and I said something suitably end-of-a-good-first-date-ish and got in the cab and I was still grinning by the time we'd got to Oxford Street, when I suddenly remembered I'd left my bag on the sofa in the club and realized I was a bit more pissed than I'd thought I was.

So the driver did a U-turn and I said, 'Two minutes . . .' and ran back into the club and though I'm not a member they were fine when I told them about my bag, and of course I found it straight away, exactly where I'd left it. It wasn't the kind of place where anybody was going to nick a bag, not even a Mulberry Bayswater – and I came out again and I don't think even two minutes had passed but I could see my cab disappearing down Old Compton Street, and I said, 'Fuck!' and a guy who had been standing outside the club having a cigarette the first time I'd left said, 'I saw that. I was a bit surprised too – but I think the driver thought it was you who got in – same hair, really similar coat. I don't suppose he felt like he could chuck her out.' And I shrugged and decided to walk round the corner to find another cab.

And I nearly bumped into Gary, but I'm so glad I didn't. It was weird the way it happened, because if I hadn't forgotten my bag ... well, anyway, everything went a bit slow-motion when I spotted him, standing in the doorway of a bar – and there was nothing odd about that: he hadn't said he was going home and I hadn't asked. No, what was weird was the fact that he was standing talking to a guy he obviously knew – they were laughing together and I was quite enjoying being able to look at Gary when he couldn't see me; he'd have had to have turned round to catch sight of me – when the other bloke, who was taller, suddenly leaned forward and kissed Gary on the forehead and then put one arm round his waist and squeezed his bum. And Gary carried on laughing and even though he removed the man's hand, he didn't pull away or look remotely put out or surprised. And then they both went inside the bar. And ... and I could feel a hot blush rising from my chest and creeping up my neck and I felt ... stupid, embarrassed.

You'll work it out ...

I'd spent the whole of my career working alongside gay men and I like to think I have a pretty finely tuned gaydar – though clearly not as finely tuned as I'd thought – so yes, I'd worked it out. Even if Gary hadn't.

So anyway, Gary did call. On Sunday evening. I knew he would; he's a nice guy. He started saying how much fun he'd had on Friday and I bit my lip while he went on about this and that and then he said, 'So, how about dinner? Thursday or Friday? Does that sound like a good idea?'

And I said, 'Gary, it would've been a good idea, if . . .' and I faltered a bit. And Gary said, 'What? What's up?!' and I just thought, fuck it, tell it like it is . . . 'if you weren't gay, Gary. It would be a good idea if you weren't gay.' And that stopped him for a moment. So I told him about going back for my bag and losing my cab and walking round the corner, and . . . and the silence was awful, but then he filled it.

'Actually, Pippa, I don't know if I am gay. But I might be. I probably am. I just don't know. But I do know that you are great and I like you a lot and I'm sorry. I'm really sorry.'

'Why are you going out on dates with women if you think you might be gay? I don't get that. It's fine for you to be gay but what the hell are you doing on Imnotinlove.com and asking me – and God knows who else – out when you should be on, I dunno, Grindr? What are you *doing*?'

'Hedging my bets? Look, I'm incredibly sorry, Pippa. I mean that. I'm gutted. I've only just found you and it looks as though I'm losing you already.'

'He was hot, though, wasn't he?'

This wasn't said with any hint of bitterness, I might add. The bloke outside the bar was hot, end of. Gary laughed. His relief was obvious.

'Yes, he was hot. His name's Niall; he's a TV cameraman. Look, Pippa, I am desperate to salvage something from this. Please can we stay in touch?'

I even considered it for a moment or two, but then (you'll be pleased to hear) I got a grip. 'I don't think so, Gary. My little pink book is pretty full. My quota of gay best friends has been met. If I needed more I'd sign up with mygaybestfriend.co.uk.'

'Does that actually exist?'

'No, to my knowledge it does not exist. But it's a brilliant idea and I might just stay in on Friday nights and set it up. Meanwhile have a lovely life, whichever path you choose to take, OK?'

And I put the phone down, albeit metaphorically, because I wasn't on a landline. So there you have it, Mum: my first internet date. It doesn't necessarily excuse what happened next but it does, I think, go some way to explaining it. I had pretty much worked it out of my system after a session in the gym on Monday morning. Or at least I thought I had.

And the four other men on imnotinlove.com? For all I know they're still trying to email me. I cancelled my subscription the next morning. And then straight afterwards I got a call from Lisa wondering whether I'd mind doing a couple of days in the shop on Thursday and Friday, because Guy had just sprung a surprise long weekend on her and his mum had said she'd take the twins and although everything would probably be fine with just Marta in the shop, she'd feel that bit more secure if I was around, if I didn't mind? And she said she'd pay me, of course. But I said I'd love to and she could donate my two-day 'salary' to charidee. And I meant it because, a) I actually love being in the shop, and, b) I've no idea what the going rate is for an independent fashion boutique manager, but whatever it is, I don't need it.

And anyway, working in Name was the perfect distraction from dating closeted gay men. I love Lisa's shop – I know you would too – because it's funky without being alienatingly super-hip and it attracts the kind of women you want to talk to. Or at least listen to, or just watch. Because it's in Primrose Hill, half the clientele are TV presenters or actresses, and that's just the half I recognize. And Marta is a sweetie and fun to be around and I like hearing about twenty-something dating hell, if only because it has alarming similarities to forty-something dating hell, though I chose to keep my counsel on that subject, even when repeatedly pressed by Marta.

And the weather seemed to have cheered up a bit, too, which meant more customers keen to shed their layers – and I absolutely love the intimacy of a shop where customers will ask the 'staff' what they think. I probably missed my calling as a stylist while I was busy booking jobs for models. Or maybe not an actual stylist, but as someone who has, as you know, always had a handle on how to shop (and the means to do it, for which I am grateful, I suppose, whatever the emotional cost of those means) it's a thrill to pass on The Knowledge.

For example, on the Friday we had a really lovely woman come in – beautiful olive skin, fabulous inky hair, excellent manicure, cute toddler in tow . . . and also about five foot two and the shape of a plum tomato. And I could see her eyeing the Hussein Chalayan rail with total longing – as well she might – and suddenly I desperately wanted her not to make a Terrible Mistake. I think she was in the toddler zone but wanting very much not to be, and we've all been there. So when she picked out a tiny sliver of a frock in a size ten – which, incidentally, there was no way she was going to get into – I felt a duty to deflect her potential misery, to reduce the huge gap between her expectations and the reality of almost certainly looking totally crap. So I did. And when she left half an hour later with a carrier bag containing a coral-coloured swathe of silk jersey from Issa, I actually high-fived Marta.

So I was in a pretty good mood. Gary was a receding memory and Alex was as good as forgotten when this woman – blonde, very striking, slim but curvy – walked into the shop when Marta was on her lunch break. She came over to the till and said, 'Hi, is Lisa around?' and I said, 'No, sorry, Lisa's gone away for a long weekend with her boyfriend so I'm just filling in,' and she said, 'Oh, OK, that sounds fun. Where have they gone? Have they taken the twins?' and I said, 'Well, I don't think Lisa knew when they set off, and no, the twins are with Guy's mother apparently, but she texted me this morning to say they were in Barcelona, which sounds pretty fab.' And the woman said, 'Oh I love Barcelona. How wonderful . . .' and then her phone rang but she missed the call while looking for it in her bag, and she said, 'Excuse me,' and wandered a few feet away and started flicking through the Hussein Chalayan rail while she made a call, and I thought: *Yup, you can wear that dress.* And then I couldn't help overhearing her conversation – she spoke quite loudly – because it was quite distracting. Here it is, or at least her side of it, pretty much word for word:

'Hey. Hello you. Look, I'm sorry I missed you last night. Best laid plans, yeah . . . But look, I think I can get away early this afternoon . . . Hook up with you at that hotel when I'm sort of on the way home . . . yeah . . . and we can grab an hour? Maybe longer . . . Um, by the way, on the subject of hotels, is The Landmark that big one on the Marylebone Road? . . . OK, no worries, I'll explain later . . . But I can only stay an hour, tops . . . Yeah, have to be home by seven . . . no later or I'll be in real trouble with you-know-who . . . Bye!'

And then she hung up and turned round and rolled her eyes at me and sort of grinned and said, 'Sorry about that!' and I said, 'No problem!' and grinned back because I could read between the conversational lines and it was pretty obvious what was going on. Anyway she started flicking through the Chalayan rail again and said, 'Actually I only popped by to see Lisa but my God, this is a great dress ...' and she picked out the same dress that Plum Tomato had looked at, and I figured she'd look great in it so I said, 'Oh you really should try that on,' and she didn't need much persuading.

I was just about to process the payment while the woman was saying how 'totally perfect' the dress was for this Do she had to go to next weekend, when Marta came back from lunch and I said, 'Look, Marta, do you mind sorting this out for me? This customer has just bought the most perfect frock, and I'm completely starving.' And I turned to the woman and said, 'Enjoy. You looked really great in it. And of course you've got it with you for the cocktail hour too.' And I winked and she laughed and said, 'No, I think I'll save it, but thanks.' And Marta came round to the till and said, 'Hi. How are you? Let's have a look ...' and peeked in the bag. And the woman, who was obviously a regular, said, 'Hi, Marta, it is the most fabulous frock and –' she turned to me – 'I'm sorry, I don't know your name ...' and I said, 'Pippa,' and she said, 'Pippa talked me into it, but it didn't take much, to be honest.'

And I said, 'Well as I say, enjoy it.' And she said, 'Thanks, I will.' And I left.

And when I came back an hour later, Marta said it had been quite a busy lunchtime since Susie had bought that dress. And I said, 'Susie?' And Marta said, 'Yes, she's Guy's sort-of-sister-in-law. Her partner is Guy's twin, Alex. They're not married but they've been together for ever and have two kids, I think.' And, Mum, I really didn't know what to say for a moment, but then I said, 'Oh, I wish she'd said.' And Marta said, 'She said the same thing to me. She said, 'Oh, I was about to tell Pippa how I knew Lisa and ask her to give her my love when I was totally distracted by that dress.' And I said, 'It's easily done.'

And though I carried on with my Friday afternoon on autopilot, my head was full of Susie. And, by extension, Alex.

My phone rang on Sunday night, quite late, about ten. And I nearly ignored it because I had a hunch it might be David, or even Gary – though there was no reason why it should be either of them – but I was glad I did because the caller ID said it was Lisa.

'Pip!'

'Lisa. Have you just got back? How was *le weekend*?'

'We stayed at this amazing hotel just off Las Ramblas and it was ... Pip, Guy proposed.'

And that was properly wonderful news. I mean really brilliant. Because Lisa and Guy are great together and even though they had had the twins, I still wasn't sure if Guy was the marrying kind, so it was lovely to know he was, because Lisa deserves that. And then I asked if she was going to be in the shop tomorrow and if so, could we have a quick lunch, possibly involving a glass of champagne? And she said, 'Absolutely. And anyway I wanted to thank you for looking after things when I was away.' And I said, 'Well, there's no way you're buying me lunch now.'

Mum, I lay in bed on that Sunday night and you must believe me – I know you would – I was in a real quandary. Whatever I may be, whatever kind of woman I have become, I am not, have never been, a gossip. If anything I am a people-pleaser, occasionally at some cost to my own happiness. And I'm also a bit naive sometimes, too, though recent events have kind of shored up a stronger side of me, I think. And so as I lay in bed thinking about Susie cheating on her nice ... well, I'd assumed he was her husband, but anyway, partner ... who, it now seemed clear to me, probably already suspected something – if indeed he didn't already know – the more I felt that that was ... well, there's no other word for it except wrong. And although I am a woman's woman, well, I'd spent twenty minutes selling a frock to Susie Whatever-her-surname-is, whom I had liked ... and about four hours getting to know her partner really quite well, even if I had done most of the talking. And he was such a nice bloke – arguably even nicer than Guy, whom I adore. And I felt bad for

Alex, understood now why he had been so muted when we'd met, why he'd barely spoken about Susie.

The following morning I went to the gym straight after dropping Hal at school. I worked out for an hour and when I got out of the shower I felt that delicious kind of physical exhaustion and mental alertness that I always get from a really good workout and which really seems to help keep me off the anti-depressants. So yes, I was in a very good mood when I got home – even singing along to the oldies on Ken Bruce while I sorted out a few emails and unloaded the dishwasher before going to meet Lisa for what I hoped might be quite a long lunch.

We met at St Germain, a few doors down from the shop, which I love – it manages to be both local and glamorous, and we ordered a bottle of champagne straight away. Lisa showed me the ring, a simple, but simply enormous diamond in a chunky platinum setting, and told me how Guy had proposed over dinner at Ca l'Isidre, which would've been too showy and public for me, but a round of applause from the other diners (and some vintage fizz on the house) is totally Guy and Lisa, and that's fine. And Lisa was glowing so much I thought she might be pregnant again too, so I asked her, after the second glass, but she said, 'Do you think I'd have ordered a bottle if I was, like, pregnant?' and I said, 'Well, yes, probably.' And we laughed and it was ... a lovely afternoon. And of course we got a bit pissed.

And that's when I told her. That's when I said: 'I met your soon-to-be-sort-of-sister-in-law in the shop – Susie.'

'Yeah, Marta said she'd come in and bought that great dress. She's probably going to wear it to Mr and Mrs Fox's golden wedding party this weekend.'

'Yes,' I said, 'but she might wear it before that I think.' And Lisa gave me a questioning look, so I said, 'Lisa. She's having an affair.'

Lisa's jaw literally dropped and she said: 'Hang on – she told you this?'

And I said, 'No, no, of course not, but I overheard a phone conversation.' And I told Lisa about Susie saying she could hook up for an hour at – and I think I got this right – the Landmark Hotel on the way home, but had to be back by seven or she'd be in trouble with you-know-who. And how that made sense of Alex's quietness the other week. And probably also why he hadn't even mentioned her name.

And Lisa said, 'Hang on, Pip. You were flirting with him. And he was flirting with you.'

And I was a bit surprised by this because I really hadn't been flirting – had I? And other than the 'yummy' comment, I don't think Alex had been flirting with me, and I wanted to make this clear, so I said, 'No, Lisa, you know me, I don't do flirting. I do *empathetic*. And if a man mistakes it for flirting, that's not my fault, is it?'

Lisa conceded that this was true. And she sat silently

for a few moments, twisting her engagement ring around her finger, and then she said, thoughtfully, 'That's probably why Alex turned up in the first place, to talk to Guy? But of course we were in dinner party mode, so they never had that conversation. Omigod, poor Alex . . .'

And I said, 'But don't tell Guy. You mustn't tell Guy. Leave it to Alex to do that . . . if and when.'

'Yes, of course. Of course I won't tell him.'

And straight away I knew she would.

I can't remember too much about the rest of lunch, but the mood had changed – and Mum, I'd changed it. I felt guilty about that, but also oddly relieved. I'd passed on something I'd learned to a person . . . (well, given I was now pretty certain Lisa would tell Guy, make that people . . .) I could trust. And more than just being people I could trust, they were the right sort of people, they were part of Alex's family so they would do right by him, because that's what families do, isn't it? And frankly it felt good to have unburdened myself because ultimately it really wasn't my problem, was it?

By the following Friday, I had four more sixty-minute sessions at the gym under my belt plus two evenings of Ashtanga, my weekly flower-delivering visit to the hospice . . . the usual busy-doing-anything routine my life has become. Oh, and Hal had got a place at College Hall, which had necessitated a Thursday night celebration supper at Carluccio's with Hal and a quick call to David, who was delighted, of course, and said that he'd be passing through London next week and would take Hal out for his own celebration. And I couldn't resist asking David if he'd bought off the school with a new IT wing. And he had the good grace to laugh and said, 'No, but maybe next year, eh?' And then he said, 'Actually I wasn't going to tell you this just yet, because we haven't had the twelve-week scan, but ...'

So, Mrs Ashford was pregnant and 'Hal will get a sibling after all'. And my good mood was, unsurprisingly, instantaneously not only broken, but totally crushed. But through gritted teeth I managed a 'congratulations'.

Maybe if that hadn't happened on Thursday evening, I would have handled the Friday phone call differently. Who knows – it's a total 'whatever'. Either way, when my mobile rang at about 11 a.m., after the gym, and the caller ID revealed a number I didn't recognize, instead of being put off I was mildly intrigued, so I answered.

'Hi.'

'Hello? Is that Pippa?'

'That's me, yes.'

'Hi, Pippa. Um, it's Alex Fox here. We met the other week, at, er ...'

'Yes, Alex. At Lisa and Guy's.'

'Yeah. Look, I know this is totally out of the blue, so I'll cut to the chase: I got your number from Guy and he said that, well ... er, look, I wondered if you were free for a quick drink later? I'm at the office till five thirtyish, maybe six . . . but, if you were free?'

'Sure. Yes. Um, look, I think I know why you might be calling.'

'Well, maybe. Maybe not, but . . .' And he named a bar in Soho, near his office. And it was with some irony I realized it was the same bar where I'd seen Gary being groped by the hot cameraman, and that felt right, somehow. In fact suddenly everything felt a lot more right than it did wrong. And I really can't explain why that is.

I spent the rest of the afternoon deciding what to wear. It needed quite a bit of thought because obviously this wasn't a date. Or at least not any kind of a date I'd ever been on, so there was no point in looking all Friday-night-up-west. I rejected loads of things – too casual, too smart, too sexy, not sexy enough . . . before I eventually hit on a combination that I felt sent out the right sort of signals: quietly confident and a little bit sexy without being remotely in your face. Black skinnies, a grey silk DVF blouse with a bit of a plunge, and my latest pair of black suede Georgina Goodman boots – mid-height heel, not too vampy, comfortable for walking, if walking happened to be on the agenda, and a lovely double-breasted Jaeger camel coat. It was very après-office – if I worked in a pretty glamorous office – so I looked like a woman of substance, but more shaggable than scary. Not that I was thinking 'shaggable', obviously, but I didn't want to look un-shaggable, either.

I got there too early, of course, so I walked around the block a few times until I was fairly sure Alex would have arrived. And when I did finally walk through the door I spotted him straight away, at the bar, fiddling with his phone, and he glanced up and smiled. Not a big beaming, teeth-baring sort of smile but quite a tight-lipped smile, and I leant in to kiss him on the cheek and he seemed, I don't know ... reticent, slightly surprised, but he asked what I wanted to drink and blah-di-blah, and I hopped on to the stool and he just leant against the bar and looked a bit distracted ... and I really didn't want to say, 'So, why am I here?', but he did it for me.

'Um, Pippa, you're probably wondering why you're here. Or at least why I asked you to be here.'

'Well, I'm sure everything will be revealed.' I wanted to sound bright and chipper but definitely not too pushy.

'Yeah. Look, Pippa, there's some stuff going on in my life. It seems to have gone from being averagely complicated – work, family, kids, the usual – to much more complicated, virtually overnight.' He sighed and stopped. I desperately wanted to fill in the gaps because he looked so ... adrift.

'Yes, that can happen. Things happen just like that. As Tommy Cooper would have said.' And I regretted *that* as soon as it came out of my mouth.

'Ha. Well, I've lost my job. Today. Just like that. And apparently my missus – we're not actually married but we may as well be, should be by now, I suppose – is, according to my brother, having an affair. It was Guy who encouraged me to call you, actually. We met up last night and he told me that you'd overheard Susie arranging to meet someone. And, in his words, he said, "You should talk to Pippa about it." And actually I wasn't going to call you because I really wanted to sort stuff out with Susie first, or at least have a conversation about it, but I came in to work this morning and . . . look, you don't want to hear all this, do you?'

'Oh but I do. Please. I owe you one anyway for talking non-stop at Guy and Lisa's, so please use me as a sounding-board.'

'Well, I was going to ask you about the Susie thing, but suddenly that seems like, well . . . literally yesterday's news. Not that it isn't important – it is, wildly important. It's just that it's been temporarily eclipsed after the meeting this morning in which our new owners . . .' and Alex went on to explain how his publishing house had recently been taken over by a big German company, and though there were rumours of pretty dramatic re-structuring, Alex had felt safe because his magazines were doing well – at least, one of them was – but this morning the newly installed German CEO had called him in for what he'd thought would be a strategy chat; instead he'd basically left with his P45. And now he was looking for a great employment lawyer, but he'd also wanted to chat to me, because he didn't feel he could talk to Susie about this ... yet, while he was still in shock about it, and especially not if she was 'having an affair! I mean, fuck! It never fucking rains but it pours. And now I'm talking in clichés.'

'Shall I get him to pour you another?' I asked, gesturing at the barman.

'Yeah. Fuck it. Let's get pissed and put the world to rights and then I shall head home to the mother of my children and break it to her gently that I know she's shagging someone else but, hey, I've lost my job and would she mind very much putting on a brave face for the sake of my parents' golden wedding anniversary tomorrow? Yeah, that's A Plan.'

And that was indeed a plan. And indeed that's exactly what happened. And by ten o'clock we were pissed, and when Alex texted Susie (he showed me the text) it said, *i'm going to be even later than I already am. sometimes a man's gotta do ... it's a work thing. tell you later.*

And back came her reply (he showed me): *save it. do what you have to do, i'm getting an early night cos 2morrow will be a late one, remember?*

And by eleven thirty we were in a cab heading back to mine, which was fine, because Hal was having a sleepover at Dom's ... and we were suddenly frantic, kissing like teenagers in the back of the cab, just insane with lust. And, Mum, believe me, just writing the words 'insane with lust' makes me blush because it sounds like one of those pulpy fifties novels with a lairy cover, but it's true, that's what we were. And we got to mine, and Alex said: 'Nice work – at least you got a great house off the hedge-fund tosser,' and it wasn't the moment to explain about the house, really, so I just said, 'Yeah. Coffee?' and he laughed and I fiddled around for ages trying to find the keys and then we were inside and I was turning on the lights ... and, literally with the flick of a switch, the moment just shifted and suddenly, through a blur of Grey Goose-and-tonic (but not much tonic) I saw Alex blink and I just knew ... I knew I'd lost him. I knew he was going to go. And I really didn't want him to go.

'Pippa. Oh God. Look. I know this is totally crap of me, but ... I don't think I can do this. Not now. Maybe not ever. Christ, what am I doing? It wouldn't be fair. Not to you, not to Susie. It would be fabulous, I know that – but it wouldn't be fair. Not now. Maybe ... Look, I've got to go. I'm so sorry.'

And it really was as quick as that. One minute he had had his tongue down my throat and his hand up my blouse, the next he was talking like somebody out of a bad film. What did 'fair' have to do with it? I didn't at that moment give a monkey's about notions of 'fair' or 'unfair'; I just wanted him. But I kind of slumped back against the wall, DVF un-tucked, Paloma Picasso's Mon Rouge lipstick smeared, and sighed. And I recognized that if I wanted Alex as much as I thought I did – knew I did – I would

77

have to play the long game and embrace delayed gratification. I would also have to be cleverer than I'd probably
ever been, at least when it came to men.

'You're right. You're as good as married; you have kids;
you've just lost your job; it's your parents' golden wedding
tomorrow. This is not the time. This would just be running
away from the cold reality of the here and now.' (I could
do bad movie scenes, too, apparently). 'So go. It's fine. I
won't hold it against you. Much as I might like to.' And
at this moment I actually (look away now, Mum) leant
over and ran my hand over Alex's crotch. Which, I discovered, was not on the same page of the script as his brain.
And he groaned.

'I'm going, Pippa. I'm going now. I'm sorry.' And then
he removed my hand from his crotch and he went.

I walked into the kitchen like a Stepford Dumpee, boiled
the kettle, made camomile tea and walked upstairs and
into the bathroom. I made my looking-in-the-mirror face,
which was slightly blurry, and I removed my make-up
slowly, with intense fastidiousness, and applied moisturizer, cleaned my teeth and even flossed, and then I got
undressed and put on my bathrobe. I walked into the
bedroom with the tea and got into the gorgeous Frette
bed linen with the stupidly high thread count – a wedding
present I was still intensely happy to have custody of –
and then I picked up my phone, wrote a text and sent it.

In the morning I woke up with a thundering headache

and all the details of the previous night – the good, the bad, the crotch-strokingly ugly – flooded back, and I reached for my phone and there it was: *Start living a different kind of life ... P :-) xxx*

And I didn't even quite know what I meant by that, but I knew it was the start of something.

I love you, Mum.

Pip xxx

CHAPTER 3

Alex

Monday 8 June 2009

From: isobel@struttbrayrush.co.uk
To: alex@foxmail.co.uk; guy@guysports.com;
             willfox@wings.co.uk

*Brothers: Just to keep you up to speed with plans for The Party
To End All Parties. (Warning: There will be bullet points!)*

* *Ma and Pa want us all at the Pink House NO LATER than 12.
  That's MIDDAY on the Sat, Guy. So no excuses!*

* *The marquee people will be there first thing. Having said that,
  I think it would be good if there were somebody on hand other
  than the folks to oversee things. Will is nearest, and has already*

volunteered. Thank you, Will. Also, photographic duties fall to Alex, obviously ... so don't forget your camera(s)!

- Ma has booked a catering company she read about in Tatler or The Lady or the Suffolk Gentlefolk Monthly, or whatev – Hot Sausage and Mustard. They will be on site by 8 a.m. and commandeering the kitchen, but will also arrive with as much stuff pre-prepared as poss. You prob don't give a monkey's about the menu but I have included it as an attachment, if you can be arsed.

- The order of play is that non-family guests (100!) should be arriving 6 for 6.30. There will be drinks and then dinner will be served 7.30–8. There are some nannies organizing ents for the kids when they start getting annoying. Afterwards there will be speeches. We are all doing speeches, btw, so please get cracking pronto! I've allocated 5 mins each. Then Pa will close and there will be DANCING! Local DJ – ex BBC Suffolk (!) – booked. Carriages at 1 a.m., etc. I have pre-booked a taxi service for the locals.

- Accommodation: we're all sleeping over, obv. Everybody's in their old room, except for Alex and Susie and the kids, who are in the stables(!).

- Sunday: Ma and Pa will host brunch, but Ma has hinted (OK, said) that we're expected to clear off by mid–late afternoon *as they will be exhausted. Won't we all?! Marquee's being taken down Monday, btw.*

• *Met office long-range weather forecast is good. Fingers crossed!*

• *Don't forget your dancing shoes! Over and out.*

Isobel x

From: guy@guysports.com
To: isobel@struttbrayrush.co.uk

You basically scare the shit out of me. Still, very impressive. 12 it will be ... G

From: alex@foxmail.co.uk
To: isobel@struttbrayrush.co.uk

Terrifyingly efficient. Expect nothing less. Off to therapy now, re stables ... A x

From: willfox@wings.co.uk
To: isobel@struttbrayrush.co.uk

Very good. I've decided to stay overnight on Fri 19th – figure the folks will get in a flap first thing o'wise. Will do Alpha Male stuff re marquee erection – tho have decided against wearing uniform. W x

From: guy@guysports.com
To: alex@foxmail.co.uk

Did you get that email from I?! Weird she never went into the Forces, no?! Call you later? G

Thursday 18 June 2009

From: alex@foxmail.co.uk
To: guy@guysports.com

Thanks for lunch. Thanks and – no thanks. You know what I mean. My head is still spinning. It's not that I'd ever been so complacent as to imagine that Susie might not be capable of whatever it is she's been capable of. It's just that you don't go looking for trouble, do you? We've been OK. Not great, I grant you, but OK. Nothing is ever the same after you have kids (as you know). But just because it isn't the same doesn't mean it has to be bad (as you know). We've just been muddling through, same as everybody. Sometimes it's a bit ships-in-the-night, but . . . I dunno. I really don't know what to think. And it's been kind of complicated by the fact that it came from Pippa. Kind of ironic, really. I mean, whatever Pippa lacks in a sense of

*humour she makes up for in . . . I don't think I have to go there,
really, do I?*

*Anyway I keep thinking about the details of it. Weird that it
was only last week. Look I'll cut to the chase – could you text me
Pippa's number? I've got to get my address book up to speed on
my new phone, having lost the other one at the bloody Landmark
when I was blue-sky-out-of-the-fucking-box with the Germans. And
I know what you're thinking but my motivation for wanting
Pippa's number isn't THAT (really!). I just feel I need to talk to
her about exactly what she overheard. God, I hate this week!*

*But I'm so selfish. It's not all about me. Congratufuckinglations
– if ever there was the perfect wife for you, it's Lisa. About fucking
time. A*

From: guy@guysports.com
To: alex@foxmail.co.uk

*I hear you. Don't go doing anything hasty . . . BUT, having said
that, it may well be a good idea if you spoke to Pippa. While I
totally trust Lisa's version of events – why wouldn't I? She's going
to be Mrs Guy Fox – I think it's prob a good idea for you to get
it from the horse's mouth, so to speak. Though Pippa's no horse.
Anyway, I'll text you her number separately as a business card.
G*

Friday 19 June 2009

From: isobel@struttbrayrush.co.uk
To: willfox@wings.co.uk

*Will, I know you're up to your eyeballs and you're racing down
to the Pink House tonight, but I just wondered if you'd heard
from the brothers this week? I've sent a couple of emails and no
replies ... I know they're not exactly wordsmiths, but I usually
get the email equivalent of a grunt in reply, so ... Anyway, see
you tomoz! Ix*

From: willfox@wings.co.uk
To: isobel@struttbrayrush.co.uk

*Spoke to G – he's been out of the loop (I quote) 'closing a mega-
deal'. Whatever that means. (Assumes Patronizing Older Brother
Voice.) Apparently we can read all about it on the back pages of
the tabloids tomorrow. In truth, I may forget to do that. Anyway,
A isn't in a good place. Apparently he lost his phone last week
and didn't back up all his numbers, so that prob explains the
radio silence, but he just called – ostensibly about tomorrow
though I could tell there was something else – and YOU MUST
NOT BREATHE A WORD OF THIS TO A SOUL because he's
keeping it under his hat till the party's over – but he's just lost
his job. He's in bits. What is called for is some sibling support
but in a hands-off sort of way, I think, for now ... I got the*

impression he wasn't going to tell Susie till after the weekend.
Having said all that, I think there's even more going on. Don't
know what – just a hunch, even though A is always pretty impos-
sible to read. Other than that, everything under control. See you
tomoz. Wx

From: isobel@struttbrayrush.co.uk
To: willfox@wings.co.uk

Oh God, I just KNEW there was something! Poor Alex. My lips
are SEALED. Though nothing is guaranteed after the second glass
of fizz. Till tomorrow. I x

From: willfox@wings.co.uk
To: isobel@struttbrayrush.co.uk

Who says there'll be a second glass of fizz?! Recessionary meas-
ures called for – isn't it going to be cava all the way after the
first glass?! Now I trust you to keep mum (if not MUMM! Look
– a champagne joke!). On the subject of which, don't even think
of telling the folks. W

From: isobel@struttbrayrush.co.uk
To: willfox@wings.co.uk
Am not entirely stupid! MUMM's the word. Gutted about the
cava, tho . . . x

Monday 22 June 2009

From: isobel@struttbrayrush.co.uk
To: willfox@wings.co.uk
Cc: Guy Fox; Alex Fox

Congratulations siblings! I don't think the weekend could have gone any better, do you? Spoke to folks first thing: tired but happy. Kitchen restored to relative normality, tent pegs/dance floor apparently haven't entirely ruined lawn and they're leaving for the Portuguese Golf Detention Centre from Stansted tomorrow a.m. Our Work Here Is Done, methinks?! Hope all well in your respective worlds ... Ix

From: alex@foxmail.co.uk
To: guy@guysports.com

Crap morning. Told Susie about work – it took a while to get her to actually hear what the hell I was saying and when she did she was pretty tight-lipped – and then I had so much on my mind, like talking to employment lawyer to sort out the redundancy package. Anyway, I got Isobel's email – glad folks OK and enjoyed weekend and will be out of loop in Golf Hellzone for a bit. Thanks for support. Talk soon ... A

From: guy@guysports.com

To: alex@foxmail.co.uk

Look mate, don't do anything SILLY, right?! Don't start making decisions when everything is a bit tits up, emotions running high ... remember, Susie is the emotional one, you're the cool one, so hold on to that. And don't worry about the Pippa sitch. One drunken taxi fumble does NOT constitute a relationship deal-breaker. Unless you want it to. Get your priorities right: sort out the work thing before you start messing with the domestic stuff. Look at it this way: you've had a relationship hiccup and what-ever Soos has been up to maybe you're now both 1–1 in extra time? But pause before you start taking the penalties, eh? Bound to end in tears otherwise. Just saying ... G

From: alex@foxmail.co.uk
To: guy@guysports.com

Thanks. Am cool, calm ... and I've collected my P45! Gallows humour always the best, eh? A

From: willfox@wings.co.uk
To: alex@foxmail.co.uk

You OK? W

From: alex@foxmail.co.uk

To: willfox@wings.co.uk

Never better! You? A

From: willfox@wings.co.uk
To: alex@foxmail.co.uk

Are you being chippy or merely sarcastic? Just offering support, like big brothers are meant to do. No need to take it ... W

From: alex@foxmail.co.uk
To: willfox@wings.co.uk

Yeah, I'm chippy AND sarcastic. Thanks for offer of support – but not required. It'll all get sorted. As you were. A

From: isobel@struttbrayrush.co.uk
To: alex@foxmail.co.uk

You OK little brother? xxx

From: alex@foxmail.co.uk
To: isobel@struttbrayrush.co.uk

Thanks, I'll be fine. Everything will be fine. Enforced change is an OPPORTUNITY, right?! It's a cluster-fuck of mid-life crises pending ... A

From: isobel@struttbrayrush.co.uk
To: alex@foxmail.co.uk

Look, I'm just saying I'm here if you need me. I know you won't but it's my sisterly duty to say it. And not only say it but MEAN it. And if you need any legal advice I know a cracking lawyer who relishes a good ruck and would leap at working with you. I x

From: alex@foxmail.co.uk
To: isobel@struttbrayrush.co.uk

Employment or Divorce?!

From: isobel@struttbrayrush.co.uk
To: alex@foxmail.co.uk

FFS! Employment! What ARE you on about? Call me between 1– 2 p.m. if you want the name/number. She's ace. I x

From: alex@foxmail.co.uk
To: isobel@struttbrayrush.co.uk

Grateful! Will call. A x

Friday 26 June 2009

From: guy@guysports.com
To: alex@foxmail.co.uk

Wassup? You still alive?! G

From: alex@foxmail.co.uk
To: guy@guysports.com

Yeah, but only just. Sorry – bastard week. Isobel put me on to one of her lawyer mates who's a proper ball-breaker and says she'll see me right (at a price). And Susie and I are ... actually fuck knows what Susie and I are. All I know is that a big box containing a pair of posh new boots arrived for her this morning and then she said she's taking the kids down to the seaside for the weekend to stay with her new best mate, that Sausage Woman from the party, formerly known as Heinous – I think you met her? And apparently she's doing this because she thinks 'we all need some space'. So hurfuckingrah – we are now officially a mid-life crisis + marital breakdown x unemployment cliché, squared. You going to the match tomorrow? A

From: guy@guysports.com
To: alex@foxmail.co.uk

Oh. Shit. But maybe a weekend apart good for all of you? And I'm not only going to the match tomorrow, I've got two golden tickets for the director's box. You on for that?! G

From: alex@foxmail.co.uk
To: guy@guysports.com

Like you need an answer? Call me in the morning with the Where and the When . . . A

From: guy@guysports.com
To: alex@foxmail.co.uk

Great re the match – should be ace. And why not call Pippa? Any port in a storm, eh mate? And it's not like you're MARRIED! (This is a JOKE!). G

Monday 29 June 2009

From: alex@foxmail.co.uk
To: guy@guysports.com

Call me asap? A

From: guy@guysports.com
To: alex@foxmail.co.uk

Look, I know we just talked for 5 mins and obv we needed longer but I just want to reiterate: don't tell Susie. Take a deep breath. Sort out your mid-life crisis. Get the Ball-Breaker to clinch you a fabulous redundo deal that will buy you a year off to re-think. Publishing not the be-all. You've been moaning about the pressure for at least 18 months, remember? In a year's time you could be totally tooled up as a photographer and living your fucking dream. Sell the house if you have to, but FFS don't rush into anything. G

From: alex@foxmail.co.uk
To: guy@guysports.com

Thanks. It's fine, really ... A

From: alex@foxmail.co.uk
To: guy@guysports.com

I just tried to call you – signal busy – but I think I need to write this down anyway because, further to my previous ... it's not fine ... last night I had the first proper conversation I've had with Susie in weeks. She came back from her girly weekend at the seaside all calm and collected and ... it turns out that the conversation Pippa thought she overheard in the fucking shop was actually Susie LEAVING A FUCKING MESSAGE ON MY PHONE. THE SAME PHONE I LOST BEFORE I'D HAD TIME TO HEAR THE MESSAGE. A MESSAGE ABOUT MEETING ME AT THE LANDMARK HOTEL, COS SHE KNEW I WAS THERE FOR THE GERMANS' MANAGEMENT THINK-TANK. FUCKITY-FUCK.

I left the fucking phone in the Landmark's bar at lunchtime on that Friday, shortly after which Susie apparently left me a message suggesting some sort of quick 'date-night' cocktail on the way home, and she said we could only be an hour or so because she'd already asked our terrifying au pair – Irish Ruby, aka You Know Fucking Who – to stay late twice that week, and she was too scared to ask her again. If you'd met Ruby, you'd know that was entirely plausible. She's like Susan Boyle crossed with Sarah Palin. But when I got home – late that night, unsurprisingly, after being forced to reinvent the wheel for the Germans and then have a 'celebratory' drink – Susie was already in bed. I told her I'd lost my phone and all she said was 'that explains why you didn't return my call. I left you a message this afternoon. But whatever.' And she just turned over and went to sleep.

Anyway, all of that would be fine, I guess, wouldn't it ... if I hadn't just spent most of this weekend IN BED WITH PIPPA.

I am fucked. Thanks, Guy. And thank your missus too, while you're at it. I can't really blame Pippa, I suppose – not now – but I think I may need some SPACE. A

From: guy@guysports.com
To: alex@foxmail.co.uk

—DELETED—

CHAPTER 4

Susie

I don't regret that weekend with Heinous in Random-on-Sea, despite the fact that it changed everything. I don't believe in regrets – why dwell on the past when there's so much future to fuck up and then pretend not to have any regrets about?

I spoke to Heinous on the Tuesday after the party, the day after I had returned from the morning school run so full of thoughts that I barely even registered that Alex was still at home, much less wearing his pyjama bottoms in the kitchen and synching his new iPhone on the laptop instead of at work (presumably that late night on Friday had earned him a Monday morning off? Whatever). Either way, having psyched myself up on the journey to school and back – all of twenty minutes – I barely paused for breath after shutting the front door before confronting him about the text message from 'P'. I took a deep breath. And then I just launched into it.

'So, Alex, um, I was just wondering, er—'

But before I'd got into my stride, Alex interrupted.

'Look, hang on, Susie – you and I probably need to talk about lots of things, but first . . .' And his voice went from calm, disengaged, distracted to, well, the opposite, really – chilly, his words like a cold shower.

'Let's just stick to the stuff that really matters. Like the fact that on Friday I . . . I lost my bloody job, Susie. Which, in case you were wondering, is why I'm sitting here in our kitchen in Queen's Park at 9.30 a.m. on a Monday morning, instead of in Soho preparing for the weekly 10.30 strategy meeting, as fucking per . . .'

And at this point he picked up his (nearly empty, thankfully) coffee mug and hurled it at the kitchen wall, helpfully painted in Farrow and Ball's near-as-dammit coffee-coloured 'London Clay'.

I know that men define themselves by their work even more than women do; however, Alex has always defined himself by his work more than most men. Which meant that an out-of-the-blue redundancy (because while Alex may have been brooding over this all weekend, which of course explained a lot, it was still news to me) was bound to test the strongest relationship. And we didn't, at this moment in time, have anything even approaching the strongest relationship. And now I had to tap dance in fuck-me slingbacks on hot coals.

'OK, Alex. This is suddenly a lot to take in. And I don't

think chucking coffee mugs at walls is really any way to—'

'Oh shut up, Susie.'

'No, I will not shut up. I am incredibly sorry – and shocked – that you have just lost your job but for some reason you are not making it very easy for me to sympathize.'

'Yeah, let's make it all about you.'

Actually, I could see that he might have a point. Thinking on my dancing feet – which still hurt from Saturday – I decided to make it All About Him. My partner had just lost his job. Out of sorts was the order of the day. Accusations about affairs were unhelpful. They could wait. Or I could even be spectacularly grown-up and just ignore them completely. So, what did I do? Farrow and Ball be damned, I put the kettle on.

The rest of the day was much calmer. We sat down and talked about the redundancy situation. About lawyers ('I bet Isobel knows someone' was easily my most helpful suggestion). We talked about the 'opportunities' redundancy represented, albeit theoretically. Alex talked vaguely about photography, his great passion, and how maybe Now Was The Time. And we talked about the kids, and how, thank God, we didn't have school fees to worry about since we had been 'fortunate' enough to pay a premium to live in the catchment for a decent, if not actually outstanding, London primary. And when Alex wanted to make a couple of calls, I snuck off to the computer and ordered those boots from Georgina Goodman, because I am a modern working woman with my own income and bank account, and fuck it . . . they were great boots. And we both agreed we wouldn't tell the kids about Alex's job because they wouldn't understand, and we'd just try to get through the next few days like grown-ups, if that was humanly possible. And I thought, 'Try to forget about "P", because "P" is not necessarily a cuckoo in our little familial nest; she may just be a red herring.'

So the week became as calm as any week that begins with a job loss and portentously simmering accusations of infidelity can be. Which is to say, not quite as calm as one may like but not entirely unbearable, either.

Ruby, our . . . well, 'nanny' is far too grand a word for someone who does three or four hours after school, and no weekends, and not quite enough of the holidays (i.e. no August, or religious festivals) . . . anyway, Ruby agreed to babysit on Tuesday night so that Alex and I could go for a quick Thai. During which I came very – dangerously – close to saying that I was on a tight deadline with this year's *100 Best Restaurants in the World* – my professional baby, the one I'd given birth to a decade ago and which was still bouncing, but fortunately I bit my tongue just in time.

Before I'd had the children I'd done a lot of the legwork on the guide myself, but these days I mostly edited, while the terrible drudgery of having to eat great meals in the world's very best restaurants was grudgingly farmed out to legions of slavering food hacks, which did a lot for my waistline and my professional popularity but I can't pretend I didn't miss it. And I'd never missed it more than while I was sitting in a no-better-than-OK local restaurant on a drizzly June evening with a partner so wound up he looked as if he might actually punch his Pad Thai unless an even softer target presented itself. Fortunately I quickly realized that any mention of my working life would, in the current context, probably ensure I was that target, so I stopped mid-sentence. But Alex seemed to be so far away, so lost in his own thoughts, that I'm not sure he would've heard me anyway.

During the five-minute walk back to the house, I had the proverbial brainwave.

'Look, Alex. On Saturday Heinous invited us, well mostly me and the kids to be honest, down to visit her in, er, Random-on-Sea,' (I had genuinely forgotten where she really lived) 'so I thought I might give her a call tomorrow and avail ourselves of her offer. Drive down after school this Friday. Come back late afternoon Sunday, if that's cool with Heinous – and you? It will give us all a bit of, dare I say it,' (I even felt brave enough to waggle my fingers in the air), '"space".'

'Yeah, yeah. Whatever.'

'Sure?'

'Yeah. Go on. Where the fuck's Random-on-Sea?'

'Um, not Brighton but down and left a bit and keep going until you're nearly in Kent, apparently.'

'That'd be the A21 then. The Highway to Hell. Take you for ever if the weather's good. Don't you remember, we went to a wedding down that way a few years ago, after Lula, before Charlie? Philip from our marketing department and that ditzy fashion editor girlie – Bridget, wasn't it? The one who was so skinny she looked like she'd faint before she got her vows out?'

For the first time in two days Alex sounded . . . normal, I suppose. And sometimes when you're adrift in the Ocean of Abnormal you have to seize on normal as if it were a passing lifesaver.

'Yes, yes, God, Philip and Bridget, whatever happened to them? It was in Battle, wasn't it?'

'Yeah. Philip set up on his own and dumb Bridget just wanted babies straight away. But she would have had to spend a couple of years just eating before bothering to have sex. Actually, if memory serves, I think they ended up with IVF triplets. Can you imagine?'

It was deliciously normal, me and Alex comfortably slagging off old acquaintances. Even if it doesn't reflect very well on us as generous and warm-hearted individuals, we all do it, don't we, inside the co-dependently bitchy bubble of coupledom? So I felt safe, if not entirely secure.

'Anyway,' Alex continued, quite perked up by now, 'yes, why don't you go and see the Sausage Woman. Report back. I like it down there. The travel links are so rubbish that you can get a lot of house for your money. I remember having the conversation with Philip.'

'Yes, that's what Heinous said too. "A lot of house for the price of a two-bedder in Media Vale".'

So the next day I called Heinous, and she said, 'Of course! Come, for God's sake. But that's rough on Alex, about the job, isn't it? Are you sure you shouldn't be at home, massaging his fragile male ego in a wifely manner?'

'No, I'm pretty sure I shouldn't, as it happens. I'll explain when I see you. Email me directions. See you supper time Friday, if that's OK?'

So, on Friday, when me and the kids finally fell out of the car at 7.45 p.m. and into Heinous's front door at the beginning of my first visit to Random-on-Sea (Alex had not been wrong about the A21 being the Highway to – or conceivably, in this case, from – Hell, especially on a Friday) the first thing Heinous said was: 'Nice boots. Cosy for the end of June, but one must suffer for such glamour.' The second thing: 'Drink?'

And as I glanced around her pretty Victorian townhouse – which was, unnervingly (this was the woman I'd hated, after all), decorated almost exactly the way I would've decorated it, in muted colours, referencing its location with seascapes and driftwood and beach stones and tongue-and-groove panelling in the loo but not theming it up too much – it felt, weirdly, a little bit like a home-from-home. Which was a very strange feeling for a confirmed Londoner who had spent a lifetime suffering from agoraphobic panic attacks whenever she ventured beyond the M25.

So that weekend all the planets were in the correct alignment for me to start my somewhat fraught affair with Random-on-Sea: my partner had lost his job, he may (or may not, we'd see) be having an affair of his own and thus an idea began to form in my mind. Just the hintette of an idea at this point, really, but one that took a more concrete – or at least bricks-and-mortar-ish – form over the next few days.

There were several compelling factors that contributed to the unfolding of my Master Plan.

1) Heinous and I got on like the proverbial burning *maison*. During the next forty-eight hours it occurred to both of us (we discussed it at length over an implausible amount of Sauvignon on the Saturday night) that one of the reasons we'd probably loathed each other at school was because we were so similar, and of course, at sixteen, entirely without the wisdom to see it.

2) I was also particularly vulnerable to the idea of a new BF since my old BF, Bella, had moved to Australia to edit the glossy magazine *Girlfriend* nine months ago. I

missed Bells more than I ever quite dared tell her during our emails because, with a deflating sense of insecurity, I wasn't sure if it was entirely reciprocated. Her emails were relentlessly enthusiastic (The weather! The city! Commuting to work by ferry from her groovy Sydney suburb! The beach-based social life! The weekends in the Blue Mountains and hip spas in Byron Bay!) while from me they were basically just more-of-the-same (Work! The kids! Alex! The kids! Work! The weather . . . the weather . . . the arsing, twunting weather!).

3) Lula and Heinous's chip-off-the-block of a daughter, Edie – just the right side of being a wildly precocious only child (and it takes one to know one) – bonded instantly. Charlie, meanwhile, took charge of Heinous's labradoodle, Sausage, and was beside himself that it took precisely five and a half minutes to get from Heinous's front door to the beach.

4) Random-on-Sea was, it turned out, a town of two halves. To the east was ye Olde Towne, all Tudorbethan beams and inglenookery and steeply winding streets teeming with a combination of beardy-boho local artists (more RAs per square foot than anywhere else in the country, according to Heinous – something to do with the light, apparently), beardy-weirdy yokels (possibly actual fisherfolk) and hip 'DFLs' – aka the Down-from-Londoners. These were either rich enough to be weekenders escaping from their pricey postcodes or self-employed creatives who

didn't need to commute and had traded the same kind of expensive alleged-lifestyle I was living – and, it turned out, Heinous had also lived in nearby 'Media Vale' with her ex – for a life of sun, seaside and bracing cliff walks on the beautiful Fire Hills.

Meanwhile, to the west of the town's seen-better-days pier was the formerly elegant and gracious, now fairly dilapidated and grungy, Victorian New Town. This was where Heinous lived, in a Grade 2-listed four-storey terrace with sea views. As conservation areas go this one was less chic than it was shabby, frankly, but I loved it at first sight. The houses may have needed re-painting, re-roofing, re-pointing and in some cases entirely re-building, but they were big and beautiful and everybody appeared to park right outside their own front doors, a major novelty for a Londoner. The area even reminded me (and if I squinted it helped) of a run-down version of London's Little Venice, with the Channel standing in for the Grand Union canal.

5) All of which was why, as early as Saturday lunchtime when we were trawling en masse for fish and chips in ye Olde Towne, I found myself peering in estate agents' windows and exclaiming, with (according to Heinous) predictable Londoner's zeal, 'Look at THAT! Five beds, garden the size of Queen's Park and all for the—'

'Yup,' said Heinous, who had been in this position every time she was accessorized by over-excitable off-the-leash

Londoners, 'the price of a poky two-bed flat in "Media Vale" ... I know, Soos. Why do you think I'm here?'

So we had had a great weekend, but I was pretty surprised by how little persuading Alex had needed about the Master Plan.

When I'd returned home excited on the Sunday night, full of tales of big, cheap houses, and *the beach at the end of the road* and how much the kids loved it, Alex and I had finally sat down and had the conversation I'd been practising again in my head on the drive home.

'Look, Alex. Um. Who is this person whose name begins with P who wants you to live ...' (at which point, yes, I did do air-quotes with my fingers) '... "a different sort of life"? A life that apparently includes smiley emoticons and three kisses?'

I was inspecting Alex closely for a reaction but there wasn't much to go on, just a slight twitch and a pursing of the lips which, even for an expert in neuro-linguistic programming (which I wasn't), would have been virtually impossible to read. I vaguely recalled that, on the other hand, Alex had learnt a bit about NLP on some ghastly management-empowerment course, back in the days when that kind of stuff was considered not only desirable by the boss classes, but a sound investment. Anyway, though it seemed an age before he replied it was probably a particularly filmic hyper-real half a second. Alex glanced up at me and made eye-contact. It was surprisingly intense. So much so, in fact, I had to look away.

'What "P"?'

I breathed deeply.

'Someone – presumably a woman – who sent you a text just before the party. Look, I'm sorry but your phone fell out of your jeans pocket when I was tidying and, uh, there it was. So shoot me.'

This sort of light-hearted 'D'oh!' forehead-slapping and eye-rolling approach seemed like a good idea. Even if it didn't sound like me.

'P? Um, that'd probably be Pippa. A friend of Guy and Lisa's. Met her at their place that night I stayed for dinner the other week, remember? Anyway, you've met her. She works in Lisa's shop sometimes, used to be Lisa's agent, sold you that expensive dress you wore to the party?'

Pippa was that nice woman who'd *sold me the Hussein Chalayan dress*? I had to think on my feet because I could suddenly recall almost every minute of my half-hour in Name, and . . .

'Well OK, but it still doesn't explain why this Pippa is sending you soppy texts with kisses and smiley faces.'

'Actually, she was being supportive about me losing my job. She was suggesting that every ending is a . . . a . . . new beginning. I'd told her at Guy and Lisa's about loving photography and I think she was just saying, go for it. That's how I read it, anyway.'

'But this still doesn't add up. How did she know you'd lost your job? How did sodding Pippa know you'd lost your job before I did? Answer me that, Alex. I'm the mother of your children!'

I know; it sounded exactly like a scene from *'Enders*.

'Because ... look, Soos, I'd spoken to her at work on Friday, OK? She called me at the office because I'd had a conversation with Guy and ... and there was something I needed to ask her about. And something I need to ask you about, too, as it happens, when I can get my head round it. But because I'd also just lost my job we inevitably talked about that ... and, y'know, she was helpful. People often are when they're not connected to a situation them-selves. And she was full of advice, for chrissakes.'

'Hang on, hang on. That's when you sent me that text: *a man's gotta do*. Did you "do" Pippa, then? And what did you "need" to talk to her about? Did you "need" to get up to speed with the spring-summer collections?'

Yes, even I could see this was going nowhere fast, but what would you have done in the heat – and the heat was now suddenly white hot – of the moment?

'No, I did not "do" Pippa. You're being ridiculous. And selfish.'

Actually he had a point. I was being selfish.

Over the next several minutes, while adopting a calm, but just-this-side-of-patronizing tone, Alex told me that Pippa had overheard me arranging what had apparently sounded like 'an assignation, a hook-up' with 'somebody in a hotel', and that 'she'd told Lisa, after that weekend in Barcelona when she and Guy had got engaged', and that Lisa told Guy. And Guy had told Alex, and Alex had called Pippa, ostensibly to find out what this was all about, but had then got sidelined by losing his bloody job.

And, during those few minutes, I was (thank God!) able to reassure him that:

A) Of course I wasn't having an affair. I hadn't had a conversation with anybody – Pippa had just got the wrong end of the stick. Because:

B) I'd been leaving a message for Alex, on his phone. Which was:

C) The same phone he'd already lost. But I wasn't to know that he'd lost it, was I? And so:

D) When I hadn't heard back from him that afternoon, I'd assumed he couldn't escape from the Germans and had just gone home and relieved Ruby and sorted the kids and, yes, spent a bit of time twirling around in front of the bedroom mirror in the Chalayan, and ...

E) I had been more or less asleep by the time Alex had eventually got home, so ...

F) *Of course I wasn't having a bloody affair.*

I mean, how laughably ridiculous an idea was that? Or rather, yes, maybe I had been trying to have an affair, if you could call an attempt to have a spontaneous date-night 'fling' with your own partner an affair. And the irony of this was that I'd tried to do it because Alex had become so distant I was worried he might be having an affair. A worry that had of course been compounded by discovering the bloody text from 'P' a week later, which had in turn haunted me for the golden wedding anniversary weekend during which Alex had been so incredibly distant, despite that thoughtful packet of Resolve. Anyway Alex's distance made perfect sense as soon as I knew he was trying to protect me from knowing about losing his job. And as for this Pippa person ... who cared? As far as I was concerned she was now *Pippa who?*

And so, improvising quickly, I said all this while Alex nodded and listened intently and didn't butt in. And with the assistance of my excellent memory, and Alex's apparent compliance, I figured all of this messy stuff could be buried pretty easily. I was confident about that. After all, Alex had lost the bloody phone, hadn't he? And with it any 'evidence'? It was a good day to bury bad news.

So that Sunday night, after I'd returned from Random and we'd had our surprisingly calm and measured and indisputably grown-up conversation, Alex was a very different Alex from the one I had left on Friday afternoon. The colour was back in his cheeks and he seemed bright-eyed and optimistic. He said he'd gone to a brilliant match on Saturday with Guy, had had an excellent conversation with the Ball-Breaker in the early evening and nearly gone out for a drink with his closest work colleague, Tony (who had inherited the magazine marketing job from Philip, of Philip-and-Bridget, and who lived round the corner from us in Kensal Rise) but then he'd decided to stay in and eat pizza and watch *Match of the Day* instead. He told me how he'd spent far too much of Sunday in bed, just thinking ... and how I had been right – the space had been good for us. Possibly even essential, because that space had suddenly, miraculously, put everything into perspective and helped him to see where his priorities lay.

And that night, for the first time in maybe eight or ten weeks, we'd made love – well, fucked, really. And it had been so good, not to mention a surprise, to recapture some of the urgent up-against-the-wall-now passion that had characterized the first few years of our relationship. Alex seemed to be alive again in a way that I found unexpectedly exciting. So unexpectedly exciting, in fact, that the Myla thong had made an equally unexpected reappearance from the back of the knicker-drawer. And when a sleepy Chuck had turned up at the bedside while we were still in the early – and still conjoined beneath the duvet – sexual aftermath, clutching his bunny and blinking and saying, 'I was woke up by big noises, Mummy. What was they?' Alex and I shared the warm collusive giggles ('*were*, darling. It's *what were they?*') of the very-happily-coupled-thank-you, before returning Charlie to his bed.

I couldn't, in truth, recall being quite this content for ages. And even though nothing changed the fact that Alex had lost his job, he seemed . . . OK. Better than OK, frankly. Perhaps I should have questioned that, but what kind of self-sabotaging fool goes searching for problems when a sufficiency of problems generally proves to be perfectly capable of seeking you out all by themselves? That would be idiotic, wouldn't it? Well, either idiotic or . . . or what – sensible? Pragmatic?

Against this backdrop, then, our summer unfolded gently and evenly. In the last week of July and the first week of August we had our usual Cornwall fortnight staying in the piggery conversion near Perranporth (actually it was probably just a normal, if slightly low-slung barn, but for some reason, now lost in the mists, we had dubbed it 'The Sty' the first time we'd rented it back when Lula was a toddler, and it had stuck). There, as usual, we celebrated both our summer babies' birthdays – Lula was born at the end of July, Chuck six days later – and settled into the easy rhythms of the English seaside holiday: namely, four glorious days of sun and sandcastles, rock-pools and pasties and rosé-soused sunsets and the kids falling asleep on our laps at dinner, followed by four days of torrential downpours, during which we would put off the (inevitable) trip to the Eden Project, before (inevitably) caving in on Rain Day Three. Once there, we would struggle sweatily through the Rainforest Biome accompanied by half of north-west London, fail to find anything the children wanted to eat in the cafe at lunchtime, cough up too much cash too quickly in the gift shop (after which something would invariably get lost/broken before we'd even got back to the car) and then spend the following day regretting Our Eden Hell, far too exhausted to do anything other than stay in the house playing Hungry Hippos and Boggle and watching Disney DVDs. And then the sun would suddenly reassert itself and the whole cycle would begin again, for another week. Bliss, really.

So, by the end of the summer Alex and I had talked a lot about relocating to Random-on-Sea, having made a few hit-and-run visits with the kids in August, when we peered in estate agents' windows and ate chips on the windy, shingly beaches. By this time, of course, we had convinced ourselves we were moving out of London for all the 'right' reasons – to start again, to paper over our domestic cracks, making the future a better, brighter, ozone-suffused place for us all.

We put the house up for sale in the second week of September and despite a sluggish property market we were under offer within three weeks. Our buyers were a lovely gay couple – two solicitors, Christopher and Christian – who hadn't been put off by the faint coffee stain on the Farrow and Ball. In turn, we knew that this meant we could still afford to buy a listed-and-stuccoed-and-corniced (with an embarrassment of garden, probably) Dream Home with hardly any mortgage. Which also meant that even with just one income and Alex's redundancy package we could afford to send Lula and Charlie to a prep school on the outskirts of Random, a school with a hundred acres of playing fields and a maximum of eighteen kids in a class. So, finally, our very own Good Life was waiting to unfold inside (as soon as we found it) our Dream Home. Who wouldn't have been excited about that? Who wouldn't have turned a blind eye to all the signs and portents that hinted at an entirely different outcome for us all? It's a rhetorical question, mind you. No need to answer.

We had a party at home a few days before we completed on the sale and moved down to our wonky rental in Random. Mid-November felt like a strange kind of time to be moving away from our home and our friends – mutual and individual. Alex and I had always prided ourselves on not being smug marrieds. Not actually being married helped, obviously, but everybody close to us had long since stopped bothering to ask us why we weren't. Or maybe they'd just forgotten. Anyway, we'd always kept our own Venn diagram of friends, with the ones we both liked – couples of the equally un-smug variety, mostly – overlapping in the middle.

November is a neither-one-thing-nor-the-other sort of month – not yet Christmassy, yet post the Halloween-and-Bonfires autumn the kids love so much and which I wished hadn't been turned into such a relentless consumer-fest, with entire supermarkets re-vamped in the Halloween-themed livery of orange and black. I wasn't a fan of the trick-or-treat, which (I was tediously fond of pointing out, every single October, ad infinitum) had never existed in this country until *ET* had introduced it to us in the early 1980s. But anyway, here we were in the very last gasp of autumn, inviting our N&D round to say goodbye with bottles of wine and slices of home-made pizza and it was only when I found myself wedged into a corner with Tony from marketing – whom I liked, but with whom relations had become ever so slightly strained since Alex's departure from the company – that I had one of those spooky, slow-motion, entirely-in-the-moment yet slightly-out-of-body experiences that made me think, 'Fuck! What are we doing? These are our people, this is our 'hood. Where are we going?'

And then it passed as quickly as it had arrived. The turnout was good, too, while all those who hadn't been able to make it had very plausible excuses. These included Guy and Lisa, who though our 'closest'– at least in terms of distance – family members, had dropped off our radar a bit in the last few months. There were obvious reasons for this, what with our respective summer holidays and Guy and Lisa both being caught up in the Pippa-and-the-overheard-conversation debacle, though I had made a point of having lunch with a very contrite Lisa shortly after Alex had explained things.

'Look, Soos,' Lisa had said after we'd both made small-talk about kids and pushed lettuce leaves around our plate and then drunk a glass of wine slightly too quickly, some time in early July, 'Pippa is a great girl, but she's also got a bit too much time on her hands, and stuff . . . But the point is, I know it was a genuine misunderstanding. I know she regrets it. She's had a tough time for a few years so we've cut her a bit of slack, but obviously that was never meant to involve—'

'Potentially fucking up my relationship with Alex? Potentially fucking *him*? Well that's very loyal, Lisa, but the fact remains that she not only weaselled her way into Alex's confidence but, as far as I can tell, exploited his vulnerability. And let's face it, she's a very good-looking single woman and, on an entirely un-sisterly level, she might be good at selling me expensive frocks but I don't want her anywhere near the father of my children.'

'I hear you,' (Lisa did enjoy an earnest American cliché) 'I *toadally* hear you, but you guys are good now, right?'

'Yeah, we're pretty good. All things considered. Alex is feeling quite positive about his, uh, mid-life crisis. We're thinking of . . . well, let's just say we're thinking of all sorts of new and interesting things. But anyway, just never mention Pippa again to me, under any circumstances, and we'll be fine. And can we please talk about wedding plans? You any nearer to fixing a date?'

So I'd ironed things out with Lisa. And I'd left Alex to sort things out with Guy. Their twin-thing was pretty much impenetrable; they had all the psychic bonds you'd expect if you've ever read ancient doctors'-waiting-room women's magazines in which 'The Weirdo World of Twins' articles are a pretty consistent theme. There was the time, for example, when Guy had had a burst appendix playing rugby when he was thirteen and at precisely the same moment Alex had suddenly fallen off his stool in the chemistry lab at their school, clutching his lower abdomen and screaming 'Guy! Guuuuy!'

This independently verified event had immediately passed into both school and family lore, to be regularly trotted out at family gatherings, often with interesting new embellishments. For example, since I'd first met them both, the story had expanded to include Guy shouting Alex's name as he writhed on the rugby pitch and Alex on the floor of the lab clawing at his stomach so much he ended up with a temporary scar, just like Guy's permanent one. Though the event itself had definitely happened, I had always been intrigued by the fact that this didn't seem to be enough to keep it interesting – that over time, both Guy and Alex had embroidered it.

I thought this said a great deal about notions of 'truth'; that basically your version of an event is necessarily your 'truth' and my version of the same event is going to be my 'truth' and anybody witnessing it will inevitably have their own version of that 'truth'. This has made me slightly suspicious of some of the more fervent claims of truthfulness, if only because truth often seems to be entirely subjective. However, the 'truth' of the matter in this case was that Lisa and Guy couldn't make it to our leaving party because they had taken the twins to visit Lisa's family in Brooklyn, and specifically her ailing grandmother – who wasn't expected to make it to next spring – and that this had been arranged for weeks, long before we even had a date for completion on the house. Yup, that was the whole truth and nothing but, so help me.

Will was a no-show too, what with being in Afghanistan doing brave RAF-type things and not due back until his tour ended at Christmas. But we had Isobel and the kids, and Nigel and Joan, obviously, and my dad and Cathy. Despite, on the surface, having zilch-zero-nada in common (certainly not golf) with either Nigel or Joan, Dad always made a fabulous effort to slay them with an onslaught of charm, not to mention the sort of urbane name-dropping you could tell they didn't entirely trust but secretly rather enjoyed. And then Dad and Nigel would eventually find some common ground, which usually involved slagging off politicians at both ends of the spectrum as well as the bits in the middle, united as they were in their dismay at anybody younger than – maybe even other than – themselves being allowed to run the country. Meanwhile Joan and Cathy always defaulted to a conversation about food and were therefore as happy as a pair of pigs-in-blankets.

So (as Tony from marketing would say, infuriatingly) 'it's all good'. And it *was* all good. We had friends, we had food, the kids were being sweet and exceptionally well-behaved – seen a lot but not heard as much as they might be – while passing around the pizza slices, and it should have been an evening of warmth and optimistic excitement laced with an inevitable poignancy that all this was about to pass. And I suppose it was all of those things, up to a point. Alex was more attentive to me than I might have predicted while maintaining his Fox-y hail-fellow cheeriness with everybody else. I was having some interesting chats, not least with Isobel (things were still simmering along with the saucy Tosser) who had also taken a very proprietorial approach to making sure that Alex had been adequately compensated for losing his job. Which, thanks to Isobel's mate, the Ball-Breaker, he had been. We could now easily get by for a year without Alex earning a penny, though obviously that wasn't the plan.

But even so, something wasn't right. I couldn't put my finger on it precisely, other than to say I was extremely aware that, for some reason, somewhere along the way, my sense of humour had recently gone AWOL. This was a worry because my default setting, my saving grace, even my USP, was always finding something funny. Not (I like to think) in a cruel, offensive, just-because-you-can-make-a-joke-doesn't-mean you-should, Frankie Boyle sort of way, obviously, but being funny was, I'm pretty sure, the very first thing Alex found attractive about me. I think he went on to find other things attractive too – well, I know he did – but the night we'd first met, by chance, standing at the bar of a Soho member's club while waiting for separate cabs a couple of weeks before Christmas a decade ago, I had made him laugh. I remember it so vividly – despite being pretty pissed at the time – because one of the staff had just come up to me and said:

'Sorry, Susie, it's a 'mare of a night for cabs. We've ordered you one but they're saying anything up to an hour. Is that OK?'

And I'd nodded, 'Yeah, no problem, that's fine.'

Then she'd turned to the man standing next to me.

'But Alex, I think yours will be here any minute.' And then she'd looked at both of us and added, 'Do you two know each other? Because maybe you could share if you're heading vaguely in the same direction?'

And, without even looking at the man and with all the insouciant confidence of a pleasantly drunk single woman of twenty-nine wearing Vivienne Westwood and feeling good, I'd said: 'Well I don't know Alex, but that wouldn't stop me vaguely heading in his direction. I'm good at directions and brilliant at vaguely.'

And Alex had laughed. 'Well I'm vaguely heading west – you're welcome to vaguely share.'

And I'd looked at the tall, handsome, smiling man in the definitely-Prada shoes and jacket I was pretty sure was Comme des Garçons, and I'd said: 'Tell you what, unless you're busy, why don't we have a drink and wait for my cab? I mean Hackney's west, right?'

And he'd laughed again, and said, 'You're funny. My mates have just headed off to a party I don't fancy going to, in Shoreditch. What are you drinking?'

And I'd said, 'Vodka and slimline. And I really live in Cricklewood.'

And he said, 'Well waddya know – Kilburn.'

And he'd ordered two vodka tonics and then we'd left together an hour later and that was pretty much that. We'd been together ever since.

Of course I've often wondered what would – or indeed wouldn't – have happened if we hadn't been standing next to each other at that bar at that precise moment, both waiting for cabs on one of the busiest nights of the year, but it's a pointless exercise. Life is invariably constructed of just such fleeting moments, piled on top of each other like Jenga bricks.

So on a drizzly day in November I found myself standing in the kitchen at our 'Goodbye London' party, moment- arily pausing and wondering if the decision to leave all this behind and start living 'a different sort of life' (and yes, that phrase still rang in my ears) wasn't in fact turning out to be the removal of the first brick in our own Jenga tower. Or perhaps a couple of key bricks had already been removed without us noticing, which had in turn made our little tower even more precarious than we thought?

But I couldn't answer these nagging internal questions. Not yet. And the fact that they were questions I was already asking made me feel weirdly ashamed. As if I had maybe already removed a couple of bricks myself without telling anybody, and then hidden them like a guilty toddler who knows they're doing something wrong but doesn't know quite what that is … and now I was waiting for the rest of the bricks to come tumbling down.

At which point Isobel sidled up to me, looking furtive, and said, 'Quick word about, er, *cooking*, Soos?' and the moment had passed.

Just under a week later, on the following Saturday morning, all was predictably chaotic as countless cardboard boxes were taped and un-taped (I'd spent a long time in particular trying to wrap the Venetian glass mirror, until Alex took over) and small pointless objects (was that a Happy Meal toy, FFS?) were shoved into them before re-taping and scribbling on them with marker, while Joan, who had 'kindly' volunteered to 'help', kept things cracking along at a predictably military pace with the aid of non-stop tea and admonishments to the kids to 'keep out of the way, you two'. Indeed, when the kettle was finally packed into the last box – and thus sensibly, albeit mostly theoretically, meant to be the first out of the van – it was still hot.

The van set off for the wonky rental just before we did,

so I spent the last few minutes wiping kitchen surfaces and skirting boards like some sort of sad Mrs Stepford-Bourgeois so that the two Chrises wouldn't think I was a slut. This despite the fact that a surprisingly moist-eyed Ruby was already cleaning the place in preparation for their leisurely arrival the following day, accompanied (I liked to think) by two posh cats, a super-king size-bed, an enormous Ligne Roset sofa and a couple of rather fabulous statement pieces of art. Admittedly this was mostly a fantasy about the domestic lives of stylish gay couples, but it was a potent one because, pathetic though this may seem, I wanted to believe that our beloved house was marrying up.

Meanwhile, we had (albeit temporarily) traded down. The rental was even wonkier than I'd recalled, its 'period features' (both the boiler and the fridge looked as though they should be listed) less stylish than eyesore, not to mention potentially lethal. Still, we had space, having sensibly pruned our belongings down to the leanest of basics – beds, sofas, clothes, pots and pans, computers – and then dispatched the rest to storage, optimistic that we'd find our Dream Home long before we ever needed even one of the several hundred packets of IKEA tea-lights I appeared to have acquired over the past decade.

The first week was a blur. Unpacking should have been the worst of it but taking two children to start a new school two-thirds of the way through a term wasn't ideal, though I think probably more stressful for us than it was for them. And at the end of the week, before we had even managed to locate the bottle opener, it was Alex's birthday, which called for an emergency phone call to Heinous who kindly offered to babysit as long as she and Edie could have a built-in sleepover, while Alex and I went to the closest entry in an ancient edition of the *Good Pub Guide*, which was about five miles away.

We walked into the predictably beam-bedecked gastro-hostelry and ordered a vodka and slimline for me and a pint of Old Tory Fart (at which point I realized that Alex – hitherto a bottled lager kind of bloke – was startlingly keen to embrace our new environment by drinking whatever it took to fit in). We found ourselves a table close to the inglenook fireplace and shrugged off several layers of smart fabrics – 'smart' as in 'intelligently warm' that is, not smart as in remotely attractive – and ordered variations on the theme of pie and chips, then sat back to check out the locals. Suddenly there was a voice we both recognized, coming from a mouth we did not. And the reason we didn't immediately recognize the mouth was that it was mostly hidden by an impressive Captain Haddock-y layer of beard, underneath which was a man, who said: 'Well I never. Alex and Susie. Long time. What the hell brings you here?'

Blimey, it was Philip – formerly of marketing and now apparently moonlighting as a pirate – which was a sort of pleasant surprise, though perhaps, if I'm honest, more of a surprise than it was entirely pleasant. Yet he and Alex fell on each other like long-lost friends rather than lapsed acquaintance-colleagues, which, I was already discovering, is precisely what happens when you're new in town and friends are scarce, if not entirely absent. Anyway, within moments we had established that Philip was on his habitual Friday night out with the boys and 'Bridge' was home with the kids, and also that we were now going to become a table of six and, hey, waddya know – it was birthday drinks and artery-clogging pies all round.

'So you've escaped the rat-race, eh? Congratulations,' said Philip's beard.

'Yeah, we're so out of all that,' said a new super-cheery, back-slapping, ale-quaffing, booming-voiced version of Alex Fox, who I had never known was quite such a social chameleon.

'That's great. Really great. You'll love it down here. Wonderful quality of life. Great for the kids. Where've you bought, then?'

'Renting at the moment, but looking in Random-on-Sea. I'm sure we'll find something soon,' said Alex.

'I'm sure you will, I'm sure you will. Fantastic houses, and all for the price of—'

'A two-bed flat in Media Vale,' said me and Alex, in perfect harmony.

'Well, exactly. Now let me introduce you to . . .'

It was handshakes all round with three other inter-changeable-looking ruddy-faced men wearing a selection of beards and fleeces, whose names I instantly forgot but who were conceivably all called Peter. And because I was suddenly a bit tired, not to say outnumbered, I sort of sat back and let the rest of the evening wash over me, occasionally dipping in and out of the masculine anecdotage about houses and work and 'the missus'. By about 10.15 I was really wishing I was back at Wonky, having a mint tea with Heinous, so I sort of nudged Alex and whispered and he pretended not to hear, so I did it again, at which point he turned to Philip – apparently now re-branded as Phil – and winked archly and said, 'The missus is suggesting we call it a night. Long week.' And I would've fallen off my milking stool if doing so wouldn't have attracted too much attention because Alex seemed to have morphed into Jerry from *The Good Life*, albeit wearing a North Face jacket instead of a blazer and turtle-neck. Anyway, Phil wasn't having any of that.

'No, sorry, birthday boy – and Susie – I'm not having any of that. It's back to the ranch for a nightcap before we let you go. Bridge will be thrilled to see you,' and even though I was nearly as exhausted as if I'd actually done something properly outdoorsy in my recently acquired smart fabric layers, I was quite intrigued by the idea of Bridget, so I agreed.

'That's the spirit, Susie. You know it makes sense,' said

Phil, and Alex helped me into my coat and gave my arm a little squeeze as he did so, as if to say, 'Look, we're new in town, we need all the help we can get . . .' and that was fair enough because it was true.

'We're only round the corner,' said Phil, and indeed they were, just around the corner and next door to the church, in – oh, glorious cliché – The Old Rectory.

'Shoes off,' said Phil as we huddled inside the elegant porch. 'Bridge'll have my guts for garters if you don't.' At which point (and not for the last time) I wondered if this extraordinary sitcom-bonhomie version of Phil was the inevitable outcome of leaving London. And then I dismissed the thought, slightly ashamed that I was being an urban snob. Anyway, we were now inside and here was Bridget. Or at least by a process of eliminating every other woman in the world I assumed this was Bridge, for just as Phil had embraced the hirsute Haddock look, so Bridget had, astonishingly, acquired about six stones and was therefore kind of a big-knicker-wearing Renée-Zellweger-as-Bridget-Jones version of the old twiglet-Bridget. It was so completely extraordinary and unexpected that I had to stop myself gaping, goggle-eyed and carp-like.

'Wow, is that Alex and Susie? Omigod. Come in. Let's have a hug, you guys.'

Judging by the expression of joy on Bridge's face I sensed she probably didn't get out much – and certainly never very far from her fridge. But maybe that was triplets for you? That, or being married to Captain Haddock.

The triplets – two boys, one girl: Theo, Josh and Daisy – had apparently just turned five and started school in September.

'Which is great,' said Bridget, over a glass of Maker's Mark straight up (an ex-fashion editor drinking bourbon? Truly the world had tipped on its axis), 'because it means I can get myself a bit of a life again.'

'Yes, Bridge has been doing some styling for *Sussex Life* – it's actually a glossy – as well as sorting out the windows of our local designer retail outlet, making sure they don't put a double-breasted camel coat over a cerise wrap-dress, eh Bridge?'

And poor Bridget, for whom I suddenly felt extreme pity, blushed slightly and said, apologetically, 'Actually, camel and cerise is a good look. But yes, I'm a bit out of the loop. Some friends asked me to help, so . . .' She tailed off, and I recalled in a flash that she had once been the deputy fashion editor of *Marie Claire*, and I sort of wanted to hug her quite tightly. Instead I asked where the loo was.

It was after 1.30 a.m. when we finally poured ourselves into a mini-cab.

'Well, happy birthday, Alex,' I said.

'I thought that was pretty great, actually,' said Alex. 'I mean, it could have been just us staring at each other all night across the cow pies, but it was really nice to catch up with Phil and Bridget, don't you think? Even if I would never have recognized them in the street, what with The Beard. And Bridget turning into the Forth Bridget. But I think it's worked out really well for them, don't you? Phil seems to have got his shit together with his own business. And Bridge has very obviously got over the eating disorder.'

'Well, yeah, she's obviously got over one sort of eating disorder.' And I glanced at Alex to see if he was joking about it being nice to see Phil-n-Bridge, but I could tell he was a hundred per cent sincere. This didn't, it must be said, immediately square with my own feelings about Mr and Mrs Phil Bingley, which were that if you prised the lid off their (admittedly lovely) Old Rectory, you'd effectively also open a can of . . .

'Bloody gorgeous house too, eh Soos? Fingers crossed we find something like that.'

Well, yes, obviously. Fingers crossed. No disagreement there.

So, here we were, a month before Christmas, living out of boxes in the Wonky Rental and signed up with every estate agent in town while we searched for the Dream Home in which the *famille* Fox would finally find themselves, both literally and metaphorically. Those were the facts and that was the truth.

Or at least it was a kind of one-dimensional version of The Truth. Seen from a slightly different perspective, The

Truth was that, as a family, we were rather suddenly and quite dramatically drifting in different directions, tugged along by seemingly hidden currents beneath the tides and attempting to grasp any passing flotsam. Yeah, I can do sea metaphors.

The thing about moving out of your comfort zone and starting over on what is effectively a sea-and-sunshine-and-ice-cream-in-the-summer whim which fuels one's escapist fantasies, is that it's tough enough when you all want the same things, share the same dreams and motivations ... and are strong swimmers. If you're not, you may just find yourself delaying – and distracting yourself from – the inevitable. Suddenly you're not waving but drowning.

Away from friends, family, neighbours, school, work, the park, the tube, the bus, the corner shop (where they automatically put aside your copies of *Grazia*, *Private Eye*, *Vanity Fair*, *Heat* and *Radio Times* and sneak your children Haribo), never mind Selfridges, Starbucks and Soho members' clubs ... away from all those things that re-inforce who you are and the life you're living and which, for all their apparent mundanity, also make you feel safe and whole and which, of course, you entirely take for granted – well, when they're gone you're thrown back on yourself and, without warning, discover you're not so much a rock-solid family of four and an island of emotional and practical self-sufficiency but an archipelago balanced precariously atop tectonic plates, so almost anything can happen. Your partner could even morph into a total stranger right in front of your eyes.

There were four and half months in between moving into the Wonky Rental in November and moving into the Dream Home, during which Christmas came to Random. Inside Poundland there was more tinsel than you could poke an acrylic fingernail at, while outside the mall in the square there was an ice rink the size of a paddling pool with a 'rustic' picket fence. I'm partial to a bit of ice skating but my centre of gravity wasn't quite low enough for this rink. Still, they had these big plastic push-along penguins for the little kids to cling on to while they were crying, which was a nice touch.

Turns out, Random's shopping mall was 'famous' for two things. First, for being built on the site of what I imagine was a lovely cricket pitch, an act of consumerist barbarism inappropriately commemorated by a bronze of a cricketer, and secondly for having a multi-storey car park of such wilful complexity that once out of the car and on foot you needed a compass to find the lifts to take you to a selection of oddly, and then again evenly, numbered levels ... which in turn connected, in an entirely arbitrary fashion, to a whole other set of levels, requiring another set of lifts to take one down, or possibly up, to the shops.

On the other hand, because disabled drivers and the parents of toddlers had been gifted relatively easy access to the retail outlets, drivers sometimes emerged from their cars wearing comedy plaster casts and accessorized by a selection of Tiny Tims on crutches in order to facilitate a relatively unimpeded pathway to the door of Bhs. Though if you didn't want to go to Bhs you were stuffed, obviously. Imagine a shopping centre designed by whoever invented Tomb Raider, but with all the fun extracted.

Anyway, having parked the car elsewhere, while browsing the mall with Heinous, child-free (and therefore as relaxed as possible when there were only however-many-there-were shopping days left until Christmas), next door to Claire's Accessories I chanced upon a new 'pop-up shop' selling only calendars. Of course, I'd not only never been inside a calendar pop-up shop before, but also entirely failed to realize that calendars are such brilliantly niched products that not only can all one's calendrical needs be met under one roof, but many of one's emotional needs, too.

'Look,' I said to Heinous. 'A Miffy calendar. And look at this Busy Mum's calendar, with stickers and everything so it doubles as a reward chart. That's exactly what I need. And I can think of at least half a dozen people I know who'd like that R-Patz calendar. OK, so I don't quite get the R-Patz thing myself, but frankly why would I? He's like twelve or something. Oh, but I have to have this Simpsons calendar.'

So after an inevitably calendar-heavy Christmas and a lost weekend of a New Year, a sluggish January was enlivened only by finding the Dream Home.

We'd jumped at it and offered close to the asking price, but why the hell wouldn't we? It ticked every conceivable box in our personal Dream Home checklist: listed, stuccoed, corniced, with an embarrassment of garden (not that I was remotely embarrassed – merely daunted), it was also a beach-pebble's throw from Heinous's house. This was indeed a Kirstie Allsopp 'Forever House', and even better than that, it was going to be ours practically mortgage-free. During the weeks before we moved, I was keeping a scribbled list-cum-diary which, when viewed in retrospect and with the volume on The Clear Light of Day turned up to No. 11, reveals just how much the tectonic plates were shifting.

There was, for example, the note headed SCHOOL stuck to the pin-board in front of my desk:

START REMEMBERING NAMES OF L'S MATES
IN YEAR FIVE AND C'S IN YEAR ONE. AND
THEIR MOTHERS! GET SOME NUMBERS
FOR PLAYDATES.

Then there was a tense scribbled exchange between me and Alex in early February, written on a scrap of paper that had originally been left on the kitchen table and which I subsequently re-discovered torn into tiny pieces in the bin and which I extracted and re-read. And, weirdly, saved.

— A, If you plan on emerging from your 'office' during today's daylight hours (or, given they're so few, even after dark) could you please phone the solicitor. Something about the survey? Am TOTALLY bogged today ... Sx

— I'm WORKING. You're working. I'll do it tomorrow. Or you can? A

— Yeah I'm WORKING and you're ... 'working'. Whatever. S

I know – not good. Then there was the fact that our social life was, so far, effectively Phil and Bridget and Heinous – only one of whom I actually liked (though Chuck adored the triplets) and because Heinous also occasionally doubled up as our babysitter it made breaking new social ground pretty tricky. Hence the following 'shopping' list, also on my pinboard:

— Supper FRI: P&B – and H? Anybody else? Not sure if ideal combo ... and food? Bridge a veggie.

And then there was the Friday in December when Charlie came home from school looking a bit crestfallen and said over supper: 'Mrs Davidson doesn't like me.'

'Oh I'm sure that's not true, darling,' I said breezily. 'Now remind me who Mrs Davidson is again?'

'My form teacher.'

Yeah, if it wasn't one thing, it was another. Inside Wonky it was rapidly turning into the winter of discontent and disconnectedness. Though surely this was inevitable?

Something had happened to Alex. At first I simply put it down to general out-of-sorts 'WTF?-ness', after all I was suffering my own version of What/Why-The-Fuck? For example, WTF were we doing in Random-on-Sea in the bleak midwinter? Or WTF were we hoping to achieve? WTF would owning the Dream Home actually mean? WTF was Alex doing spending every minute of the day, spare or otherwise, glued to his bloody Mac? (Answer: 'Learning how to use Photoshop.' But *for twelve hours a day*?)

In fact, Alex had already been given a little photographic joblet: to take some moody pictures of Random for the website of one of Phil's local business clients, a boutique B&B, which was lovely and everything, apart from the fact that he was being paid £250. So while I had my doubts about photography being the sort of profession you could easily, never mind lucratively, crack in middle-age while based in Random-on-Sea, I figured it was probably best to keep them to myself. Anyway, Alex had squillions of magazine contacts and he was an arse-kicking Alpha Fox, so presumably he'd be fine.

And then there was the weirdness of Alex being in the house all the time, yet also strangely absent. I have always been a great believer in the absence/fond heart equation, so this new omnipresent Alex, always here yet, oddly, not,

forever behind a closed door, was a new and entirely un-
familiar concept and not one, if I'm honest, that I was
coping with particularly brilliantly. Some of that was due
to the fact that he was so tetchy whenever I mentioned
the word 'work' in almost any context. As far as Alex was
concerned, if he woke up, had a piece of toast and coffee
and went into his office, emerging briefly at lunchtime
and then disappearing again, finally re-emerging to do
the school run, it was because he was (bring on the air-
quotes) 'working'.

Meanwhile, I was working very hard. Admittedly my
work isn't always an eight-hour day, five days a week; more
often it comes in bursts which can involve several weeks
of very long and frenetic days followed by periods of relative calm. Currently, though, I was in headless-chicken
mode because I needed to nail the new restaurant guide
by the end of January in order to meet the publisher's
deadlines. This meant pushing the guide's writers to meet
my deadlines while trying to squeeze in quick sprints up
to town for meetings about how best to expand the guide's
website, which had recently won a 'Webbie' award. These
were four-hour round-trips on the train, never mind the
meetings, so while I hadn't imagined the logistics of living
in Random would dramatically affect my work, after a
two-week period during which I was commuting to London
almost daily, I realized this assumption was hopelessly
wrong.

And I don't know if this was just my perception or if it was actually true, but there seemed to be very few other mothers at the kids' new school who worked. I'd drop off Lula and Chuck at 8.30 and watch the mums gathered in their chatty cliques in the car park while I wheel-spun out on to the main road in order to catch the 8.53 up to the Smoke. Occasionally I'd find myself making small-talk with one of them in the corridors while trying to work out which child belonged to which parent, and which of those were the children's friends. And it turned out that quite a few of these women *did* work – sort of. There were a lot of those part-time, recession-friendly mumtrepreneurs, doing interior design for their mates or cupcake-baking . . . not the kind of jobs I considered to be 'proper' careers.

One day I fell into conversation with another mother while we were both attempting to locate our youngest children's PE kits. Her son, Liam, was also in Year One; I'd heard Chuck mention his name. It was she who suggested the boys had a playdate.

'That would be lovely,' I said, genuinely. 'Obviously we haven't been here long and it would be really great for the kids to start making a few friends they can see after school occasionally.' And I gave her my mobile number. 'Please call me. I'd take your number now too if I wasn't racing to catch a train. Sorry!'

'Ah, another busy working mum, then,' she said with an empathetic grin.

The following week, I picked up Chuck from his first playdate with Liam. Over the obligatory cuppa in the immaculate kitchen of a big modern house on a small estate near the park, I asked Liam's mum about her work.

'Oh, well, I'm really excited because it's starting to take off a bit,' she told me enthusiastically. 'What I do, you see, is paint people's names – or just their initials – on to attractive stones I've found on the beach. I'm really pleased, actually, because one of the nicest gift shops in the Old Town have said they'll take a whole alphabet's-worth. And of course it costs me practically nothing to make them but they'll retail at £5.99, so that's £155 right there. And now I'm thinking of selling them on the internet.'

And of course I made very enthusiastic noises, while thinking to myself: *Fuck, it's like feminism never happened. That's not a job, that's a bloody hobby.*

So, forgive me my post-feminist workaholic sins but, y'know, I've always been a grafter, not to mention a bit old-school and Protestant-ethic about what constitutes work. And this obviously extended to Alex because, as far as I was concerned, sitting in front of a computer is really only work if you're getting paid for the end result, while sitting in front of the computer and having a quick look at Net-a-Porter/updating your Facebook status/emailing a mate is very obviously recreation. And while I was sure Alex was doing the digital-photography equivalent of hunting for the Higgs boson, I also didn't think it was remotely possible he could be doing it non-stop all day and quite a lot of the evening, five – sometimes even six – days a week. I got pretty tired of knocking on his door while bearing tea and being forced to talk to the back of his head.

'Hi. How's things? What are you up to?'

'"Up to?" I'm working. What do you think I'm doing? Surfing porn?'

I had no idea; that's why I'd asked. And it was depressing to always be met by a talking back who answered a question with a question.

And then there was the time in early February when I came upstairs to the little attic room he'd co-opted as his office (mine was downstairs in the wonky 'conservatory/dining room', overlooking the gone-wonkily-to-seed 'garden') and I forgot to knock and just walked in with tea and something sweet made by Tunnock's and saw him speedily clicking the corner of a webpage, and as it whizzed into his toolbar he turned and with a face like, well, February, really – though a little bit more pink around the ears – said: 'For fuck's sake, Soos. Knock, would you.'

And it was obviously a guilty face, but guilty of what? This was the point when the name *Pippa* started to haunt me a little bit and I lapsed into my old pattern. Previously it had been his phone; now it was his computer.

Investigating the Mac was altogether trickier, though, because Alex had a password when his screen was asleep. Two days later, however, history had a chance to repeat itself and I had an opportunity to satisfy my curiosity when Alex came off the computer and rushed out, late for the school run he'd assured me he wanted to do and without having shut down the Mac.

I stood in his office doorway for a moment, torn by the prospect of trespassing, eaten by pre-guilt and the very likely prospect that if I did find something, I wouldn't necessarily like what I'd found.

I hovered over Entourage but then clicked on Safari, and then again on History. The first thing on the list was a website selling camera equipment, the second a Google search about lenses, the third ... Facebook.

This didn't look great. As far as I knew Alex didn't even have a Facebook account. He'd always said he despised it ('I don't have enough time for my real friends, never mind people I was at school with. What's the point?'), so I went a bit hot-and-cold and was all set to click on it when I stopped, realizing that if I did so it would appear in his history. So, very slowly, while having an intense interior dialogue along the lines of 'yes', 'no', yes', 'no', 'yes!'... I went back downstairs to my laptop and my own Facebook account, where I searched for 'Alex Fox'.

And inevitably there were quite a lot of Alex Foxes. At first glance none of the headshot-type pictures were obviously Alex, though there were also lots using abstract kind of photos or who hadn't bothered to upload anything yet, so short of befriending them all I had no way of knowing if any of them were him.

This wasn't good news at all. If I'd found Hot Chixxx.com, for fuxxx sake, I'd've been ever so slightly less mortified, because I'm not a prude even if degrees of mortification are pretty much imperceptible. Our sex life was, after a couple of months of going at it like small mammals, very much in another quiet book-at-bedtime phase, and I know that men – most men, anyway – have an entirely different outlook on sex than we – most women, that is – do. I get that they can successfully separate their here-and-now relationships from the recreational pleasure of cruising HotChixxx.com. That it is in effect their Net-A-Porter. I understand all of this intellectually, of course. Emotionally not so much.

But still, *Facebook*? These days I used it pretty infrequently (I'd befriended Heinous, for example), and in fact I was just starting to enjoy Twitter. Still, I also knew Facebook was a sneaky spouses' first port of call for extra-marital shenanigans. Hadn't I recently read somewhere that it was cited in one in five divorces?

But just then Alex arrived home with the kids, so I shut down the Airbook and slipped effortlessly (oh, who am I kidding? effortfully) into mum-mode.

Charlie was sporting the head teacher's Good Work

sticker on his blazer and had had his name read out in assembly, while Lula had earned ten points for her House by scoring a hat-trick during a hockey match. As a pupil at a London state primary she'd obviously never played hockey before we'd moved to Random – and entirely guilty of imposing my own baggage on my children, when she did I'd assumed she'd hate it with a deep and powerful loathing simply because I had spent several years loitering resentfully in goal with a copy of *Jackie* stuffed down my shin-pads. But it so happened that she absolutely loved it and, even more surprisingly, was good at it, too.

So I said: 'Yay. Congratulations, Fox posse. Who fancies going out for pizza?'

And over the top of the deafening screams of assent, Alex winked at me and grinned and said: 'Good idea, Boss.'

And I thought: Oh God. What am I doing prising the lid off the bloody can? This is good. This is what it's all about . . .

And of course sometimes this *was* what it was all about. But at other times – most of the time, if I'm really truthful – it wasn't.

Because the truth of the matter – proper capital-T 'Truth' now – was that even if, when he wasn't online perving over state-of-the-art camera equipment, Alex was spending most of his 'working' day befriending who-knew-who on Facebook, well . . . maybe that was just karma?

Or, rather, karma for me. Because I wasn't entirely un-guilty of creating the emotional climate in which that kind of thing might happen. And I don't just mean by leaving chippy little scribbled notes about phoning so-licitors because I was too busy working, as opposed to 'working'. And I don't even mean by being an unsupportive partner to a man who had recently been made redundant and was still, quite obviously, reeling. No, I don't mean that kind of stuff, I mean that on an almost daily basis I was still haunted by the fact that, well ... OK ... that Pippa had been right about her interpretation of the over-heard phone conversation. That, yes, I had been arranging 'an assignation'. And that this 'assignation' had not been with Alex.

I *had* left Alex a message that Friday afternoon the previous June, but that wasn't what Pippa had overheard. I'd called Alex later, after I'd left the shop. And I hadn't left him a message attempting to book a spontaneous 'date night' for that evening but, instead, a made-up excuse about why I would probably be late home. And the only reason I had been able to think on my feet fast enough to turn Pippa's overheard 'conversation' into Alex's over-heard 'message' – and had got away with it – was because Alex had lost his phone. Though that phone was not, in fact, quite as 'lost' as it might be.

The reason I knew this is because on the day after I'd finally confronted him about 'P', the week after he'd lost his job, I'd gone in the afternoon to the hotel where the Germans were holding their think-tank – The Landmark – and I'd spoken to the concierge and asked if anybody had found an iPhone, lost during the Guthenberg & Partners Blue-Sky-Think-Tanking session a couple of weeks back? And the concierge asked me a few probing questions – who was I? for example. Which was fair enough. And then he said, 'I'm very sorry, Mrs Fox; it sounds like the same phone but we handed it over this morning to Mr Fox's PA, so you might want to check with her, or your husband?'

'Um. So you gave it to a . . . her?'

'Oh yes, definitely. She said she was a temp and would return it to Mr Fox later, so no problem. Crossed wires, I think.'

And I said something like, 'Yes, a little bit crossed, but never mind. Thank you. I was just trying to be helpful to my, er, husband.'

'Of course. Have a lovely day, Mrs Fox.'

So I left. And I was initially a bit confused because Alex's former PA was Gorgeous George, The Gay Geordie, and though deliciously camp, by no stretch of the imagination was George likely to be mistaken for a woman. So whoever she was, this woman was definitely not 'Mr Fox's PA' – or even a mysterious temp, because George had been away on holiday at Easter, but not since then. I couldn't be entirely certain who she was, though I had a hunch.

And though I didn't much like the hunch, over the next few days it provided me with an extraordinary sense of focus. And it was that focus, coupled with a compelling need to put this domestic hiccup behind us that resulted, albeit partly by accident – thanks to Heinous – in Operation Random-on-Sea. So here we were.

'Yay. Pizza. Bring it on.'

CHAPTER 5

Pippa

Dearest Mum,

After I sent that bloody text I won't bother pretending I didn't spend a few days regretting it. Of course I regretted it (particularly the :-) and the xxx's) but not necessarily for the reasons you may think. I didn't, for example, regret it because it was such an obvious come-on to a man who was as good as married – but because it wasn't as obvious a come-on as I think I really, deep down, intended it to be. It was actually slightly ambiguous. And sometimes men aren't good with ambiguous. Sometimes they just need to be told not only what you want, but what they want, too. Don't you agree?

'Start living a different kind of life'? Well, let's face it, that's the kind of advice you might easily offer a man who'd lost his job. A *carpe diem*, a bit of self-help-cum-therapy? What it didn't really say – at least when I woke up and read it the following morning, hungover – was 'Come on, big boy, finish what you started in the back of that cab'. And that's truthfully what I wanted to say, because even though I know men can be exceptionally lazy about the getting of sex – that if it's there on a plate they'll often just help themselves – it was precisely the fact that Alex had walked when he could have stayed which made it clear to me that far from it being merely an opportunistic drunken fumble in the back of a cab, it had messed with his head sufficiently to make him feel guilty. Which meant, by extension, that he cared. And not, weirdly enough, just about Susie, but very likely about me, too.

I became completely convinced of this over the next few days. I felt that Alex's silence, far from indicating a lack of interest, actually hinted at precisely the opposite. But I wasn't going to contact him – no way. Instead I would play the long game, because if Alex was about to start Living A Different Kind of Life, then I surprised myself by how much I wanted to find out what sort of life that could be.

Anyway, that weekend, the one after Alex had bolted, I felt the opposite of what you might expect – which would be embarrassed, flustered, guilty, that kind of thing – and instead felt an incredible sense of calm. This was pretty counter-intuitive: I'd just spent an evening with an insecure man who had confided in me and then stuck his tongue down my throat and his hands down my knickers with all the desperate abandon of a hormonal sixteen-year-old. A scenario from which any women's magazine advice column worth its salt would, quite obviously, advise me to 'run, lady, run a million miles ... and fast!' Instinctively, however, in the case of Alex, I felt this would be entirely wrong. I would effectively run to him; he just wouldn't know I was doing it.

The weekend was pretty normal. Hal had a few things to do – a rugby match on Saturday morning, which I planned to attend with a few home-made biscuits to keep up parental morale on the touchline, and in the afternoon he wanted to rifle through the Jack Wills rails in Selfridges with a couple of mates and his monthly allowance, which I was happy enough to let them do while I lost myself for a while in Womenswear. So, after a late lunch at Pizza Express, me and three large boy-men wandered down to a cinema in Leicester Square. While they were watching the third part of a shoot-'em-up trilogy of which I had cleverly avoided seeing parts 1&2, I slipped into the screen next door for one of those rom-coms in which Jennifer Aniston plays a weirdly winsome fortysomething who looks thirty-four and has a disastrous-art-imitates-love-life.

And then Sunday was ... Sunday-ish. I made a roast because (as you well know, Mum) I have always been obsessed with family Sunday lunches, and nothing will change that, certainly nothing as straightforward as not having a family. And then afterwards I dropped Hal round to Dom's in order, no doubt, that he might appreciate the farther reaches of YouTube without too much parental supervision, Dom being the youngest of four boys and therefore pretty much free-range. And Dom's mum, Patsy, said she'd drop Hal back, fed and watered, by 8 p.m., which meant I had four hours at home with the papers. And ... whatever.

Between 4 and 8 p.m. I spent quite a bit of time staring at my phone. And with that came the feeling I always get when I'm waiting for an overground train at a busy station and a non-stopper roars past the platform and for a moment – a mere millisecond – I think I won't be able to *not* chuck myself in front of it. Which, incidentally, has nothing to do with wanting to commit suicide and everything to do with ... I dunno, seizing the madness of an adrenalized moment? In the case of the phone, it was of course text-related. I felt as though I may not be able to stop myself sending a text to Alex that I would actually end up seriously regretting. Something entirely unambiguous, like 'Fuck Me Now! P'.

But of course I didn't. Partly because I knew that Alex was away for the weekend at his parents' house, celebrating their golden wedding anniversary, surrounded by family and old friends, and I wasn't going to risk interrupting that. I didn't want to freak Alex out any more than I suspected he already was; I wanted to retreat while also moving forward. There's almost certainly some sort of military terminology for that kind of manoeuvre. Not that I know what it is, obviously, but Alex might.

Anyway, instead of doing the proverbial Something Silly, I decided to do Something Sensible. Even though this 'Something Sensible' mostly just involved *not* doing Something Silly.

I didn't have that long to wait before I heard from Alex. Just over a week, in fact, because, the following Saturday, while I was rearranging my walk-in wardrobe with the slightly OCD efficiency you'd expect of a woman who antic-ipates a long, slow, child-free weekend (Hal was away with his dad and stepmother, being gently – or in reality prob-ably brusquely and insensitively – introduced to the concept of a sibling, albeit one who was still only a scan), I received a text:

P. Wondered if you might be free this evening? I am ... A

And I found myself doing that thing only women do, which is to read (and re-read and re-re-read) a couple of handfuls of words searching for some deeper meaning. After about twenty minutes of this fairly pointless activity I drew the conclusion that there was no deeper meaning. The meaning was already as deep as it could be, which is to say all the information I could have required (at least for the moment) was right there in front of me.

Having almost ruled out the possibility that this text had been sent to the wrong person – the clue was in that 'P' – just to be on the safe side I decided to rule it out a few more times. Although Alex probably knew several 'P's, eventually I had to assume this 'P' was me. If only on the grounds that to not assume this would make me certifiable.

Wondered if you might be free this evening? There was nothing terribly ambiguous about that. Though I suppose 'evening' could be interpreted to mean 'early' while if he'd said 'tonight' it would have been even less unambiguous. So: 'I am . . .' The most interesting bit of this sentence – apart from the statement of his availability, obviously – was the ellipsis. I actually Googled 'ellipsis' and found the Wikipedia definition:

'A mark or series of marks that usually indicate an intentional omission of a word in the original text. An ellipsis can also be used to indicate a pause in speech, an unfinished thought, or, at the end of a sentence, a trailing off into silence (aposiopesis). When placed at the end of a sentence, the ellipsis can also inspire a feeling of melancholy longing . . .' (My ellipsis, not theirs.)

'A pause', an 'unfinished thought', 'a trailing off into silence' and 'A FEELING OF MELANCHOLY LONGING' (my capitals, not theirs). So I finally replied. Or at least I started to reply because the response actually took me another five minutes to construct.

I started with:

I'm free! What's your plan?! . . . P

But that seemed too exclamatory, too John Inman in *Are You Being Served*. So:

I have no plans at the moment . . . P

But that one seemed a bit too stand-offish, as though I was waiting for the best offer before I'd commit, which was foolish because you should start as you mean to go on in a relationship; this was my best offer and I wanted Alex to know that, though not in a needy way. So:

Good to hear from you. I have no plans . . . P

Which seemed to strike the right note (I'd rejected 'nice' and 'lovely' as, respectively, too banal and too needy) while the ellipsis introduced a similar note of 'melancholy longing' to the original text. And then I agonized for another three minutes about adding an 'x':

Good to hear from you. I have no plans P

Or:

Good to hear from you. I have no plans . . . Px

Or:

Good to hear from you. I have no plans! Px

Or even:

Good to hear from you. I have no plans! . . . PXX

But in the end I rejected all the 'x's because an 'x' was implicit.

So:

Good to hear from you. I have no plans . . . P

I hit Send. The reply came within a minute:

Great. OK if I turn up at your doorstep 7ish? I remember your address. A

I was slightly thrown by this. I'd assumed we'd probably meet on neutral territory and take it from there. But on the upside, any ambiguity I might have been searching for had abruptly evaporated. So:

Sure. See you then.

I looked at my watch. It was 4.28 p.m. I figured I'd better get my head – and my house – straight. Weirdly, I also wanted to cry. But there you are, unexpected emotions sometimes creep up on you.

The first thing I did was go straight back to finishing what I'd started in the wardrobe department, partly to be better organized and because the process of organizing helps clear my head and I hate things being half finished, and partly because it would give me some space to think about the evening that lay ahead. Instead, however, opening my wardrobe doors was a bit like opening a portal to a shadowy, half-forgotten world. And that was even before I found – or rather, technically speaking, re-found (because I've carried it with me wherever I've lived for nearly thirty years now) the old brown shoebox labelled 'Memory's' (sic). Which, in turn, took me straight back to Tuesday 8 April 1984, when I had been sixteen for a week and was getting ready to walk from our house in the north-west London 'burbs to the High Street for some 'essential' purchases – magazines, magazines, magazines and if my stock of cherry-flavoured lip-gloss was running dangerously low, possibly also a little light-fingered perusal of the Miss Selfridge Kiss 'n' Make-Up counter.

On that day – which I suddenly recalled as vividly as if it had been last week – I was wearing black liquid eyeliner and an asymmetric haircut (a coppery-tinted bobbed homage to the Vidal Sassoon oeuvre) accessorized by an equally asymmetrical attitude. Having rejected a black lacy mini-dress, second-hand black stilettos and your gorgeous white fox fur stole, Mum, as perhaps slightly too outré a look for an overcast weekday morning, I finally settled on a pair of black ski pants, black suede ankle boots with a white rubber Cuban heel (do you remember those? From – cue sharp intake of glamour-breath – Paris!), plus one of my favourite charity shop finds: that Chrissie Hynde-ish boxy jacket in butterscotch-coloured suede which was so stylish it barely mattered that some of the seams were reinforced on the inside by double-sided Sellotape.

For any sixteen-year-old girl every morning is a fashion crisis in waiting, and it was no exception for me as I attempted to make a stylistic shift from early 1980s New Romantic towards something a bit more Edie Sedgwick. This wasn't simply a case of staring at hangers and working out which items of clothing would work best together, there was the weighty nature versus nurture debate to be taken into account, for I was blessed with you, Mum –

The Stylish Mother – which was only really a blessing until I suddenly become two inches taller, not to mention a shoe size bigger than you, having shared the same dress size for a clutch of months between the ages of twelve and fourteen. Then the blessing evolved into ... if not a curse precisely, a gauntlet-chucking challenge. Which is why you can't take all the credit for creating a Frauken*steen's* little monster of a daughter who dreamed of appearing in *Vogue*, though preferably not while wearing Sellotape.

Anyway, I sat there on the floor of my 'closet' staring at my 'Memory's' from 1984 and recalled that even the apparently simple act of sauntering to the High Street to buy the new issues of *Honey* and *Cosmo* (*Honey* was cooler, *Cosmo* was fatter) called for a very carefully considered look because I would be seen by the boys who congregated on their Yamaha FS1 lawnmower-mopeds – 'Fizzies' – at the end of the road. Most evenings they raced past my house executing squealing, rubber-burning wheelies while I sat nonchalantly on my bedroom windowsill with a cuppa, watching the potential drama unfolding like a suburban Capulet confronted by a bunch of boy-racing Montagues.

Do you remember how many of the moped boys were called Mark, Mum? And though the Mark (two parts Nick Heyward to one part Martin Kemp) for whom I carried a flaming torch of unrequited lust was entirely immune to my charms, another Mark – one who truly, deeply and properly loved me – was spurned as cruelly, casually and consistently as only a teenage girl can spurn a teenage boy who worships at her second-hand soles.

Despite being the only Mark allowed over the threshold and into my bedroom (though not my bed, oh no), despite being infinitely kind, funny, long-suffering and wearing his unrequited devotion as lightly as he did his PVC bomber and brushed pale denim parallels – not to mention being the only one of The Marks to have entirely charmed you, which was no mean feat – Mark One was, as far as I was concerned (and probably for all of these reasons), merely 'friend' rather than boyfriend material. Something of which I would regularly remind him when the bedroom lights were dimmed (overhead bulb switched off, Anglepoise switched on), curtains drawn and the Eurythmics' 'Sweet Dreams' was playing on your appropriated music centre (wood veneer-effect dashboard, smoked plastic turntable lid), creating an atmosphere of almost unbearably – for Mark, anyway – sophisticated erotic suspense.

So, back in April 1984, merely setting foot outside the house not only needed to take into consideration the potential presence of The Marks, but also the mystery boy who had recently moved into the street diagonally across from our house and who often sat in his window staring into mine.

He wasn't a Mark (well he could have been; I didn't know his name, but he definitely didn't have a Fizzy or hang out with the other Marks) and even with the benefit of my 20/20 vision, he lived just a bit too far away to be checked out very closely from my bedroom vantage point. But he definitely had boyfriend potential, if only because he had noticed my existence, which was sometimes all it took. So I suddenly, conveniently, found a lot of letters that needed posting very urgently, which in turn meant walking down his road to double-back along the road that ran parallel to his, where the (second-nearest) post box actually was. This was years before I'd heard the term 'stalking', obviously.

But beyond running the gauntlet of the local Marks, there were other hazards to be encountered en-route to shopping nirvana, notably the branch of Oxfam at the bottom of the road that was at the bottom of our road. Do you remember it? Next to the bookies? All the other local girls seemed to be unimpressed by the shop's stock of 1960s cocktail dresses and shoes, so I quickly learned how to mix high street purchases with charity shop finds (while borrowing whatever still fitted from you) creating an eclectic 'style'. Or, alternatively, just a collision between garments in exciting drip-dry fabrics and challenging colour combinations.

My successes included:

A pair of Miss Selfridge black PVC jeans teamed with a black sleeveless chiffon blouse.

A truly fabulous sleeveless cream jersey shift with broad horizontal bands of brown and orange and gold lurex – which, having racked up three snogs with three different boys (only one of whom was called Mark) on the only three occasions I'd ever worn it, I considered to be a 'result' dress so potent it needed to be deployed carefully and only ever after dark, preferably alongside a Pernod-and-black.

So, here I was with the beaten-up shoebox labelled 'Memory's' in cursive felt-tip, looking at the neatly folded copy of *The Face* magazine – the one I'd spotted in WH Smith and for which I'd ended up excitedly rejecting both *Cosmo* and *Honey*. *The Face* seemed suddenly to be my Proustian 'madeleine' – I was right back there: hormonal, fashion-and-boy-and-hair-obsessed, both scared by and optimistic about the future, but obviously not with the faintest idea of where I'd be now, twenty-five years later. Or with a clue as to the trajectory that would take me here, to this precise moment, when I was sitting on the floor of the 'wardrobe' sobbing all over an old magazine and waiting for a date with a man who belonged to someone else.

What do you think of me, Mum? What do you really think of the woman I have become? . . .

And yes, if you're wondering, that is a melancholy ellipsis.

Eventually I pulled myself together. Sorted out the tangle

of hangers, folded some sweaters and put them in bags, in drawers. Rediscovered some spring/summer pieces from last year that I thought I'd wear again and made a quick note about the gaps I felt needed plugging, for which I'd probably shop next week. And then I ran myself a big hot bath and started the auto-pilot process of middle-aged beautification/maintenance: depilate, body scrub, moisturize . . . and I thought, not for the first time, that none of these words sound as good as they feel, that in fact they're all so perversely and ironically ugly they might as well be 'moist' or 'gusset'.

By 6 p.m. I was done, scrubbed up, looking pretty good. Maybe even 'hot', and, dare I say it, possibly even MILF-y. Not that any of this made me love myself any more than I'd loved myself when I was twenty and properly, as opposed to peri-menopausally, fuckable.

The problem with being someone who was once 'professionally' pretty is that it coincided with those years when I wasn't feeling remotely pretty on the inside. You know how reluctant a teenage model I was, Mum; how much I hated my four-year 'career'; after all, you hated it too. You particularly hated the fact that it contributed to me flunking my A-levels and stopped me 'fulfilling my potential' and going to uni (my head teacher's words, not yours, to be fair). Instead I was living in a model flat in Tokyo and hating every minute. And it's not like it was a glittering career. Sixteen catalogues, five pop videos, two covers of *Just 17* and three campaigns for Laura Ashley do not a 'Super' make.

I know you were relieved when I stopped at twenty-one, but disappointed that I didn't change direction. We had that huge row, I remember, when I told you I wanted to poach not game-keep and you accused me of 'frittering' my life away. But even though I hated modelling I actually loved being an agent. Loved being able to help 'my girls' (even though I was still pretty much a girl myself), enjoyed being able to give them the heads-up about the head-fuckery of the business – and then enjoy their successes much more than I ever did my own. And I really liked being a team player at the centre of a fondly bickering 'family'.

So, you know, no regrets. Not really. It wasn't a brain-dead job at all (stupid agents don't get covers and campaigns for their girls), even though I know it could seem frivolous from the outside. I suppose the only thing I do sort of regret is not grabbing that fleeting moment when I could've set up on my own, with a handful of the 'big' girls, like Lisa. But instead I married David and if I hadn't done that I wouldn't have Hal, and of course life without Hal is unimaginable. So, you know …

Anyway, even though I suppose it didn't really matter, it ended up taking me nearly an hour to decide what to wear. And that was after I'd narrowed it down to the category of 'non-slutty dresses it's easy to get out of quickly'. So, a DVF wrap dress it was, then.

When I heard the doorbell, I was downstairs in the kitchen, checking on the progress of the white wine cooling process, then uncorking a bottle of red just in case, and seeing if I still had any tonic to go with the vodka I never drank at home and which, on closer inspection, appeared to be nearly gone, which was odd. And then I ran up the stairs three at a time, bare-footed, pausing to catch my breath before I opened the door.

'Hi,' said Alex. 'You don't mind this, do you? Me turning up on your doorstep? It occurred to me after I'd sent the text that maybe you'd prefer to meet somewhere else.'

'No, it's fine, totally fine. Come in. Thanks.'

Alex was bearing flowers. One of those ready-made supermarket bouquets with the price tag half torn off – cheap but actually very pretty. And in his other hand he had a bottle of Barolo: not so cheap. I was touched. I was also, for a moment, slightly scared. Flowers and wine said 'date'. 'Date' said single. Only one of us was single. Or maybe not?

'I was just opening a bottle downstairs but that one looks much nicer than mine. Come down . . .' He followed me into the basement. I could see him checking out the room and tried to picture it from his perspective. I had a vision of his – or actually Susie's – kitchen and that vision wasn't this. Three months previously my newly revamped kitchen had been on the cover of *Elle Deco*. The shoot had been nothing to do with me, really – the architect had known the editor – but I had enjoyed the process.

'This is a beautiful room. Why do I feel like I recognize it?'

I hadn't really wanted to have the *Elle Deco* conversation but Alex had been a magazine publisher until about five minutes ago, so he probably did recognize it.

'February issue of *Elle Deco*?'

'Blimey, yes. Susie ... uh ... we ... I subscribe.' I could tell he immediately regretted mentioning Susie so I pretended I hadn't heard.

'Yes, it scrubs up pretty well.' I didn't want to look flash.

'It's stunning.' He ran his hand along the seamless Corian work surface. 'Really beautiful. It must have cost a—' He checked himself.

'It did. But it's a kitchen for life, really, so I figured it was money well spent. I came into some money a while back, so ...'

And I didn't want to have this conversation, either, though I could see I was probably going to have to.

'The hedge-fund bastard, I presume, doing right by the mother of his child? Good for him.'

I took a deep breath.

'No. Not quite. Not really.'

'Ah, OK, scratch cards?'

'No. No ...' Another breath. 'No, my parents both died a few years ago. Together. On the same day.'

Alex immediately looked flustered – and flustered wasn't how I wanted Alex to look, but even though this was not a conversation I had wanted, or even anticipated having, I thought I'd better just go for it. So I told him, Mum. I told him about you and Dad.

'Thailand. Boxing Day 2004. The tsunami. They were on the beach and they drowned. My father died trying to save my mother. The irony is that they had been divorced for years – my father had moved to Thailand and married again in the late 1980s – but they'd recently sort of reconciled, as friends anyway. And my father had invited my mother for Christmas to cheer her up after her second marriage had gone down the pan ... and we'd all – that is, me and my brother and sister – we'd all encouraged her to go, even though she wasn't sure she wanted to. But she flew out on Christmas Day, and sent us a text saying *I'm SO glad I'm here! Thank you for making me do it! Lots of love, Mum XXX*. And she died the next morning and ...' I paused, choking slightly. 'Dad came home in a box three weeks later, but they never found Mum. Or maybe they did, but if so she couldn't be identified. So we never got her back. I still wake up in the night wondering where she is. If you've never been there, I can't tell you how incredibly difficult it is not to have a ... a body. And a place to put that body.'

This was not the way I'd scripted the evening. Alex was ashen.

'Christ. I don't know what to say, Pippa. And anything I do say will sound shallow and meaningless, but, given that – my God, I'm so, so sorry.'

'Thank you. Thanks . . .' I wiped away a tear, poured two glasses of the Barolo and attempted a slightly cack-handed mood shift: 'But apparently life goes on. So, anyway – you're right about one thing: the house was actually in the divorce settlement from The Bastard, but the kitchen was down to my parents. I have quite a lot of money. More than I need.'

'And . . . your brother and sister?'

So I told him about how Simon had flown to Thailand to identify the bodies – *body* – and that, apart from Dad's funeral, he never really came home; how he lives in Thailand now, trying to fight his demons, right the wrongs, do Good Works, and all while drinking too much. And I told him how Beth, who had been skiing in the Rockies that Christmas with a couple of mates, had got engaged to a ski instructor within a month of Mum and Dad dying and now lived in Jackson Hole, managing chalets. How instead of bringing us closer, your deaths had the opposite effect; that the three of us – eaten up with the survivors' guilt (illogical guilt, but guilt nonetheless) of having encouraged you to go in the first place – dealt with it individually rather than collectively and now barely spoke, and that we all preferred it that way. At least for now.

And I suppose it was a conversation so suffused with tragedy that it speeded up the process of what was, surely, going to happen anyway, though possibly not as fast as it did. For it turned out that within twenty minutes of arriving nervously at my door with a smile and flowers and a bottle of wine, Alex suddenly kissed me passionately before untying the belt of my wrap dress, unfastening my bra, sucking on my nipples and then, after sinking to his knees, sliding his tongue hungrily between my legs. Then he turned me round, bent me over the kitchen island and fucked me so hard and fast from behind that I gasped with a combination of shock and pleasure.

'More,' I whispered. 'More.'

'There's . . . plenty . . . more,' said Alex breathlessly. And there was.

It was only later – much, much later – that I started to wonder whether it had been me that Alex had found so irresistible, given he'd resisted me before, or whether it had been my story and my obvious fragility and vulnerability when telling it that had seduced him to seduce me? But as soon as that thought emerged, I buried it again, fast. I was very good at burying unexpected emotions.

Alex eventually left just after lunchtime on Sunday. Before that we had fucked a further four times (not including assorted fore-and-after-play), eaten an Indian meal I'd phoned in, had a shower and a bath, watched a movie, and, somehow, even managed to talk.

Alex was relentlessly attentive and tender. Tender, that is, when he wasn't being a complete animal. And I was fine with animal. It had been ages, after all, and I fancied him wildly. And when we did, briefly, leave each other alone, one of us would soon seek out the other and then we'd be off again . . . God, it was the best sex I've ever had. I had no idea if I'd ever have more of it, but for now – for then – it was enough. And then our conversations, when we found time for them, were so easy, too. There was none of that awkward staccato rhythm that usually signifies two people trying to get to know each other, punctuated by retreating into silent, distracting sex. Everything flowed. Everything joined up. It all made sense.

When Alex finally left, I had just a couple of hours to acclimatize to his absence, to the delicious physical ache that comes of having been . . . there's no other way to put it: *completely fucked* . . . and to rediscover my mum-head in time for Hal's return, and whatever emotions he was going to be bringing home with him.

I needed that time, as it turned out, because Hal was . . . well, broadly fine, but considerably quieter than usual – 'quiet' never being a word one could normally use to describe him. After he arrived home and dumped his ruck-sack in the hall, along with his jacket – the pegs in the lobby apparently remaining entirely invisible to anybody under, say, the age of twenty – he sloped down to the kitchen and raided the fridge and then the larder, making a pile of the kind of grazing foods I would normally ration more strictly (crisps, yoghurt corners, fizzy drink, the token piece of fruit to fend off my criticism and which would mysteriously remain uneaten), but I sensed this was a classic case of comfort-eating and if that was what it took to ease him back into our shared life as opposed to his dad's (mostly unshared) life, then so be it.

'So, good weekend?' I said brightly, albeit in a Don't Mention The War Until He Does kind of way.

'Yeah. S'OK. Um. Mum?'

'Yes, darling?'

'Why didn't you and Dad have more children?'

Woaah. I hadn't seen this one coming.

'Um, well. Ah. I think we sort of didn't have time, really. We were so busy with you, and stuff, and then by the time we might have started thinking about it, well we sort of weren't really together so much.'

I was aware that I was speaking to Hal the way I might speak to an eight-year-old rather than a pubertal proto-teen who was almost certainly going to overtake me in height within months.

'My sister ... Um, I have a sister – half-sister – on the way. You knew that?'

'Well yes, I did. But I also knew that Daddy wanted to tell you himself. And Nina, too, of course. So ... is that exciting?'

'S'pose. Saw the picture. She looks like a prawn.'

'Yes, well, they do when they're only twelve weeks. You all look the same, really. I've got a picture – a scan – of you as a prawn. Do you want to see it?'

'Dunno. Maybe. Yes. OK.'

'Come upstairs. I keep all the baby stuff in my room.'

So we went upstairs and I dug around in the wardrobe to find another box of 'Memory's'. This one wasn't an old shoebox but a rather lovely pale blue leather jewellery box from Smythson and inside it was all my Hal-related pregnancy and birth ephemera: the faded pregnancy tester that confirmed he actually existed as a clutch of cells, all of the scans, our tags from hospital and one crispy dried-blood-coloured rose from David's bouquet, which looked a bit umbilical. I handed Hal a scan.

'Look. Here you are as a prawn at twelve weeks, same as . . . Nina and Daddy's baby.'

Hal took the slightly crumpled paper and peered at it.

'This is black and white. Nina's baby is in colour and kind of 3D.'

'Well, the technology's come on a bit since our day, like TV.'

Hal handed it back. 'Yeah, we haven't even got HD Sky, Mum. Can we get that? Everybody's got it.'

'Yes, I expect we can. I'll call them tomorrow. So everything's OK? With Daddy and Nina and stuff?'

'Yeah, s'pose. But Nina does this really annoying thing.

168

She keeps saying you're my "tummy-mummy" and she's my "other mummy".'

'Does she? That's pretty nauseating. I'm your mum and she's Nina.'

'I know. Is it OK if I phone Dom?'

'Sure it is.'

And that was that. But that was also the moment I suddenly realized my nearly thirteen-year-old was starting to slip out of my grasp. The feeling that he was internalizing emotions I could no longer access was as overwhelming as the sense that asking him to articulate them was completely futile. My boy was moving into manhood, and with that he was also, inexorably and inevitably, starting to move away from me. I wanted to hold him very tight, right there, and I think he knew that. I also knew that he didn't want me to.

'OK. So . . . not too many snacks, Hal. I'm going to get us a Chinese later, if you fancy it?'

'Yeah, cool.'

But he was already halfway out of the door. He was going. Gone. I sighed a sigh so deep and long and pregnant with expectation that it reminded me of breathing during labour.

After our Chinese, after Hal had taken himself off to bed at the frankly unnervingly early hour of 8.45 p.m. without so much as a prod from me, I'd tried to interest myself in the kind of lush feel-good Sunday-night period

TV drama I normally adore but, despite writing and acting that shouted 'BAFTAs all round', it just didn't hold my attention. After a desultory flick through the Sunday supplements, tearing out a photo of a pair of shoes – fuck-me slingbacks by any other name – from the *Sunday Times* Style section, which shouted 'buy me', I went downstairs and resorted to rearranging cereal packets so that you could see their spines. And then, at 10.47, a text:

P. Need to speak to you tomorrow. A

Which didn't necessarily sound good. I was only slightly mollified by the second text-ping:

That should have read . . . A x

OK I replied. Then a second text: *P x*

And I decided I might want to watch that drama after all.

The call came just after ten the following morning. Alex sounded breathless, distracted.

'Pippa?'

'Hi. Yes, that's definitely me.'

'Look. Lot of things going on . . . I . . . look . . . I don't think we can see each other. At least, not for a while. And please don't take this the wrong way – please don't. The weekend was amazing. You are fabulous . . .'

'But?'

'Well yes, there is a "but". I wish there wasn't but there

is. Susie . . . I've made a mistake. You've made a mistake.
In fact we've both made a mistake.'

'Go on. Go on, Alex. Get it off your chest.'

'Look, I've had a conversation with Susie, about the
conversation you overheard. Except it wasn't a conversation. It was a message. It was a message to me on the
phone that got lost, so I never picked it up. It was a message
trying to arrange a kind of date night, *between me and Susie*.
She was leaving a message for *me*, Pippa. She's not having
an affair. Or rather, she was trying to have an affair. *With
me*. Trying to put some spark back into our relationship,
y'know?'

That 'y'know' was almost pleading. He desperately
wanted me to understand, clearly needed me to let him
off the hook. And yet even in that moment, with all this
new information piling up through the ether, I could
vividly recall overhearing Susie in the shop and I remained
just as certain as I had at the time that she wasn't leaving
a message. Or, to put it another way, even if she was leaving
a message it wasn't a message for Alex.

'But—'

'No, Pippa, I can't hear your "but". I know it's unfair
but I just can't. I know what you think you heard, but
I also know Susie. And deep down I trust her. We have a
. . . bond. And that isn't to say you and I don't have a bond,
but it isn't a ten-year-old bond. It's barely more than a
ten-day-old bond. And please don't imagine that I am not

crazy about you, that ... Oh God, Pippa. I've really fucked up. I need some space. At least for a bit. Do you understand?'

Yeah, of course I understood. But understanding didn't stop me wanting to punch a wall with my bare hands and howl a self-pityingly primal scream of 'Why *meeeee*?' And yet I may just have had the best sex of my life with Alex, but I was also old enough to know that this didn't necessarily 'mean' anything. It certainly didn't mean that this ... thing ... was going anywhere. So I just said, quietly: 'It's very ironic, isn't it?'

'What is? What?'

'Well, you effectively started having an affair with me to ... maybe, I guess, even up the score? Except it turns out there was no score to even up. But you only found that out after the event. It feels pretty ironic to me.'

'Please don't, Pippa. I don't even want to use the word "affair". It's not *Brief Encounter*, it's the twenty-first sodding century. And I wanted to see you again because you are a beautiful, intelligent woman with whom I have a bond.'

'Just not a bond that's as strong as—'

'I have kids, Pippa. I have a family.'

'OK, so go, Alex. Thanks for your honesty, but you can go now.'

And I ended the call. The phone rang again straight away. Against my better judgement, I answered.

'Pippa, please try to see it from my perspective. Just give me . . . I dunno, some time?'

'I do see it from your perspective. And I am giving you some time. All the time you'll ever need. So go, Alex.'

And I ended the call again. And then, just to be on the safe side, I turned off the phone. And I seriously thought about punching a wall, but I kicked a cushion instead. And then I put the kettle on. And I stared at my sleeping phone. And then I had an idea.

The phone. Alex's lost phone. He'd told me that he'd called the hotel when he realized he'd lost it but that they hadn't found it so he'd just made an insurance claim and upgraded to an iPhone 3Gs. But I wondered how lost that phone really was. Wondered if there wasn't a chance – admittedly a long shot – that it had actually been found and that somehow its rediscovery had been overlooked in the chaos of Alex's last couple of weeks at work? The thought intrigued me. Not to mention the knowledge that long shots sometimes pay off.

Which is why, within an hour of my conversation with Alex, I found myself on the north side of the Marylebone Road, pacing the pavement just outside the Landmark Hotel, summoning up the courage to be a convincing liar in an act of folly which while not quite qualifying as stalking, came pretty close. And yet I felt compelled to do it. I felt it was the right thing to do. And I justified this because even if I never saw Alex again – though this didn't seem entirely likely, to be honest – I needed to satisfy my curiosity.

Inside the hotel, the concierge was Italian, super-smiley, with hyper-whitened teeth and a winning way with eye-contact that was just the right side of oleaginous – i.e., pretty much what you expect of a concierge.

'Ah yes, hi. My name is Caroline Smith and my boss, Alex Fox – I'm his PA – asked me to check if you'd had a phone handed in. He was at the Messerschmidt . . . no . . . the *Guthenberg* meeting a couple of weeks ago and lost his phone, and though I'm sure he's contacted you previously, I was, uh, just in the area and I thought it might be worth just checking with you again. Because you never know, do you?'

According to his badge the concierge's name was Giorgio Massimo, which sounded like a snigger-worthy pseudonym. He eyed me levelly and then dazzled me with his teeth: 50 per cent smile, 100 per cent ring of confidence.

'Ah, Ms Smeeth. The thing is, I call Mr Fox's former PA, George – I remember 'im because I too am George – just today because yes the phone is 'ere, returned by a guest who only just discover he 'ad two iPhones in 'is bag. 'Owever, Mr George is not returning my call. So.'

A shrug. And because that 'So' was presented as a kind of challenge, some quick and creative thinking was called for.

'Well yes – Mr George . . . George . . . is probably not

picking up messages because he's on holiday. I am Mr Fox's regular temp. So . . .'

This 'So', on the other hand, was as bright and breezily uncomplicated as somebody who has never had an acting lesson in her life could muster. Feminine wiles could potentially disarm even the most professional five-star concierge, so I simply smiled: 'But of course I quite understand if you'd prefer to leave it for George to sort out on his return from holiday, in three weeks. Totally understand. Thank you very much for your help, Signor Massimo.' I leaned down to pick up my handbag and made as if to turn away.

'Miss Smeeth?'

'Yes?'

From underneath his concierge's pulpit, Giorgio produced an iPhone.

'I trust you will ensure this gets to Mr Fox?'

'Oh I will. Thank you very much.'

I smiled. It was time for 'Caroline Smith' to go.

For a while after the phone-heist I felt slightly dazed and a bit criminal. Indeed, I tried to weigh up just how criminal I may have been and the evidence was fairly compelling: posing as someone I wasn't, passing myself off in a job I didn't have, taking somebody else's property under false pretences . . . though in the grand scheme of criminality it did seem to be more at the *Hustle* end of the spectrum rather than, say, the Great Train Robbery. Nonetheless, there was no escaping the fact that I was both officially a liar and a thief, albeit (at least as I saw it) a thief for the greater good. Well mostly *my* greater good. So not Robin Hood, I grant you.

When my heart had stopped pounding and I had stopped pounding the pavements in syncopated time and settled in Starbucks on Baker Street with a grande skinny latte, I looked at the phone – which was of course uncharged and also, I presumed, blocked or locked, or whatever. Now I knew phones could be unblocked/locked, though I had no idea how it was done or where you went to do it, and I also suspected that this sort of thing fell vaguely into the realms of the weird new *Hustle* life that suddenly seemed to have replaced my previously un-criminal existence of thumb-twiddling Belsize Park-mummying. But I was on a roll. And I was enjoying it.

It turns out that it's not very hard to access somebody else's iPhone. You just go to an independent phone shop in one of the more 'vibrant' areas of town and flutter your eyelashes a bit, go away, come back in an hour, hand over some cash and hey presto – as if by magic, Derren Brown's your uncle. And then you're ready for the school run.

It was a long, thumb-twiddling, Belsize Park-mummying afternoon and early evening before Hal absented himself upstairs and allowed me to investigate my – that is, Alex's – freshly recharged phone, which I did in bed, accessorized by a cup of peppermint tea instead of a pint of Dutch courage.

It took only moments to touch the phone icon, and then the voicemail icon, and see the list of the last few voice messages left on Alex's phone on the day he lost it, which included two 'Unknown's, one from 'Guy' and ... yup, there it was: one message from 'Soos'. I took a deep breath. I tapped 'Soos' and listened. And then I marvelled at how little time it had taken – maybe less than twenty seconds – for Alex's phone to reveal its secrets.

Hi, it's me. Hope all's OK with the Germans ... Look, I'm probably going to be a bit late home tonight, but maybe you'll be even later? Anyway, um, Ruby's covering for me and I should be back by about 7.30, after this bloody meeting the guide publishers have just shoe-horned into an arsing Friday evening. Call me if you pick this up before say, 4.30? Otherwise I'll see you later ... and I'll probably grab fish and chips so let me know if you want some too, otherwise I'll assume the Germans have force-fed you bratwurst and cabbage down the bier-keller and therefore you're fine. Byeee ...

Just the one message from 'Soos', then. The kind of ordinary message left by thousands of people every day on their partner's phones. Nothing sinister about it, just domestic trivia. Or then again, maybe not. Because in no way could Susie's message to Alex be construed as a date-night invitation – more like a date-night obfuscation. I had 'evidence', sure ... but I had no real evidence of anything concrete. And then just thinking about my oh-so-casual use of the word 'evidence' gave me an involuntary shiver. 'Evidence' hinted at a scene of crime, called to mind *Silent Witness* and forensics sorts in paper suits moving around dead bodies, wielding dusty brushes. And whose crime scene was this, anyway? It was starting to feel like mine.

I was also disarmed by the fact that listening to Susie's message on Alex's phone and therefore hearing what I wanted to hear – what I'd believed I would hear – was so intensely disappointing. I now knew what I'd needed to know and yet of course I still 'knew' nothing. I didn't know the truth. And why had I even needed to know? What did I seriously think I could achieve by finding Alex's phone, which only that morning had seemed so unlikely?

And of course even when I had my hunch confirmed, it didn't change anything. What was I expecting to do with information that had, quite literally, fallen into my hands? Was I going to call Alex and say, 'Look, don't ask me how or why, but I have your old phone. And I can tell you that Susie did not leave the message she claimed she'd left, but a different message, saying she'd be late home.'

And did that message even mean that Susie was having an affair? Not in and of itself – of course not. And even though I *did* think she was having an affair, maybe that just said more about me than it did about that simple, funny, garbled message from a woman to her long-term partner?

The fact is, I didn't feel remotely clever or enlightened; I felt like a fool. In the space of one day I had somehow gone from being merely a woman spurned to, at worst a petty criminal, at best a sneak. And either way, undeniably also a thief. Somehow I was now a woman reduced to stalking other people's lives in order to fill the yawning chasms in her own. That would be the therapist's version, I guess; the version of my 'truth' that would probably help me not to hate myself too much – if only I ever dared share it in therapy. Except ... I don't do therapy.

But though I felt completely grubby, even inside my crisp, clean, high-thread-count Frette sheets, I could also see a way out of this, a way I could potentially absolve myself of responsibility for what now very clearly looked to be a kind of momentary madness, albeit a form of madness born out of loneliness.

There, I said it, Mum. Because only properly lonely people with time on their hands and no sense of perspective do the kind of things I had just done. Who the hell was I to interfere in Alex and Susie's domestic life? I could maybe blame Gary the gay financier, I could conceivably blame you, and Dad. I could even blame Alex for flirting with me over a bowl of chilli at Lisa and Guy's – if indeed he had, and even that was open to debate. But mostly I had only myself to blame. Never had that old cliché about being 'careful what you wish for' felt more apposite.

That night, I slept the sleep of the restless dead and

woke up feeling and looking zombie-ish. Downstairs, Hal was already making himself sweet porridge. A bowl of sugar-loaded carbs looked very attractive.

'Enough for me?' I asked my son, aware a subtle reversal of roles might be underway. He looked pleased.

'Yeah, I made loads. Have some.'

So we ate a convivial, silent breakfast together, me and my handsome five-foot-eight son; three-quarters boy, one-quarter man, with his inky hands and messy cowlick, just like his dad's.

'Busy day today?' I asked him, the way I'd probably ask a grown-up Man of the House, if there were one to ask.

'Yeah, y'know. I'm taking my guitar 'cos I'm going round to Dom's after, for like band practice?'

'Band practice? I didn't know you were in a band!'

'We just started it.' He shrugged.

'That's very cool. So, who's in the band? What are you called? What do you play?'

'Dom sings, me on guitar, Charlie G on bass, even though he's a bit crap, and Dom's brother – y'know Jules? – on drums. He's good, Jules. He's better than all of us.'

'Well, yes he would be. He's sixteen. So what are you called?'

'It keeps changing. Yesterday it was still Expelliarmus, but Jules says that's lame. He wants to change it to Expelled.' Hal shrugged. 'I don't really care about the name, to be honest; I just like playing.'

'And the music?'

'Oh, really old music – Nirvana, sick stuff like that, but Dom's rewritten the lyrics to "Smells Like Teen Spirit". He says they don't make sense.'

'Well yes, rock lyrics often don't. That's probably the point.'

'Yeah. So that's OK tonight, Mum? Band practice?'

'You bet. I'm all for band practice. Lock yourselves in a garage, turn the amps up to eleven and make your eyeballs bleed, then write an anthem and become a rock god. I mean, what's not to like? But maybe we should have a conversation about the groupies and drugs? And you'd better be home by eight. It's bed by nine on a school night, even for a rock god.'

'Shut up, Mum!'

But he still looked pleased. And I was pleased that he was pleased. I was, indeed, all for 'band practice', even for a boy who was still a fortnight shy of thirteen. So the day got off to a better start than I'd expected and the rest of it was spent doing something so predictable, so feminine and so entirely in-character that within moments of setting foot in Selfridges, where I was intent on serious, focused self-gifting, I felt instantaneously better. And as the week progressed, day by day I reclaimed a little bit more of myself, sloughed off Monday's weirdo Pippa, a woman who slept with other women's partners, 'stole' their phones, hacked into them and listened to messages she shouldn't. What kind of madness was *that*? And now Alex's phone was stashed away in the back of my wardrobe. A trophy from my crime scene. Gone from sight but far from forgotten.

By the following weekend my memories of the previous one had almost completely faded into a dreamy blur. It's a weird thing, sex. I mean of course it's weird, but the strangest thing about it is its transience. I've always been struck by the fact that you – well, I – can have proper mind-bending, chandelier-swinging sex and while you're having it the focus is so intense and consuming that everything else in the world is completely blotted out. You forget you're a mother (maybe it's essential that you do?), forget that you have friends and a life or a job and a million thoughts that would normally consume you. And then later, when it's passed, the memory of the person you had the sex with may remain strong and powerful but trying to recall the sex itself is almost impossible.

Maybe it isn't like that for everyone but it's always been like that for me. Maybe that's a good thing, if also a bit sad? Perhaps that's also what keeps people sane because that kind of sex is just too 'trippy' to assimilate into real life; before you know it you'll be leaving each other messages about whose turn it is to get the fish and chips and which one of you needs to be home in time to relieve the nanny.

So anyway, by the weekend I had convinced myself it

was better this way, even though I'd still bought the pair of fuck-me slingbacks I'd seen in the *Sunday Times*. I do believe there are old habits you really can change, but I think most of them die pretty hard.

I miss you so much, Mum.

Pippa xxx

CHAPTER 6

Alex

Friday 27 November 2009

From: guy@guysports.com
To: alex@foxmail.co.uk

Morning, mate. How's your new manor? Hope not too grim dahn sarf? Still living out of cardboard boxes or are you getting sorted? Business as usual here. Kids fine, missus fine. Still can't agree a date for the wedding but we'd better crack on – L's getting twitchy now the novelty of engagement has worn off. She brought home a copy of Brides *the other day and left it lying around. I think this is prob some kind of hint, no? Whatever. Love to you all. G*

From: alex@foxmail.co.uk
To: guy@guysports.com
Yeah, all OK here. Very different ... but we'll get the hang of it

eventually. Kids seem to be settling in at school and we're regis-tered with every estate agent within a twenty-mile radius so hope-fully we'll find the dream home sooner rather than later. Yup, copy of Brides *definitely more than a hint. Get on with it, man. We could do with another party. A*

Friday 4 December 2009

From: Isobel@struttbrayrush.co.uk
To: alex@foxmail.co.uk

Alex. Hope things going well for you all in Random-on-Sea. I'm sure it will all make sense in the spring cos winter prob a bit grim at the seaside, I think? Anyway, wondered what your plans are for Xmas? The folks are expecting us all as usual but Mum is also finding the prospect of the whole catering-for-everybody business a bit tiring and is being slightly martyr-ish. Perhaps we should sort of take over? Do it at theirs but let them put their feet up? Mind you I don't spose Ma will be able to let go. Maybe Susie has some ideas? I know how brilliant she is at doing Xmas – she was ace that time the folks went to the Florida Golf Detention Centre. Is that really five years ago?! Anyway, maybe we should all book into B&Bs in Random and do it at yours? Just a thought. Scream if you want to! Ix

Monday 7 December 2009

From: alex@foxmail.co.uk
To: Isobel@struttbrayrush.co.uk

Isobel. I think you can probably hear my screams from here. It's not that Soos wouldn't do a brilliant job – she would – it's just that the house isn't geared up for entertaining on a Christmas scale. At least, not a Fox-style Christmas scale. I'll run it by her but I can guess what she'll say, which is: why don't we wait until next Xmas when we're bound to be in the Dream Home and gagging to entertain you all? Yup, I'm popping down Ladbrokes to put a fiver on it even now ... Look, let's do it at the folks' but lock Ma out of the kitchen. I'm sure that's do-able. Is Will going to be around this year, btw? A

From: Isobel@struttbrayrush.co.uk
To: alex@foxmail.co.uk

OK, apols for brusque – off to a client meeting. Yeah, let's go with that idea. Makes sense. And yes, Will's back on the 23rd, I think – and Luke too! x

Tuesday 8 December 2009

From: alex@foxmail.co.uk
To: Isobel@struttbrayrush.co.uk

Roger that. A

Sunday 27 December 2009

From: guy@guysports.com
To: alex@foxmail.co.uk

Man, was Christmas a total fucking nightmare or what?!

Monday 28 December 2009

From: alex@foxmail.co.uk
To: guy@guysports.com

Pls don't get me started. OK, get me started ... Look, it could have been worse. I think we've all had a tough year. Well, OK, you haven't but the rest of us have. Couldn't have foreseen Isobel's meltdown re the twunting chef. Didn't think Mum was going to morph into Fanny Cradock ... with Susie in the Johnny role. But frankly I did expect Will to be his usual holier-than-thou patronizing self. Can't imagine why Lisa is still so hell-bent on being a Fox, but you'd better marry her quick before she changes her mind! Bottom line – the kids had fun. Christmas = kids. Better luck next year, eh? On the subject of which – what are you up to for New Year? A

Tuesday 29 December 2009

From: guy@guysports.com
To: alex@foxmail.co.uk

Funny you should mention it – I think Lisa and I are going to do The Deed in June. She seems to have A Plan – and the Plan doesn't appear to include marquees at the Pink House, so breathe easy mate and ... watch this space! We're going to a party on NYE. You? G

From: alex@foxmail.co.uk
To: guy@guysports.com

We're going to a party at Phil and Bridget's. As we have precisely three 'friends' here and two of them are Phil and Bridget it's been a pretty straightforward process of elimination. Spose you'll be hanging with the sporting A-List again? Beckingham Palace this year, perchance? A

From: guy@guysports.com
To: alex@foxmail.co.uk
Yeah, Beckham's constantly texting me, begging us to come.

Apparently we're on Elton's table – but if I don't get to sit in between Liz Hurley and Patsy Kensit, I'm SO outta there. Meanwhile, in the Real World ... actually I don't even know if I should tell you this but ... sod it! We're going to Pippa's for New Year. She's having a party. You cool with that? She's one of Lisa's best friends ... G

From: alex@foxmail.co.uk
To: guy@guysports.com

Yeah, course. Water under the bridge. How is Pippa? She OK?

From: guy@guysports.com
To: alex@foxmail.co.uk

I haven't seen her in months but I think she's fine. She's seeing someone ... so that's good. Tell me that's GOOD?!

From: alex@foxmail.co.uk
To: guy@guysports.com

Yeah, sure. Who's she seeing?

Wednesday 30 December 2009

From: guy@guysports.com
To: alex@foxmail.co.uk

Ah, knew I shouldn't have mentioned Pippa. Leave it – it doesn't matter!

From: alex@foxmail.co.uk
To: guy@guysports.com

Go on, tell me!

Text from Guy Fox to Alex Fox: *Leave it! Wish I hadn't prised the lid off the can of worms ... Again!*

Text from Alex Fox to Guy Fox: *You're a bastard – just tell me!*

Text from Guy Fox to Alex Fox: *FFS! Call you in 5 ...*

Saturday 2 January 2010

From: alex@foxmail.co.uk
To: guy@guysports.com

Holy Mary Mother of the baby Jesus – I still have the hangover from HELL. You got to hand it to them, they REALLY know how to party down here in the sticks – cos there's sod all else to do. Can you believe we were still going at 5 a.m.? Susie nearly passed out with shock when Bridget sidled up to her at about 10 past 12 and said 'Fancy a toot, Soos – for old acquaintances' sake?'! So there we all were inside Ye Olde Rectum, knocking back the fizz and . . . snorting charlie in the lavs, like it's the 80s! I didn't think I still had it in me, but apparently I do cos I'd still fail a drugs test now. Am staying on the subs bench . . . Hope you had a good one?! . . . A

From: guy@guysports.com
To: alex@foxmail.co.uk

Who knew you could even get Class As in rural Sussex?! I am properly shocked and appalled, mate. And maybe a tiny bit impressed. But don't try and fool me with your leading questions . . . the party was fine, ta. But if there was any coke-snorting in the lavs I def missed it! G

From: alex@foxmail.co.uk
To: guy@guysports.com

*I need more than that and you know it. Don't be a complete C***!*

Sunday 3 January 2010

From: guy@guysports.co.uk
To: alex@foxmail.co.uk

How's the head, Scarface?! Look, the party was good. Pippa's a great hostess. She seems on good form. She asked after you, OK?! I said you were fine – ALL OF YOU were fine. And that's the RIGHT answer, innit?

From: alex@foxmail.co.uk
To: guy@guysports.com

I'm not sure that was the right answer, no. I don't know what the right answer would have been but I don't think it would have been that. But I'm glad she's OK. She deserves to be OK. She's ... special. And I hope her bloke treats her right. I wish he wasn't treating her at all, if you want the honest truth, but hey – we make our beds and we lie on them. And there's almost certainly a joke in there, somewhere, but I'm not in the mood for jokes. A

Text from Guy Fox to Alex Fox: *Call me*

Monday 4 January 2010

From: willfox@wings.co.uk
To: alex@foxmail.co.uk
Cc: guy@guysports.com

I hear you'll be in town tomorrow night? Any chance of meeting both my brothers for a swift half down The Gas Mask and Parachute? W

From: alex@foxmail.co.uk
To: willfox@wings.co.uk
Cc: guy@guysports.com

Yeah, I guess. Pretty busy though … A

From: willfox@wings.co.uk
To: alex@foxmail.co.uk
Cc: guy@guysports.com

Just thought it might be worth our while. Sibling ties … W

Tuesday 5 January 2010

From: alex@foxmail.co.uk
To: guy@guysports.com

Cc: willfox@wings.co.uk

I'll be at Charing X just after 6. Pub by half-past . . .

From: guy@guysports.com
To: alex@foxmail.co.uk
Cc: willfox@wings.co.uk

*Copy. Roger. Don't forget your flak jackets in case of Friendly Fire
. . . Overandout.*

11.46 p.m.
Text from Alex Fox to Guy Fox: *Cover my arse mate cos I'm
staying over in town tonight – I just texted Soos to say I was
staying with you. So I'm STAYING WITH YOU. Do NOT fuck up!*

11.51 p.m.
Text from Guy Fox to Alex Fox: *FFS. yr not doing a clever or
grownup thing but that figures cos yr not clever or grownup. i'll
watch yr back but don't make a habit of this. yr a wanker*

Wednesday 6 January 2010

From: alex@foxmail.co.uk
To: guy@guysports.com

G. Smug bastard, our brother – but actually I had a laugh last night. As smug bastards go, he could be worse. And it's easy to forget the shit that goes down in A'stan. Hate to say it but all that killy-death stuff sure puts the domestic grind into perspective. Maybe that's what pisses me off most about him – that he's living A Real Man's Life and still has his Widowed-in-Action Single Dad halo polished?

Do you think he's seeing any action? I don't mean the combat shit! S'times I think he's gonna leap out of the closet one Xmas Day, just after the crackers and before Dad dishes out turkey and we'd have to watch Mum swoon dead away and Isobel crack a bad joke about loving a man in uniform. Actually sod photography, maybe I'll try writing sitcoms?!

Seriously tho', thanks for the chat after Bravo-Two-Zero left us to go home and dust his Airfix collection. You were good, man, REALLY good, but it didn't make any difference. I called P five minutes after you left. I was gonna leave a message but she picked up straight away – which totally threw me. And she was alone and so we talked and … whatever. So that's where I was last night. But you knew that. If you tell Lisa – if you tell anybody – I will kill you. End of. Thanks for being my brother. A

Text from Guy Fox to Alex Fox: Like I say, you're a wanker. Like I say, don't make a habit of it. I love you but you REALLY piss me off sometimes

Text from Alex Fox to Guy Fox: Too late, mate.
Thursday 7 January 2010

From: willfox@wings.co.uk
To: alex@foxmail.co.uk

Good to see you the other night. Filial bonds not entirely broken,
esp after four pints of Old Twat and a bag of pork scratchings.
As ever, the twin-bond is so tight I always feel like a gooseberry.
But at least you weren't talking in tongues and sharing appen-
dectomies. Take care. W

From: alex@foxmail.co.uk
To: willfox@wings.co.uk

Ha! Good to see you too. Keep safe in 'Stan, man ... A

CHAPTER 7

Susie

When you move away from everything you know to
a place where you know nothing and pretty much
no one and you attempt to create a new life for yourself and your family, it would be highly unusual if
there wasn't some stress.

I wrote that in a rare piece of non-food-related freelance
for a women's magazine, one of a series of monthly
columns entitled 'Living the Dream'.

Our Middle-Youth generation is so restless, so driven,
so consumed by consuming the stuff we think will
make us happier, even as we know deep down – or
if not actually know then certainly suspect – that no
amount of Cath Kidston, Farrow and Ball or artfully
arranged seashell collections on windowsills can ever

compensate for the things you lose when you move
away from your old world ...

I wasn't entirely sure this was the angle they were looking
for, but hey. And never mind the interior-decorating
triumphs, it turned out not to count for much when your
friends – your real, warts-'n'-all, two-decades-and-counting
mates – pitched up at your place for the obligatory seaside
weekend break (which, believe me, only happens in the
months after the clocks go forward, because between
November and March you may as well have moved to
Kyrgyzstan). And after they'd piled out of the 4x4 it was
mere moments before they were falling into predictable
raptures over the Grade 2-listed cornices and infinite sea-
views and cute shell collection on the loo windowsill ...
And how awesome it was that you'd now got THREE loos
to choose from in your to-die-for house that (OMG!) cost
the same as a two-bed flat in ...

So yes, for a few weeks after we moved into the Dream
Home at the beginning of April, we were the most popular
people we knew. For our beloved visitors (because we were
genuinely pleased to see them – and then equally pleased
to see the back of them) it was presumably a pleasurable
mini-break. However, after about six weeks of relentless
socializing, it became a bit like running a boutique seaside
B&B. Weekends that could – probably should – have been
about finding our own place in the Random-on-Sea

'community' were spent making sure we had sufficient duvets and blow-up mattresses, travel cots and baby bottle sterilizing equipment, not to mention cupboards full of the kind of organic wheat-free snacks and raisin permutations that our own children wouldn't touch anymore.

It's not that we didn't have fun, exactly – especially when the kids were asleep and we were cooking, cracking open the wine and catching up with our guests' lives in the Smoke – but were you really meant to wake up exhausted every Monday morning and then spend hours stripping beds and doing two loads of washing before rounding up your visitors' discarded dummies/cuddly toys/memory sticks/underwear and getting them to the post office asap because so-and-so's child would 'probably die of grief if they don't have Bunny by Tuesday, at the latest'?

Pretty soon we were exhausted even before we were allowed to start our own week. Actually, I was exhausted, because the new Real Ale-drinking Alex was suddenly proving himself to be predictably, if depressingly, male when it came to domestic trivia. Either way, it's not as if we were being paid to run Random-on-Sea's newest B&B.

My fortieth birthday at the end of April was a case in point. I quite fancied having a party but, frankly, didn't really feel like organizing it. Dropped hints – hints dropped so loudly, indeed, that they sounded like a canteen of cutlery hitting a stone floor – apparently fell on Alex's selectively deaf ears. For about a millisecond I entertained the fantasy that this was because he had a thrilling Secret Plan, something that conceivably involved being whisked away (for isn't 'whisking away' always a good thing in relation to Secret Plans?) to a place of loveliness for a weekend of middle-aged pampering or relaxation or indulgence or hot thongy sex – or even all of the above ... but in my more sanguine, sensibly middle-aged moments I recognized that this wasn't going to happen.

Because even though I felt I deserved a fortieth Do (five years ago I'd arranged a fantastic surprise party for Alex) I was slightly terrified by the idea that if I waited for him to take the initiative he wouldn't and we could end up in our local pub, The Horse and Groom (inevitably 'The Doom and Gloom'), drinking bad red wine and eating Golden Wonder crisps with Heinous, Phil and Bridge. Clearly, this was not to be countenanced. Clearly I deserved better. But, equally clearly, I figured the only way I was going to get anything better than a night of carbs-and-ale in a pub with too many beams-and-beards was to organize it myself.

Which is how we ended up hosting a party in the Dream Home that was as exhausting as it was chaotic. Not that it wasn't also fun but, after every sofa, bed, and sofa-bed had finally been vacated, it was also the tipping point vis-à-vis running the Dream Home as a B&B.

About thirty friends and relatives came down from

London, about two-thirds of whom checked into proper local B&Bs, while the remainder ended up scattered around the house, with the result that the morning after looked like a modern-(un)dress version of *Caligula*.

We also managed to round up about twenty or so locals. Besides Heinous and Phil and Bridge, there were now a few new people we had met (at Heinous's, at Phil and Bridge's) whom we found were not too piratically beardy, or rune-castingly-weirdy. People, in fact, with whom we appeared to have quite a bit in common and therefore who seemed kind of promising in the long term, for it turned out that Random was awash with other DFLs who had also sold their houses/warehouses/flats in Muswell Hill/Hackney/Dulwich and decamped to the seaside for a 'better' life. Or, at the very least, a life with a lot more sea in it. They were also the kind of media/creative types we'd known at home (and yes, I still referred to London as 'home': thirty-nine years is a lot of habit to break) and though we'd never actually known any of them when we lived in London, we were all about one degree of Kevin Bacon away from each other and now drawn together by a shared set of circumstances/coincidences – and the fact that Random was a very small town with a higher-than-average incidence of beards.

Making new 'friends' in a small town in early middle-age was, I discovered, a lot like making friends in London in one's teens, when the tribal shallowness and sheer ignorance of youth means a 'friend' can easily describe either your same sex soul-mate or simply somebody who is toting that week's coolest 12" single and wearing a pair of shoes you covet.

But while friendship is a pretty mutable business when you're young, over time it's fair to say the definition becomes a bit more stringent. Nonetheless, when you move out of your comfort zone all bets are off again. Suddenly you take your 'friendships' where you find them – even if you find them at the bar in the 'Doom and Gloom' or in the loos tooting a line of charlie at Phil and Bridge's hedonistic New Year's party, in the first flush of enthusiasm for all things Random, when over-heated acquaintanceships really do look like proper friendships. And when the wine is flowing and a dinner party is underway, you find yourself surprised by how easily you allow for the differences of opinion, those tiny, jarring moments which highlight how little you really know these new 'friends' – and perhaps also why you never knew them in any of your previous incarnations.

So . . . my fortieth was 'fun', and drunken and in many respects well worth the effort involved, but there were more than a few WTF? moments. The moment, for example, when Sean, a successful and amusing illustrator who was married to an edgily modernist architect of Balkan extraction with an entirely unpronounceable name, decided to engage a group of reluctant DFLs on the subject of

Zimbabwe. I was just refilling everybody's glasses when he said:

'So many things are inaccurately reported. In many respects Mugabe has always had exactly the right idea.'

The intakes of breath were so sharp it was a miracle nobody ended up in A&E. I peered at Sean to see if he was aiming – and misfiring – for blackly comedic effect ... but no, he was smiling blithely, alongside his equally toothy wife. Apparently still oblivious as the small group fragmented around them, he turned to me and said:

'Really, Susie, there's just too much misinformation.'

Yeah – starting right here, I thought to myself. But instead of slinging them out on their ears, I bottled it, smiled and said, 'More wine?' before mentally crossing them off the short list of potential new soul-mates.

'Alex,' I hissed, interrupting his tête-à-tête with a – hold the front page – freshly beardless, fleece-free and therefore rather dapper-looking Phil. 'I've just overheard the most appalling thing. Sean and his wife with the unpronounceable name ...'

'What about them?'

So I told him, but instead of looking shocked and appalled, he just laughed.

'Oh come on, Soos. He's obviously joking.'

'Some joke. And anyway he wasn't.'

'Well, you know what? I really wouldn't go jumping to any conclusions if I were you. I like Sean and ... thingy.'

I stared at Alex, gobsmackery written all over my face.
'Are you serious?'

'Actually I'd rather not be serious at the moment, if it's all right with you. It's a great party. Lighten up.'

Then Alex – a card-carrying member of the Labour party – patted me on the bum (yes, really) and in that moment was lost to me. Up until then I'd had no idea I was living with Woody Allen's *Zelig*.

I wandered around the house for a bit, trying to forget about the increasingly unrecognizable Alex and mad Sean (presumably he hadn't always been a moron) before shrugging it off and going in search of Heinous, who had of course once been a moron but had Seen the Light. Or had she?

I found Heinous by accident. She was in the top-floor bathroom, which, thanks to the broken catch on the door, not only revealed her at a time when she very much didn't want to be revealed but also quite horribly compromised. Don't get me wrong, it would have been fine – if mildly embarrassing for both parties – had I merely stumbled across her sitting on the loo, but this was worse, for, there in the bathroom, illuminated only by the shaft of light from the bright full moon shining through the window, I could clearly see Heinous on her knees 'pleasuring' a standing man who was – inescapably and without any shadow of a doubt – Phil.

And though I could only make out Heinous from behind

(and believe me I was willing it to be Bridget not Heinous, though vis-à-vis arses there was no comparison, size-wise), Phil was facing the doorway, where my expression – shock, horror, amusement, disbelief, whatever – appeared to hasten the inevitable.

'Oh baby. Oh ... *Oooooh* ... Susie!'

'What?' This from Heinous, whose 'job' was clearly done.

'Sorry,' I blurted before shutting the door and retreating very swiftly downstairs to locate Bridget who, mercifully, was a full three floors below, in the kitchen, chatting to Lisa, with whom it turned out she'd once worked in her previous fashion-editing incarnation. I refilled both their glasses and gave a slightly surprised Bridget a tight little squeeze round the shoulders.

'How lovely that you two know each other! And can I just say, Bridge, that you are looking very gorgeous tonight. I totally love that dress; is it Boden?'

'Thanks, Susie – yes, clever you, it is Boden. Their stuff is very forgiving of the fuller figure, I find.'

And Bridget gave a nervous little laugh. Lisa, meanwhile, smiled the slightly baffled smile of the righteously and permanently slim and said: 'I was just saying to Bridget that she might want to get involved with what we're planning on doing with the shop, which is to increase our online presence. I'm hoping she's still up for some styling.'

Bridget looked so much as if she might burst with joy

that I could've cried. Instead, I gave her another little squeeze and said: 'I think that would be a fabulous idea, Lisa. I think you need Bridget and Bridge needs to spend a bit more time up in the Smoke, hanging with the fashion crowd.'

And then I left them to it and escaped into the garden and stared up at the moon and thought: this place is properly mad-bonkers. And I am now forty. And I have no idea what to do – if indeed there is anything to do – about the Heinous/Phil/Bridge triangle so I'll just stick my head in the shingle and, at least for the moment, completely ignore it.

As our first summer kicked off by the seaside, aka officially 'home', I began to stop thinking about some of the things I never imagined I wouldn't care about for the rest of my life, such as Selfridges. And to those friends who made the effort to come and visit and then left us, sighing, it was probably best to pretend that yes of course it was worth turning around and driving back up the Highway to Hell, if only because there wasn't enough room for all of them here.

On a beautiful Monday morning in June, just after the weekend clear-up and a handful of days before Lisa and Guy's wedding, I was sitting on our front steps with a pint of coffee, staring at the glimpse of sea between the trees, and I realized I'd had enough of hotel-keeping, at least for a while. At that moment Alex was somewhere inside the house, drilling, having recently developed an unexpected but increasingly OCD interest in Dream Home-related DIY. Last week Charlie had started calling him 'Dad the Builder', but Alex hadn't been amused.

'There's a lot of work involved in maintaining a house like this, you know,' Alex had explained to Charlie, totally seriously.

'Can Dad fix it? Yes HE CAN!'

'For God's sake, shut up, Charlie,' barked Alex, then swung round and pushed his son away. Chuck – unused to being called Charlie – looked shocked and then his face crumpled into tears.

'Alex ...' I shouted and then marched off, a sobbing Chuck in tow.

'Daddy's mean, Mummy.'

'Yes, Daddy was a little bit mean but I think he's just tired,' I said, though the truth was I felt sick to my stomach.

On the stoop, I recalled this scene and the tears welled up. I shivered, went back into the house, poured a cup of coffee for Alex and eventually located him on the top floor, wearing a martyrish expression while fitting roller-blinds in the third – count 'em – bathroom.

'Coffee. Um, Alex? Do you think it's the best use of your time, forever wielding your power-tools?'

'And what does that mean?'

'Just that the house is fine. It's not falling down. Maybe the DIY should be shoe-horned into your free time?'

'This is my free time. I don't have a job, remember?'

'Well yes, but maybe putting up blinds is just a distraction from the more important stuff? This bathroom isn't overlooked. In fact we don't even use it. And without any blinds you can see the moon ...' I trailed off, already regretting instigating this conversation.

'It's the guest bathroom. And seeing as we apparently run a hotel these days ...' Alex sighed. 'Look, just let me do stuff my way, OK? Stop hassling me every five minutes. Maybe I need some time to think about the rest of my life – our lives – and if I do that while I'm also putting up blinds, what bloody difference does it make to you? We're OK for money. What's the problem? Why are you always on my case?'

'I'm not.' But I was.

'You are. It's as if you're disappointed in me now I'm no longer the "Big Magazine Publisher"'. This was unnerving: he was using air-quotes again. 'It's as if you think I'm now some sort of sad burden instead of an asset. Not Alpha enough for you anymore? That's what it feels like.' Alex put down the coffee, picked up the drill and turned away.

'Please don't turn your back on me. I really think we should carry on talking.'

'And you can stop fucking well speaking to me as though I'm six years old.'

'Alex. What the hell is going on? You're different. Can't you see you're different? Where's the sense of humour I loved so much? Where's your sense of fun? You're bloody miserable to be around, forever sniping at the kids. It's like you have the weight of the world on your shoulders instead of a beautiful house and a family who loves you and the possibility of a career that will fulfil you more than it stresses you out. It feels like you're slipping away from us, Alex . . .'

The words were rolling out now – an unstoppable seven-month incoming tide of words breaking on the shores of Random-on-Sea.

'Alex. Are you having an affair? Are you seeing Pippa?' Silence, but for the drill.

'Alex? ALEX, turn the fucking drill off!' I leaned over to the socket and flicked the switch. 'Alex, will you please talk to me? I just asked if you were having an affair . . . with Pippa?'

Alex's expression was unrecognizable. Or, more accurately, he was unrecognizable as the Alex I knew, though the expression was recognizable enough. It was one I was getting to know quite well. He put down the silent drill and leaned against the dove-grey tongue-and-groove bathroom wall, just to the left of the windowsill artlessly decorated with seashells and pebbles.

'No, Susie, I am not having an affair. Not with Pippa or anyone else. But if I was having an affair I'd hardly be likely to admit it, would I? In the same way you wouldn't admit it if you were having an affair. And you talk about me having changed? Ha. Pot, kettle, black. You might want to take a look at yourself. As for your sense of humour, well you're pretty insufferable to be around a lot of the time. Maybe I just didn't see it when we weren't under the same roof, all day, every bloody day, but I'm sure as hell seeing it now. And I like it about as much as you like the unemployed version of me.'

'Alex . . .'

'Don't "Alex" me. Just leave me the fuck alone for a bit. Oh and by the way I'm out later, with Phil, so don't bother cooking for me tonight, OK?'

And Alex turned his back and picked up his drill and I couldn't think of anything to say that wouldn't make things a lot worse than they already were, so I left the bathroom and walked slowly down several flights of stairs to the basement utility room and even more slowly emptied the washing machine of its first load of bedlinen and filled it with the second. Trying hard not to think, I sought sanctuary in doing.

Alex went out about 7 p.m., before the kids were in bed. This had never happened before, much less on a Monday.

'Where are you going, Daddy?' asked Lula, freshly bathed and sitting at the kitchen table in a new pink, satiny nightdress – posh pyjamas having recently been firmly rejected in favour of nightwear that looked like something Jodie Foster might have worn in *Taxi Driver*. She was drawing pairs of shoes in glittery pen.

'Out,' said Alex. 'Night night. Be good for Mummy.' And he patted her on the head, distractedly.

'Night night, Daddy,' said Charlie, leaning forward in his chair for a hug. But Alex didn't seem to notice. Instead he checked his phone, glanced at his watch and patted Chuck on the head without making eye-contact.

'Night, Big Man, be good.' He glanced at me: 'I won't be too late.' And then he was gone.

'Why's Daddy going out on a Monday, Mummy? He never goes out on a Monday,' said Lula as she filled in a wobbly-looking stack-heeled stiletto with purple glitter.

'I don't know, darling. Biscuit?'

Later, when the kids were in bed, I microwaved some cauliflower cheese leftovers from their supper the night before, ate a bag of Revels and drank a large glass of Sauvignon before taking the second one outside on to the front steps, where, in the balmy June evening, I sat and looked at the clear star-studded sky. And then because there was no longer enough to do, inevitably I started to think. And because I really didn't want to think, I had to find something to do. Briefly I considered texting Alex – I wrote one but then thought better of it. Then, on the spur of the moment, I wrote another, different text. And this one I did send.

Call me? S x

Now? x

Yes please x

The phone rang less than a minute later.

'Susie?'

'Yes. That's definitely me.'

'What's up? What's wrong? Something must be wrong.'

'I don't know. I mean, yes, something's wrong, I just don't know what. I'm sorry – have I interrupted anything? Are you busy?'

'No, not busy. It's a good time for me. But maybe not for you?'

'It's all going wrong.'

'How do you mean, "wrong"? I thought it was all going right – for all of you?'

'On the surface it is, but underneath, not so right. I don't think it's going to work. I've really tried. And I'm sure Alex has too, in his way, but it's no good. Something's shifted. Do you know how sometimes newspapers print wrong, so that you can see the layers of words and pictures but can't make them out properly? It's like that. We're out of register. Kind of together, but not properly joined up. And I've had two glasses of wine, by the way, and not much food. So . . .'

'What can I do?'

'I don't know. I don't know what you can do. I shouldn't even be speaking to you, should I?'

'That's fine. You know you can speak to me whenever you want. I seem to recall it was you who said you shouldn't – and wouldn't unless it was absolutely necessary. Do you remember?'

'Yeah, I remember. As if I could forget.'

'But you know I'm always here for you, if you need me. Not like that. Not like . . .'

'I know, I know. Not like before.'

'Not like before.' There was a very long pause. 'Unless . . .'

'I think I need to see you, Will . . .'

Please don't judge me. OK, whatever – judge away. You'll think what you like and that's fair enough. I've been a domestic criminal in the past, and the worst sort, too: a woman who has slept with her partner's brother. But I've been 'clean' – we've been 'clean', Will and I – for ages. Or rather, it had been ages . . . years . . . until we both fell off the wagon. But maybe I should explain. Or perhaps I just *need* to explain. Then you can still judge me, but at least you'll have all the facts. And I don't know why, exactly, but that's important to me: that you know the truth.

It was because of Will – because of what happened between us – that I never allowed myself to marry Alex, despite being engaged, despite him practically begging me to marry. And it's not as if I was raised mired in Catholic guilt or anything, but . . . nobody has the monopoly on guilt, do they? Of course, what I failed to understand, at least until it was too late, was that Alex probably felt I was somehow punishing him, for crimes unknown. I wasn't, though – and that's the truth. I was punishing myself.

And of course the terrible irony is that long before I betrayed Alex – and isn't 'betrayed' a truly horrible word? – I had betrayed Will first.

I met Will just over a year before I met Alex. My best friend, Bells, was dating an RAF officer – she always had the proverbial thing for men in uniform, was even briefly engaged to a copper before she saw the light and realized that not all uniforms were equally sexy – and during the three or four months she was seeing Tom she gave a couple of very-much-out-of-her-comfort-zone dinner parties for Tom and a few of his mates.

Bells was (and presumably still is) a lousy cook, so she needed me onside, both practically and emotionally. Originally the plan had been to stow me away in her tiny galley kitchen and keep the guests in the living room and then she could take all the credit for whatever I dished up. My only caveat being that I wasn't going to tell her what I was cooking, so she'd have to wing it – which we both thought was hilarious, because we were twenty-eight. However, my cover was blown when Bells was in the loo having a lip-gloss crisis and a guest suffering a corkscrew crisis wandered into the kitchen.

'Hi, I'm Will. Who the hell are you? And why are you hiding in here?' I'd have made a lousy spy; I confessed immediately, while Will, who thought this mad plan to impress Tom was very funny, decided to play along.

It was a great evening, if a little *Abigail's Party*, and then I was eventually allowed to reveal the truth alongside my strawberry pavlova. All the eight guests thought it was very funny, too – apart it must be said from Tom. In fact, for Bells, our stunt backfired because Tom finished with her a week later, citing 'immaturity'. Fortunately Bells is not a grudge-bearer and shrugged it off with: 'He'd already started saying "no" to my requests to wear his uniform in bed, so the writing was on the wall. And I think he'd stopped enjoying my – how shall I put this? – insurrections in the ranks and just wanted me to start taking orders.'

So when I told her that Will, who had asked for my number, had called me and that we were going out, she was genuinely pleased.

'Word of warning, Susie: he probably just wants you for your delicious meringues.'

'You are slightly tragically sex-obsessed, Bella, and in a weirdly old-fashioned way. You're the Jilly Cooper heroine who got away.'

'Er, who said anything about sex? I was talking about your fantastic puddings, but if you want to talk about sex, well, let's face it, you do have great tits.'

Twelve years ago I did indeed have 'great tits'. I knew this because for about fourteen years prior to this I had

had men of pretty much all ages, sizes and racial config-
urations tell me, over and over, in no uncertain terms.
Sometimes this would be in a relatively appropriate and
intimate context; at other times it would be while I was
standing at a bus stop or queuing in a shop or anywhere
in the vicinity of scaffolding. And because I wasn't actually working in porn movies, statistically more often 'great
tits' would be hissed, shouted, muttered or whispered
randomly, in public. Thus my 'great tits' were both,
depending on my mood, a source of feminine pride or a
terrible cross (your heart bra) to bear. But having had my
34E burden since the Lower 4th, becoming the first girl
in the year to wear a bra because she had to rather than
because she wanted to, meant I'd long since forgotten a
life pre-tits, great or otherwise.

And I really really hated the words 'tits'. In fact usage
of the word 'tits' was effectively a deal-breaker when it
came to blokes. If a man really loved me (I'd decided) or
even just liked me quite a lot, he'd climb down off his
metaphorical scaffolding and call my chest almost
anything other than 'tits'. Except for 'hooters', obviously,
or 'fun bags'.

Anyway, it turned out that Will wasn't a 'tit' man. Or
rather, he was a 'tit' man but he always referred to them
as 'breasts', which meant I sort of loved him straight away.
Not that he was talking about my 'breasts' straight away,
obviously – but when he was eventually introduced to

them it was clear he respected them, which in turn meant that he respected me, which also meant he was probably a Gent. And when I was twenty-eight I hadn't met too many Gents who weren't either my dad or my dad's friends. And actually, several of my dad's friends had struck me as definite 'tit' types – but I digress.

Will says he asked me out because I 'made him laugh'. Which is obviously better than 'because you have great tits', but almost as predictable. When it came to chalk versus cheese we were, quite obviously, the White Cliffs versus Pule (it's a Serbian donkey cheese that costs €1,000 a kilo, though you'd have to pay me more than that to eat it). Verily the definition of opposites attracting, at the time we met Will was a widowed RAF officer of thirty-six with a seven-year-old son, whose disparate list of re-creations included fly-fishing, contemporary American literature and tinkering with his classic pillar-box-red 1974 Jensen Healey (apparently a kind of car). I, on the other hand, was a flighty twenty-eight-year-old singleton, living in a flatshare in Crouch End and working as features editor on the newly launched *Fine Dining* magazine, whose re-creations included becoming tired and emotional in so many of the capital's clubs and bars that, some time around 1995, against a backdrop of Blur and Oasis, Bella had nicknamed me 'the carpet inspector'.

On paper, Will and I should have amounted to no more than three dates, two shags and one slightly strained but fabulously polite conversation about why we couldn't see each other anymore, what with having nothing in common. But instead, something strange happened – strange for both of us – which is that at precisely the point when everybody we knew thought we'd be breaking up, we did exactly the opposite and fell in love.

I'm not sure which of us did the 'falling' first, but given my predilection for getting horizontal it was probably me. Still, it was a close thing and, cheesily enough, it happened on our first – and as it turned out, last – Valentine's Day, which was spent in the kind of high-end chintzy country house hotel that had yet to embrace modernism in either design or attitude, much less gastronomy, and was, we both agreed, oddly all the better – not to mention more 'romantic' – for it.

This was also the day Will gave me a present. It was an unusual present for Valentine's Day – no long-stemmed roses or petrol-station teddies for Will – and it was completely extraordinary. As I tentatively pulled the paper off a large flat rectangle – a picture, surely? But of what? – the 'picture' was in fact revealed to be a very old and very beautiful Venetian glass mirror. It wasn't one of those trendy copies but the real deal, complete with foxing and scratches. After I'd unwrapped it and stood staring at it, speechless, for what was clearly too long, Will said, 'Bloody hell, Susie, do you hate it? Is it the most completely wrong thing ever?'

'No. No, it is easily the most magnificently beautiful thing I've ever been given. I'm just genuinely lost for words. Jesus, Will, it must've cost a—' I stopped. How crass could I be?

'Ssshh. It didn't cost anything. I don't know if that makes it better or worse, but I've had it for a long time and it's been waiting for somebody who I knew – OK, hoped – would properly love it. Marianne used to say it was the most flattering mirror in the world. I wouldn't know about that, but—'

'You had this mirror when Marianne was alive?'

'If I told you it had been her mirror, would you take that the wrong way? Would you think I'd fobbed you off with my late wife's leftovers? Have I completely fucked up? I have, haven't I?'

I can see that, for many women, being given something precious that had once belonged to their boyfriend's dead wife would have meant that, yes, Will had fucked up. Luckily he'd waited to give it to a woman who didn't think that at all, indeed whose first thought was: *Oh my God. I don't deserve this. I haven't earned it. But I'm going to.*

I was incredibly moved. And confused. Not least because taped to the glass was an envelope containing a plain piece of card, and on the card was written: *Mirror, Mirror . . . I look at this and now I start thinking of you. W x*

I turned and hugged him, buried my head in his chest and heaved a sob.

'Hey. It was meant to be a happy thing. No tears, Susie
– please,' said Will.

'I am happy. I'm just overwhelmed.'

It's the only time in my life I've ever cried when I've
been given a present, whatever that means. And yet one
day can accommodate many moods and so while I'd like
to pretend that this February 14th continued in an appropriately Mills & Boon-ish vein, it didn't.

At this time, Will was stationed in Norfolk, while his
son, Luke, whom I'd never met, had already been boarding
for a term and a half. In fact it was Luke's schooling arrangements that prompted our first ever row, if you could call
it a row, over dinner that night. Will didn't really do rows;
he just sort of clenched his teeth and glowered slightly,
which in some ways was worse – and he was particularly
clenched when, tongue loosened by champagne, I shared
unsolicited parenting 'advice' and started berating Will
for sending 'a tiny little boy off to boarding school, like
it's nineteen-sodding-ten!'

Will suffered this rant for a bit longer than he needed
to, frankly, before he said: 'Susie, not only have you never
had the benefit of meeting Luke to judge precisely what
kind of "tiny little boy" he is – which is to say, not very
tiny and also exceptionally mature and level-headed for
his age – but perhaps you don't entirely grasp the complexities of single parenting in the armed forces, where one
could at any time be sent off thither and yon, which in

turn would be infinitely more disruptive for a "tiny little boy" than the warm and friendly environment of weekly boarding at a school where the majority of the pupils are from precisely the same background. And then Luke spends most weekends when I'm not around either with his maternal or paternal grandparents, who not only happen to live a mere fifteen miles away from each other but have also been close friends since before I was born, so . . .'

So that told me. And the fact that at no point in his measured 'argument' had Will said 'you're not a parent' was not lost on me, either. Will was never condescending or patronizing, even if I deserved it. Instead he was kind and patient and loyal, which would make him sound like a golden retriever if he wasn't also in possession of a wit so dry it could have been shaken and accessorized by a twist of lemon. And did I already mention that he was – is – also six foot two with buns of steel and was – is almost certainly still – the most incredible, imaginative, unselfish lover? No, I didn't think so.

After our Valentine's supper, during which I had behaved like a graceless idiot, Will took me back to our room and showed me a thing or two about how a man can love a woman even if a woman doesn't necessarily deserve it. And after that, when we were lying in the ridiculous four-poster that was so high and vast it had steps, Will called room service and ordered more champagne and then did such magnificently erotic things with it that I felt as though it was me, not Bells, who was the Jilly Cooper heroine. After all that, I lay in his arms and said: 'I love you, Will. When can I meet Luke?'

And Will said: 'Would you mind very much if we separated those two sentences and dealt with them individually?'

And I said: 'No, of course not. Which one do you want to start with?'

But Will didn't answer. At least not verbally. Instead he peeled away the mille-feuille of blankets and eiderdowns under which we lay and started to lick gently between my legs, sliding his tongue slowly up and across my stomach and onwards, upwards towards my . . .

'Susie, you have the most beautiful breasts in the world. Now turn over. I'm going to fuck you hard.'

And because he was an officer and a gentleman, obviously I did as I was told.

So what went wrong? Well, nothing went wrong. With Will, nothing ever really went wrong in the usual way of things going wrong in relationships, but something definitely went . . . and it was, inevitably, Will. He left me for his job. Or rather, his job took him away from me, abroad three months later, and seven months after that, after I had moved out of the Crouch End flatshare and into my own bijou rental in Cricklewood, Will was still away doing excellent manly things with planes in horrible desolate places, and though we spoke as often as possible I missed him like a crazy woman and I longed for his kisses to the point where the mere thought of them had me shivering with Proustian pangs ... and then suddenly it was December and I was standing at a bar in a Soho members' club, wearing Vivienne Westwood and feeling fine, if a bit too single for comfort, and while waiting for a cab that never came I was chatted up by a good-looking bloke called Alex.

No, I don't know what the odds are either. Somewhere there will be a set of statistics about the likelihood of people coincidentally hooking up with their partner's sibling whom they'd never previously met but only heard of, though I've yet to stumble across that website. By the time Alex got around to the family conversations, which was basically the day after the night before when we found ourselves in a Pitcher & Piano attempting to blot out our terrible hangovers with protein and carb over-doses, and when I asked his surname, not only did he shock me with:

'Fox. But I remember yours.'

And then swiftly – too swiftly for any degree of comfort – revealed that he had a twin brother, an older sister and an older brother called Will who was in the RAF and currently 'away on a tour, making the world a better place, if only in his dreams'. And I was so stunned by the reve-lation that I just kept *schtum*. To do anything else would, at that point have been plain daft – I was probably still technically drunk – so I just nodded and smiled and said: 'Oh, really, that's so interesting. What's it like having a twin? I've often wondered.'

And as Alex trotted out all the biographical details about his family that I already knew, albeit from an intriguing new perspective and with his own spin, I just kept nodding and smiling, smiling and nodding, until: 'Are you OK? Am I being incredibly boring? Tell me to shut up if you want. Or, better still, tell me about you.'

Which, under the circumstances, seemed like a good idea, so I did.

When Will returned from his tour three weeks later, there was a 'crisis meeting'. Even now, many years on and having acquired at least the veneer of maturity en route, the mere thought of it makes me blush. Some parts I have even managed to block out completely, though broadly speaking it was conducted at lunchtime in a Café Rouge in a postcode that may have been New Jersey for all I knew of it. Never mind the MoD, MI5 would have been impressed by my 'undercover' operation – and certainly the buttoned-up Burberry mac I'd chosen for the assignation. I stopped short of glasses and a trilby, though.

Anyway, our conversation was brief:

ME: Will. We need to talk. I have missed you so much. But . . .

WILL (*with a sigh*): I think I can guess, Susie. It's an occupational hazard of my beloved bloody job.

ME: Well yes, you can probably guess, but actually it's kind of even worse than that.

WILL: Worse? You're pregnant?

ME: Stop it, Will. No, I'm not pregnant. But I am seeing someone, and ...

WILL: How long, Susie?

ME: Not very long, Will, but the point is ... um.

WILL: Come on – spit it out. Frankly, if I have to make a choice, I prefer the short sharp shock to the drawn-out kind of shock.

ME (*deep breath*): Well, OK. Look. I'm seeing someone and it's your brother, Alex. And I had no idea he was your brother until after we'd ... um. Anyway. No idea at all. I would never do that to you. It is a bizarre coincidence. And up until then I had been completely faithful, Will – I hadn't even thought about the possibility of not being faithful. I love you. I loved you. I'm ... I'm all over the place, frankly ... And no, please don't do that face, Will. Don't do that, and please say something? *Anything*?

And after this it really is all a bit of a blur, but Will didn't say much. And then after he hadn't said much he got up and paid the bill and he left. And it was all over in about ninety seconds, albeit ninety seconds that felt like a couple of incredibly crap lifetimes lived back-to-back.

And when he'd gone, I sat there staring at my cappuccino, fighting the inevitable tears. And then about five minutes later I received a text from Will, which said: *You deserve each other. Have a lovely life. Wx*

And that was particularly awful because far from being a bitter and twisted message suffused with rage and hurt, because I knew Will – knew how kind he was – I suspected he really meant it, and not in a horrible way. Not that I could ask him, of course. Not now. And that made it worse even as it somehow made it easier, too. Made it much easier to walk out of that City branch of Café Rouge and into the cold thin light of an early January London day and get on the tube back home to my bijou flatlet in Cricklewood and pack a bag of clothes and walk the half-mile or so to Alex's basement pied-à-terre in Kilburn and sit on the wall outside and wait for him to come home, which he did at 6.37. And when he saw me, he looked surprised, of course, but also – and this was obvious – pretty delighted. And he said:

'Susie. What the hell are you doing? It's freezing! Why didn't you call? Come in, come in . . .'

And I did. And the next time I went back to Cricklewood it was to pack my stuff – including the mirror, which, judging by the face that stared back at me, no longer seemed to want to flatter – and bring it all back to Kilburn.

Despite being introduced to the rest of the Fox family the following weekend at Careless, it was well over a year before I saw Will again. From Alex – who still had no idea about any of this, and I vowed he never would – I heard that his brother Will had been re-posted twice and was apparently seeing a forty-something divorcee called Lynda. (Lynda with a 'y': I could just picture her.) And when we did finally meet, sufficient time had elapsed for me not to want to actually die of the horror of it all. Alex and I were very much a couple, it was Sunday lunch at Careless and Will (plus Lynda, who looked almost exactly as I'd imagined she'd look, which is to say not a bit like me) and was also very nice (and not a bit like me) and Luke (who was ten, and not remotely little but just as handsome as his dad) were the last to arrive and the first to leave and as we were effectively being 'introduced', we barely spoke, and then only very politely and distantly.

And it was almost entirely bearable, really – right up until the very last minute anyway, when, just as they were about to leave and were saying their goodbyes, Will leaned in to kiss me on both cheeks and said, in a normal, cheery I've-only-just-met-you sort of voice: 'Lovely to have met you, Susie. Good luck with Alex – you'll need it!' and then swiftly whispered: 'You look beautiful. And very happy. I'm glad. I'm happy too.'

And then he squeezed my arm and with that he was gone. And the next time I saw Will, a year after that, I was pregnant. And Lynda was history.

'I think I need to see you, Will.'
'Is that really a good idea?'

'You know what? I don't really give a fuck if it's a good idea or not. I don't even know what a good idea is anymore.'

'If you need to see me I will drop everything, within reason. But I'm also concerned that you're over-reacting and that all the changes in your life mean that you're not giving this your best shot. It's tough for all of you, but relationships have these hiccups. You know that. You're not stupid, Susie. And the fact is . . .' Will paused and sighed. 'I'm worried that if we meet we'll be creating more problems than we'd be solving.'

And I knew what he meant by that. It had been barely more than a year since we'd fallen off our respective wagons, shortly after an entirely chance meeting in Charing Cross Road. I had just grabbed a coffee in Pret when I saw him walking out of the National Portrait Gallery, and we had small-talked awkwardly in the street and then went to a pub in Covent Garden ('just one drink'). And then, insanely, twenty-four hours later, after a flurry of texts and just a week before the golden wedding party, we found ourselves – because it really did seem as though we were not in control, that someone else was pulling our strings – in a bed in an anonymous hotel near Regents Park. Not a million miles away from the Landmark, as it happens. And then, during our second hook-up, the night before the party, at the same hotel, we didn't have sex because we knew it would be too magnificent and entirely wrong, but had talked a lot and had still been so confused that we'd both effectively run for the hills. Or rather, straight after the party, Will had actually run for the hills and returned to his air-force base in Wales, while I had begun to engineer Operation Random-on-Sea.

So what was I doing asking to see him, with all the potential problems that could – and almost inevitably would – present? All I know is that I was now on my third glass of wine and hadn't eaten enough. My kids were asleep and my partner was out on the lam on a Monday night with Phil, and my new best friend – Heinous – was turning out to be the kind of woman who gave blow-jobs to other women's husbands on their friend's fortieth birthday (not that I was in a position to judge, but . . .). And I missed Bells and my London friends, and I thought I might just keel over with self-pity and loneliness. And all of this while sitting on the steps of my bloody Dream Home at a point in my life when I should have been feeling something akin to content, if not actually downright happy.

'I'm sorry, Will. I'm a complete fucking idiot. It'll be fine. You're right. And I'm sorry I even called.'

'No need to ever apologize or explain, Susie. I take you as I find you. And obviously I'd like to help but I think my help may prove more of a hindrance, that's all. Hang on, though – we'll be seeing each other on Saturday anyway. The wedding? Don't tell me you forgot about that?'

And of course at that precise moment I had completely forgotten about Guy and Lisa's wedding. Though I was genuinely delighted that they were finally getting hitched, the prospect of Alex's twin brother getting married this very weekend in front of a crowd that would – I assumed – include Lisa's great friend, Pippa, wasn't exactly making my heart sing. In fact it was making my heart sulk like a hormonal teenager, made it want to slam doors and shout 'Whatever' and 'You just don't understand me!' Yup, the prospect of scrubbing up and hanging with the Fox family for a long day and evening made me want to crawl under a duvet with a huge bar of Dairy Milk and stay there for at least a week.

'It actually did slip my mind for a moment, you're right. But of course I'll – we'll – see you on Saturday. And thanks. Thanks very much for just being at the end of the phone. I'll try not to make a habit of it.'

I was determined to sound cheerful and on top of things. It seemed to work.

'Always here if you need me though. Night, Susie.'

And so I tipped the second half of the third glass of wine down the sink and crawled under the duvet and slept for at least eight hours. And I had no idea when – or indeed if – Alex got home, but he certainly wasn't there by the time I got up.

By the following Saturday morning I had somehow psyched myself into the Wedding Zone. I had a slither of brand new day-to-evening, sexy-but-not-too-sexy Vivienne Westwood 'Anglomania' on a hanger on the front of the wardrobe door and a new pair of Georgina Goodman sale sandals sitting on the floor below it. On Thursday I had also managed to bag a miracle last-minute cancellation at John Frieda in town so I could see my genius colourist, because I'd long since decided that even if I was moving out of the Smoke for good, the day I started getting my hair done at Upper Cut on the High Street was indeed the day I would Curl Up and Dye.

And so we set off, *en famille*, at 11 a.m. on Saturday in order to make the 3 p.m. ceremony at Kenwood House in Hampstead with room to breathe, because above and beyond the fact that Alex was Best Man, lateness was not and never had been a Fox option. Apart from Guy, that is, who was habitually late for everything but hoping to break the habit of a lifetime today.

I don't want you to feel cheated by my description of the wedding, because I'm warning you right now: I'm keeping it brief. We all love a good wedding, after all, and of course I'd love to paint you a suitably 'romantic' picture of the beautiful ex-model bride in her elegant column of halter-necked cream silk by Vera Wang, accessorized by a simple ponytail 'Do', discreet make-up and a small bouquet of peonies. I'd love to bang on at considerable length about the perfection of the weather and the fact that Guy wasn't late (though of course Lisa was), and how the civil ceremony was a minimal yet heartfelt delight – and all the more so for being over in fifteen minutes. And I'd love to tell you how Pea and iPod were divine in their roles as ring-bearer and flowergirl and how I got just the right amount of teary, which is to say a bit, but not to the point of being either smeary or snotty. And then how the sit-down lunch for 120 was magnificent, and the speeches trod just the right delicate balance between sentimental and offensive. And how we then all danced and drank and caroused until the cows came home to Kenwood for about the first time in 150 years.

I'd love to tell you all of this but I may have to leave it to someone else to do that, because I wasn't actually there.

It's not my proudest moment but somewhere along the Highway to Hell, in a petrol station forecourt near Tunbridge Wells, Alex and I found ourselves in the middle of a stand-up row triggered by the fact that Charlie had wet himself. And despite the fact that I distinctly recall having a second pair of trousers on hand just in case, they were nowhere to be found. And then one of us remembered that they'd been put on the roof of the car for a second or two before one of us also remembered that they'd never been removed from the roof of the car before we'd driven off. And so something which, between a couple sharing the same emotional as well as physical journey, might have been a trigger for shared giggles and shrugs and the emergency purchase of a pair of pull-ups, instead became a metaphor for all our separate stresses and highlighted the fact that we were now moving away from each other at high speed, both literally and metaphorically.

Which is also how, twenty very shouty minutes later, Alex and (a visibly distressed, for which I hated myself) Lula – and her bridesmaid's dress, hanging in the back of the car under plastic – found themselves driving on to the wedding while an equally visibly distressed (not to mention visibly wet) Chuck and I found ourselves ordering a cab to take us back home to Random. Like I say, not my finest hour. But then these are the kind of irrational decisions a couple in crisis will make when their lives stop being an 'us' kind of relationship and instead become a couple of separate 'I' relationships, forever stuck in No Man's Land and intent on self-preservation.

So Chuck and I never made it to the wedding (though I did eventually see some photographs, which is how I know about the dress and the flowers). Instead we spent the afternoon trawling rock-pools on Random's beach, after which I sent a brief text to Heinous, saying 'Heeeeeelp! Am going bonkers!' or something to that effect, and she texted back 'Kettle's on . . .' and we pitched up at hers, and because Edie was in London with her dad for the weekend and Chuck was exhausted and conked out on her sofa in front of *Toy Story*, Heinous and I were able to have a proper child-free heart-to-heart for the first time in weeks – and definitely the first time since my birthday. And that was . . . interesting.

'So, this isn't looking great, if I may say so, Susie,' said Heinous.

'No, not great. I think Alex and I have reached some kind of point of no return.' But I wasn't about to elaborate in detail. While Heinous was the closest friend I had in Random it didn't automatically follow that she was the closest friend I had in the world. I had never, for example, told her about Will. The only person still in my life who knew anything about Will and me was Bells, and she was 12,000 miles away.

'So where do you go from here?'

'I'm not quite sure. In fact never mind "quite", I'm not even remotely sure. Things are moving so fast. On the subject of which . . .' and I fancied a change of subject, so I peered at her quite intently. 'Ah, you and, er, Phil. Is it a "don't mention the war" situation? A moment of madness fuelled by the intoxicating high of celebrating my fortieth birthday? Or?'

I let the question hang. Heinous looked momentarily flustered. Surprisingly flustered, really. I'd assumed that the Phil–Heinous conjunction had been an alcohol-fuelled *carpe-diem* moment seized by both parties to assuage some small-town boredom at the end of a long winter. But now I could tell just by looking at her that I'd completely misread the situation. That it was far more complicated than I'd imagined. Not that I'd done much imagining, frankly, because the sight of Heinous giving Phil a moonlit

234

blow-job was not an image I wished to have burned into my cerebral cortex for all eternity.

'I shouldn't be telling you this, Susie. I really shouldn't, but ... Phil and I ... we're ...'

'Oh bloody hell, Harriet. What are you doing?' This first-name formality seemed entirely appropriate.

'We're in love. Phil's leaving Bridge and we're going to be together. You may as well know now because by Monday everybody will.'

'For fuck's sake! What are you doing? What do you mean, "We're in love"? You're not eighteen. They're married, they've got small kids, they're a family. What is he doing? Leaving Bridge this weekend and shacking up here?'

'That's about the size of it. He'll be round tonight. Carrying a suitcase full of guilty clichés.'

'Christ, H. Are you mental? You've only known each other for six months.'

'How long do you need? And marriages break down every day, as you may have noticed. I don't see that we're doing anything demonstrably more mental or selfish than, say, shouting at each other in a petrol station fore-court and heading in different directions on the day of a family wedding – somebody else's big day which you have now both effectively blighted. Anyway, Bridge and Phil haven't fucked since 2007.'

'Says Phil. Come on, you can't be that dumb? You know what men say. I'll bet he and Bridge are still at it. And

Bridge will be devastated. Confused first, and then devastated. And *three kids*.'

I felt very strongly that Heinous was doing the wrong thing, but of course how hypocritical was I? The woman who had just four days previously phoned her ex-lover, her partner's brother, in desperation ... Who, every day, wondered how she'd fucked up her life to the point where, despite now living in the house of her dreams, the man she'd assumed she'd be with for the rest of her life was increasingly a stranger and she felt miserable most of the time.

At that moment, Heinous's phone pinged with a text. She scrutinized it carefully, before pulling a :-/ face and saying: 'OK, wow, looks like the proverbial shit has hit the propellers sooner than I'd expected. He's on his way.'

'OK, so we're out of here.'

I scooped up a still-sleeping Chuck from the sofa and grabbed my bag and we left. Even with the dead weight on my hips, it took about three minutes to get home – we really were that close. 'Home.' Home was where the heart was, right? As I fumbled for the keys on the steps of the Dream Home and waved a cheery 'Hi!' at a car-washing neighbour, my heart – which had stopped being a sulky teenager and was now just the heart of a deeply saddened middle-aged woman – sank even further.

An hour or two later, at about 8.30 p.m., when Chuck was in the bath and I had poured myself a glass of something cold and white and very attractive-looking, the phone rang. It was Alex, clearly a bit drunk.

'OK, the reception's underway so I thought I'd grab a moment to call you. You're a fucking disgrace, Susie. You're a selfish bitch and despite having a good go at ruining my brother and sister-in-law's wedding you didn't succeed because it's fucking great and everybody's having a fabulous time. And you know what? Nobody could give a fuck whether you're here or not because, funnily enough, it's not all about you. And in case you're interested, Lula's had a lovely time, despite everything. And we'll be back sometime tomorrow, but I don't know exactly when because we're in no hurry.'

'No need to hurry. No need to hurry at all.' All the energy seemed to have drained from my body. 'Oh and by the way, Phil's just left Bridge for Harriet.'

'Yeah, I know, he just texted me. I knew he was going to do it. We were up until half three last Monday talking about it. Good luck to them! I don't know how he stuck it with fatso for as long as he did. Mind you, to be fair, being fat is one thing she could've changed; being boring and stupid wasn't. And while we're at it, I think this relationship has probably run its course too. And I can tell you straight away that I'm keeping the house so you'll have to leave.'

'Typically charming, Alex.' Interesting that in the same way as the children became 'my' children when he was feeling distanced from them, so the Dream Home was now 'his' when he was distanced from me.

And the phone went dead. An hour later, when Chuck was asleep and I was at the bottom of the third glass, the phone rang again.

'Will?'

'Susie. Are you all right?'

'I'm ... Yeah. Whatever. I don't know. No, I'm not.'

'I'm on my way.'

'Don't be ridiculous! Of course you're not. It's your brother's wedding, for fuck's sake.'

'They won't even notice – they're in their own little wedding bubble. Everybody's fine. I'm on my way.'

And I touched 'End Call' and stared at the phone. And then, within a minute or two, it rang again, the caller identified as 'Bridget'. I watched it ring for a while, guiltily, before letting it go to voicemail. I wanted to speak to Bridge, just not right now. Instead, very slowly and deliberately, I poured myself another glass of wine.

CHAPTER 8

Pippa

Dearest Mum,

As fast as possible, I determined to put all the Alex nonsense behind me, even if I was tiring of constantly putting things behind me. I was even briefly tempted to extract the bloody iPhone – the *body* – from its hiding place and wander along the Grand Union canal under cover of darkness before discreetly dumping it. However, in the end I couldn't quite bring myself to dispose of the phone, even though its presence, even its invisible presence, tucked away in my wardrobe, still felt like having one of those 'trophies' that murderers like to hang on to as a scene-of-crime keepsake.

And even if, as 'crime-scene trophies' go, Alex's iPhone wasn't exactly up there with the lock of hair or the bloodied knife, it was nonetheless properly haunted by the sound of Susie's voice – and, what's more, Susie's voice lying – which gave it an extra shivers-down-my-backbone quality, because I felt as though I was hanging on to a ghost of Susie's DNA, captured in the ether. Not of course that Susie was dead, or planning to be, and not that I wished her dead either. I am, you'll be relieved to learn, not suddenly about to reveal a secret that exposes me as part-time Belsize Park yummy-mummy, part-time killer. No, all that had happened was that I'd 'acquired' my ex-lover's lost mobile phone in order to listen to his old messages and discover if his wife was cheating on him, that's all. Could have happened to anybody, right?

Anyway, as the summer wore on, I successfully distracted myself from those rapidly receding memories and their concomitant moments of madness, and lost myself in the here-and-now. I spent two out of my three child-free August weeks while Hal was at his dad's place on the Côte d'Azur, staying at the same hotel as Lisa and Guy and the twins, in Ibiza – where I indulged in a lot of sleep, three novels, a few gallons of Rioja and (to my considerable surprise), after being chatted up over a margarita at sunset by a man with a nice smile and a winning way with a cheesy one-liner, an unexpected fling with a recently divorced ex-DJ d'un certain age, called Nik.

Nik had apparently been converted to the Balearic lifestyle after 1988's 'Second Summer of Love' – a pop cultural event (one amongst many) that had entirely passed me by because I'd been living in a shoebox in Tokyo at the time. I also suspected that Nik called me 'babes' because it saved him the bother of having to remember my name. But that was fine because even though he'd tragically lost his 'c', Nik was sweet and funny and undemanding (apart from when he was demanding, although that was fine too) and obviously there's nothing wrong with having a holiday fling with a fiftyish DJ, even one called Nik who in turn calls you 'babes' ... especially if you're a forty-whatever 'babe' who assumed that her shagging-on-the-beach days were behind her. Hurrah, in fact, for Nik, who was also conceivably the only fiftyish bloke on (or even near) the Balearics who wasn't busily hankering after twenty-year-olds. Of either sex. Or both.

'Nah, not my style. I prefer women to girls,' said Nik after I raised the subject of his unfashionable predilection while we were poolside and post-coital at his villa near St Joan. 'Course, a youngster's flesh may be a bit tauter, but so fucking what? Your *brain* is taut, babes – and you've got a great arse.' Nik made me laugh and the sex was fun without ever being earth-moving. He was just what the doctor ordered.

'You have a lovely life, babes – you deserve it, big style,' he said to me when he saw me off at the airport, unsentimentally but not un-sweetly. He gave me a present, too – a simple, rather lovely silver bangle with a tiny Ibiza-shaped charm attached – and then he gave me a kiss and, finally (clever, this), instead of waiting for me to turn around and walk away from him through passport control, which is what somebody who loves you does when they say goodbye, Nik simply winked and smiled before turning away and wandering off through Departures. I didn't expect him to turn around and, as far as I know, he didn't.

By the time I got home, under a cloud of warm, dense summer drizzle, to my empty, pristine house, Nik was already a blur, if not actually a Manga-ish cartoon of the whole concept of a modern middle-aged 'holiday romance'. But thanks to the miracle of digital photography, once I'd downloaded my snaps on to the laptop the essence of Nik came sharply back into focus, and then, of course, I sort of missed him.

Photographs have an extraordinary capacity to rose-tint our inner spectacles. War photographers or gritty documentarists aside, most of us take pictures of nice stuff: of pretty places, of people we like, looking, for the most part, happy. It's why those photographs you see in newspapers in the context of some dreadful crime are, for all their bromide banality, so painful to look at. The three freshly ironed and hair-brushed siblings in their school uniform, captured grinning against a photo-studio backdrop of clouds, for example ... all of whom, one discovers, were dosed up on Calpol and then bludgeoned to death by their devoted dad shortly before he set the family home alight, the kids' mum and, finally, himself. Those sort of formal, posed photographs tell so many ... if not lies, precisely, then certainly untruths. Here, for example, were Nik and I cheek-to-cheek, grinning, snapped by Nik in an arm's-length close-up. And of course if you'd shown somebody the picture and told them we'd been married sixteen years (rather than shagging for six days, at that point), there's no reason why they wouldn't have believed it.

So I've always been wary of photographs. Some of that must be to do with my professional relationship with photography, but not all of it. Modelling itself wasn't particularly painful, just boring, though I suppose it gave me an insight into the potential gulf between a picture and the 'moment' it purports to capture. In fashion, that gulf can be huge, of course – a model may be standing in front of the camera nursing her period pains, hunger pangs and a tongue like the bottom of a birdcage, not to mention having had three hours' sleep/three grams of coke the night before, but all the viewer sees – indeed wants to see, or is meant to see – is just how perfect her legs look ... how great that frock is ... how awesome those shoes are ... and that's how it should be. It's showbusiness, after all.

Anyway, after August's high-jinkery, I even started to forget about the iPhone, presumably simply as a result of having worked so hard to 'forget' about Alex. I couldn't, in fact, completely forget Alex, memories of whom sometimes bounced themselves into my frontal lobe unbidden, but whenever this happened I could – and did – actively choose to put them to the back of my mind, and thus Alex found himself a kind of semi-permanent hiding place alongside all the other things which, over the years, I've decided need to be 'filed'. You, for example, Mum. And Dad of course. And even Simon and Beth. Basically, I just got on with stuff.

In the second week of an Indian summer of a September, the day after an afternoon's paintballing with his mates and an evening of turning their guitars up to at least 11, Hal started at his new school, College Hall.

I'd assumed the transition would be pretty effortless because several of his friends were moving on to the same school. Not only was it close by, it was effectively more of the same, at least in theory. Obviously it would take a bit of time for Hal to settle in simply because he'd been at his previous school since nursery. However, I assumed – because I think parents of freshly minted teens, especially boys, do an awful lot of 'assuming' on the grounds that there's not a lot else to go on if you don't speak 'grunt' or communicate via text – that all would be well by half-term, if not before.

But it wasn't. Hal was a classic 'Only' – resourceful, mature, a bit too comfortable in adult company, slightly secretive – but all these traits were exacerbated in the first few weeks of Big School. Far from embracing the grunting and door-slamming years, he started becoming a bit clingy. At first I kind of liked it because any parent of a turbo-teen with go-faster stripes is likely to enjoy the novelty of having one hang around on the same sofa as them, actually watching the same programme while bonding over the nachos-dipping. But after we'd moved into the third week of it, I had to say something.

'Hal, you haven't sat and watched a cookery programme with me ever in your entire life. It's not that I don't like it – I do – but maybe we should talk?'

Hal swiftly defaulted to teen – shrugged, dipped a nacho in the guacamole and said, 'Maybe I like cooking?'

'Well, maybe you do. And if so that's great; let's go and cook – but maybe you don't? Is something wrong? Is it school?'

That was all it took. There I was, busily respecting Hal's newly erected teenage boundaries, not wanting to pry, and it turns out he just wanted to be asked.

'Yeah, Mum. I don't like it. It's ... different.'

'Course it's different, Hal – it's secondary school. But you've probably met half your year group somewhere or other, over the years, at parties or matches, or ... ?'

Hal shrugged. 'Whatever. I don't like it.'

'But specifically what don't you like about it? It obviously takes time to settle in.'

'Well I don't like being called "Gaylord" by a bunch of Year Tens every single break. I don't like that much. And Dom is now best friends with Zak Brody. And Zak Brody is, like, a complete arse and totally up himself.'

'Dom is best friends with *Zak Brody*?'

Now this was news. Far from being just another privi-leged, privately educated north London thirteen-year-old, equal parts RP and a sense of entitlement, Zak Brody was a privileged north London thirteen-year-old blessed with RP, a sense of entitlement and ... a three-film deal with Disney. A child actor since he was six, when he was eleven Zak had been plucked from the relative obscurity of a CBBC sitcom to star in the 'Now a Major Motion Picture' adaptation of the cultish *Sick Boy* series of children's books. The movie had been a huge hit last year and having just filmed the second during the summer holidays, Zak was now back at school – Hal's school. The same school, inci-dentally, where Zak's dad (a so-so ex-soap actor turned excellent teacher) just happened to be Head of Drama.

And now, according to Hal, Zak was 'playing guitar – my guitar. Well not my actual guitar; he's got his own' in The Expelled, formerly known as Expelliarmus, from which, there being no call for two lead guitarists in any group, it appeared Hal had himself been expelled. I don't consider myself to be a particularly competitive mum, but I felt this was a pretty horrible thing to have happened to Hal, because being thirteen is tough enough even before you have to get to grips with the arrival of a new sibling – due in December – or your best mate since Reception dumping you for the shallow thrill of sharing his amps with a movie star.

'Oh Hal, that's rubbish, Dom doing that. Properly rubbish. I might call Patsy.'

'No, please don't, Mum! No way. Whatever you do, don't do that.'

Hal looked almost panic-stricken, and why wouldn't he? Mums may conceivably make those cringey sort of phone calls on behalf of their kids when they're still twelve, but apparently not at thirteen – and probably never again. Anyway, the point was that this was merely the first of several conversations I had on the same subject with Hal, and then – after revealing he'd had phone conversations on the same subject with his dad – I had to have them with David, too. All of which eventually resulted in a three-way Skyped summit meeting and then, after much driving to visit schools, a mutual agreement – though I had to be talked into it – that Hal would leave College Hall at Christmas and, come January, would head for Somerset and his new, very groovy (not to mention staggeringly expensive) co-ed boarding school.

So many thoughts, not the least of which was that I hadn't expected to be a nearly-empty-nester just yet. I'd resisted it of course, selfishly, when Hal had mentioned boarding. But I came round eventually, though only once I'd established that Hal's desire to board wasn't a passing £30,000-a-year fad, or an over-reaction to some typical (if you factored out the movie-star element) teenage argy-bargy and name-calling. Children seem to be hyper-aware about 'bullying' though I'm a bit more old-school about what it actually constitutes. Kids can be pretty tough on each other, after all, and though the vocabulary may be different, I do hold with the old 'sticks and stones' adage. It's tough out there in the grown-up world; the sooner you develop a few hard edges the better.

Anyway, after establishing that he wanted to go for all the 'right' reasons and given that money wasn't exactly an issue and I really liked the school, I gave Project Boarding my blessing. What else could I do?

Hal's half-sister, Kiki (a pretty name, unless it instantly calls to mind the frog from *Hector's House*, which it did for me) was born in December and so at the end of term Hal flew out to meet her and spend Christmas with David, the current Mrs Ashford and the rest of the Ashford clan, leaving me to what I fully anticipated was going to be a write-off of an un-Christmas, home-alone wearing elephant-arsed jogging bottoms and with nothing but a turkey 'crown' and Sky Plus for company. However, I figured that if I was going to sit around wearing old jogging bottoms and pushing food around my plate, I may as well do it in style, so I seized the moment and booked five days at a spa in the Canaries.

A few days before Christmas and a couple of days before I left, I was invited round to Guy and Lisa's for ye olde traditional pre-Christmas spag bol – a 'tradition' that was all of three years old, admittedly, but you have to start somewhere. I hadn't seen very much of them for months, as the whole Alex business had driven a wedge – or had appeared to, at least – between us. But enough time had now elapsed ... and anyway I was keen to know if they were any nearer setting a date for their alleged wedding.

It was a fun evening, calling to mind another evening of the not-too-terribly distant past, but for one distinct difference.

'So, how is, um, Alex? And, er, Susie?' I whispered at Lisa as I followed her into the kitchen, in search of a napkin. I was on my second glass, I felt relaxed, I didn't particularly need a napkin but I also didn't feel this was a wildly inappropriate question to ask, six months down the road. However, Lisa attempted to furrow her brow – always a bit of a challenge for the cosmetically-tampered-with, though I got the general idea.

'You know they moved to the seaside, right?' Lisa all but hissed.

'I didn't know that, no. How would I know that?'

'Well, ah, you might still be in touch with Alex?'

'No, no, Lisa – absolutely not. Not my style.'

'Well, OK, I figured probably not, but scratch the surface and you never know what's going on in other people's lives, do you?'

'No. And I didn't know what was going on in theirs. So ...'

'Yeah, they've bought a fuck-off gorgeous Grade 2-listed house with sea views. Alex is practically welded to a drill when he's not busy on the computer. And Susie, well, I guess she's ... busy. She's always busy. So ...'

'Which seaside? Brighton, I assume?'

'You assume wrong. No, they're in Random-on-Sea. A town where East Sussex bumps into Kent. My God, it takes forever to get there but I gotta say that when you do it's totally another country. You'd never know it's only sixty miles from London.'

'Well, whatever, that's great for them. So about this alleged wedding ...'

It was time to change the subject but at the same time my brain was busily multi-tasking. So, Alex and Susie had decamped to Random-on-Sea. Who'd've thought it? I had Susie down as the kind of woman who might start clawing at the air as a precursor to a coronary if she was ever forced to venture beyond the M25 – or indeed anywhere further than walking distance from a flat white. And it wasn't as if Alex was exactly Mr Small-Town, either.

But why, of all places, I wondered, had they chosen Random-on-Sea? Did they have friends there? Some sort of family connection, maybe on Susie's side? Had I ever mentioned anything to do with Random-on-Sea to Alex? I wracked my brains but couldn't recall a thing. Then again, why would I? My connection to Random was not only ancient, but long-since severed, while my memories of the town were practically sepia-tinted. Nonetheless, I had spent quite a bit of time in and around Random-on-Sea as a kid, because that was where Nana lived. *Your* mum.

As kids we saw Nana quite a lot. I remember she died in her sleep – which is as it should be – just the week after Elvis died, in the summer of 1977. She was seventy-seven. I had always liked the fact that she was the same age as the century. Nana managed not only to stick around long enough to celebrate the Queen's Silver Jubilee but (she was pretty plugged-in, Nana) also to 'tut-tut' over the Sex Pistols being at number one.

Anyway, the last time I'd been anywhere near Random-on-Sea was to attend Nana's funeral in a pretty little village church nestled in a valley somewhere to the east of the town. Though I couldn't recall the funeral itself, I had vague memories of us all driving home after a sumptuous and very un-funereal tea of which Nana would have approved, and of we kids being respectfully far quieter than normal while wedged into the back of the mustard-coloured Volvo estate.

I hadn't really thought about Random-on-Sea for years, and when I had it had been in relation to Nana. In fact up until now Random had only ever existed in relation to Nana, though of course I was now slightly curious about the place.

I couldn't remember too much about it, other than the

fact that Nana had lived in a little doll's house with far too many stairs on a steep street in the picturesque Old Town. I'd loved Nana's house as a kid, partly because it was on a Wonderland-meets-Portmeirion sort of scale and made me feel Alice-ish, if not exactly 'Prisoner'-y, but also because it was full of Nana's lovely things, and lovely smells, too – of bracingly briny sea air gusting through open windows and, particularly, of a combination of baking and potpourri. Indeed, the only potpourri that smells remotely like Nana's uniquely heady mixture is the gorgeous and insanely expensive Santa Maria Novella, to which I treat myself at Christmas.

Anyway, much later back at home and fuelled by a glass or two, I started searching through some of your old family photograph albums, Mum, unearthing all those faded snaps I hadn't recalled looking at since shortly after they'd been picked up from Boots in 1970-whatever. Here we all were: you and Dad, me and Simon and Beth, squinting into the sun in front of the Volvo; presumably Nana had taken that one? And again, with Dad taking the picture and Nana inserted into the group. And here were some of us in Nana's tiny sun-trap of a walled garden, and of us kids wearing shorts and eating toffee-apples on the pebbly beach, with those distinctive black fishermen's net huts in the background. For a while, I was intrigued by the pictures but soon enough the old photography-phobia set in and I couldn't look at our smiling faces without seeing all of our futures ... Mum and Dad splitting up the year after Nana died, Me and Beth falling out over a 'shared' boyfriend in our teens, Simon leaving home to live with Dad ... and worse.

And though looking at old pictures didn't – couldn't – reveal any of these forthcoming seismic shifts and schisms, the images' mosquito-stuck-in-amber quality both thrilled and, it must be said, slightly terrified me. Three of the people in these pictures were of course now dead, while the other three were ... what? Walking wounded?

I sighed and packed the pictures away. I'd only started looking at them in order to trigger some old memories of Random – memories which, I suppose, (had I thought any of it through, which I hadn't) I imagined could bring me somehow closer to Alex's 'surprise-surprise!' of a new life. But of course there were other ways of doing that, which is how, the day after Hal had flown off to be with his dad and the day before I flew to the Canaries, I found myself negotiating hellish mid-morning cross-town traffic, negotiating the Blackwall Tunnel while trying not to think too hard about the Thames doing something involving disaster movie-ish SFX above my head and then driving down the A21 to Random-on-Sea. For the first time in over thirty years.

Out of season, even the loveliest seaside towns and villages have a slightly desperate Last Resort feel about them and Random-on-Sea was not, on a gloomy day in

December, one of the loveliest seaside towns. Whereas I'd imagined a sort of pocket Eastbourne – twee and Tory – Random's front line reality was un-pretty, pretty gritty and whatever is the opposite of twee.

And though the architecture was of the once-gracious variety, the atmosphere was gloomy, down-at-heel, border-line seedy. It was hard to imagine Alex here, or Susie – actually particularly Susie, who had 'smart Metropolitan chick' written all over her – though I supposed they were tucked away in some lovely middle-class enclave, not here on this frankly miserable-looking chippie-and-chip-paper-strewn promenade.

Things perked up a bit in the Old Town, however. Its homely proportions and villagey atmosphere were, certainly for a woman from Belsize Park, much more attrac-tive than the bleak and windswept multi-storey rows of Victorian stucco terraces further west. The Old Town also felt less transient, with a proper community nestling among its shabby-chic, vaguely boho little shops. There certainly hadn't been any organic bakeries and vintage clothes shops when Nana was alive. In fact, 'organic' and 'vintage' weren't even words in common usage, much less words that applied to shopping.

I parked in a near-deserted car park directly facing a bleak, gunmetal-grey sea at high tide, and then I wandered for a while along the seafront, gulping ozone and feeling my internal cobwebs clearing. En route to wherever, I passed a couple of joggers, plenty of drunks and several young girls pushing buggies. With a start, I realized I was a long way – much further than the sixty-odd miles on the odometer – from Belsize Park and that these sweet-faced teens were – *d'oh!* – not au-pairs but mothers.

It was easy to find Nana's old house. I'm a great believer in 'muscle memory', effectively trusting your body to do something when you think your brain has forgotten how. Even after the best part of a lifetime it turned out that my brain could easily remember where Nana lived; my muscles simply got me there.

I couldn't quite believe that Nana had died well over thirty years ago. I think she had already been a widow for about ten years by then, so the house was sold out of the family and the money divided between you, Mum, and Auntie Pam. When Pam died of breast cancer in the late 1980s, leaving no children, her share passed straight to us and was kept in trust until we were eighteen, when we three grandkids ended up with about £10,000 each. I used my money as a deposit on the purchase of my first tiny flat in Shepherd's Bush so, when I set eyes on 'Nana's' house – now even prettier than I remembered it, having been re-pointed and the old back door repainted a hot pink – I realized I had a great deal for which to thank Nana, quite aside from the best lemon drizzle cake I have ever tasted. And perhaps it was also an old 'muscle memory' that, in a very out-of-character moment, found me spontaneously knocking on the front door.

I suppose a part of me must have expected the door to be answered by a Nana-ish old lady, not by a stylish, Ugg-wearing (and wasn't that a pair of Seven For All Mankind jeans?) thirty-whatever brunette with her hair piled messily on her head and decorated with tinsel. Just behind her lurked a toddler, clutching her mother's thigh.

'Oh, hi!' I said. 'Look, ah, I'm so sorry to just, er, bang on your door like this. Actually I half expected nobody to be in – which makes it even more mad, really – but, anyway, I was just sort of passing and the thing is, my grandmother used to live here, and she died in 1977, and, well, I was just curious.'

'Oh, wow. Do you want to come in and look around?' She glanced at my handbag and boots. 'You don't look as if you're casing the joint. Not that there's much to case. And if you are, I'm fresh out of Chloé bags, more's the pity.'

'Oh yes, well, that would be lovely. Are you sure that's OK? Thanks very much.'

So here I was, standing in a stranger's hallway and predictably paralysed by Englishness. It wasn't even as if I had the excuse of being sent by an estate agent; instead I was patently just nosy. But my accidental hostess didn't seem to mind.

'You said 1977? Well in that case, after your Nan died

I think this house must have been sold to my parents-in-law, though they've since decamped to a bungalow in Bexhill. My husband and I have lived here about three years now and we've done it up bit by bit. It's nearly finished but I don't suppose it looks very much as you remember it?'

'Well, yes – and no.'

I peered around, drinking in the house's loveliness, the white-painted floorboards and walls, highlighted by pale greys, in contrast to Nana's wall-to-wall carpeted swirls, dark wood furniture and heavy curtains.

'The proportions have changed a bit. Or rather, my proportions have changed, so I'm having a kind of *Alice in Wonderland* moment.'

'Well if you want to have a "Drink Me" moment, I was just about to make a cuppa.'

'Are you sure?'

'Sure I'm sure. Zoe – this is my daughter Zoe, who is two-and-a-bit – Zoe I were about to do some baking. Which makes me sound like some sort of yummy-cliché though I do feel I ought to point out, even to a woman with a Chloé bag, that we have never done baking before, on the grounds that I am usually working and Zoe is either at nursery or hanging out with her gran. In fact the baking is kind of my fantasy of what being a good mother is all about, though of course it's probably not Zoe's. I'm Ruth, by the way.'

'Hi. Yes, I'm Pippa. Baking – how lovely.'

I was totally disarmed by this woman's – Ruth's – friendliness and openness. I couldn't imagine it happening in London. And yet Ruth was so sophisticated I couldn't imagine her not being a Londoner, which, I realize, says more about me and my deep-seated metropolitan prejudices than it does about either Ruth or Random-on-Sea. Nonetheless, I sort of needed to know.

'Have you lived here long?'

'Well, as I say, nearly three years. Three years in February.'

'No, sorry, I meant here in Random-on-Sea?'

'Yeah, a while. OK, my whole life, apart from uni – and even then I only got as far as Brighton. Sad, isn't it?'

Why did I find it so surprising that a woman born and raised sixty-odd miles from London might also know her pukka jeans brands and be able to spot a Chloé bag?

'Sorry, of course, why shouldn't you? I am dumb. And such a Londoner!'

'No worries. We're not all horny-handed sons and daughters of toil, soil or, uh, fisherfolk. But you –' Ruth did air-quotes while smiling – '"DFLs" do tend to think we are.'

'DFLs?'

'Down-from-Londoners.'

'Oh, OK. I am such a DFL. Apologies.'

'No problem. I'll make some tea while you poke around

upstairs if you want. I only wish I'd baked some madeleines.'

'Ha. Yes I am having a bit of a Proustian moment. You really don't mind if I go upstairs?'

'You'd be mad if you didn't, now you're here.'

Having knocked on Ruth's door on a whim, I felt very privileged to have been rewarded with something that, far from trampling on my childhood memories – or indeed my memories of Nana – somehow enhanced them. Ruth's house was not to Nana's personal taste, but I knew Nana would've recognized that this version of the house was also somehow 'right', if only because it had been achieved so lovingly and with such attention to detail.

'Your house is beautiful,' I said to Ruth when I came down again.

'I'm glad you approve. Admittedly I've only known you for five minutes but already it seems to matter that you like it on behalf of your grandmother. What was she like?'

'Pretty much the blueprint for grannies. She also baked brilliantly. Exceptional lemon drizzle. If you try baking that she may not be able to resist returning to give you a hand.'

'Well, that might just work. Waddya think, Zo? Shall we get Pippa's nana to help us bake?'

And Zoe nodded and smiled and, to my surprise, walked round the table and clambered on to my lap. So I drank tea and chatted to Ruth while her daughter sat on my knee in, of all places, Nana's house – Ruth's house – and then Ruth suggested starting to make the cakes with Zoe, so I said: 'I'm so sorry to take up your afternoon. I really must tear myself away.'

'No need to go on our account; we're enjoying the company, aren't we, Zo?'

'Well, that's very kind but I should probably crack on back up to town. I'm actually flying to Lanzarote tomorrow.'

'Blimey, lucky you. Away for Christmas?'

'Yeah. I'm not a massive fan of Christmas.' And I paused for a moment, close to launching into why I didn't like Christmas before I checked myself. 'Anyway my son's with his dad this year so I thought I'd just treat myself.'

'Don't blame you. Christmas is for kids – but without them, as far as I'm concerned, Christmas is for sleeping.'

'Well, thanks for the tea and everything. Really lovely to meet you. Both of you.'

'Likewise. I'm so glad you knocked. Most days you'd have got an empty house – my husband and I are both pretty full on with work.'

'Do you mind if I ask what you do?'

'I'm a midwife and my husband's a GP. But you should see us if Zoe so much as trips over and scrapes a knee. Pathetic excuse for medics, both of us. And you? What do you do?'

'Well, I'm mostly a mum these days, albeit nearly a redundant one since my thirteen-year-old has decided he wants to start boarding. But I used to work in, uh, fashion.'

'Cool. Hence the Chloé?'

'Just a by-product. And sorry, but are those Seven jeans?'

'They are. And there's not much call for them when you're up to your elbows in the birthing pool, I can tell you.'

I was halfway out the door by now, but we were still chatting.

'Yes, I can imagine. Really good to meet you, Ruth. I love what you've done with the house, I really do. Nana would've totally approved. Thanks so much.'

'Pleasure.' Ruth dug around in the back pocket of her Sevens and produced a business card:

RUTH ABBOTT BSc
Independent Midwifery
bornfree@ruthabbott.co.uk

'Here, take this. I'm not suggesting you need my professional skills but if you're ever in the area knocking on strangers' doors do please come and see us again. I mean it. Bring your son sometime; I'm sure he'd be interested to see where his great-grandma lived, but if he's not there's a Go-Kart track round the corner and a very cool new skate park up the hill. So . . .'

Ruth shrugged and grinned.

'Thanks very much. Really. You've been very kind.'

And then after I'd walked thirty yards or so down the road I turned around, and there they both were, Ruth and Zoe, still waving from their doorstep. And I felt a strange but not entirely unpleasant butterfly-wings sensation in my solar plexus, a feeling which, funnily enough, reminded me of Hal's first fluttering foetal movements all those years ago.

Mid-afternoon in December, the streets were quiet in the Old Town and dusk was descending fast. I walked back to the car, chilled by the strong sea breeze gusting from the darkness on the edge of town which contrasted with the maniacally bright lighting and loud 'kerchings' emanating from Slots of Fun. Funny old town, this, I thought, though I could see its charms, too.

In the car – my great big cliché of a Range Rover – I felt safe and swiftly warmed, with Steve Wright burbling quietly in the background as a light spray from surf I couldn't actually see spattered the window. On the spur, I fished my phone out of the pocket of my parka, and sent Ruth a brief email:

Lovely to meet you and Zoe this afternoon. Thanks so much for your hospitality – hope the cake is a triumph! Happy Christmas and New Year. Pippa x

And then I wrote a short text: *Random-on-Sea is lovely . . . x*

And I hit Send. And I waited. And within a couple of

minutes back came a reply: *Who is this? Don't recognize the number, sorry*

And I stared at it for a moment before deleting it, just as Alex had clearly deleted my number. And then I turned Steve Wright up a bit louder, reversed out of the parking space and began the long journey home.

My spa trip was restful, regenerative. More books, no blokes and lots of yoga. I also successfully avoided eating turkey and every day was sunny enough to fall asleep beside the pool, if not to actually get in it. When I got home on the 28th, the day before Hal, I felt both restless and relaxed enough to come up with yet another out-of-character idea – though given that out-of-character ideas were now becoming such a regular default they were, of course, redefining my character.

I decided to have a party. I couldn't actually recall the last time I'd had a party at home – any of my homes – that hadn't been for Hal. I don't 'do' parties, and I don't know any other single people who do them either. I mean, I go to them, of course – but hosting? I guess I'm old-fashioned enough to think that every hostess needs a host, even if he is just lurking in the background with a corkscrew and a bowl of Kettle Chips. But I suddenly wanted to have a party, and I figured that at thirteen-and-a-half, Hal was old enough to wield a corkscrew and make polite small-talk with adults before retreating to his room with a mate or two for a sleepover. How hard could it be to give a party, after all? Even a New Year's Eve party? People were always going on about how New Year's was such a nightmare if you were over about twenty-one. I could do the kind of New Year's Eve party that divided into two parts – the people with kids but no babysitters could do the early shift from say 6 to 8, then the hardcore singles and those blessed with sitters could tip up later, and then if they got a better offer they could all bugger off elsewhere. I really didn't mind. In fact I quite liked the idea of having a bit of a bash then being in bed by 12 watching Jools Holland's *Hootenanny* – even though the pleasure of that show had dimmed since I discovered it was recorded weeks in advance. Whatever. With a bit of luck I'd probably still be dancing by midnight. And it turns out it's far easier to organize a party than I'd thought it might be – why hadn't I done it years ago? – and Hal was gratifyingly enthusiastic.

'This is an awesome idea, Mum. Can I help?'

Can I help? I wasn't entirely sure I'd ever heard Hal utter the phrase before. Anyway, he could and he did. We made a trip to the Majestic wine warehouse in St John's Wood to load up the Range Rover, and raided Waitrose for every conceivable nibbly/crunchy/dippy thing we could find. And then Hal decided he was going to turn DJ and sort out some tunes on the MP3, almost certainly including such prehistoric stuff as Nirvana, though I did beg him to include a few things everybody could dance to if the mood grabbed us and steered him towards my doubtless amusingly retro collection. I couldn't recall buying a single CD in the past five years.

'Mum, you've actually got some cool stuff here. Did you know that?'

So I'd pretty much nailed the party-giving thing, really . . . apart from the all-but-insignificant business of choosing the guests and then actually inviting them. Would I find anyone at all at such short notice? Maybe I was just setting myself up to fail? My friendships were so scattered and compartmentalized and many were now so lapsed that I barely knew how to corral them under one roof. And then I wondered how it would be if I glanced around the room and suddenly felt like a gatecrasher at my own party, because the problem with being the hostess is that you can't really leave when you've had enough.

I made list after list. I trawled through my phone and emails to recall old colleagues, old dates and old (as in a long time ago) mates. Then I narrowed it down to the people whom I'd either actually seen or had really wanted to see in the last five years, because my life was very easily divided into pre-and post-2005 and I knew that however much I may have 'moved on', I much preferred that the pre-2005 version of me should remain compartmentalized.

In the end the list ran to about sixty people, of whom maybe half might reasonably be expected to turn up at such short notice, in which case it would be a shuffling around the kitchen with the drinks-and-nibbles sort of party, while if the figure miraculously ended up closer to sixty then we'd probably actually be up for some dancing. And then of course it took me the whole evening of the 29th just to invite everybody via text and email, and then about halfway through that process I started feeling like a complete arse. After all, who even considered organizing a party for NYE precisely two days in advance? Perhaps only the sort of person who, secretly, deep down, hoped nobody would turn up?

Ha! Turns out that the over-thirty-fives are, pretty much to a man and woman, actually gagging for that last-minute alternative to the pub or over-priced local restaurant. Don't ask me how but, come 11.30 p.m., Lisa, me and Marta were doing a version of Beyoncé's 'Single Ladies' dance in the living room in front of (a pseudo-appalled but actually finding it quite funny) Hal and a couple of his mates, plus some rugby players brought along by Guy and Lisa, whom the boys actually recognized but to me just looked like big blokes who were exceptionally bad at dancing. Then there was another bunch of people downstairs, including – astoundingly – half the booking desk (still there, still booking and, presumably, also still bitching for Britain) from my old employer Model's Own. I'd've imagined they would have had much better offers for NYE but we always assume other people are leading a different sort of life from the one they actually are, don't we? Personally my own 'best' New Year's Eve had occurred in 1988 when I was twenty. Up until then I'd always hated New Year's Eve. As a teenager I just hadn't got the hang of enforced 'fun', preferring to have my fun a bit more off the cuff, on my own terms rather than everybody else's. Anyway, on the 31st December of 1988, when I was living and working in Tokyo, one of my flatmates, a German model called Claudia (her nickname: 'But-Not-Schiffer') said: 'I hear there's a private party somewhere in Roppongi. It might be a laugh. It's for . . .'

But-Not-Schiffer named a hugely famous British pop band who were currently touring Japan and my interest was admittedly slightly piqued, partly because I was a fan but mostly because it was already 10 p.m. and the prospect of a quiet night in with the TV and But-Not-Schiffer was suddenly unbearable.

I peered at clothes, sighed and was uninspired. Tonight was not, I felt, a night for making mad London-girl fashion statements but for keeping it simple with some basic black Body-Con by Azzedine Alaia and the essential late 1980s slash of red lipstick (think Robert Palmer's 'Addicted to Love' video). Plus a pair of false eyelashes, just because.

By 11.15, But-Not-Schiffer and I found ourselves in a predictably sweaty basement in Roppongi. The New Year's Do turned out to be a band member's birthday party, while the hostess – a friend-of-a-friend-of – was unfazed by yet more crashers. Anyway, in Tokyo even a couple of *gai-jin* catalogue models were usually granted Access All Areas.

And so I hovered, nursing a fluorescent drink and attempting to shrug off my habitual anti-New Year apathy, pointy stilettos toe-tapping at the edge of that dance floor, waiting for a tune that would impel me on to it ... when I spotted him. A capital-H Him, as it happens. And even at the moment when our eyes locked and stayed locked (if it had been a film everything else would have gone slow-motion and blurry round the edges) and despite being entirely 'in' the moment and savouring it, and suddenly realizing that my prospects for New Year's Eve 1988 (not to mention very early 1989) were looking up quite dramatically, I also knew this was one of those moments I was going to remember forever, whatever happened next.

What actually happened next was that I walked on to the dance floor and straight up to the handsome man, who was also famous – what with him being in the band and the band being massive and everything – and despite the fact that there were people dancing around him, both literally and metaphorically, I just stood there and waited for what felt like minutes but was actually about a second, before he smiled and said: 'You have very beautiful eyes.'

I probably rolled my (very beautiful) eyes, but I also smiled the sort of smile that said, 'Even I know that in terms of cheesy chat-ups that is the very ripest of Camembert, but I don't mind, mostly because I actually believe you. And of course I do have beautiful eyes. And I really hope to God you don't find out about these eyelashes too soon.'

But obviously I didn't say any of that. I just stood there, staring at him, until the moment kind of snapped and we were hurtled back into the 'ten, nine, eight, seven, six . . .' and 'woo-hooh!'s and popping champagne corks, and whatever the next record was. I should remember what the next record was, of course, but I don't. I could cheat and make one up – Prince's '1999' seems pretty likely – but that would be to diminish the Moment, which was perfect just as I remember it.

Anyway, of all the so-called 'romantic' moments of my life – and there have been a few, despite having had such a car-crash of a 'romantic' life – the moment Johnny Stone told me I had 'very beautiful eyes' in the middle of a Tokyo dance floor at about 11.55 p.m. on New Year's Eve 1988 remains one of the very best. Because 'romance' is, after all, mostly about context. And I couldn't have written this one any better myself. For me, 'romance' should have some sort of slightly filmic quality and preferably a script to match; it should also tick certain boxes – the 'right' timing, location, weather even – and should preferably (not that I'm picky, much) occur at exactly the right moment in your own story. For me, locking eyes with Johnny Stone happened in just the right place: in the middle of a dance floor in my decade of dance floors.

Mind you, in terms of a relationship it was going nowhere. I was in Tokyo, he was touring the world, mobile phones had barely been invented – much less text or email. Complete non-starter then, and probably for the best. It would only have ruined what was already a perfectly beautiful moment, though we did manage to make that moment last until just after midday on January 1 by judicious use of an old-school hotel 'Do Not Disturb' sign and the removal of the suite's numerous phones from their hooks.

And now I was here in my own home, over two decades later but dancing like a twenty-year-old and surrounded by people I'd forgotten I knew and people I never had known, with my teenage son not yet quite so horrified by it all that he'd packed his bags and left. I could scarcely believe I was again enjoying myself on NYE without recourse to Jools Holland. I pondered that fact as I refilled my glass and a wobbly-looking Lisa sidled up to me, grinning, and, half conspiratorially, half plain pissed (and apparently wholly apropos nothing), whispered: 'Look, Alex has been asking after you, so Guy told him you're seeing someone. And Alex asked who, and Guy said it was a rugby player mate of his. And y'know he just made that up to, like, protect you both from each other? So don't have a go at him, OK? And anyway, if you did want to start seeing a rugby player I think you might be spoilt for choice tonight.'

And with that she winked and wobbled off back upstairs in her Choos. And I thought, in as much as I was capable of coherent thought at all: 'Uh-oh. Alex . . .'

And some time after that, Hal retreated to his room with his mates to play on the Wii and, for all I knew, conduct terrible drink-mixing experiments with horrific stomach-pumping consequences. The thought of this alarmed me for a moment, until I remembered that after imbibing dangerous amounts of cider sometime circa 1982 I had once vomited all the way from the top to the bottom deck of a Routemaster bus and that the sheer horror of it all had ensured I never drank cider ever again in my life. And then I wondered, drunkenly, if Hal had ever even been on a bus. I couldn't think of an occasion when he might have been.

'Do you know what?' I said to the tall, broad-shouldered and hoveringly attentive man standing next to me, whose name I couldn't recall but who was nonetheless kindly refilling my glass for the zillionth time, 'I don't think my son's ever been on a bus! Isn't that appalling?'

'Appalling,' he agreed. 'Now where's the best place to kiss you?'

'I find lips are a good place to start.'

So he did.

The next morning didn't really exist. The afternoon, however, hove into view like a desert mirage, promising more than it could ever deliver. Hal, meanwhile, was fabulous. He and Dom (the irony of Hal and Dom rekindling their friendship just as Hal was about to depart for Somerset wasn't lost on any of us) sweetly if ineffectually started to tidy up, while I had a long shower and attempted to recall various fleeting memories from the night before, such as wondering who the Mickey Rourke-alike (if Mickey Rourke hadn't had Stallone-alike plastic surgery, that is) might have been. And when and where had he gone, precisely? And I was still wondering this when I'd emerged from the shower and was suitably dressed for stuffing bin-bags, and Hal said, casually: 'So, Mum, did you end up, like, kissing *Richard Woodhead*?'

'What?'

'I think you did. How cool is that.'

'Is it?'

'Dur. Yeah. Eighty-six caps and fifty tries for England. He was staring at you, like, all night.'

'OK. And eighty-six caps and fifty tries – that's good, is it?'

'Mum, it's the record.'

'Well, good for him.'

'More like good for you.'

At which point the doorbell rang. It was Guy. And a man who looked disconcertingly familiar.

'OK, Pippa, Lisa's asleep, the twins are watching *Finding Nemo* on the sofa with Marta – whom we have to hope isn't asleep – and we are at your disposal for an hour or so, to do any manly disposing-of-things you may require.'

'Hi,' said Richard Woodhead. 'I slept over in Guy and Lisa's spare room and I felt bad about having plied you with so much of your own alcohol and then leaving you behind to take out the empties, so ... I hope you don't mind?'

'Wow, that is kind. OK, come in.'

Even though I really wished I'd had a bit of advance notice so that I wasn't wearing a six-year-old Juicy Couture tracksuit and my hair in a scrunchie.

'She doesn't mind,' said a voice behind me.

'Richard, this is my son, Hal. Hal, this is Richard.'

'I know. Eighty-six caps and fifty tries for England.'

'You play rugby, Hal? Maybe it's time to try buses?'

And while Hal looked more star-struck than he did bemused, Richard made up for his slightly cheap shot by asking what position Hal played. At which point Guy winked at me, and I wondered if it was remotely appropriate to sneak off and slip into something less comfortable. And I also found a tiny multi-tasking moment in which to wonder:

a) Whether Richard Woodhead was going to turn out to be this century's Johnny Stone?

And:

b) Did I actually have any bin-bags?

So far, I liked the look of 2010. I particularly enjoyed the novelty of the next hour and a half, in which men did bloke stuff in my house while I made tea. I really liked that. And I also liked it when Hal, who had more than done his bit, said:

'OK if I go round to Dom's now, Mum? I'm sleeping over, remember?'

And quick as a flash, Guy said: 'OK if I go round to Lisa's now, Pip? I'm sleeping over there too.'

And while I laughed, Richard said: 'But is it OK if I stay right here for a bit longer? Unless you'd rather I went, of course?'

To which my response was: 'No, I'd much rather you stayed. But I'd also love it if I could get out of this track-suit.'

Fortunately I was the only one who heard his sotto-voce reply: 'I'd love it too.'

On January 3rd, I was still busy embracing New Year indolence until I realized it had been a week since I'd done any yoga and at least two weeks since I'd been anywhere near the hospice, all of which made me feel pretty guilty until I started to feel annoyed by my perpetual and predictable default-to-feeling-guilty, which in turn ended up outweighing the guilt.

On the 4th I was back in the January swing, no booze and a detox underway, ninety minutes of Ashtanga under my belt and fresh flowers in the lobby of the hospice in Highgate where Auntie Pam had spent her last few weeks.

Meanwhile, Hal was particularly chipper. In five days

he'd be starting his new school and in the meantime he seemed to have developed a fetish for packing and re-packing his cool new camouflage-embossed trunk. He was also asking a lot of questions about Richard.

'Is Richard your boyfriend, Mum?'

'Um, no, I think I'm a bit too old for boyfriends. And Richard is definitely a bit too old to be one.'

'You know what I mean.'

'OK, yes, I know what you mean. I don't know yet. Too early to say. Maybe?'

'Maybe by half-term?'

'Who knows? Now go away and do some more folding, like the thirteen-year-old of my dreams.'

'You make me sound like a girl.'

'I'm liking your feminine side.'

'Stop it, Mum!'

We were in a collective good mood. I had had a couple of texts from Richard, who since retiring from rugby fifteen years previously, had returned to his first love – flying. A former pilot, he had (rather thrillingly) flown Concorde for BA and now combined training new pilots with a line in after-dinner and motivational speaking and some charity work and all-in-all would have been living the perfect life of a National Sporting Hero (retd) if his wife hadn't left him six months ago for some TV chef, a situation that had apparently entirely underwhelmed their grown-up kids, a son of twenty-two and a daughter of

twenty. There seemed to be something of an abandon-
ment theme among the middle-aged men I was meeting.
One more case study and I'd probably have a thesis.

So maybe I shouldn't have been too surprised when I
got that call from Alex the following evening. After years
of waiting, men were suddenly arriving at my door like
the buses my son had never caught.

It was late, after 11 p.m. At first I thought it could be
Richard, but we weren't really in a phoning-after-11 p.m.
sort of situation. Not yet. So when I saw the caller ID 'Alex',
I was surprised, even though I knew I'd been on his mind
because Lisa had told me at the party. And of course there
was the amusingly ironic fact that he had thought I was
seeing a rugby player at a time when I wasn't, but now I
was actually seeing an ex-rugby player. In truth it was the
perfect time for Alex to call me because I was in the proverbial 'good place'. My heart wasn't lurching; sufficient
time had elapsed. I was fine. I'd moved on. I still had Alex's
old iPhone upstairs in a box in my cupboard, granted, but
no skeletons other than that.

'Alex Fox. Pleasant surprise, stranger, if a little late in
the day.'

'I know. I'm sorry it's so late. I hope it's OK? I've just
had a drink with my brothers and . . . they've gone home
and I was thinking I could either catch the 11.15 from
Charing Cross, or talk to you for a few minutes and catch
the 11.45. Or . . .'

'Or what, Alex?'

'Or. I dunno, Pippa. How are you? How have you been? Are you happy? Did you have a good new year?'

He was slurring a bit, but not so much that a conversation was pointless, so . . .

'Yeah, I'm good, Alex. I've been . . . fine. I'm pretty happy, yes. I had a lovely New Year. Usually I hate them but I threw a party, which isn't a very "me" thing to do but it was fun. And you? How are you? You live by the seaside now, I hear.'

'Yeah, I do. And you know I do, because you sent me a text telling me you did, a couple of days before Christmas.'

'Right! Well, yes, but . . .'

'I pretended I didn't know who it was from. Pretended I'd deleted your number. I thought it was the best idea, at the time. Then I started regretting it.'

'Oh, OK. Well that makes sense. I was in Random-on-Sea for the first time in over thirty years, as it happens. My mum's mum – Nana – lived there, and I spent a lot of time there as a kid before she died. Nice place for you . . . for you as a family. Good for kids. And stuff.'

'Yeah. Maybe. Look, Pip, I can't tell you how tempted I was to call you and persuade you to meet me in Random – assuming you were still there when you sent it.'

'But you didn't.'

'No, I didn't. But I'm doing it now. I really would love

277

to see you again, Pippa. Not like that ... not like before. Just ... just *because*.'

My head crowded with so many thoughts and I could feel myself stepping off firm dry land into something that looked suspiciously like quicksand. I could suddenly feel everything that had been safe and sure and certain starting to sink and slide and I felt wrong-footed. Even slightly scared. But I felt excited, too. So shoot me.

'So come on then. Come and see me. You remember my address.'

And without waiting for an answer, because I knew what the answer was, I touched 'End Call' and walked slowly downstairs and – screw the detox – picked out a nice bottle of Merlot and uncorked it. Then the Merlot and I stood very still and let ourselves breathe.

Sorry, Mum.

Pip xxx

CHAPTER 9

Alex

Wednesday 23 June 2010

From: alex@foxmail.co.uk
To: guy@guysports.com

Hey Mate,

As I write you're in Bali on your honeymoon. I just went on the Amanusa website and . . . well, I think you'll probably just about manage to struggle through your fortnight, especially if you've got one of those suites with your own pool. You deserve it.

Your wedding was a cracking day. Bad start – for me, anyway – but we made it, and you two made it and the weather was perfect and you both got your vows – and each other's names – in the right order, which was a relief because, let's face it, Lisa could so easily have ended up married to me. Unfortunately she got you, but all of life is compromise, right?

She looked beautiful. We all know she's beautiful but she looked above-and-beyond ... and so fucking happy, even though she obviously picked the wrong brother. When you had the first dance (Van Morrison?! Who knew!) I thought I'd never seen anyone look as happy as you two did. It was a day that (and forgive the uncharacteristic lapse into sentimentality) oozed love and optimism and it kind of gave me hope, even as it made me realize that Susie and I would never be able to feel like that together – probably never had. And (on a parental note!) I was proud of Lula. She'd been so upset when Susie and Chuck had bailed at the service station and I worried about her all day, but she's a great kid, growing up fast and she did us all proud. I'm only sorry that Chuck wasn't there to share it. But Susie? Frankly I couldn't give a shit. Anyway, thanks for the loan of the house. Lula and I have left it just as we found it (OK, apart from the pizza boxes) and Marta has the keys. At least I think she does ... (joke!)

I've often wondered why Susie and I didn't marry. I asked her (again and again) and she sort of said yes, so we 'announced' our 'engagement' (you remember? Mum asking me a bit too loudly if I'd really made the right decision and Susie ending up in the loo in tears?), but then she'd change her mind and say no and eventually I just gave up. We had the kids, we had the scary mortgage, we had the whole quasi-marital shebang going on so what difference was a bit of paper ever going to make? I don't know why I felt like I wanted it so badly, but maybe it's a bloke thing? Maybe the more she said no, the more entrenched I became, the more I wanted her to change her mind? But don't think it hasn't also occurred to me that if she'd said yes and we'd gone ahead and done the deed eight years ago we'd probably be divorced by now.

I know this isn't the kind of thing you want to flag up to a newlywed, much less your blissfully-happy-in-Bali newlywed brother, but I genuinely don't know how people sustain long relationships anymore. I look at the folks and I look around at our generation and I wonder how many of 'us' (and of course you can count me out) will ever celebrate golden weddings? You and Lisa will have to live to your nineties, for starters.

But the upshot of all of this is that Susie and I are splitting up. It's been on the cards for a while, to be honest, but her behaviour on Saturday was the proverbial last straw. I think moving to Random was a last-ditch attempt by both of us to save something that was already under threat of collapse. I think (I know) I sought some kind of sanctuary with Pippa ... and maybe I'll carry on seeking it. Pippa wasn't the cause – she's totally not to blame. The problems between me and Susie were already there but I think – OK, I know – that losing my job hit me harder than I'd actually realized. With redundancy it's not so much the day-to-day doing of the job that you miss, or even the money (no, really!), it's the sense of belonging to something. Unlike Susie I was never cut out to be freelance or entrepreneurial. I'm your dyed-in-the-wool traditional company bloke. If I'd been born a *few decades earlier I'd've signed up at twenty-one to, I dunno, J. Walter Thompson or IBM or some other Sixties icon-of-whatever and by now I'd have been promoted to a corner office and be looking forward to the full-salary pension while commuting in to Kings X from a 1930s detached-and-thatched in Hertfordshire.*

I was never meant to be a risk-taker. I'm not like you. I hate putting my neck on the line. I like taking care of business and keeping things rolling along. I'm the proverbial safe pair of hands. So it's pretty ironic that I lost my job in a recession, a time when you'd think that keeping me would be the easiest thing to do. It's not like I fucked up. At least I'm pretty sure I didn't fuck up; after all it's not me that's responsible for print journalism being a dying trade. But they said I didn't seem 'sufficiently committed to the future of multi-platform'. Bollocks to that. But maybe I am 'old school' already, at forty-five? I suppose I must be because they only went and hired a thirty-year-old to do my job.

One of the problems with Susie and me is that she always saw me as an Alpha. I'm not, I just do a good impression of one because if you're six-foot-whatever and have your own teeth and hair, people – women especially – assume you're King of the fucking Jungle. In Dad's case and your case and Will's case, they'd be absolutely right; they'd even be right in Isobel's case, and Susie's, too, come to that. But I'm a fucking sheep in wolf's clothing. I don't want to 'Play up! Play up! And play the fucking game!' anymore. I don't want to have to compete in the 'King-Kong Chest-Beating' and 'Loudest Tarzan Roar' competitions. I don't want to have to endlessly strategize my head off during company 'away days' and then run across hot coals in my bare feet shouting, 'Because I'm Worth It!' I'm forty-five. I just want to do eight hours' work and get home to see the kids and have a nice dinner with the missus and sink half a bottle of wine and fall asleep in front of Question Time. What's so fucking wrong with that, eh?

But now, somehow, I'm an unemployed ex-magazine publisher living in a rundown seaside town that's too far from London to commute and is stuffed with, so far as I can tell, nutters. Honest, mate – it's heaving with people who are all running away from something (and I'd include me and Susie in that, for sure, even if the only thing we were running away from was ourselves). They're escaping from old partners, old jobs, old drug habits, old unrealized hopes and all-too-real fears. There's a real sadness about it – and for all the summery cheerfulness and big houses and having the sea at the end of the road, you should see it in February. It's the Last Fucking Resort.

Anyway, I'm digressing. Suddenly there seems to be so much I want to get off my chest. I don't suppose I'll send you this email because I think in the end it's more for me than it is for you. It's the closest I'll ever get to therapy, believe me.

So me and Susie are calling it a day. We had a row on the phone when the slow dances were underway. Since then we've been maintaining frosty businesslike relations. I'm in the spare room, of course, and I've told her that I'm not leaving the house, so fuck knows how that's going to work because I'll have to buy her half out. I've earned this fucking house and I'm not going

anywhere – no way. So ... That's about it, mate. I'm an unem-
ployed forty-five-year-old who is splitting up with the mother of
his children. As mid-life clichés go, I'm only a few million dollars
and a couple of dozen prostitutes short of being Charlie fucking
Sheen.

   Love to the missus. Love to the kids. Love to you.
A X

[Entourage will place this message in the 'drafts' folder until you
send it]

Thursday 24 June 2010

From: willfox@wings.co.uk
To: isobel@struttbrayrush.co.uk; guy@guysports.com;
        alex@foxamil.co.uk

PLEASE call/text/email me asap. Dad's in hospital in Faro – he's
had a heart attack. Mum's with him and I'm on my way to
Stansted now – there's an EasyJet flight at lunchtime. Hope you
can get here Guy. Fingers crossed. W

CHAPTER 10

Susie

The thing about me is that I'm very decisive. Except when I'm not. Or rather, I'm very decisive when I've actually made a decision – no looking back then – but until that point I'm about as decisive as ... as ... no, sorry, I can't decide on a simile. Or even a metaphor.

Thus my decisiveness about ending things with Alex was uncharacteristically decisive. I'd beaten myself up a lot, of course, conducted endless internal dialogues berating myself for bailing on something – specifically Project Random – that had only just begun. But this mood didn't last long. Instead, I focused on how to get out, and where to go. Meanwhile, Alex and I were attempting to live separate lives under the same roof, which, I hardly need point out, was 10,000 kinds of incredibly difficult, especially as the kids knew something was up – particularly Lula, who is a bit of an emotional sponge. I mean, they're not stupid. Mummy and Daddy were sleeping in different bedrooms, and then when they weren't sleeping apart they were arguing or being elaborately polite, as if caught up in some kind of overly complicated eighteenth-century dance in which neither partner knew who was leading or where they were headed, much less when and how it would end.

Then there were the practical problems. For example, if I was to be the one doing the leaving (and apparently I was), then Alex would have to buy me out of my half of the Dream Home – not entirely straightforward given he was effectively unemployed. And then there were the emotional 'issues' – dizzyingly multi-layered and almost entirely unexpected, at least by me. When communications first broke down I was disarmed by how little was said by either of us. Which makes me sound like an idiot, given that non-communication involves a great deal of not communicating, but in a long relationship you just get used to the low-level domestic hum of day-to-day communication and when that starts to disappear the silence that replaces it is particularly heavy and surprisingly silent.

In between the silences we tried to conduct our lives 'as usual'. I had work to do, as ever, and that was OK; it was safe and easy to navigate. The things I found I couldn't handle quite so well were things I hadn't expected to have to: people's responses to the news, for example – baffled, brisk, dismissive, overly empathetic, the works. And then there was the way the landline stopped ringing almost overnight. And the fact that we now received individual non-couple-ish calls on our mobiles, which necessitated leaving rooms and speaking *sotto voce*, which just exacerbated the separateness.

I'd wondered how to tell people. And who to tell? I called my dad and Cathy on their landline and decided that whoever picked up would be the one I'd spill it to. And I got Cathy, which was a relief because she's better on the phone than Dad – she's a woman – and I knew she'd be kind instead of inadvertently judgemental. Not that my dad isn't kind in his own way, just that he invariably manages to make me feel as though anything that goes wrong in my life is entirely my fault. He's probably right, but sometimes you don't want home truths seeping down the line from your parents, you just want through-the-ether hugs.

'Oh sweetheart, I'm so sorry,' said Cathy, emphatically and sincerely and through-the-ether-hugging. 'Is there anything we can do?'

I assured Cathy that bowls of homemade chicken soup were not required, mostly because I had my own small stockpile in the freezer. It was a terrible oversight by both our fathers not to have married Jewish women. I was always intensely jealous of my primary school best friend, Rachel, whose otherwise exceptionally welcoming house I could never visit after school on Fridays, but where, nonetheless, I acquired a lifetime's addiction to *cholla*. Anyway, once I'd assured Cathy I was OK chicken-wise, everything she said, and the way in which she said it, was the right sort of thing to say. Often that's all you need.

Then I phoned my mother. You'll have noticed that my mother makes only a fleeting appearance in this narrative, largely because she's made only a fleeting appearance in mine. If your mum goes to live at the opposite end of the earth when you're a teenager and returns only occasionally, to cuddle a grandchild while suggesting that the colour of your living-room walls leaves something to be desired, or that those jeans really don't suit you, or that teething is best dealt with by rubbing brandy on baby's gums, then her innate sense of maternal entitlement – undimmed by distance or time – may not be matched by your own desire for her input. To put it politely.

After all this time, my 'relationship' with my mother had become a bit like that between a child and a fondly remembered godparent or aunt. Sometimes I found it very hard to remember how life had been when we had lived together. And though I could effortlessly recall our flat – the smell of the kitchen (with its Aga ours would have been in a minority of London mansion flats, I'd imagine), the texture of the carpets under bare feet, the faded patterns on the cork tiles in the kitchen, the colour of the bathroom walls (Cadbury's Dairy Milk, so stylish with the avocado suite), my mother herself had become a slightly vague and spectral figure, though in real life she was far from either.

I'd last seen her shortly after Chuck had been born. She'd swooped in, piled high with presents and, inevitably, unsolicited advice about breastfeeding and naps, despite the fact that my having given birth twice to her once automatically conferred upon me 100 per cent more experience in the art of baby management. No matter, my mother was – is – a capital M sort of Mother. And, occasionally, a Mutha.

So I phoned Mum on a weekend when Alex had spontaneously decided to take the kids to Careless, during which he was planning to break the 'bad' news. I'd packed a bag with three spare pairs of trousers for Chuck, just in case, and thought to myself that the kids had never been away from me for a whole weekend, much less 'alone' with Alex for that long. But this was how the future would inevitably be so they – we? – may as well start getting used to it.

I'd expected to find Mum at home, busily smiting redback spiders among the bottlebrushes in the arse-end of New South Wales, but instead I got Bruce. And was surprised to discover that my mum was in Byron Bay, the best part of 1,000 miles away, 'enjoying a long weekend of girly spa pampering, with your friend Bells'. None of these words sounded right coming from Bruce, who was probably reading them from a Post-it note crib-sheet help-fully left by my mother.

And she was with Bells? Who, as it happened, had been next on my list of people to call. Perhaps I shouldn't have been quite so surprised by this, particularly as I'd put them both in touch with each other when Bells had emigrated, but I was. Of course it made perfect sense, Bells bonding in Byron with my 'daughterless' mother, but still, it felt wrong. Obviously I didn't have a sister but this news made me feel as though I did and, what's more, that she was the favourite. I made a mental note to maybe call Bells's mum, Jane, at her home in Lancashire. Or had she moved to Yorkshire? And then I thought 'as if . . .'

Instead I had a little chat with Bruce, with whom I'd always got on, inasmuch as you can get on with someone you barely know any better than, say, the bloke in the newsagent's. And then Bruce is your archetypal Aussie male – smiley and monosyllabic. And I sort of flagged up the fact that Mum might want to give me a call about, like, stuff – but made sure that Bruce didn't think it was very pressing because I'd decided that a call from my mum at this point may end up opening a can of worms I'd rather stayed very firmly shut, at least until I'd got my head around the Mum-and-Bells situation.

Then I called Heinous, who didn't pick up either her mobile or her landline so I texted: *give us a call! S x*. Nothing. And then I checked Facebook and saw that she and Phil were away for the weekend and had posted some 'lovely' pictures of Chesil Beach. And I wondered why she hadn't told me.

Then I considered calling Bridge. Undesirable though that conversation probably was in almost every conceivable way, I definitely owed it to her to do the right thing. I'd left a couple of messages and sent a breezy text or two in the last couple of weeks but full contact was now uncomfortably overdue.

'Hello, is that you, Susie?' Bridge sounded breathless and (I very much hoped this was not the case) possibly on the brink of tears.

'Yes, look, Bridge, I'm so sorry for being a crap friend and not calling and stuff. But I've had ... and I know it's no excuse really, but ... I've had a bit on my plate too.'

'No problem, Susie, I know you have. It's really nice of you to call now though. Really nice.' There was quite a big pause.

'So Bridge, I'm really sorry about Phil. Men can be so crap sometimes.'

'It's OK. I'm fine. We're fine. Really we are. We're just cracking on. It'll all come out in the wash.'

'I'm sure it will. But still. If there's anything I can do? Or if you want to meet up for a, like, coffee or a drink?'

'That's so kind of you, Susie. And ... well ... I don't know what you're doing now but, um, if you wanted to come over?'

This is the point where the horrible, selfish part of me wanted to say 'Sorry, actually I'm in Papua New Guinea', but then the nice bit of me prevailed and asserted itself: 'You know what? Alex is away with the kids at his parents so I'm sort of at a loose end, if you really wanted me to come over.'

'That would be lovely, Susie. And could I ask you a massive favour? Would you mind bringing some milk? I'm sorry but we've run out and I can't seem to get dressed and round to the Co-op. Is that pathetic?'

'Not pathetic at all. Anything else?'

'No, no, thanks. We're fine for wine.'

On first impressions, Bridge's place was like a glimpse into some sort of twenty-first-century Farrow-and-Balled Rectory-bound version of Bedlam, a seventh circle of domestic middle-class marital breakdown hell. It was also a heads-up for the kind of single-parenting potential future I sincerely wished to avoid.

Bridge answered the door wearing an 'outfit' that unless she were in her first week post-partum, should've given even a recently dumped former fashion editor pause for thought. On her grey marl hoodie there were the sort of stains that have nothing to do with living alone with five-year-olds – maybe not even vomitous newborns – but instead hinted at the dread phrase, 'letting herself go'. Bridge looked as though she hadn't slept for a week and her hair made being-dragged-through-a-bush-backwards look fashion-forward. On the upside, she had easily lost a stone on the failsafe Misery diet. Nonetheless, it's sisterly to lie in such circumstances, so:

'Hey Bridge, you look well! Milk.'

'God, you're sweet, I look like a wreck, but thanks for the milk.'

The kitchen recalled the aftermath of New Year's Eve.

'Sorry about the mess,' said Bridge, half-heartedly removing a few bottles from work surfaces and dropping them into black bin-bags. There were an extraordinary amount of bottles.

'OK, let me give you a hand with this!' I said brightly. 'Where are the kids?'

'Stagecoach. Another pushy would-be stage-mum has kindly taken them, so I have precisely two hours to get my shit together. Which is about twenty-two hours less than I need. Coffee?'

As Bridge boiled a kettle and located a used cafetiere in the dishwasher, I busied myself with bottle removal.

'Lots of bottles, Bridge. Looks like a party.'

'It kind of was a party. It seemed like a good idea. Sorry you didn't get an invitation – it was quite spontaneous.'

It felt wrong to probe the circumstances of a recently separated mother-of-young-triplets throwing a spontaneous party, so I decided to walk gently over the domestic eggshells. And there were actually a lot of eggshells, on the floor, near the bin-bags.

'But it's great that you felt up to having a party. And, uh, are you in touch with Phil at all?'

'Sort of. He's away with the Mad Bitch this weekend, right?'

'Is he? I'm not up to speed. My friendship with Harriet seems to have faltered.'

'Well, I think they're in Dorset. Phil's parents live there . . . Oh hi, Vladimir. This is my friend Susie. I was just telling her about the party.'

I turned. And then I had to stop myself doing a Looney Tunes-style picking-up-of-a-jaw-from-the-floor. For there, standing in the doorway, was a young man of such intensely stupendous physical perfection that, at least for a moment, I couldn't speak. Six-foot-ish, wearing boxers and a wife-beater vest, 'Vladimir' leaned against the doorframe, yawned and raised his arms – his strong, lightly tanned, well-muscled arms – in an elaborate stretch, which, in turn, revealed a taut six-pack and a curly whorl of jet black hair just above the waistband of his boxers. As my blush rose, I really wished I wasn't wearing . . . whatever I was wearing, even if whatever I was wearing made me look like Cheryl Cole in comparison to Bridge. I couldn't really think straight.

'Susie, this is Vladimir, from the Ukraine. He's our new "manny".'

'Wow. Yes. Hi. Blimey.'

'Hi Susie,' said Vladimir, extending a (big, strong) hand.

Mine felt limp and dead-fishy, but he squeezed it and then balled my hand in his before uncoiling his fingers and fist-bumping my flaccid appendage. There was nothing remotely flaccid about any of Vladimir's appendages. And I had clearly come over all *Carry On Au-Pair*. I thought I might faint.

'So, that's great. How long have you been, er, helping Bridget?'

'I am here being four weeks already. I am learning English. I love children. In my country I am learning to be – how you say? – a kindergarten teacher of children.'

'Wow. That's great. I always think it's such a shame there aren't more men teaching in primary schools. Especially for the boys.'

'I think too. You have children?'

'Yes, a girl and a boy. Nearly ten and nearly six.'

'I would very much like to meet.'

'That would be lovely. So how did you and Bridge . . . ?'

'I put an ad on Gumtree for an au-pair and I got Vladimir,' said Bridge, as casually as if that sort of thing were par for the course for a recently separated middle-aged mother of three. 'Would you two mind very much if I disappeared into the shower for five minutes? Coffee's ready and there are croissants somewhere too.'

'I will make warm the cressents,' said Vladimir, turning on the oven and indeed everything else in his orbit. I was conscious that I was wearing an expression with my eyebrows hovering in my hairline, calling to mind Caroline Quentin in a primetime BBC sitcom.

'So, how are you enjoying England, Vladimir?'

'Very much am enjoying your country; I am very lucky to be much enjoying Bridget.'

It was too much.

'Yes, Bridget is very enjoyable.'

'I think she is wonderful woman and mother. And her husband is idiot.'

'Absolutely, couldn't agree more. Now, where are those cressents?'

Five minutes later Bridget reappeared with her freshly washed hair under a towel turban, wearing pedal pushers, a Breton-striped jersey and Tods. This Bardot-Bridget was unrecognizable (not to mention unstained) – at least compared to the previous Bridget, who had herself been unrecognizable in relation to the Bridget of old. I was suddenly feeling quite tired.

'Now I must enter the shower also,' said Vladimir.

'OK, Vee,' said Bridget, her tone indefinably intimate.

'So,' I said as Vladimir's footsteps receded, 'things not as bad as they might be then, Bridge? What with Vladimir?'

'No, things are very much better than one could ever have expected, obviously.' Bridge met my wide-eyed gaze with a large smile and I noted that she had particularly fine teeth. I'd never noticed before. Perhaps I'd never really seen her smile? 'Vee is great with the kids, and with me. I'm having the best sex I've ever had in my life. So, bit of a result really.'

I choked lightly on some cressent, and coughed politely. 'Understatement. And sorry if I'm over-stepping the mark but, Jesus, Bridge – he's hot.'

'Insane, isn't it? When we first spoke on the phone, after he answered my ad, I'd already decided he sounded perfect – in terms of the job, I mean – so when he said he was emailing me his full CV and a picture I just thought, fine, great, whatever. And even though the picture didn't remotely do him justice I could see he was fit and I thought "Shit! My dormant inner cougar may have just been unleashed." But obviously being a fat, recently separated thirty-eight-year-old mother of three, I banished the thought to the back of my mind. At least until I picked him up from Gatwick.'

'I'm surprised you didn't pass out when he walked through Arrivals.'

'I nearly did. And then I decided that of course he must be gay because no Eastern European manny could ever be that stupidly handsome and actually be straight. And if he were then he'd be wearing snow-washed denim and a mullet. And I carried on believing he must be gay right up until the point when it was clear that he wasn't.'

'Would you mind very much telling me how that manifested? Broad brushstrokes if you'd prefer?'

'Well, it was about five days after he'd arrived, and the kids – who took to him instantly, it must be said – were finally in bed and I had made lasagne and was opening a bottle of wine and planning to watch re-runs of *Location Location* ... like a saddo, when Vladimir came into the kitchen and apologized for being there and asked would I mind if he stayed for a chat because he was feeling lonely and missing his family. Apparently he had only decided to au-pair in the UK on a whim to help him recover from breaking up with Monika, his fiancée, whom he had been with since school, and blah-blah.

'So I said "Of course", and "Breaking up is very hard, and I should know". And I asked him about Monika and he showed me a photo of her on his phone – and she looked like Katie Price with a Kate Middleton makeover, absolutely gorgeous – and apparently she'd dumped him for a Ukrainian footballer. So we talked about broken hearts and I tried to reassure him that all might not be lost and if it was meant to be it was meant to be, and other clichés. And then we had a couple of glasses of wine – he'd never really drunk wine before, which may have had something to do with it – and we were on the sofa watching the ten o'clock news when he just sort of lunged. But in a really sweet way, like a nerdy teenager. And, ah, that was sort of that, really.'

'Wow. But what about the kids?'

'Oh they have no idea. We're very careful about that.

They miss their daddy, but God knows I don't. The Mad Bitch is welcome to him.'

'Well yes, I can see that Vladimir would definitely help fill the gaps. But in the long term?'

'One day at a time, sweet Jesus. But you know what? I have a funny feeling this one may be a keeper.'

Had poor (and yet not so poor) Bridge lost her mind?

'Really? Are you sure? I mean he's obviously the perfect rebound, but he's how old?'

'He's not a teenager, he's twenty-four. And OK, fourteen years is a bit of a gap, but he's asked me to marry him.'

'OK! But that's because he wants to stay in England, surely? I mean ... Fuck, sorry Bridge, don't get me wrong – you're definitely a catch – but frying pans, fires?'

'I know. I sound like a lovesick teenager, right? But we're good together.'

At which point Vladimir reappeared in the kitchen, now dressed – though barely – but far from clamming up, Bridge reached out a hand towards him and said: 'Vee, I was just telling Susie how good we are together but I'm not sure she believes me.'

So Vladimir slipped one of his (lovely, strong, lightly tanned, well-muscled) arms around Bridge's rapidly decreasing waist and kissed her tenderly on the forehead.

Later on Saturday afternoon and still ever-so-slightly stunned, I was pottering round the house and cruising property websites while pondering the fact that one's life (or in this case Bridge's) can take an unexpected turn at any moment, and not always for the worse, when the phone rang. I didn't immediately recognize the number.

'Hello?'

'Susie, it's Joan. You'll remember me? The woman who wasn't your mother-in-law but who nonetheless still treated you like a daughter? Your children's grandmother?'

Her tone was hard to read until I suddenly twigged: it was gin-and-tonic-o'clock. I would have to tread carefully. This could go anywhere.

'Hello, Joan.'

'Yes, well, hello to you too, young lady. And what do you think you are doing, leaving my son, apparently on a whim? I have always known you were selfish, though that's probably not your fault, seeing as you were an only child. But this beggars belief. What on earth are you thinking? We don't do "divorce" in the Fox family.'

Fire with fire? Hm. Maybe not.

'Well, as you have just pointed out, Joan, I'm not actually in the Fox family so there won't be a divorce. And while I may be leaving the house, your son is the one who suggested it.'

'You know exactly what I mean. Selfish, *selfish* girl. Breaking Alex's heart like this and destroying those children's lives!'

'Hang on a minute, Joan, you might want to run that idea by Alex because I think you'll find I'm not doing anything of the sort. And as for "destroying the children's lives"? What a thing to say. Parents split up all the time. Nobody seeks it out, children do suffer, but "destroying their lives"? There's no chance of that while they have two parents who love them.'

'Don't patronize me, Susie.'

'I wouldn't dream of it, Joan. But what on earth are you doing calling and saying this stuff now? Alex must've only just told you himself.'

'I'm in the garage. I had to call. Alex was crying earlier, Susie. Crying over the pavlova, in front of the children.'

'Really? I'm surprised. He's seemed very cool about it all so far. Are you sure he wasn't actually crying *about* the pavlova? Look, Joan, I would be grateful if you'd let me and Alex work this out for ourselves like the adults we allegedly are, rather than ranting at me as if I were a naughty child. Splitting up was his idea. And all may not be quite as straightforward as you think, in that respect . . .'

'And what precisely does that mean?'

There was a definite slur. I could picture Joan and her G&T swaying around the garage. All she needed to set her off on the full Joan Crawford was to stumble across a wire coat hanger.

'It means that your son may well have been having an affair. So I wouldn't bother being quite so judgemental, frankly.'

This was cheap of me, given that I wasn't exactly blameless, but needs must.

'Affair? You are an impossible girl, Susie Poe – the Foxes don't do affairs. I think we ought to meet over lunch and discuss this properly.'

The Foxes don't do affairs. If only she knew.

'Fine, Joan. When you've sobered up and finished comforting your heartbroken son, why don't you give me a call sometime?'

And I ended the call. And (so much for putting up a feisty frontage) then I started to cry because Joan's tipsy rant was the moment that the finality of it all truly hit home. Though I had never technically been a member of the Fox family (even if we were linked in more ways than most of its members would ever know) this was clearly also the moment when any tenuous membership was now beginning to be unravelled. It was one thing to never really want to be 'a Fox', but quite another to have that opportunity removed for ever. But of course this was how it would be now, if only because the matriarchal Joan never did anything by halves, at least not when it came to her family. Blood was of course thicker than water, but also infinitely stickier. Anyway, I had barely recovered from Joan's onslaught when the phone rang again. Great: my mother. It was a matriarchal avalanche.

'Darling, I just spoke to Bruce –' just? It must have been about 2 a.m. in Australia – 'and he tells me you called and that you sounded as if you needed your mummy.'

I am absolutely sure I wasn't imagining the slurring. Was my 'mummy' on a bender in Byron with Bells? As if my heart hadn't already sunk enough for one day.

'Mum. How nice to hear from you. But it must be very late where you are?'

'It is a bit, darling, but I'm off the leash for the weekend and a girl's gotta do what a girl's gotta do.' (For the record, my mother is sixty-seven.)

'Well, OK, great. I hear you're in Byron Bay with Bells? That sounds fun.'

'It is so much fun. And oh how we wish you were here! Just before I spoke to Bruce, Bells and I had been talking about you, saying how much we missed you.'

This was increasingly surreal.

'Right, well, that's lovely and everything, obviously, but – OK, I don't know if now is the best time but I doubt there is ever a best time to tell your mother that you're splitting up with the father of your children. So that's about the size of it. Alex and I are no more. Or, at least, not as a couple. Perhaps we'll get to the "friends" stage eventually but it seems to be some way off.'

There was a pause. I hate phone pauses. Even ordinary conversational pauses can be hard to read, but with a distance of 12,000 miles and an echo on the line a phone pause is an impossible thing to read successfully. Inevitably we both started speaking simultaneously.

'No, go on, after you,' I said.

'I was just saying, darling, that it's terribly sad, especially for the children, but from what I can see it was always a relationship on borrowed time.'

'Really?'

'Oh yes, darling. Terribly weak man, Alex, beneath all the bluff and bluster.'

'I never knew you thought that. I don't think I even thought it myself until recently.'

'It's not something one goes around saying to one's grown daughter, is it, darling? But he was never right for you. Though from what I hear his brother – Will, isn't it? – may have been. So unfortunate that that never worked out, apart from your beautiful children of course. Then I suppose there was always the possibility of having your cover blown once you became involved with Alex? A successful relationship really needs a foundation of trust and honesty on which to build and you never had that, really, did you, darling?'

It was my turn to be silent for a while. I could almost hear the tumbleweed rolling through Main Street and the swing doors of the saloon squeaking on their hinges.

'OK, right, so how long have you known about Will? I suppose Bells told you?'

'Only about a year. And of course she did, darling. And I'm glad she did because there have been so many gaps I've needed to be filled. I feel I know so little about you as an adult, so who better to paint me an accurate picture of the woman you grew into than your best friend?'

'Quite. On the subject of whom, is she there?'

'She is. And I know she'd love a quick word. Bella, darling – I've got Susie on the line!'

'Soos!'

There was a definite tone to Bells's voice. Sheepishness or vodka?

'Bells.' I didn't feel the need for exclamation marks.

'Wassup, babe?!'

It was vodka. At the sound of Bells's voice, I melted a bit and felt a lump rise in my throat. My best mate. I missed her. 'I miss you, you mad cow,' I said warmly.

'Squared.'

'But why did you tell Mum about Will? And why the fuck are you away with my mum anyway?'

'I told your mum because, because ... shit, I know I shouldn't have, I know that, but we're so far away and it feels like another country.'

'It is another country, you moron. How pissed *are* you?'

'Stop it. Only a bit pissed. I love you. We love you. *We miss you.*'

'Spare me the sentimental-drunk stuff. So we all miss each other. And Alex and I are splitting up. And he's having an affair with a woman called Pippa who sold me a fabulous dress that I can't even look at anymore – may, in fact, have to destroy. And I think she knows about Will. God knows how. And I've just had Joan on the phone calling me 'impossible and selfish'. And all this after a morning at Bridget's house – Bridget as in Phil and Bridget – and Phil's run off with Heinous Harvey and Bridge is now shagging her hot new au-pair. And the world's gone completely fucking mental.'

'Wooooah! Hang on! Bridget's *gay*? And where the hell has Heinous Harvey sprung from? And you and Alex? Omigod. Are you all right, Soos? Are you OK, babe?'

'No, I'm not OK. I'm crap. And it's all falling apart. And I can see that if this was all written down it might look quite funny, on paper, but in real life it's not funny at all. None of it.'

'No, I can see that. Now, take a deep breath –' Bells sounded rather sober – 'and just listen for a moment. I'm coming back, in a month, for good. And I'm bringing your mum for a visit. We were going to surprise you, me and Pauline, but we're not now, so . . . Hang on a mo, Soos.'

There was some muffled conversation in the background before Bells returned.

'Yes, anyway, so I'm jacking in the job.'

'I thought you loved it. Your emails, raving about the place?'

'I know. Positive spin. Had to give it a go. Some things are absolutely great here – this place, Byron, isn't bad for starters – but you learn things about yourself when you travel and to be honest I've learned that I'm a homebody.

And without your mum I would've gone mad. Does that sound weird?'

'Yes, it sounds beyond weird, of course it does. The idea of my mother keeping you sane.'

'Well she has. And she's been a brilliant surrogate mum, and I think she feels shit about being so far away from you for so long. Actually I know she does, and she's used me as much as I've used her, but in a nice way. So anyway I'm coming home. I've been offered a job by a German publishing company who are expanding in Britain. So . . .'

There was such a lot to take in that it felt very much not the right time to ask if the German publishing company was called Guthenberg, though I had a hunch it might be.

'That's great. And no, Bridget is not gay. The hot au-pair is called Vladimir. And Harriet Harvey, of all people, sort of became my new best friend, mostly because my old best friend fucked off to Australia. And Heinous was instrumental in "inspiring" (Bells couldn't see my air-quotes, but I knew she could hear them), our move to Random-on-Sea, but I kind of went off her when I caught her giving Philip-from-marketing a blow-job in the loo at my house on my fortieth birthday.'

'She's entirely untrustworthy. She stole your Keith Haring Swatch, remember?'

'No, that was Hunchback. Whatever. Water under the—'

'Bridget?' said Bells. And I truly and deeply loved her for being able to finish my sentences far better than I could finish them myself.

'You're great. I'm so glad you're coming home.'

'I am great. And I'm so glad I'm coming home too. Me and Pauline will sort you out, won't we, Pauline?'

I could hear affirmative-sounding noises in the background, followed very clearly by my mother saying, 'Actually would you be a darling and make that a double?' It was clearly time to go.

'Please tell me you and Mum aren't in some club being scary and Cougar-ish?'

'No, darling, boutique hotel bar. But we are having a highly inappropriate lesbian affair. You cool with that?'

I laughed so hard I got hiccups. Sometimes you have no idea quite how much you've missed somebody until they've come back.

I was very buoyed up by speaking to Bells. The effect lasted for days. It got me through Alex returning from his weekend wearing a thunderous expression and accompanied by our frankly frazzled-looking, discombobulated children, clearly unused to the traditional male hands-off approach to parenting, manifesting in little things – or indeed not-so-little, depending on your viewpoint – such as Lula wearing the same outfit she'd been wearing when she left, with unbrushed hair and too many stains, and Chuck, who is catnip to scrapes and bruises, returning with several more and telling me, half gleefully and half guiltily, that he'd 'jumped out of a tree and landed wrong'.

'Where was Daddy?' I enquired as lightly as I could while applying the too-long-after-the-event arnica. And I tried to pretend that Chuck's shrug didn't matter, but it did. I hadn't ever thought for very long about Alex's skills – or indeed lack of skills – as a father. Of course I knew he loved the children very much but, the more I thought about it, the more I realized how very little he'd had to do with them day-to-day, how much he'd managed to avoid the mundane stuff, the relentless clothes and school uniform organization, the homework, sorting their social lives, visiting doctors and dentists, solving the infinite variety of childcare crises. It was never Alex who had agonized about MMR when Lula was a baby or dropped everything in the office to race to school when she was sent home with a stomach bug at lunchtime. I worked full-time too, of course, but realized I had made myself responsible for virtually all the tedious details of the domestic landscape, and (at least as far as Alex was concerned) that apparently included the children. It's your classic post-feminist fuck-up, mistaking the desire to have it all with the need to do it all. And, perhaps like most men of his age, Alex simply colluded. His contribution to our shared domestic life had, I worked out, extended to:

- Bins, emptying and removal thereof.
- Electronic meltdowns, of all kinds, across all media.
- Drainage and plumbing issues, especially those involving S-Bends, which essentially amounted to a lot of sighing and swearing and, ultimately, phoning a Professional
- Anything to do with drills.
- Anything to do with cars.
- A few – maybe two? – years of taking the children to Queen's Park on Saturday mornings, for a maximum of two hours (in good weather), and a minimum thirty minutes (in average weather), so I could 'relax'.

I genuinely believe that Alex thought the Saturday morning arrangement was my time for lying in a hot bath surrounded by Diptyque candles and indulging in elaborate exfoliation and depilation routines while flicking though *Easy Living* with a spare third hand, though the truth of it was that I usually ended up loading and unloading the dishwasher, putting on a clothes wash and deputizing on the bins. Anyway, I had never again even considered the possibility of 'relaxing' after that time, late on a balmy early summer's morning, when Alex returned from the park, smiling and bearing newspapers and croissants, with Lula scootering behind him, and I'd said:

'Croissants! Lovely! Where the hell's Chuck?'

And Alex had turned white, spun on his heel and disappeared at a never-before-or-since-witnessed speed. Of course, our five-month-old son was just where he'd been left, asleep in his stroller next to a bench in the park under the kindly and watchful eye of a full-time-mummy playground acquaintance who (when I subsequently ran into her and thanked her effusively, scarlet with embarrassment) had (she helpfully admitted) been mere moments from phoning the police.

'But Lula, what about Chuck? Didn't you notice Daddy had forgotten him?' I asked our five-year-old daughter.

'Yes, but every time I said "Daddy, Daddy!" he kept saying "Shush, I'm on the phone!"'

I had forgotten about this episode until I saw the children pile out of the car on Sunday afternoon, and when I did remember I felt a chill of something faintly resembling foreboding and wondered if this was the fabled maternal instinct – the thing that essentially separates Us from Them? I've never kidded myself I'm the most fabulous mother in the world and certainly never made parenting my fetish, but I do think I'm probably good enough, and sometimes a great deal better than that. As for Alex – frankly, who knew? Despite having children aged nine and five, when it came to hands-on parenting, for Alex it was clearly early days.

'How was it? Did you have a lovely time?' I chirped as

the kids disembarked, and before I'd discovered the bruises. Lula glanced briefly – nervously? – at her father, but smiled and breezed past me while choosing to keep her counsel, though Chuck raced straight into my arms. Meanwhile, Alex frowned.

'Bloody handful, your kids.'

My heart sank. Once we were no longer uneasily cohabiting and I was finally out of this bloody house – and Alex's daily life – my future almost certainly included never knowing exactly what was going on when he had access to the kids. We had, in advance, already tentatively negotiated a traditional every-other-weekend at Daddy's in the future, but a long one, starting on Friday afternoons and including Alex doing the Monday morning school run, though he had already indicated to me that this probably wasn't going to be often enough.

'I'm their father, for fuck's sake! Why would I automatically be relegated to the role of junior partner? I'm not happy about it at all.'

I'd bitten my lip. How could I get away with articulating the truth? Which was: 'When it comes to the kids you've ALWAYS been the junior partner. Name all the contents of Lula's PE kitbag and then tell me what day she plays hockey. And while we're at it, give me the names of Chuck's latest "best friend" and his favourite teacher.'

But I didn't say any of this. Instead I said, soothingly, 'I'm sure everything is negotiable ...' Not rocking boats was a new discipline for me, and one at which I wasn't exactly gifted. I could, however, see that the future would include a lot of it.

And then just days after this, shortly after Nigel and Joan had decamped to 'Golfditz', Nigel Fox was preparing a putt at the eighteenth (the devil is in the details) when he had a heart attack. And then the following morning, surrounded by his wife and three of his children – Guy hadn't managed to get there fast enough from Bali – poor Nigel died, at which point the boat wasn't so much rocked as had hit a 'berg and started sinking fast, with all hands.

The funeral was held ten days later, in early July. Initially, Alex was adamant that he didn't want either me, or the children, to go. Then he changed his mind and said he wanted the children to attend, but not me. Then he changed his mind again, prompted, no doubt, by tears from Lula, who was particularly close to her grandpa (and he to her) and who had been hit very hard by the whole tragic business:

'I want to go and say goodbye to Grandpa. I love Grandpa. And I want Mummy there too. I won't go if Mummy doesn't come . . .' Accompanied by a stamped foot from my little chip-off-the-old-block.

As for me, in this – if only this – I was prepared to do as instructed: if it was considered 'appropriate' by the Fox family (of which I had never felt less of a member) I'd go – if not, I wouldn't. Simple. And yet, not so simple at all. Alex didn't want me there.

'I don't need your fucking idea of "support", though the children probably will,' he conceded.

In the end we reached a compromise. I'd come with the children to the actual funeral but then I'd take them home while Alex went on to the wake, at Careless, afterwards. He made a point of telling me that the wake was 'for family and close friends only'. And presumably I could read into that whatever I liked.

Either way I was dreading it. Alex and I hadn't spent any length of time together in a car since Guy and Lisa's wedding, and that had only been forty minutes. The prospect of driving to Suffolk filled me with even more gloom than was provided by the journey's already mega-gloomy context. In the short period since his father's death, Alex's mood had been at best unpredictable, at worst morose – and rarely more than monosyllabic.

Inside the Dream Home the tension was almost unbearable whenever I tried to do something to lift it – mostly for the sake of the children, who had been infected by Alex's distance and abrasiveness while struggling to understand its cause and who were now acting up. Chuck had started having bad dreams, coming into my bed at all hours of the night and asking, 'Where's Daddy? Why isn't Daddy in bed too?' while Lula had just retreated into herself to the point where I became increasingly concerned.

One night, a few days before the funeral and just before I went to bed, I'd snuck into Lula's room at about 11 p.m. to kiss her sleeping forehead – as I had done every single night since she'd moved into her own bedroom when I'd stopped breastfeeding her, at five months old – and I found the light on and Lula staring fixedly at the wall at the end of her bed. On her bedside table was a small, framed photo of her sitting on her grandpa's knee, taken when she was about six or seven. I didn't even know she'd had it.

'It's very late, darling; why are you still awake?' I said gently.

'I can't sleep. I'm scared if I turn out the light, I'll die. But if I die I might see Grandpa again, so I don't know what to do.'

'Sweetheart. You're not going to die. You won't die until you're incredibly ancient – much, much older even than Grandpa. And even then he'll still be waiting to see you, sitting on his big cloud, because he's your grandpa and he loves you. So there's no hurry.'

'But I love him and I miss him.'

'I know you do, darling. I know you do. And he loves you too, he just can't tell you how much at the moment. He hasn't got a . . . a phone.'

Tears pricked my eyelids. I don't know why, but I hadn't cried for Nigel. Now, however, I was crying for Lula.

'That's a lovely picture of you and Grandpa.' I picked up the photograph. It was indeed lovely, taken by Alex, under a willow, on, I now recalled, a pleasant summer's Sunday at Careless.

'Daddy gave it to me.'

'Yes. That was a good idea of Daddy's.' I wiped away a tear. And another. 'Would you like me to stay with you until you get to sleep? Would that help?'

'Yes, that would help.'

And so I lay close to my daughter, in her white princess bed with her teddies still ranged at the foot, and I stared at a picture of Cheryl Cole on the wall and realized I hadn't done this in ... so long. How long? A year? And as my beautiful daughter closed her eyes and I felt her relax and her breathing deepen as she succumbed to sleep, I saw that she was probably just a few months away from putting her teddies in a cupboard and adding a picture of Justin Bieber to her wall. And the thought made my solar plexus heave, and I wanted to squeeze her very tight and apologize for everything. Not least for failing to give her the childhood she deserved, which was always meant to have been nothing less than perfect, whatever 'perfect' was.

In the event, the journey to Suffolk the following Friday was conducted in almost total silence. A heavy sort of silence. Lula was playing Angry Birds on my new iPad; Chuck was asleep. It was almost as if nothing had changed since the last time we'd made this journey together, as a family – and yet of course almost everything had. We still stopped for coffee and a wee at 11.30 a.m., out of habit, I think, rather than any particular need.

Once again we were the last to arrive in Suffolk, albeit this time at the church, St Mary's, which was less than a quarter of a mile from Careless. And this time too, of course, there was no Nigel to greet us at the door with his usual brusque but heartfelt platitudes. Instead, a hearse containing Nigel's flower-laden coffin was already parked outside the lych-gate. If I had been dreading all of this before, the sight of the Fox family exacerbated my fear far more than I'd anticipated. And as for the sight of Will . . .

I had of course seen Will quite recently, after Guy and Lisa's wedding, when he had called and, against all expectations, driven straight down to Random, arriving on the Dream Home's doorstep just before midnight. Until he'd actually appeared, I hadn't really believed he would, but there he was, still suited and booted and buttonholed, smiling a tentative smile – for Will anyway, 'tentative' not really being part of his emotional repertoire.

'Susie . . .'

'Will. You came.'

'I said I would. Did you really think I'd change my mind?'

'No. I don't know. Maybe. Why did you come?'

'Because I had to.'

'OK.'

'Beautiful house, Susie.'

'Beautiful house, yes. But "inside every dream home a heartache", to sort-of quote Bryan Ferry.'

'Come on. Come here.' And Will enveloped me in a hug, which, inevitably, went on for too long. And which, just as inevitably, I didn't want to end. And nor, it seemed, did he. Later – after a conversation which, aside from his observations about The Wedding ('Lisa looked beautiful, Guy was on cloud nine; I've never seen him so chilled. And you would have been so proud of Lula . . .') surprised and disarmed me at every turn, leaving me with more questions than answers – Will went to use the bathroom while I sat in the living room, head teeming with thoughts. Can = worms. And when he returned:

'Susie. The mirror. You still have the mirror.'

'Of course I still have the mirror. Why wouldn't I? Quite aside from being the most flattering mirror in the world, it's one of my favourite things.'

'Yeah, there's no reason why you shouldn't have it; of course there isn't. Maybe I just assumed you wouldn't.'

'Why? You know how much I love it.'

But more to the point, why was Will talking about the bloody mirror when there were so many other more important things to discuss?

'I don't know. But seeing it just now took me to . . . another place.'

'William Through the Looking Glass?'

'Yeah, something like that. Anyway, forget it.'

So I did. And then we made love on the sofa – fast, guilty, passionate love – and afterwards I cried and Will held me so tenderly that instead of stemming the flow of tears it just exacerbated them. Neither of us said a word until the moment – and it was a long moment – passed. Even then, we didn't say much. Had I written a screenplay for the scene this would have been the point where Will and I declared our undying love, but this was far from being a ninety-minute rom-com. Our emotional business was, for both of us, obviously unfinished but without the benefit of a script it was obvious that neither of us had a clue where we should go from here. Anyway, at about 3 a.m., Will finally left and I went and sat in our – Alex's – east-facing kitchen and drank more wine, waiting for the sound of seagulls and the first streaks of sunrise.

And now, a mere fortnight later, here was Will at his father's funeral, wearing his dress uniform and radiating an aura of being in charge. And next to him, leaning on his arm, was Joan, looking suddenly less like the all-powerful matriarch than a small, pale, frail, elderly widow, an effect set off by the stark simplicity and elegance of her black shift dress, grey pashmina and a pill box hat.

And here too were Guy and Lisa, holding hands, tanned but drawn-looking, and Isobel, doing the time-honoured maternal wet hankie routine as she removed smudges from

Jack's cheeks. And then there were the children and assorted relatives and friends of the family . . . and everybody looked over as we arrived and then everybody looked away from me, or straight through me, and turned their attention to Alex and our children, while I hovered, uncertain of the etiquette, a few feet behind as they all hugged and kissed. I wanted to run but I was rooted to the spot. I felt a bit like Sarah Ferguson must have done when first confronted by the royal family post toe-sucking.

Eventually somebody had to acknowledge me. To my surprise it wasn't Will – not straight away – but Joan, who walked forward and kissed me lightly on both cheeks and said:

'Thank you for coming, Susie. I know Nigel would have wanted you to be here.'

'Thank you, Joan. And I'm so very, very sorry. It seems terribly unfair . . .'

Joan nodded and gave a wan half-smile: 'It is. But then life very often is unfair, isn't it?'

And she moved back to lean against Will – how I yearned to be able to do that – who, in turn, reached out and squeezed my upper arm, very gently, and perhaps for slightly too long. I felt that everybody was watching this, though of course they probably weren't – and if they were, it was a perfectly normal thing to do under the circumstances, wasn't it?

'Mummy, I need a *poo*,' said Chuck, perfectly on cue. As I led him into the adjacent church hall, exceptionally relieved to be released, I kissed him gratefully. He looked pretty surprised to be kissed for wanting a poo.

The service was long, but not unbearably so, and moving. All the Fox offspring read or said something. Alex was up first, reminiscing touchingly and amusingly about Nigel reading *The Chronicles of Narnia* to him and Guy at bedtime; Isobel spoke of the bond between her father and his only daughter; Guy read an excerpt from P.G. Wodehouse – Nigel's favourite author – and Will read Ralph Waldo Emerson's 'Concord Hymn', which (and I had never known this until now, and it seemed about a decade too late) was apparently Nigel's favourite poem. It floored us all.

After an intimate address by Nigel's longstanding friend, the Rev Brian Bostock (who – another revelation – had not only christened all the junior Foxes but had also offici-ated at the wedding of Will and the sainted Marianne), we moved outside for the 'Ashes to Ashes, Dust to Dust' part of the proceedings. It was immediately obvious there wasn't enough room for everyone around the grave, so I nudged Alex, placed a child's hand in each of his, and sloped round the back of the church for a fag. After a ciga-rette-free past five years, I'd started smoking again just last week. It was a temporary lapse, I'd promised myself. But I hadn't given myself a deadline to stop, either.

When it was all over, I left with the children as discreetly as possible. But then nobody was looking anyway. The children were quiet as I three-point-turned the old Audi, which I noticed was suddenly looking a bit past its sell-by. I supposed I'd have to leave it with Alex and buy something for myself soon – an oddly exhausting thought, all things considered. How did one buy cars anyway?

Whatever. As I glanced in the rear-view mirror, I could see Will assisting Joan over the churchyard stile as the Fox posse made their way back across the single field that now separated Nigel from Careless. It was ineffably sad, but for some reason I still couldn't cry. Instead, I parked in a lay-by and handed out sandwiches, crisps and fruit to the kids, making a point of not complaining when the backseat started to resemble a *favela*.

And on the drive home – disrespectfully to the memory of Nigel, who I seemed to be having trouble realizing was actually dead – all I could think about was Will. In his uniform, the description 'dashing' didn't even come close and it disturbed me that the sight of my nearly brother-in-law grieving in a pair of super-shiny Oxfords, air-force blue kit and hat, sent tiny shivers up my spine. He looked like he'd been sketched for the cover of a 1960s Mills & Boon, entitled *The Sky's The Limit* . . .

Despite his pain, dashing RAF Officer Will Fox had never looked more handsome than he did on that summer's day . . . a beautiful day but for the fact that it was also his father's funeral.

While his frail widowed mother leaned on him for support

during the interment, and as the Reverend Bostock intoned the lines 'Ashes to ashes, dust to dust . . .', Will allowed himself the very briefest of guilty glances over his shoulder, catching sight of his secret, forbidden lover, Susannah – his own brother's wife . . .

This was a 1960s Mills & Boon, after all . . .

. . . who was standing some way behind the crowd of mourners, leaning against a tree and dabbing her eyes with a monogrammed handkerchief. She had never looked more lovely than she did at this moment, thought Will. And in many ways, more than he cared to count, she had never been further from him than she was now – the time, he realized with a start, when he needed her the most . . .

For God's sake, woman – get a grip.

The next few weeks of cohabitating with Alex was like living with an acquaintance. If he had been hard to communicate with before Nigel died, he was virtually impossible to get to now. I tried to reach out occasionally, attempted to talk, but he invariably brushed me off. Any conversations we did end up having were conducted in the style of an oddly formal and old-fashioned sort of meeting, papers and lists spread out on the kitchen table, discussing finances, 'arrangements' and all the tedious minutiae that inevitably comes with disentangling a relationship, and in a peculiarly stilted and overly polite fashion. We were, by now, leading almost entirely separate lives.

Some things were, of course, made easier by Nigel's abrupt departure. There was a legacy, and even after death duties it was a larger one than Alex had expected – enough for him to buy me out of the house without having to secure a mortgage, plus a bit left over for the proverbial 'rainy days'. But having the financial pressure lifted didn't appear to alter Alex's mood, set to a semi-permanent 'morose'. He spent even longer alone in his office, more time wielding drills to no particular effect and he was out as many evenings as he was in. Eventually I stopped asking where he was going.

I decided there was no point in waiting for the estate to be settled – it would take a few months – so after we'd consulted separate solicitors and drawn up an agreement that he would buy me out at the current market value, I decided to start hunting for a house. Not to buy – I wasn't yet ready for that – but to rent for a year or two while I worked out what would be best for me and the kids. Would I stay in Random in the long term, or head home, back up the Highway from Hell?

My heart told me to run, but my head said 'stay'. If I left it would be too much for the kids and they'd be too far from Alex ... and then the decision was effectively made for me when I started looking at property on the internet and learned that, in the areas I would want to live in London, I could probably afford a two-bedroom garret. Though a fan of apartments, the journey from the

Dream Home to a small London flat was just a bit too far. For the moment we'd clearly be staying put in Random, but where?

After a few days of desultory searching on the web, I registered with a couple of the better agents in the area and though neither currently had anything that was right for us – a lot of soulless executive homes in neat cul-de-sacs on the outskirts of town, or dinky holiday rentals that were too small to swing a hamster – three days after I'd registered I got a call from Karen at Stopp & Stiff, known locally as Stop 'n' Sniff, because you make your own pun-fun in a small town.

'Hi Susie, something's just come on – literally this morning – that might interest you. I know you said you weren't particularly sold on the Old Town, but there's something about this place I think you might like . . .'

Carpe the bloody diem: she was right, I wasn't convinced by the Old Town – more because of the lack of parking than the preponderance of ye olde beamage – but I viewed the house with Karen that afternoon, just before the school run.

It wasn't remotely what I'd been looking for. In fact, being a tall thin house on a steeply winding street with a suntrap courtyard garden, it was pretty much the opposite – but I loved it. Unfurnished, there were four bedrooms, two singles for the kids, a surprisingly spacious 'master' with an en-suite shower, a tongue-and-grooved family bathroom and another little room with sea views tucked in the eaves that could easily be an office. Downstairs there were two square receptions and a surprisingly large basement kitchen. It was immaculate, too, painted in whites and pale grey, with stripped and painted floors and plantation shutters. French doors opened out on to a walled courtyard, which was on two levels. A fig tree climbed one wall; clematis crawled up another. It was so obviously loved that this had to have been somebody's own Dream Home. Karen read my mind.

'Actually, I know the people who used to live here – lovely couple with a little girl – but they sold the house a few months ago and the new owner isn't looking to live in it for the foreseeable; it's just an investment. They haven't done much to it, as it happens – just a lick of paint.' Karen paused. 'It's actually quite odd seeing it empty; the last time I was here was over Christmas, for dinner. You'd be surprised how many people you can cram in it if you want to.'

I glanced around the kitchen, noting how well it was laid out: the all-important triangle between the cooker, the fridge and the bamboo-topped island.

'How much?'

'Nine hundred and fifty a month. That's a lot here, by the way, though I think I might be able to get it down for you. I have a feeling that money isn't a huge issue for the owner, that they'd rather somebody nice was living in it.'

'That's sweet of you.'

'Not all agents are tough as old boots and fixated on the bottom line. Some of us actually get more of a buzz from finding the right person for the right house, and vice versa. Personally, I'd take it like a shot. It has a happy vibe.'

'It does. It feels good. If you can get it nearer eight hundred and fifty, I'll take it.'

Karen smiled. 'I'll see what I can do. In fact I'll see what I can do right now . . .' and she went upstairs with her phone.

'Ah, you see – there's not much of a mobile signal down here – that's got to be a potential deal-breaker, right?' I shouted after her. She laughed.

She was back downstairs within a couple of minutes.

'Sorted. All yours for eight hundred and seventy five. Nightmare not having a phone signal in the basement, especially when you work from home, right?'

'That's brilliant, Karen. Thank you so much.'

'No problem. My client is delighted we've let it so quickly. The terms of the lease are that we're responsible for all the maintenance issues. You've got a hands-off landlady, but we'll see you right. And anyway, I don't anticipate too many problems – the whole place was renovated over the last couple of years: new wiring, the works. I hope you and your family will be very happy here.'

'So do I. I think we might be . . .' It was my turn to pause. '. . . Eventually.'

'Divorced myself five years ago. It's never easy. But it gets better.'

'Yes, that's what they say. We'll see. And thank you again. This feels right.'

'Do you want to pop back to the office with me now and go through the paperwork?'

'School run beckons, I'm afraid. I'll swing by in the morning, if that's OK?'

'Fine by me, but call first, in case I'm on a viewing.'

'I will.'

'Tell you what – and I really shouldn't be doing this – but why don't you hang on to the keys and drop them back to me in the morning? Maybe you could show the kids after school? Or just come back this evening by yourself, bring a tape measure, get a feel for the place?'

So I did, but I didn't bring Lula and Chuck. Alex and I hadn't yet sat them down and had the 'Mummy and Daddy love you very much but we don't love each other enough to stay in the same house anymore' conversation, or words to that effect. Because I'd been reading some 'how to help the children when you break up' style stuff online, and apparently you have to tell kids how much you love them and that it's not their fault, though I've never quite understood why they would think it was, to be honest. It didn't cross my mind for a moment that it was my fault when my parents broke up; it was very obviously theirs. But even without that conversation it seemed a bit much to present the children with their third new house in under a year without preparing them first. So I picked the kids up from school and then had a quick word with Alex, asking if he would be in that evening to babysit – I was nervous in my dealings with him these days – and when he said he would be, I told him I'd found a house and I needed to go and spend some time in it with a tape measure, to see if sofas would fit, that sort of thing.

'And what sofas do you think you're taking from my home, precisely?'

I hadn't really expected this. It was still our home, they were our sofas – we had two, plus a sofa-bed – and I would probably take only one because my new house was smaller than the Dream Home. Of course, I would be taking other stuff, too ... beds, kitchenalia, books, pictures ... I'd assumed that we'd sit down and have some sort of terribly civilized, very British conversation about the division of our 'marital' hardware. Now, however, Alex obviously wanted to shore up his fragile emotional state with a ballast of *stuff*, so this could be tricky.

'Well, I really only need one. I thought the old Chesterfield would be fine. You've never loved it quite as much as I do.'

'No, you're right, but I seem to remember I paid for it.'

'OK. Well, I think you probably paid for all the sofas, if memory serves, but I definitely bought the fridge and the dining table and chairs and the rugs ...'

'Well you can't take the fridge. You can have the dining table if you have to, but I need some rugs.'

'This isn't sounding like a negotiation, it's sounding like you laying down the law. Which is unfair.'

'You fuck up my life, Susie, you pay the price.'

'I'm sorry?' I couldn't believe what I was hearing.

'You heard me.'

'Yes, I heard you, but I don't understand what you're talking about. I didn't "fuck up your life" – we both fucked up our own lives, together. It usually takes two to fuck up a relationship and I take responsibility for the bits that I did fuck up. But you need to take responsibility for the bits you fucked up, too.'

My voice was rising now. I was desperate to keep things quiet, 'for the sake of the children', but it was almost impossible. This man I was living . . . no, cohabiting . . . with was scarily close to becoming the enemy. How did that happen? And how did it happen so fast? We had loved each other, for years. Where had all that love gone?

'I'm not having this conversation now. Go and see your house. I'll get the children's supper and put them to bed.'

'But . . .'

'Shut up, Susie. Go.'

'I'll just have a quick word with the kids, if that's OK?'

If that's OK? I was asking their father's permission to speak to my children? What kind of madness was this?

'I'll speak to the children. I'll tell them you're . . . I dunno, seeing Harriet. But go. Now. I don't want you around here. You're driving me fucking mad.'

'I'm just going to grab a tape measure—'

'FUCK OFF!'

And you know what? I actually went. And I'd driven to Tesco Extra and bought a bloody tape measure before I realized that I hadn't, of course, measured the sofa, so I would have to measure the wall I thought it might fit against and then come home – home? Ha! – and measure the fucking sofa. And he thought *he* was going mad?

Maybe the signs were always there. Maybe I had just chosen not to notice that Alex was a bully. Or maybe he hadn't always been a bully? But that didn't seem to matter much because he sure as hell was a bully now. Even taking into account his father's sudden death and his wobbly employment status, this situation now seemed a great deal worse than I'd ever imagined it could be. I didn't have a blueprint for break-ups from long-term live-in relationships, but even if I had it wouldn't have looked like this.

At the house, early evening sunlight washed the as-yet-unmeasured walls of the sitting room. I sat on the white-painted floorboards, staring at light shafts playing against the cool grey of the chimneybreast, imagining the Venetian glass mirror against it, with invitations – to what? From who? – lined up along the mantelpiece and buttressed by Diptyque candles.

I sat on the floor for a very long time without moving, until the sun had dipped below the rooftops opposite and the room cooled. And with it my optimism about this womb-y little place. I loved the house, but I didn't love what it represented. I hadn't ever expected to be dancing a jig of joy when we moved in but I had hoped it would feel somehow right to be here. Now I wasn't so sure that I would feel 'right' wherever we were. But this was a scary thought so I pushed it to the back of my mind, rose to my feet and – finally – measured the bloody wall. The Chesterfield would probably be OK but I doubted there was room for a table next to it. Whatever.

Back 'home', just after 10 p.m., I found Alex in the kitchen, writing a list. When he handed it to me in silence it turned out to be an 'inventory'.

ALEX
LEATHER SOFA
SOFA-BED
FRIDGE
THREE HABITAT RUGS
COFFEE TABLE
CASTIGLIONI FLOOR LIGHT
TOM DIXON MIRRORBALL
VENETIAN MIRROR
TEMPUR SUPER KING BED
FRENCH LINEN PRESS

KIDS' BEDS
ALL WHITE GOODS
HALF THE KITCHEN STUFF
BOOKS/CDs/DVDs/PICTURES TO BE DISCUSSED

SUSIE
CHESTERFIELD
SPARE DOUBLE BED
IKEA RUGS
ERCOL CHEST OF DRAWERS
ERCOL NEST OF SIDE-TABLES
KITCHEN-AID FOOD PROCESSOR
YOUR DESK
THREE TABLE LAMPS
DINING TABLE AND CHAIRS

I stared at this for an absurdly long time. For some reason I couldn't really 'see' it properly. Then:

'That mirror is mine. You know it's mine. I had it before I met you. And you bought the posh bed for me when I was pregnant with Lula. And why do you get to keep the kids' beds when they'll mostly be with me?'

'Who says they'll mostly be with you? And I told the kids, by the way ...'

'What? You told the kids *what*?'

'I told them you were leaving Daddy and taking them with you but that Daddy and Mummy, though Mummy's not here to say it right now, love them very, very much. There were a lot of tears, Susie. A *lot*.'

And it was my turn to pick up the nearest object – a full glass of red wine, as it happens – and throw it, hard. It hit the wall but only just missed Alex.

'You absolute fucking complete and utter bastard. You despicable low-life piece of *shit*.'

I gasped for breath, my heart racing so fast I thought I might actually faint.

'Pot-kettle-black, Susie. And sorry, but I'm afraid I'm definitely keeping that beautiful mirror you love so much. Or more accurately, I'm keeping what's left of it.'

I was lost for words. Alex was now smiling a terrifying sort of rictus-grin like something out of a horror movie – *Heeeeeeere's ALEX!* – so I turned on my heels and ran upstairs to the living room, where, as I'd anticipated, my beautiful mirror now lay on the floor, split into three pieces, with a spider's web of cracks across the glass and shards all over the rug. *Alex's* rug.

So I carried on upstairs, to the children. Thankfully, whatever had happened earlier, Chuck was now fast asleep in his habitual pose, rumpled but relaxed-looking, flat on his back, arms flung out behind him on his pillow, but Lula's light was still on, her door ajar, so I tiptoed into the room, where I found her awake, staring at Cheryl Cole.

'Lula . . .'

She turned, appraised me for a moment in her usual, almost glacially composed way. Then she said: 'Go away, Mummy. Just go away and leave me alone.'

It felt as though my heart had been ripped out of my body.

A week later, after seemingly endless, exhausting and circular conversations – with Alex, with the children, with Alex and the children – on the morning of the day that we, that is me, Lula and Chuck, moved out of the 'Dream Home' and into the womb-y rental, I stopped by the letting agents to officially pick up the keys from Karen, despite the fact that I'd had one set all week.

'OK, the standing order's sorted, your deposit's cleared, everything's signed and counter-signed in triplicate, so you're good to go. Oh and there's this . . .'

Karen handed me a shoebox done up with masking tape. I must have looked puzzled. She shrugged.

'I'm assuming it's a bunch of guarantees and warranties and how-does-your-boiler-blow type boring paperwork. The owner asked me to pass it on to you. Like you probably haven't got enough boxes in your life already . . .'

'OK, one more for the pile. Thanks, Karen. I'm incredibly grateful for your help.'

'No problem. I promise you it gets easier. But before it does, I hope you'll be very happy in the house, all of you. It really suits you.'

'Thanks. And once I've bought a kettle please do swing by for a cuppa if you're passing. Seriously.'

'I might just do that. Take care.'

And what with one . . . no, thirty . . . things and another, such as unpacking and getting the bloody BT broadband up and running so I could send emails with my new address, I was spending a lot of time with the children, trying to mend things. Hearts, for example, not to mention a broken mirror. I was trying so hard to make our new domestic triangle the right sort of triangle.

After all of that, almost another week had passed before I bothered to open the box. Which, as Karen had predicted, contained precisely the kind of boring paperwork I could never be arsed to look at – that had always been Alex's domain – but which I supposed I would have to start to take on board, albeit reluctantly. But that wasn't all. Inside the shoebox was another box. Small, very posh, pink leather – blimey, it was Smythson – and inside that was an iPhone, and an envelope with my name – just 'Susie' – written on it in what looked to be fountain pen.

Dear Susie,

Firstly, welcome to your new home. I'm the mysterious owner, but I hope to God that doesn't put you off. It's a lovely house and I hope you'll all be very happy in it for as long as you want, or need . . .

Secondly, we all make mistakes – and I enclose one of mine. The phone belonged to Alex – it's the one he lost at that hotel last year, just before he lost his job. I had a hunch it might not be permanently lost and that hunch was proved correct. Do not for one moment imagine that I'm proud of the fact that I stalked Alex's phone and listened to your message, but I did. However, I never – HONESTLY – told Alex I had it, much less told him about the message.

I totally understand if you are furious about all this – about this letter, the phone . . . all of it, really. I appreciate it must feel completely wrong and I'm not proud of my role in any part of it. And I'm also being incredibly selfish – I'm doing this not because you need or want me to but because this letter seemed the most appropriate place for me to start living a different kind of life.

I am not with Alex. I never really was with Alex. And I'm sorry.

Pippa

I read the letter three times before walking downstairs to the kitchen, putting it in the Belfast sink and setting light to it. Ashes to ashes . . . Daunting though it seemed, my future appeared to be starting right here and now, in front of a sink and a small funeral pyre, in somebody else's Dream Home.

CHAPTER 11

Pippa

Dear Mum,

By the time Alex finally arrived, close to midnight, I had drunk a third of the bottle of Merlot, changed my outfit three times and spent at least twenty minutes distractedly wiping and re-wiping the already-immaculate kitchen work-surfaces. When the bell finally rang I still wasn't ready – mostly because I didn't know what I needed to be ready for.

On the doorstep, Alex looked slightly flushed and beery, a tiny bead of perspiration hovering indecisively between his brows.

'Pippa.'

'Alex.'

To say the atmosphere was awkward was to understate things to a Samuel Beckett-ish degree. It was already all about the pauses but who knew what was happening with the plot? Now he was actually here, I certainly didn't have a script – and nor, apparently, did Alex.

'Come in. Then you can tell me why you're here.'

I opened the door extra-wide. I didn't want to seem furtive or apologetic, or as if I'd changed my mind. Alex crossed the threshold, dropped his bag on the floor and closed the door, with a bang.

'I love you, Pippa.'

I sighed.

'No I don't think you do, Alex. I think you probably love the idea of loving me. But let's talk about that. Glass of wine?'

'Yes, thanks. But please don't go all chilly on me. I know I've been a total dickhead – it's my great skill – but please hear me out.'

'Of course I will. Come downstairs.'

I poured us both a glass of the Merlot. And then I moved to the other side of the island. I needed to put a bit of space between us.

'So, Alex. How's it hanging?'

'Oh for fuck's sake.' Alex took a gulp of the wine, leant on the island and put his head in his hands. 'Look, I've fucked up every single area of my life. I lost my job, I slept with you ... not that that was a fuck-up ... and I'm probably losing the mother of my children. Susie will be out of the door any minute because I can't communicate with her. And the irony of that is that I have tried to do the right thing ... I wanted to be with you – if you would've had me – but I decided that was –' Alex waggled his fingers to make air-quotes – '"wrong". Because me and Susie and the kids are – were – a family, and families are meant to stick together.'

'Well that's the general idea, but if you look at the statistics you'll see it doesn't often pan out like that. Look at me. I'm effectively a family of two. And my son is about to go to boarding school ...'

'Is he?'

'Yes. He hated his new school. He wants ... a different kind of life.'

I shrugged. Alex peered at me closely.

'Yeah, we all want a different kind of life. Why is that? Why can't we ever be happy with the one we have? Why do we have to keep trying to change it all the time? Why isn't anything ever enough? My parents, for example – they've lived in the same house for nearly fifty years. They're happy with what they've got.'

'OK, you really want an answer? We live in an insanely consumerist, wildly secular culture. We don't believe in anything anymore except ourselves. But because we don't know who we are anymore, we think happiness means unlimited credit and climbing the property ladder to the en-suite bedroom of our dreams. That's what I think, since you asked. But I'm not sure that's the conversation you came here to have.'

'No, you're right, it isn't. But that's pretty smart of you. And I probably agree.'

'And of course it's very easy for me to say, standing here in my fuck-off house with no need to work. So shoot me.'

'I don't want to shoot you, I want to fuck you.'

'Oh Alex. Come on. That's just sex.'

At which point Alex walked round to my side of the island – would that it had been an archipelago – and put his hands gently, very gently, up to my face, and said: 'No, it isn't "just" sex. It's more than that, Pippa. It's about feeling alive.'

And the thing was – as much as I tried to deny it – Alex made me feel alive, too, so it was inevitable that we would have sex. It had always been inevitable because we seemed to trigger something that the other needed, even craved. When it came to Alex, my head said one thing, my heart quite another and so the sex was passionate, swift, and almost – but not quite – painful. Not physically painful, but . . . anyway, I knew why this was because, afterwards, when we had moved upstairs to my bedroom and lay spooned against each other, with Alex behind me, breathing heavily, I broke the silence:

'That probably had to happen, Alex. And I'm very glad it did. No regrets, but I think we both know we're finished, it's over. That felt to me like some sort of . . . sorry, but I can't think of a better word right now . . . closure?'

Behind me, Alex remained silent but for his breathing,

heavy and laboured. After the storm came the calm, albeit a kind of dead calm.

'Yeah. I knew I couldn't ever be good enough for you. But I needed to check.'

I rolled over.

'Stop it, Alex.'

'I'm serious. Quite apart from all the obvious things, like being unemployed and cheating on the mother of my children, I just don't have what you need or deserve.'

'That's bollocks for starters. You don't know what I need or deserve. And I don't think I do.'

'So, how is your rugby player?'

I wasn't fazed by this. I knew Guy had told Alex I was seeing somebody.

'He's good. It's very early days. We have a laugh. I have no idea where it's going, if anywhere.'

'Lucky bastard.'

There was no need to reply, not verbally anyway. The second time we had sex, we made love. Tender, slow and infinitely generous to each other – and that seemed very important. When I came, it was with the kind of orgasm I'd only ever read about ... exquisite waves rolling, all of that ... I lost myself in it, became submerged.

Afterwards, it was Alex who spoke first.

'You're extraordinary, Pippa. You are an extraordinarily wonderful and beautiful woman. And the fact that I can make you feel the way you clearly just felt ...' He paused, slightly self-consciously. 'Maybe that's enough of a memory to hold on to.' And then he turned away from me, but not before I saw his tears. We fell into a fitful sleep, eventually, and when I woke in the morning (late for me, 8.40 a.m.) Alex had gone. As I knew – had, I suppose, even hoped – that he would've.

I lay in bed until ten. Unheard of for me but necessary. Alex's smell – two parts grape and grain, to one part sex – clung to my pillow and I drank it in, re-ran the night before the morning after in my head. I felt OK.

Downstairs, I made coffee and mopped up a puddle of spilt Merlot – when had that happened? – and then went slowly back upstairs to what I grandly referred to as 'the study' (perhaps one I day I'd actually study something in it) and logged on to the computer. Just a handful of emails, most of them spam or from shopping websites, but also one that intrigued me, from Ruth Abbott.

Hello Pippa.

I hope you don't mind me emailing you out of the blue like this – and I hope you had a lovely restful Christmas at your spa. I tried very hard not to be consumed by jealousy but I did have a twinge or two on Boxing Day when we sat down to the leftovers ... plus a lovely lemon drizzle cake. I really hope your nan would have approved!

Anyway, the reason for this email is that I have been thinking about you a lot in the last couple of weeks, because

when you turned up at our door it seemed somehow fateful
... I'll explain!

I came close to telling you when you were here but it
seemed a bit presumptuous and I didn't want to put you
on the spot or make you feel awkward – anyway the fact
is that me and my husband, Tom, were already planning
to put the house on the market in the New Year. I'm actually ten weeks pregnant, so it's not official, but – all being
well – it will be soon ... And though we love this house,
with two kids we really want a bigger garden – big enough
for rabbit hutches and trampolines! – and easier parking
... So we're actually looking near Tom's folks, in Bexhill.

So anyway, the house is going on the market next week
with Stopp & Stiff (aka Stop 'n' Sniff!) – an old mate of
mine from school works there. But before it does, I wanted
to give you the heads-up, just in case you – or somebody
you know – was remotely interested. It just seemed wrong
to sell your nan's old house without you knowing.

There's no need to reply to this, of course. I really just
wanted you to know. But if by any remote chance you WERE
interested, it's going on at £285K. We did the usual thing of
having three valuations and that was the second-highest ...
Anyway, as I say, I hope you had a lovely holiday – and
have a very happy 2010!

Love,

Ruth and Zoe (and Tom, in absentia) X

I glanced up at the pin board over my desk where Ruth's business card was tacked next to last year's Mother's Day card from Hal and I picked up the landline and dialled the mobile number. It was answered after three rings.

'Hi, Ruth? It's Pippa. I just got your email . . .'

'Blimey, that's quick! How are you?'

'Very good, thanks, and all the more so after hearing from you. Look, I'll cut to the chase because I'm feeling in that kind of mood, frankly. Why don't you save yourself the agent's fees and let me buy your house, for cash, at the asking price? No chains, no fuss. I'm sort of OK for money. I think agents describe it as being "in a strong position".'

'Are you serious? I don't know what to say. I just sent the email on a whim, really. Because you never know, do you?'

'You never do, no. Look, I promise I won't mess you around. I'm good for the money and I'm not planning on moving to Random. Not yet, anyway. For the moment it's just an investment, but who knows – I may yet end up down your way.'

It's amazing how fast a sale can progress when there's nothing to impede it. After a few more phone chats with Ruth, and Tom, we exchanged and were due to complete in the middle of February, which happily coincided with Hal's half-term.

I was fifteen minutes early to pick Hal up from

Paddington Station on Saturday morning, and when he finally emerged – last – from his train, I almost missed him. He seemed to have grown about three inches, his shoulders were broader and his hair had been cut in a kind of diluted schoolboy's version of a Hoxton fin. He looked ... handsome, *grown up*. It was hard to believe he was still only thirteen.

'Hey,' he said in a flat teenage monotone, guitar case slung over his shoulder. Way too cool for school – but thank God his voice hadn't yet broken.

'Hey yourself,' I said, resisting the urge to smother him in a Mummy-hug – or indeed, to high-five him in an equally tragic act of parental un-coolness. 'So what do you fancy doing? I've cleared the decks. I'm all yours.'

A hint of ... what was that expression? Embarrassment? ... flitted across his features, which he swiftly rearranged.

'Awesome. But I just got a text from Dom ...' he tailed off. I hadn't been prepared for this. Six weeks without my son and now that he was here I could tell he was about to vanish. And I only had him until Tuesday evening, when David would get his own parental fix for the next four days.

'OK, whatever, that's fine.' I tried to sound as though it really was. 'Let's grab a bit of lunch and you can get me up to speed with stuff and then you can go over to Dom's, or he can come to ours?'

'I think I've gotta go to his ...' Hal shrugged his guitar-case.

'OK, so the band members have put aside their musical differences?'

'Yeah. Zak got the sack. *Za-ak got the sa-ack.*' Suddenly Hal was very much thirteen.

'So why was that?'

'Zak got the sack cos he's a twat.'

'That's nearly a rhyme. Although "twat" is not a good word.'

'Really? It means idiot.'

'It doesn't, actually. It means ... well, it's just one of those words we should probably avoid.'

'What, like "wanker"?'

'Actually, you know what? I think I'd marginally prefer it if you called Zak a wanker instead of a twat.'

'OK, sure, whatever.'

I desperately wanted to kiss him. Instead, later, after the compulsory pizza, Hal disappeared to Dom's, shortly before Richard turned up on my doorstep. This was becoming a part of our pleasantly predictable routine. Unless Richard was doing an after-dinner speaking gig we'd usually spend Friday evenings together then go our separate ways to attend to our own domestic trivia for most of Saturday, before reconnecting in the early evening and spending the rest of the weekend together, though never Sunday nights. It was all very easy, undramatic and in complete contrast to any of my dealings with Alex.

With whom I'd had a couple of brief exchanges since early January. For example, I'd thought it best to flag up the fact that I was buying Nana's house. I hated the idea of being in Random and bumping, randomly, into Alex, or indeed Susie, and having them think – either together or separately – that I was some sort of psycho-stalker. If anything, I had more of a claim on Random-on-Sea than they did, though I could see how it might look. Anyway, I got a pithy one-line response to this news: *Small world – wouldn't want to paint it. Be happy.*

Hard to tell if this was as cheery as it appeared – I hoped so – or perhaps it was sardonic, or bitter? However, my days of over-analyzing Alex's texts were behind me. It wasn't as though I didn't care about him anymore – I did, very much; Alex had re-ignited something inside me and helped me reconnect with the kind of emotions from which I'd cut myself off for so long, albeit without ever realizing I was doing it. But, at the same time we were no good for each other. I didn't like the person I became around him – the phone-stealing, trophy-hoarding obsessive, a woman who slept with other people's partners, somebody who seemed to be out of control with her emotions. That stuff was exciting but it wasn't 'real'. I really wanted 'real' – and as far as I could tell the way to find it and keep it and then actually treasure it was to recognize that while colliding with Alex had opened a gate to a potential 'different kind of life' he was definitely not – and never could be – waiting for me at the end of the path. Now, Richard, on the other hand . . .

'Where's Hal?' said Richard. 'I thought you were getting him back this morning?'

'I was. I did. He's gone already.' I shrugged. 'Teenage boys; they're not exactly charms on their mum's bracelets, are they?'

'Which of course means you've done a brilliant job.'

'Do you think? I don't know. I suppose it's just a succession of "goodbyes" from here on in.'

'We males have stuff to do: continents to conquer, wars to fight, girls to . . . well, now we have the house to ourselves for a bit, come here . . .'

The next day, I had both Hal and Richard on my turf. An embarrassment of males, which, come to think of it, could very well be the collective noun. Neither had spent an entire day with the other, though they were off to an easy start, talking tries and tackles and whatever else constitutes a discussion about rugby (I may have watched a few matches in my time but the finer points of the game – and all team sports, really, being a tennis fan – still eluded me). I was intrigued as to how our time together would pan out, especially as I had A Plan, of which Richard had already been primed.

'OK, Hal – and Richard – how do you fancy a trip to the seaside? I know it's February, but I thought you might want to see a house I've just bought, Hal? And not just any house but a part of your heritage. It used to belong to your great-grandmother.'

Hal glanced up from his poached egg. 'Cool. Where is it?'

'Random-on-Sea. Down from London and left a bit, right at the end of East Sussex, before you hit Kent. I spent a lot of time there as a kid, before Nan died in 1977.'

'Elvis died in 1977.'

'Er, yes, he did. Nan died after Elvis, but she was older.'

'Yeah, Elvis was only forty-two. He died on August sixteenth. Which happened to be my eleventh birthday,' said Richard. I hadn't known that.

'Cool,' repeated Hal. 'Not the dying on your birthday bit, though. When are we going? Are we moving there?'

'No, we're not moving there! I'm just kind of keeping it for a rainy day. And we should go now. Although it's Sunday the previous owners very kindly agreed to meet us at the house with the keys at midday – and it usually takes a couple of hours, so let's get cracking.'

I had assumed Hal would spend most of the journey incommunicado, hooked up to his iPod Touch; I had assumed wrong. Hal's new school already seemed to have assisted him in becoming the kind of teenager who was happy to make conversation with adults for periods in excess of, say, five minutes, rather than retreating into monosyllables, though I suspect Richard's presence may have contributed to that. It also occurred to me that since I'd split with David, Hal had never spent much time with me and any adult male who wasn't his dad. He was making up for it now, though, and I loved how well he and Richard were getting on and how Richard was so easy with Hal, treating him mostly like a slightly shorter equal.

We drove past the sign that said 'Welcome to Random-on-Sea!' – somebody had spray-painted a sarcastic 'You're' just above it, though I was pleased they'd punctuated correctly – and on through the 'burbs, down the hill, past the park and the shopping centre, after which we hit the seafront. When I turned left for the Old Town, Hal had been silent for about ten minutes.

'What do you think, Hal?'

'Weird place. Kind of sad.'

He wasn't wrong. At midday on a chilly, overcast February Sunday, Random was not at its perkiest. The tide was high and as the waves slapped against the groynes, a silty grey spume spilt on to the road. Very few people were on the streets, just a couple of hardy joggers and heads-down families swaddled in layers, carrying just-in-case umbrellas.

'I know what you mean. But if you can find a way to appreciate it like this, believe me, you'll be completely charmed by the place in July. What about you, Richard?'

'Put it like this, Pippa: the only way is up.'

'Look, I know it's not exactly Santa Monica but give it a chance.'

We parked easily on the Old Town seafront, opposite the shut-for-the-season dodgems and ghost train, although Slots of Fun was still open, plying its tacky trade.

'We'll have to walk from here because the parking's a bit iffy. It's not far.' A few metres inland and the atmosphere changed. Even on such an unprepossessing day, the Old Town looked warm – well, warmer – and welcoming.

'I feel a pub lunch coming on,' said Richard.

'Sick,' said Hal.

'Hopefully not *too* sick,' I said.

Off the High Street we turned left and right and right again. There were lights on inside Nana's house. I knocked and the door opened to reveal Ruth Abbott, Zoe clamped to her thigh, and behind her a tall, pleasantly smiling man I assumed must be Tom. Inside we made the introductions.

'Richard,' said Richard, reaching a hand out to Tom.

'Yeah, I know! Good to meet you. If I'd anticipated meeting a sporting hero I would've brought a ball along for you to sign. I'm involved with a local charity auction for the NSPCC.'

I tended to forget that, to many people – my son included – Richard was a bit of a 'ledge'.

'I suspect I may have a spare ball kicking around somewhere, though rather than throwing it back to you I'll have to rely on the Royal Mail.'

'That's very kind, Richard. Much appreciated.'

'I know you're not moving in,' said Ruth, 'but I still wanted the place to feel homely so I forced Tom to light a fire. And there's a bottle of something in the fridge.' She reached out and touched my arm. 'Pippa, I can't tell you how happy we are that you've got this house and, whatever you decide to do with it, it's great to know it will be loved, even from a distance. Your nana would approve.'

'She would. And it will. What do you think of the house, Hal?'

'It's like a doll's house but I still like it. It's cool.'

'From a man with a haircut as great as yours there is probably no higher praise,' said Tom, 'and look, obviously I don't know what your plans are and we don't want to intrude, but why don't you spend a bit of time here and then join us for a pub lunch round the corner, at the Dragon?'

'This man is speaking my language. But first, Pip, we really must do some of that traditional knocking-on-ye-olde-walls and opening-of-ye-cupboards.'

Richard was great at this. I could've hugged him.

'Yeah, we'll just poke around for a bit, if that's OK. And then we'll pop down the pub and ask for a ten grand refund.'

While Ruth and Tom laughed, Hal looked mortified. 'Mum!'

'It's a joke. Come upstairs and see Nana's old room. And

I'll show you where me and Beth always used to sleep, in the attic.'

'Auntie Beth? You haven't mentioned Auntie Beth for years, Mum.'

Out of the mouths of teenagers. Hal was right. I hadn't.

'OK, that's true. And I don't know why I haven't because I should've. Come on.'

'You go upstairs with your mum. I'm going downstairs to knock on some walls and check out the fridge . . .' said Richard, correctly intuiting that this was a mother and son moment. Here was the thing: even after just six weeks together Richard didn't make my solar plexus churn like a cement mixer and my head fill with helium every time I saw him, but nonetheless, every day we spent together I realized he was beginning to break down my defences and patch up my heart.

Which was just as well, because on a Saturday morning just four weeks later, shortly after Richard had left for the day, I found myself on my knees in the bathroom and retching into the loo. Again, and again.

After which I lay flat on my back on the chilly lime-stone and stared at the ceiling for what may have been half an hour – or possibly five minutes. It was hard to say. Eventually, I went downstairs to the kitchen and made a piece of dry toast and boiled a mug of water with a slice of lemon and went back upstairs to bed and reacquainted myself with the ceiling.

For quite a while I had assumed I was a grown-up simply on the basis of being in my forties. Like an idiot I thought it just came with the territory, but clearly this was not the case – patently I was still a teenager trapped in the body of a middle-aged woman.

Contraception hadn't really been a part of my life for a long time. Initially it was because I didn't need it. After Hal had been born, David and I were both keen to get a football team under way, but, despite our best efforts, nothing had come of it. By the time I had finally started visiting a fertility specialist in Wimpole Street, when Hal was four, and discussing IVF with an increasingly distant David, he had – although I didn't yet know it – already moved on to a younger, presumably more fertile model. Shortly after Hal's eighth birthday, in 2004, he'd gone. At the time I had assumed this was because I couldn't give him what I thought he wanted – more babies – but later I realized this wasn't the case. Turned out my obsession with having more babies far outweighed his desire to have them. There had, for example, been one terrible dinner party when Hal was six, during which our hostess – Wendy, a good friend, though also an ex of David's from uni – had announced that she was twelve weeks pregnant while proudly patting her midriff as she divided a *tarte au citron*.

Despite my having already guessed – Wendy hadn't had a drink all evening and her face had that wonderful natural Botox look some women get in early pregnancy – my involuntary, hormonal response, tears, and clearly not of joy, shocked even me. David was solicitous in our host's company. 'I think Pip was hoping to beat you to it! But obviously that's wonderful news! Congratulations!' However, once we were out of the door (within fifteen minutes, as it happened) he didn't bother disguising his anger:

'For *chrissakes*, Pip, the world is heaving with pregnant women. You've been one yourself, for fuck's sake! It's not like we don't already have a perfectly wonderful child. Get a bloody grip.'

It had, needless to say, been downhill from there and David was gone within a year. While that same year – 2004 – went on to end far worse than it had begun. After all of which, I now realized, I'd shut myself down, and not only to the possibility of more children, obviously, but also to the possibility of ever being in the kind of place where more children might even be contemplated, much less conceived.

So here I was at forty-three and long-since resigned to the situation . . . except the situation I had taken for granted for so long was clearly no longer the situation, and I was slightly stunned by how very unprepared for this situation I appeared to be. Though I figured I'd probably better do a test. After which I would cross the bridge that was the paternity issue – a bridge which seemed infinitely long, a Golden Gate to-the-power-of, and not entirely stable.

I must say that being forty-three and buying a pregnancy testing kit in my local Boots on a Saturday morning wasn't helped by the girl at the till – who looked about seventeen but might have been twenty-one – being pregnant herself.

'Oh that's the one I used. Hang on, there's a two-for-one on those.'

'Thanks,' I muttered. 'And sorry,' I said to the queue of six people behind me. 'For my daughter,' I added, pointlessly.

Back in the twentieth century, when I had been pregnant with Hal, you could only do an accurate test with the first pee of the day. No longer. These days it seems you can test within minutes of a potential conception, at any time of the day or night – at which point a Poppins-ish maternity nurse will undoubtedly magically manifest on your doorstep, *tut-tutting* about soft cheese consumption and offering maternity yoga options.

But I wasn't in a rush to have the answer to the question posed by the 'Ferti-kit', mostly because I was pretty sure I knew what the answer would be. Now I came to think of it, I hadn't had my period since Christmas. How I hadn't noticed this was beyond me – I'd been able to set my watch by my cycle since I was twelve – but then perhaps I had noticed, deep down, and chosen to ignore it? Whether the outcome was good news or bad news, as yet I had no idea because there are some intellectual processes and responses that are entirely bypassed by biology. It would be whatever it was.

So forty minutes later, after much prevarication – and it was suddenly a matter of urgency that the dishwasher be unloaded and re-loaded and a (very small) pile of washing be addressed – I had the answer I knew I would get: positive. Pregnant. At forty-three. And though the statistical evidence pointed to Richard being the father, I knew he wasn't.

Richard was a stepfather – his ex-wife Sarah's children (a twenty-two-year-old son, Danny, was currently bartending in Brisbane and a twenty-year-old daughter, Siobhan, was in her final year at Bristol. Needless to say I'd not met either of them) were the product of Sarah's brief first marriage. One evening in late January, when Richard and I were still feeling our way into a relationship, sharing our complex emotional CVs over spag bol and far too much wine, Richard had told me he couldn't have kids. It had never been a huge issue, apparently, because after he had split up with his long-term girlfriend, Liz, he had met Sarah when her children were still small and had loved being a stepdad. When he and Sarah's efforts to conceive had failed, they had done some tests and discovered that his sperm count was almost comically low.

'Mostly it was just a huge blow to my ego. I was still playing rugby at the highest level and apparently oozing testosterone on a daily basis, but I'd had an inkling that something wasn't right for a while, to be honest. I'd been in a relationship for five years before I met Sarah and during that time we had become careless about contraception, though there had never been even the hint of a scare. Of course it could have been Liz's problem, but I always felt deep down that it wasn't. We never discussed it – we were young and it wasn't yet an issue – but I sort of knew.' Richard shrugged. 'Of course nowadays they'd probably be able to do something about it, but when I met Sarah she was very much out of baby-ville, though still in the small-children zone. Frankly, I wasn't disappointed being spared the broken nights and dirty nappies. And though I went from nought to sixty in what felt like seconds as a stepdad, I think I got most of the good bits of parenting and was spared some of the grief. I've always loved them as if they were my own. They're cracking kids. You'd love them, too.'

'I'm sure I would. Now, how do you feel about a second bottle?'

Recalling this, I felt an involuntary wave of guilt. Poor foetus – it was probably pickled. And I was now an 'elderly gravida', with all the additional complexities that implied. I could already see the disapproving expression on my imaginary Poppins-ish maternity nurse's face. And then, of course, there was the fact that Alex was obviously the foetus's father.

That afternoon I did something I very rarely do in the

daytime: went back to bed. I tried reading and sleeping to distract myself but mostly I just lay there, ignoring the 'ding' of texts arriving on my phone. There were cracks on the bedroom ceiling that not only had I never noticed before but which, after an hour or two, I had got to know infinitely better than the back of my hand. Which, to be honest, I had never been entirely convinced I would be able to identify in a Back-of-the-Hands line-up.

It was dusk when I finally heaved myself out of bed, showered, dressed and checked my phone. Four texts:

Lisa: *Hey. Fancy lunch tomorrow? X*

David: *Just to confirm I'll be picking up Hal and then we'll get the Heathrow Express straight from Paddington on Good Friday?*

Richard: *Still OK for tonight? X*

Richard again: *Heeeeelllllooooo. Anybody there?! X*

Straightforward stuff: Two *yeses* and one white lie of a *Sorry! Phone was recharging . . . See you 7ish? X*

By the time Richard arrived, I thought I was doing an incredibly good impression of somebody carrying minimal emotional baggage, much less a baby. But I hadn't credited Richard with quite so much 'feminine' intuition.

'You OK? You look . . . well you look beautiful, as ever, but tired. How was your day?'

'It was . . . a day. But Jesus, Richard, you're good. I thought I'd be able to wing it for a few hours at least, but apparently not. I think we need to talk.'

'Yup, that's the dread phrase no man wants to hear. So dump me – but please wait until you've had a glass or two of this because it's magnificent.'

And, today of all days, Richard proffered a bottle of Bordeaux with a distinctive label that read . . .

'Château Margaux? Blimey Richard, it's only a Monday-night lasagne. I didn't even know they had a lottery draw on Sunday nights.'

'Well, as far as I know they don't but I had a great piece of news about work today and it's worth celebrating, though clearly not if you're planning on dumping me.'

'I'm not. But . . .' By now we were downstairs and Richard was rifling through a drawer in search of a corkscrew.

'But what?'

'I can't drink it. Well, I can. I can easily drink it, but I shouldn't.'

Richard stopped.

'You're pregnant?'

I bit my lip and looked him in the eye. 'I am that thing. I had no idea, obviously, until today. And I'm a bit all over the place, for all the obvious reasons – and some less obvious ones too. And I'm so sorry, Richard. I am so fucking sorry.'

'OK, enough with the sorries. How far along are you?'

'Um, I think about ten or eleven weeks, maybe.'

'And the father? Does he know?'

'He doesn't know. Look, it was—'

'Stop. Just let me pour this glass. You could have a sip?'

'Maybe I could have a sip, yes.'

Richard poured a large glass for himself and an inch for me. Then he said: 'Sit down.'

'It's fine. I'm not feeling—'

'No, no that's not what I meant. I didn't mean "sit down because you're pregnant", just sit down because maybe that's the best way to have a proper conversation.'

'OK. So . . .'

'Look, before you start trying to explain, you don't need to. You and I met on December the thirty-first and whatever was going on in your life at that point is of no consequence. For what it's worth, I was sort of seeing someone then too. It was nearly over but not quite. In fact it only properly finished at the end of January because I wanted to be with you. I didn't feel the need to spell that out and there is no need for you to, either: we're grown-ups, shit happens. As far as I'm concerned, I'm only worried about being dumped. But it would be a hard woman who dumped a man who turns up on a Monday night with a bottle of . . . this . . . to accompany the lasagne. Admittedly this wasn't a conversation I'd prepared for, but now we're having it . . . look, Pippa, if you still want me in your life, I still want to be in it. But if you don't, I won't be. If you need to be with the father . . .'

'I don't need to be with the father. We're very finished. Not that we'd ever really begun.'

362

I paused, leaned forward and took Richard's hand. 'You know, I don't make a habit of sleeping with other women's husbands, partners, whatever. That's not who I am. But in this case I did. And it's now very over. And though I am probably incredibly selfish because I suddenly really want this baby, it is also very much *my* baby, I think. And I'm even more selfish than that because I want you in my life too, Richard. All the more so now because you are without any shadow the most decent and mature man I have ever met.'

'"Decent and mature" – it doesn't exactly make your heart sing, does it?'

'Stop it. You know what I mean. You are those things and more besides and if I lost you now I would feel ... actually I don't even want to articulate it. Look, I know I can bring up this baby by myself if I have to, but if you thought you were even remotely up for it, I'd much rather do it with you, if you could bear to? There may be sleepless nights and nappies, though obviously you're excused all that.'

'But maybe I don't want to be excused all that?' And Richard got up and walked round the table and squatted beside me and said, 'Look, I think I'm a pretty good dad, even to other men's children.'

'I didn't think they made them like you anymore.'

'Broke the mould, baby, broke the mould ...'

I giggled. And then, after kissing me very gently on

the forehead, Richard pushed forward the glass of Margaux.

'Given the amount we've put away over the last few weeks I suspect another sip will be fine. But absolutely no more after that. And if you think this is my caring-sharing "feminine" side asserting itself, you're wrong. It's my greedy selfish masculine side. I'm very happy to finish the bottle by myself.'

'I never thought that the evening would go this way, Richard. I expected slammed doors and the wrong sort of tears.' I wiped my eyes.

'And do you know why that is?'

'No, why?'

'Because, despite evidence to the contrary, I think your glass has always been half empty.'

I was dreading Guy and Lisa's wedding, for a number of reasons. Not least because I was five-and-a-half-months pregnant and feeling every minute of my forty-three years. There's a very good reason why you're meant to pop 'em out in your twenties, isn't there, Mum? I'd thought I was a bit past it with Hal, but that had been nothing compared to this. I felt like a Victorian consumptive – only nowhere near as thin, obviously.

Most of my afternoons were spent on the sofa, guiltily dozing, or watching *Loose Women* and repeats of old property programmes in which couples apparently selected for their inability to express an opinion were cajoled by bouncy presenters into buying off-plan holiday villas in those bits of Spain that everybody else had ignored. It was all very pre-recession, the idea that owning any old compromise of a house, anywhere, was better than not owning one at all.

Thus my days rolled into one another: eating, sleeping, watching bad telly and wandering very slowly to the shops to buy pints of my recently discovered pregnancy food-fetish, mango sorbet. And so much for my assertion that I could've handled this on my own just fine; without Richard, who had proved himself to be the Mount Rushmore of emotional rocks, I could very easily have turned into one of those sad people who live alone in rooms piled high with newspapers and are eventually consumed by their own cats. Not that I had a cat, though it was only a matter of time.

So Richard kept me just the right side of feral. And he was brilliant with Hal, just as Hal was brilliant with him. I'd told Hal about the baby during the Easter holidays, around the time my stomach stopped looking merely bloated and developed the firm tell-tale curvature that indicates that whatever lies within probably isn't wind.

I'd been pretty nervous about telling Hal. Having only recently acquired his first half-sibling there was plenty of potential for a properly nose-out-of-joint reaction. But I'd underestimated my son – something I'd have to start learning not to do – because he was nothing short of great. I picked my moment, which was over Hal's favourite Sloppy Giuseppe pizza.

'So, look, ah, Hal, here's a thing. I seem to be having a baby.'

'Cool. I thought you were looking a bit ... er ... big?'

'Thanks. But is it really cool? Or does it make you want to go upstairs, plug in your guitar, start playing minor chords and end up with a song called "My Mum Sucks"?'

Hal laughed. 'No. I mean, yes – I might go upstairs and plug in the guitar, but you never know, the song might be called "My Brother Rocks". When are you having him?'

'Wooooaaah, hang on! He might be a Her.'

'I'm pretty sure he's not a Her. I knew Kiki was a Her but I think this is a He.'

'OK, well if you want to place a bet I will happily relieve you of some of your birthday money. In the meantime, he or she is due in the early autumn.'

'Cool. Maybe he could arrive before I go back to school?'

'Maybe he – or she – could, but it doesn't tend to work like that. They just come when they come.'

'Whatever. And Richard is the dad?'

Just a tiny pause while I braced myself for a white lie that, I figured, could never hurt anybody. 'Yeah, Richard's the dad.'

'Cool. I like Richard.'

'Well, I'm cool that everything appears to be cool. But if you have any questions?'

'Yeah, can I go paintballing tomorrow with Dom?'

'That's not quite what I meant but, yes, why not?'

'OK. And now I'm going upstairs to write a song called "The Boy with No Name". He hasn't got a name yet, has he?'

'No, neither She nor He has a name yet. You want to think of some?'

'I already did. I'll think of some more and make a list.'

'That would be cool. That would be very cool, Hal. And Hal?'

'Yeah?'

'I love you more than you will ever know.'

'Yeah. Love you too. Thanks for the pizza. You can go and lie down now.'

So Hal was suddenly onside, Richard was my rock, David had been exceptionally pleasant about everything ('That's great news, old girl. Take it easy, you deserve it'). Meanwhile, Lisa and Guy were particularly delighted. So all was fine, but for a couple of niggling things. The first of which was going to a wedding at which, obviously, I would see Alex. And more to the point, Alex would see me and my bump and my boyfriend. A couple of weeks before the wedding, I'd had lunch with Lisa, at St Germain. The many contrasts to our lunch there the previous summer were not lost on either of us.

Somewhere between my second and third course (I was eating like a Suffolk Punch while Lisa, apparently half a dress-size off her wedding day target, was not), I casually raised the subject that dared not speak its name.

'So, I guess Alex knows about . . .' I patted my stomach.

'Yeah, I haven't seen him for ages, but Guy has. So . . . that's cool isn't it?'

'That's cool,' I said breezily, 'we're all in a different place now.'

'I figured. And he's got a lot going on anyway. So, any names yet?'

'Well, Hal's convinced it's a boy and he's very sweetly come up with a list. But what do you think of Esme? And Fraser?'

And so we whiled away most of the rest of the meal in convivial, girly chat about baby names and wedding trivia, and that was good.

On the morning of the wedding, alongside the kicks, I had butterflies in my stomach.

'Eat something that doesn't contain mango?' suggested Richard.

'No, I'm fine.' And I was fine until I got an irrational craving for an Egg McMuffin en route to Kenwood and ate it in the car while attempting not to get yolk-drips on my dress. Hal made charming gagging noises from the backseat.

'That's so gross, Mum.'

'Tell me about it. I am gross. The sooner this baby is out of here the better, frankly.'

'Not too soon,' said Richard.

'When he's ready, I guess. But I'm ready when he is.'

'Or she?' said Hal.

The wedding was a delight. I was used to Lisa's beauty – I'd been studying its evolution for years – but nothing had prepared me for the extreme and distracting beauty of Lisa as a bride. Nobody could take their eyes off her, least of all her husband. I had never seen Guy look quite as at-ease with himself as he did that day. It was the blueprint for weddings: perfect weather, perfect ceremony, perfect everything, really. And then, bolstered by Richard and Hal, I was even ready for Alex and Susie. Except it turned out there was no Susie, just Alex, resplendent in his best man rig with his (very beautiful, and very much a Fox) daughter, Lula. Where was Susie?

After the reception, before we sat down for lunch – and long before I spoke to Alex, who had given me a polite nod of acknowledgement when we'd arrived at the church – I was talking to Guy and Alex's brother, Will. I'd only met Will a couple of times and we'd never really talked before, but he exuded warmth and a grown-up in-charge-ness, so when we fell into an easy conversation over the canapés while Richard was backslapping with Guy, I chanced my arm.

'I would have expected to see Alex's wife and his son here too, today.'

'As did we all. Not quiet on the domestic front, I believe. I haven't had a proper chat with Alex about it, but apparently they all parted company in a service station near Tunbridge Wells.'

'Blue Boys.'

'Sorry?'

'No, I'm sorry. It's the name of the service station. I know the A21 quite well and it was probably there. Forgive my pregnancy-brain.'

'Forgiven! It's a shame. The only blot on an otherwise beautiful landscape – but Alex seems to be bearing up. And doesn't Lisa look stunning?'

'Never more beautiful.'

And so we moved on.

It was early evening when we finally spoke, long after lunch and the speeches (very funny from Alex – I felt a sort of unfocused, irrelevant pride) and just as the dancing was getting underway. I was standing at the edge of the dance floor, feeling like a reluctant Weeble while resisting Richard's attempts to get me to do some sort of elephantine shuffle, when Alex arrived in front of us, all smiles.

'Belated congratulations, Pippa.' He leaned in and, awkwardly navigating the bump, kissed me on both cheeks. Then he turned to Richard. 'And to you too, Richard.

Eighty-six caps for England may just fade into insignificance next to this.'

Stupidly, I hadn't really thought about the fact that Alex would know who Richard was, though a lot of men seemed to. And Guy was a sports agent. Pregnancy seemed to be making me exceptionally dim; obviously Alex and Richard could have met countless times. They certainly seemed very easy with each other.

'Thanks, Alex. Yeah, I'll have my work cut out, but whatever they say it can't be as tough as scoring a try against the All Blacks.'

'Of course it's a new one for you, isn't it? Danny and Siobhan are Sarah's, aren't they? They must have been very young when you met?'

'Yeah, three and eighteen months. Too young to remember their dad, sadly, though in some respects it probably made my job easier. Anyway, I'm looking forward to having a crack at the nappy-stuff this time around.'

'You're a braver man than me. I tried to avoid it . . .' At which entirely unexpected point Alex patted my stomach, very gently. Beside me, I sensed Richard tense. 'So you and Sarah never fancied having kids of your own?'

I may have been wrong, but it felt as though Richard left it just a heartbeat too long before he answered, though when he did he rose brilliantly to the challenge.

'No. We had our hands pretty full back then, so I had the snip.' Another pause. Alex and Richard were looking right into each other's eyes and there passed between them a frisson of something I didn't recognize but that was very distinctly male, and from which I was therefore entirely excluded. 'And by the time we changed our minds and I had the vasectomy reversed, it turned out that moment had passed.'

As, thank God, did this one.

'Well anyway, this is brilliant, mate. Best of luck – and to you too, Pippa. You look . . . you look *wonderful*.'

'And wonderfully big. But thank you, Alex.'

'Big and beautiful. Like a galleon in full sail. So glad you could come. Have a lovely evening.' And then he was gone.

I glanced at Richard. His expression was hard to read.

'Come outside for a minute? Fresh air?' he said, taking my hand and squeezing it.

'Suits me. I'm not really in either the mood or the shape for dancing.'

Outside and in silence, Richard led me quite far away from the building, towards a bench overlooking the park.

'Here OK?'

'Fine by me.'

We sat. I waited for Richard to speak.

'Look, Pip, I'm only going to ask this once and then we can either talk about it or not, depending on whether you want to. Is Alex the baby's father?'

I really didn't want to have this conversation now. Didn't

want to have it ever, to be honest. But here it was – and at just the same time as the baby shuffled around, adjusting himself beneath my ribcage.

'Was it that obvious? Yes, Alex is the father. But only . . . technically. It's over.'

'I can see that. But it's still quite close to home, isn't it? Guy is one of my closest friends.' This conversation could have scared me, I suppose, but because Richard's tone wasn't angry – though possibly confused – it didn't. It was a lot for him to process, I guess.

'I know. I don't think I'd thought it through. I didn't know you knew each other, though of course it now seems obvious that you would. I'm sorry. But I can't reiterate strongly enough how very over it all is. We've had no contact since . . . since then. Because that's when it ended.'

'I believe you. I just needed to know because when he touched you it was . . . there was a palpable sense of owner-ship. And then I thought he knew.'

'He may have, but I don't think so. He thinks you and I have been seeing each other for longer than we have. Even if he suspected the baby could be his, I guess he believes it's statistically improbable. Or even if he doesn't, maybe he just doesn't care. To be honest, I don't need to know and I don't want to know.'

Richard sighed. 'Either way, it doesn't matter. That you've been honest with me is what really matters. Subject closed. Dance or ice-cream?'

I squeezed his hand and he squeezed mine back.

'Definitely ice-cream. And then maybe we could go home?'

'Yeah, that's a plan. Let's do that.'

As we walked back up to the house in the dusk we heard the sound of a man a few metres away, pacing the gravel and talking into his phone. Alex. I quickened my pace and gently tugged Richard's hand. But even though we were moving away from Alex, we could still hear a snippet of his conversation.

'... despite everything. And we'll be back sometime tomorrow, but I don't know exactly when because we're in no hurry ...'

His tone was both aggressive and defensive, underscored by a drink or two. It was obviously Susie on the receiving end and I felt an unexpected surge of empathy. But, at the same time, this really didn't feel like my problem anymore. It all felt a long, long way away, and moving even further.

After saying our goodbyes and as we walked to the car with a strangely reluctant Hal in tow, I spotted another lone male figure, this one enjoying a cigar on the terrace. It was Nigel Fox.

'Goodbye, Mr Fox. It was such a beautiful wedding.'

'Wasn't it just? Now if I could get Isobel married off, I'd die happy. You take care of that bump, young lady ...'

We all laughed. It was just a throwaway remark. However

a fortnight later, when I learned what had happened to
Nigel Fox, I cried. It must've been the hormones because
I'd never even met him before. Bizarrely, it was only later
that I realized this deceased virtual stranger had also been
my baby's grandfather. And, as Richard's parents were both
dead, the baby would now never have a grandfather, biolog-
ical or otherwise. Maybe it was thinking about this – and
the fragility of families – that forced me to make a few
decisions I may otherwise have delayed. Or maybe it was
just the hormones. Either way, over the next few weeks,
it became clear to me that nesting in pregnancy needn't
just involve climbing precipitous stepladders with feather
dusters to root out hitherto unseen dust and cobwebs, but
that I needed to clean away the metaphorical dust and
cobwebs too.

And that process started immediately after a call from
Alex the day after the wedding. Part of me had assumed
that the sight of me pregnant on the arm of another man
would underscore how over it was between us. But another
part of me was unsurprised when my mobile rang while
I was in the kitchen, obsessively compulsively wiping the
dishwasher smears off wine glasses.

'Alex.'

'Pippa. Look, don't panic. I'm not going to make trouble.
I just wanted to say that you looked properly radiant
yesterday and I am genuinely pleased for you. And
Richard.'

'Thank you. That's very kind and decent of you.'

'Yeah, well, they are not attributes I tend to be credited with very often but I can occasionally step up to the plate.'

'And you did. And I'm grateful. And I know – well, I think I know – that you're having a difficult time, so I'm even more grateful.'

'Don't be grateful for anything.'

'Well I am. I'm grateful for more than you know.'

Why did I say that? There was a pause – a very pregnant pause. Then: 'OK, Pippa. And I'm grateful to you too. And what will be will be. You've taught me a lot.'

'Have I?'

'Yes. More than you know.'

I exhaled silently. 'OK, well that's good, I guess. We seem to be all square then?'

'Yes, we are. Best of luck, Pippa – with everything. Looks like you got "a different kind of life" after all.'

'I did. And in many respects that's down to you.'

'Well it's good to know I may have been some kind of help.'

'You were. You are.'

'OK, look, I'm going now.'

'OK. And thanks. And take care, Alex. I mean it.'

'Yeah. You too. Bye.'

And that was it, Mum. I instinctively knew that wherever it was me and Alex were heading, it was in entirely different directions. Maybe I should have felt guilty about that? I don't know. I still don't know. And perhaps it was some sort of residual guilt that made me head straight upstairs to the dressing room and retrieve the box containing Alex's phone from the wardrobe. I still didn't know what to do with it, but I knew it had to go.

Happily the decision was made for me, and far quicker than I'd imagined. Having effectively denied Stop 'n' Sniff their sales percentage when I'd bought Nana's house, I'd decided they should get the rental gig. I'd only been down to see the house twice since Richard, Hal and I had visited. I'd given a set of keys to Paul, a painter and decorator recommended by Ruth, and then accompanied him to the local trading estate while he picked up several litres of matt and eggshell to spruce up the woodwork before I let it out. The next time I'd gone back, a fortnight later, in early June, it was to retrieve the keys, pay Paul and meet up with Ruth's friend Karen, from Stop 'n' Sniff.

'It looks lovely,' said Karen. 'And it's a good time to let, too.'

'Sure, but I'm in no big hurry. Leave it a few weeks, if you don't mind. I might pop down and spend some time in the house myself. And is it OK to let it unfurnished, do you think? Any excuse not to go to IKEA suits me.'

'It's absolutely fine as it is, yes.'

If I'd decided to let the house immediately, things would obviously have turned out differently. But when I finally got the call from Karen in early July, the day after I'd given her the go-ahead to let, and though I gave an involuntary shiver as I listened to her, I also knew that this was absolutely right. Call it Truth and ... well, if not Reconciliation, then Reparation.

'Hi, Pippa,' said Karen. 'Look, I've just shown a lady round the house – we're still here actually; she's in the kitchen and I'm in the bedroom – and she loves it. Newly single mum of two youngsters and definitely not DSS. Lovely woman. But you know what? She works mostly from home – I think she's a writer – and there's a real problem with the mobile signal here. I was wondering, given that Susie's so perfect, whether you'd allow me to move down on the rent a little?'

Susie. A writer and newly single mum of two. Well of course. Who else would it be? I took a deep breath.

'Absolutely. Go right ahead. Whatever figure you decide. Susie sounds like the perfect prospect.'

'She is. You'd really like her. That's great, Pippa. I'll suggest £975, if that's OK?'

'Totally fine by me. It's tough being a newly single parent.'

'Isn't it? Been there myself. Anyway thanks again. I'll be in touch about the contract.'

'And thank you, Karen. One thing though: if you wouldn't mind, I'd prefer it if you didn't mention my name to, er, Susie. Not unless you have to. I'd really appreciate it.'

'No problem. You're the boss.'

As Susie was clearly about to vacate the big house she and Alex had bought, I figured she deserved to move into another house she clearly loved. And that afternoon, I wrote Susie a note, which took nearly two hours and several drafts, but I got there in the end. And then when I'd finished that project, I went straight into the study, fired up the laptop and started writing *this* ...

It started off as a letter to you, Mum, and it took nearly three months, right up to the birth. And over time it evolved from being 'just' a letter – or at least an exorcism disguised as a letter – into something more than that: another tentative step towards my 'different kind of life', albeit not the kind of life I'd imagined. But as you very well know, wherever you are, life rarely pans out the way you expect it to.

PS:

The labour was fast and furious, the maternity unit was busy, an anaesthetist was unavailable, working on a C-section elsewhere ... None of which would have been a problem if it hadn't suddenly all gone wrong.

It took me nearly three months to get around to Googling the words 'shoulder dystocia', which I finally did last week. The first result I read explained that this was 'a very scary, potentially life-threatening complication that can occur during labour and birth'. Which is all anybody who isn't a medical student needs to know. However, in layperson's terms it means the baby has got stuck on the way out.

'Now listen to me. Listen, Pippa ...' said Sophie, the midwife, 'you really need to concentrate now.'

It was a dull, overcast autumnal day and the flat, thin English light could barely force its way through the grimy window on which I was choosing to fixate. Richard had just been asked if he wanted to leave the room. 'Go, darling,' I said. 'Please go. It's not pretty.' So he had.

Around me, the emergency crash team, who had arrived after Sophie had pressed the panic button, operated in an atmosphere of efficiency under duress. Time warped. I had no idea how long this was taking. It felt like hours.

At one point, I found myself detaching from my body, floating up to the ceiling and, bizarrely, looking down at myself while Sophie held my hand and made soothing, if not entirely convincing, responses to my plaintive 'Where's my baby? Is the baby OK?'

I'm pretty sure I wasn't dying. I think this was my shocked and ripped-apart body's way of saying, 'You're better off out of this for a minute or two. Just pop up there and take it easy while I finish the job.' It's an extraordinary sensation but not one I'm in a hurry to repeat.

Then, having finally released the baby from my pelvic

clutches (how did they do that? Rhetorical question. I didn't really want to know), the crash team started work in silence on the other side of the room.

'He's a big beautiful boy. I'm sure he'll be just fine,' said Sophie soothingly. But he still hadn't cried. And then they took him away.

Richard and I sat in silence together. He held my hand very tightly.

'It'll be OK,' he said, focusing on my face while, down there, a nurse stitched for so long she might have been reworking the Bayeux tapestry.

Still no sign of our boy in the flesh, though they brought us a photograph of the justifiably furious-looking ten-pound baby hooked up to all the technology in the Special Care Unit. It was three hours before we saw him and, when we did, Sophie handed him to Richard first.

But I didn't mind because it had all turned out OK in the end, even though the words of the consultant who had got the baby out, and whose face I saw for the first time when he appeared on his rounds at my bedside three days later, will resonate for months, if not years.

'In case you are wondering, you should know that it doesn't get any worse for us than a birth like that. If you ever feel the need to talk to me about it, we can arrange it. Just call my secretary.'

'Thanks so much, Mr . . . ? Um, I'm so sorry, I don't even know your name.'

'And there's no reason why you should. It's Douglas. Douglas Fraser.'

Of course.

As my beautiful Fraser was out of Special Care four days later – and they hadn't had to break his collarbone during delivery – why would I ever want to make a fuss? However, last week I finally called Mr Fraser's secretary and, slightly apologetically, explained that perhaps I might like to have that chat after all, maybe in the New Year? I think I may even have used the word 'closure'.

'Of course,' said the PA, 'that's no problem at all. I'll have a look at Mr Fraser's diary and call you back tomorrow, if that's OK?'

I came off the phone and turned around to retrieve a happily sleeping Fraser from the arms of a woman who understood my need for 'closure' as well as I did. Probably the only woman in the world who did.

'That was totally the right thing to do, Pip. Life's too short,' said my sister, Beth.

'Yeah,' I said. 'Yes, I think it was. I don't want to waste any more time living in the past; I just want to hurry up and embrace whatever it is life is going to throw at us all.'

'Very sensible, but you always were the sensible one. Come on, Pip: let's round up Hal, pick up Simon and Richard from the pub, grab some Tesco flowers, wander up to Highgate cemetery and let Fraser hang out with his grandpa for a bit.'

So that's what we did, Mum. Your family, all of us, together.

All my love always,
Pip xxxxxx
26/12/2010

CHAPTER 12

Alex

Friday 24 December 2010

From: alex@foxmail.co.uk
To: willfox@wings.co.uk

Will. I'm writing this to you from Khao Lak, just north of Phuket. It was one of the worst-hit areas during the tsunami – nearly 4,000 people died here. Not that you'd know it now because the beach is just as serene and beautiful as you'd expect a Thai beach to be. Extraordinary really. The locals say that most of the year life goes on as it ever did, and the main reason tourism has been hit has less to do with the tsunami, much more to do with the economy.

If you know where to look, however, there are a few things that will remind you of what happened here. Just yesterday I visited an orphanage specifically for children who lost their parents during the tsunami. Many of the kids are in the process of finding new homes, but many are not ... You've been close enough to disaster zones that you probably don't need me to tell you how hard it was to keep focused on the job.

I photographed one of the women who works at the orphanage. She told me that after she and her two-year-old daughter were swept off the beach they floated for nearly eight hours, clinging on to a piece of wood from a broken boat. Eventually, they were rescued by fishermen. Her daughter is now nearly ten, but despite still living close to the beach she has never set foot in the water since. Her mother told me that for several years she would scream if she were ever made to have a bath or a shower.

And then there is a graveyard a couple of kilometres away from where I'm sitting now – the Bang Muang Cemetery, where nearly 400 unidentified bodies are buried and the small, numbered, concrete headstones are quite hard to see; weeds now cover most of them. Very sadly, it's quite badly unkempt. Apparently the bodies are buried in metal coffins inside concrete chambers. The idea was to preserve the DNA, but because 90 per cent certainty of identity is needed before a body can be returned to a family, despite once being subject to the world's biggest forensics investigation these are the bodies that, quite literally, didn't measure up. The authorities keep records of their DNA on file in Bangkok, just in case.

Given that both she and Pippa's dad died at Khao Lak, it's not unlikely that this is where Pippa's mother is laid to rest. The first time I visited, I took flowers and left them on a grave. It didn't really seem to matter which one. And I've been back a few times since.

My project is going very well. It's more than just photographs now; it's a proper 'body of work'. I've sent some shots to various magazine and newspaper contacts back home and the feedback has been incredibly encouraging. One of my mates is helping to curate a major exhibition entitled 'After The Event' at the Hayward – portraits of people who have been through extraordinary experiences – and my picture of the woman at the orphanage has been selected. That's incredibly gratifying because there are some very big names involved, but that's not why I came. It's just a journey I had to make.

Obviously the next couple of days will be testing. Though the stoicism of the Thais is unbelievable, they will certainly allow themselves to remember, and mourn, on Boxing Day.

I'm staying here until New Year, then I'm going on to Sri Lanka for more of the same. I'll be meeting Marta in Colombo. Did you ever meet Marta? She worked at Lisa's shop, did a bit of nannying and babysitting for – irony of ironies – both Lisa and Pippa. We had been seeing each other for a few weeks before I came here. It was all very easy and – dare I say it? – fun. Who knows where it will go? I try not to plan ahead too much these days.

But enough about me.

There's so much I want to say but I don't know if I can manage to say it all. I'm sitting on a beach at sunset, nursing a cold beer, so ... But I'll have a bash at it.

I know you've been keeping an eye on Susie. And believe it or *not, that's fine by me. It wasn't fine, of course, not for a long, long time – ten years in fact – but it is now. When Dad died, something shifted and lifted. I no longer felt the need to keep up the pretence of being yet another Alpha Fox. I'd always felt I was trying to compete with you for Dad's affection, even though Mum was always on my team. Meanwhile, Guy just didn't seem to be caught up in any of that stuff, and I envied him for it.*

And I know about you and Susie. And maybe you even know why – and how – I know? Perhaps there's no need to go there, but . . . maybe there is? Call it closure. Call it whatever the hell you want, Will, but maybe it's time, especially as Dad is no longer around to pass judgement.

It was the mirror. Because even though I wasn't exactly hanging around yours and Marianne's very often, I knew that mirror – for the simple reason that I was with Marianne when she bought it. You may recall that she came home one Saturday afternoon with the mirror in the back of the car and told you how she'd been to an auction with a friend and fallen in love with it and been persuaded to bid far too much for it, against her better judgement, but that she was delighted she had?

Well, I was the 'friend' who persuaded her. And I was the 'friend' whom she dropped off round the corner just before she came home to you. And yes, I was the insecure, jealous little brother who thought that seducing your girlfriend was a clever game. But Marianne had the measure of me, eventually. She dumped me, committed to you and that was the end. We'd had our fun but Marianne had the last laugh. At least for a while.

And I forgot about the mirror for a long time. Right up until it arrived in my flat, along with Susie and about 100 bags of clothes and shoes. At first, of course, I assumed it was just an incredibly similar mirror, but it didn't take long to find out the truth. And it wasn't Susie who blew the whistle, obviously. No, it was such a silly, simple thing. The thing Marianne had loved most about the mirror wasn't what it looked like, or even what it reflected – though she did say it was the most flattering mirror ever – instead it was something you could see on it. You probably never even noticed it yourself but on the back there was a tiny metal plaque with the words: 'For M . . . From A' engraved on it. We had no idea who 'M' and 'A' were, but Marianne felt it was meant to be. It was our little joke.

When I finally identified the mirror, about three weeks after Susie had moved in (it was covered in bubble-wrap and it wasn't my place to unwrap it), I was shocked – what were the odds? – and I did a bit of detective work, like asking Susie where she'd got it. She was very dismissive.

'An ex gave it to me. Isn't it beautiful? He's very much an ex, but I kept custody of the mirror. Where do you think it should go?'

And I resisted the urge to say 'Out with the fucking rubbish' because I may be many things but I'm not a hypocrite. This was clearly my quick karmic pay-off for the Marianne situation – because I also knew you'd never part with anything of M's unless there was a very good reason – and now it appeared that Susie was the reason. My hunch was confirmed the 'first' time you two met, officially, at Ma and Pa's. I watched you both like a hawk.

You both went so far out of your way to appear uninterested in each other that you may as well have announced that the opposite was the case. But of course only I could see that because I was the only one watching. I've always wondered what it was you whispered in Susie's ear when you said those overly formal 'goodbyes'.

But I loved Susie and time passed and we were together. For example, I never had a moment's doubt that our children were my children. And I never had any doubt that she had moved on from you, towards me. Until, that is, I did have doubts. At Ma and Pa's anniversary, for example, when you asked Susie to dance and I watched you while I was talking to Guy, and you were both trying so hard to look comfortable together ... well, it was very obvious – if only to me – that you weren't comfortable together, even after all that time apart. And then when you left the marquee together I had to resist the urge to run after you both, because I knew.

And the only reason I can tell you all of this now is because I HAVE moved on. Really. Susie and I had ten mostly-good years together – and two beautiful children – and that is, I now understand, more of a cause for celebration than regret. Now, though, it's time for all of us to start living a different kind of life ... so, Happy Christmas.

I love you, mate. I always have. I just got distracted for a while.

Alex X

ACKNOWLEDGEMENTS

Many thanks to my wonderful editor, Jane Wood, for being both miraculously hands-on and hands-off at exactly the moment when I needed one or the other the most. Thanks also to everybody else at Quercus for their hard work on behalf of this twitchy first-time novelist.

I am also grateful to my incomparable agent, Jonny Geller, for sending me my favourite email of 2011. I subsequently forwarded it to some medieval monks who very kindly illuminated it on parchment ... and it now reads even better in Latin. Thanks also to everybody at Curtis Brown for their enthusiasm and hard work on my behalf, particularly Lisa Babalis, Melissa Pimentel, Rebecca Ritchie and Jo Rodgers (all fluent in Latin ... probably).

Thanks also to my friends in Random-on-Sea (it really does exist), especially Maria Ludkin, for helping me to remain just the right side of sane while I had these, er, *voices in my head*. Finally, special thanks to Julian Anderson – mostly, in this context, for reading the first chapter and saying 'so, what happens next?' Out of politeness, I thought I'd better find out.

Separate Lives
Reading Group Questions

1. At the beginning of the book, Susie sees Pippa's text message to Alex – what did you think of her reaction? Do you think there was another way to handle that situation?

2. How did you feel about Pippa when you first encountered her in the book? Did that change as the story progressed?

3. What did you make of Susie's decision to leave Alex on his own for the weekend after his redundancy? Did you understand her reasoning?

4. Did you feel that the 'Dream House' in Random-on-Sea was ever destined to make Susie and Alex happy?

5. Do you believe that Susie always held a candle for Will, or was her renewed love for him a symptom of things going wrong with Alex?

6. How do Pippa, Susie and Alex's pasts affect the decisions that they make over the course of the book?

7. Both Susie and Pippa have 'absent' mothers. Do you think this may have affected some of their decisions?

8. Would you describe Susie and Pippa as 'good' mothers?

9. At the end of the book, all of the protagonists are leading a 'different kind of life' - do you think that they will be content in their new realities?

10. The book explores different notions of what a family is. Which one, if any, seems to work best?

A Writer and Reader's Life
Q&A with Kathryn Flett

Why do you write?
I've written ever since I can remember so I suppose it must be a sort of terrible obsession/compulsion. I've obviously been very lucky to be able to turn it into a career because I genuinely have no idea how I'd be earning a living otherwise - though I'd love to own a little shop.

How do you write? On a page, or on a screen?
I write on an Apple Mac desktop, in my 'office' at home. Unless it's a shopping list, I've almost forgotten how to write longhand.

When do you write?
Whenever I have to, though rarely for 'pleasure'. By which I mean if there's something great on TV, I'll find a way not to write. Many years in journalism mean I'm pretty disciplined about deadlines and know when I have to stop looking for displacement activities and just sit down and get the job done.

What's a typical writing day?
Every day is different, depending on what it is I'm writing, but normally I'll be up at 7.30 a.m., get the kids ready, do the school run and be back by 9.30 a.m. After a couple of pints of coffee, I'll catch up on emails, have a quick look

at Twitter (and try not to get distracted!) and then write from about 10 a.m. through to a quick lunch break at about 1.30 p.m. If I'm on a tight deadline, I'll keep going until 3 p.m., before the next school run, though I often have a post-lunch energy/concentration dip (which is when I go to the supermarket). Luckily, I'm quite fast, so I've learned not to force myself to write if I'm not really in the 'zone' because I'll invariably end up having to re-write it all later. These days, I find I'm usually too tired to get much writing done in the evenings after the kids are in bed, so I prefer to switch off . . . usually by switching on the telly.

Having said all that, writing fiction turned out to be a very different process to writing journalism. Very few people knew I was writing *Separate Lives* and because my 'deadline' was self-imposed (it took me about seven months to write, part-time) some days I ended up writing 2,000 words I was really happy with, while on others it might have been 500 words I'd find myself rewriting from scratch the following day. I was basically learning on the job, though I did make myself start at the beginning of the story and write straight through to the end. That may sound slightly obvious, though I've discovered that not every author likes to work in a very linear way. I started writing with an ending in mind, yet the one I finally reached turned out to be very different - and (hopefully) better.

Best part of writing?
Knowing when you've nailed it - whatever that particular

'it' may be. It could be a sentence, a paragraph, a chapter, a piece of dialogue, a plot development - whatever, but you'll know when it's right even if it's not necessarily what you set out to do.

Worst part of writing?
Not nailing it! And isolation. Writing isn't a very inclusive business so it's important to find a balance between the world unfolding in your head/on-screen and the rest of your life. I can sometimes feel a bit punch-drunk when I have to speedily remove my writing-head and replace it with my mum-head, for example.

What's the best piece of writing advice you've ever received?
Don't talk about it - maybe don't even bother thinking about it - just do it. (Advice, incidentally, that wouldn't work for everyone!)

What's the first book you fell in love with?
The Chronicles of Narnia. All of them.

What's the last book you read?
Capital by John Lanchester (as of late April 2012): very clever; very 'now'.

Which book do you wish you'd written?
Rebecca by Daphne du Maurier. It's a perfect piece of storytelling and I re-read it every few years.